# Praise for *Married to a Perfect Stranger*

"The perfect blend of interesting, emotionally complex, and openhearted protagonists… In a story of personal growth and excited rediscovery, both characters must overcome scorn and opposition from their family and colleagues in order to come into themselves, appreciate each other, and turn a naively arranged marriage into a loving union."

—eview

"Ashford's tale of a couple separated and reunited after no challenges readers' emotions. This is a totally heartwarming story."

—*RT Book Reviews*, 4 Stars

"It's a pleasure to have Ms. Ashford writing books again. Regency fans can look forward to an author who knows her period."

—*Fresh Fiction*

"Ashford's latest flawlessly written love story is a quietly compelling tale… The author's ability to create truly memorable characters while getting all the historical domestic details exactly right ensures that romance readers picky about authenticity will be well rewarded."

—*Booklist*

"Great research and snappy dialogue, buoyant writing, and exceptional characterization."

—*A Fair Substitute for Heaven*

"Totally charming."

—*Bookeden*

# Also by Jane Ashford

Once Again a Bride
Man of Honour
The Three Graces
The Marriage Wager
The Bride Insists
The Bargain
The Marchington Scandal
The Headstrong Ward
Married to a Perfect Stranger

# Charmed and Dangerous

# JANE ASHFORD

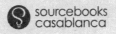
sourcebooks
casablanca

Published by Sourcebooks Casablanca, an imprint of Sourcebooks,
Inc.
P.O. Box 4410, Naperville, Illinois 60567-4410
(630) 961-3900
Fax: (630) 961-2168
www.sourcebooks.com

Originally published in 1998 by Bantam Books, a division of Bantam Doubleday Dell Publishing Group, Inc., New York

Printed and bound in Canada
WC 10 9 8 7 6 5 4 3 2 1

# *One*

*Vienna, Austria, 1814*

GENERAL MATTHEW PRYOR SAT RAMROD STRAIGHT behind his desk, demonstrating to his visitor the proper posture for an interview with one's superior in the diplomatic corps of the British Empire. But the hint was wasted on the man who lounged in the armchair opposite. He continued to lean back, his legs negligently crossed, and watch the general with a hooded, uncomfortably sharp gaze.

You couldn't label it insolence precisely, the general thought. The man *looked* attentive. And yet something about his manner clearly implied that he didn't expect to learn anything of importance during this conversation.

General Pryor gritted his teeth. From the moment he had heard that Gavin Graham was to be assigned to His Majesty's delegation at the great diplomatic congress in Vienna, he had foreseen difficulties. Graham was trouble. He was known for evading orders he disagreed

with. He was notorious for becoming too involved
with people in the countries to which he was posted,
particularly the female members of the population.
He was reckless and arrogant. Unfortunately, he was
also very, *very* good at uncovering information vital to
British interests and cementing alliances made at conference tables a thousand miles away. He had to be good,
General Pryor thought sourly. He wouldn't have been
tolerated otherwise, and he wouldn't be sitting across
the desk now looking pointedly patient at the delay.

"You must know why I summoned you," the
general snapped.

Graham spread his hands, indicating ignorance, and
irritating General Pryor even further. He knew damn
well, the older man thought. Lack of intelligence had
never been Graham's problem. "Sophie Krelov," he
added angrily.

"Ah."

"Indeed." The general waited for some other
acknowledgment, and got none. "The woman's an
acknowledged spy," he continued tightly. "It's well
known she worked for Boney until we packed him off
to Elba. She's connected to the Russians, too, through
that husband of hers, the so-called 'count.' You've
absolutely no business hanging about her, Graham."

"Such a stunner, however," murmured his visitor.
"That hair, those—"

"Vienna's full of beautiful women. Particularly
now, with this congress going on and half of Europe
here. If you cannot restrain your...instincts for the
other sex, fix them on some better object. You are not
to pursue Countess Krelov."

Graham met his eyes. General Pryor, who had commanded battalions in the field and seen death at close quarters, experienced an odd tremor. Was the man going to defy him? he wondered. What did he mean by that hard, measuring stare? "That is an order," Pryor added harshly.

"I see."

Gavin looked away, and the general experienced an unsettling mixture of rage and relief. The things he had heard about Graham had not been exaggerated, he thought. Just the opposite. Colleagues had told him that he'd be ready to throttle the man within a day; in point of fact, it had taken only twenty minutes.

"Sophie picks up a good deal of information," Graham said. "It might be quite useful to have a... connection with her."

The general snorted, well aware of the sort of "connection" Graham had in mind. "The woman's unscrupulous and completely untrustworthy. I don't want to worry about what sort of information she's getting from you."

Graham's face went stony. "I can assure you, sir, that I—"

"Yes, yes. I've heard all about your famous 'methods.' Riding off into the hills with bandits. Forming 'connections' in the most outrageous quarters. I won't have that sort of thing on my watch. Understand? We will carry out our mission like English officers and gentlemen. We will uphold the standards that make England great. We will not go sneaking—" General Pryor realized that he was ranting and broke off abruptly. He would not allow this man to rattle him, he thought. "I am in charge of this section of our delegation," he added more temperately. "And I shall decide how it is to be conducted." He met Graham's cool gaze again. "Is that clear?"

"It is."

"Good. And you will give me your word that you will not pursue Sophie Krelov?"

Graham frowned.

Now he had him, General Pryor exulted. Gavin Graham was famous for never going back on his promises—and for making damned few of them.

"If you like," said the other evenly.

"I do."

The stare he received in return was even more intimidating, but the general did not allow himself to look away.

"I give you my word I shall not pursue Sophie Krelov."

Pryor released a breath he hadn't realized he was holding. He'd won—the battle, if not the war. Because, of course, Graham had some scheme in mind that would allow him to do precisely as he pleased. He always did.

But he'd met his match this time, the general thought. Pryor had planned beyond the direct assault. He had something in reserve. "Heard from my wife this week. She's arriving in a few days from London."

Graham murmured his felicitations.

"Bringing Laura Devane with her," the general added, hoping it was true. His wife hadn't thought much of the idea, but she'd promised to try to get the girl here.

Gavin gazed at him in silence.

"You remember Miss Devane," prompted the general finally, feeling like a man who has lobbed a bomb that failed to explode.

"Umm."

"Damn it, man, you offered for her. Must remember her."

So he had, Gavin recalled; a decade ago, in another life. Laura Devane, the only woman who had refused him anything since…well, since he was in short coats trying to dominate two high-strung older sisters. Gavin eyed the general again. What the devil was this about?

"Thought you could show her around Vienna," said the man.

"I'm sure your wife will make a far more pleasant companion," said Gavin.

"My wife will be occupied with…er…duties and obligations. Won't have time to take the girl about."

Gavin managed to restrain himself from inquiring why the deuce she was bringing her, then. "Miss Devane did not marry?"

"No, no. Never did."

The older man threw him a glance apparently meant to be significant. Gavin nearly laughed aloud. Was he supposed to believe that Laura Devane had been pining for him? She'd shown no signs of it when he had given in to his father's nagging and offered for her those years ago. *Offered for her fortune*, a sardonic inner voice corrected. Neither he nor his father had been interested in anything else about her. And then that fortune had been lost, he recalled. He couldn't remember how. He had been in India by then, a bitter and reluctant junior diplomat. "What has she been doing all this time?" he wondered aloud.

"Ah, er." The general made a vague gesture. "This and that."

Living off some relative, Gavin supposed, his momentary curiosity fading. It didn't matter. He wasn't about to be stuck squiring a virgin of—what, twenty-nine?—through the glittering social whirl that the Congress of Vienna had become. He had far more important, and enjoyable, things planned.

"Appreciate it if you'd lend a hand," Pryor said.

Graham raised an eyebrow.

"With Miss Devane. Make her feel welcome."

Gavin experienced a familiar flash of anger and an equally familiar move to repress and control it. It was something he had learned to do quite well in the last decade, as a man who hated taking orders working in the service of his king. "I see," he said. General Pryor hoped to distract him from Sophie Krelov with Laura Devane. That was why he was having her brought here—at a good deal of trouble and expense no doubt. Mental images of the two women rose in his mind— Sophie, red-gold and voluptuous, one of the most sensuous women he had ever met; and Laura Devane, skinny and anxious, pale as milk. It was the most ludicrous plan imaginable. He started to say so, then reconsidered. If the general thought he had outwitted him, well, let him think so. It would keep him out of the way. And it would be simple enough to get rid of Laura Devane.

"Very well, sir," said Gavin. "I'll show Miss Devane Vienna."

◆

"Not pink," said Laura, waving aside the fashionable modiste's assistant and the gown she was holding out for Laura's approval. "I don't care to see any pastels. Perhaps a rose or bronze or dark green."

Catherine Pryor, the general's wife, examined her companion with covert amazement. What had become of the colorless, practically invisible governess she had gone to visit two weeks ago? She knew this was the same woman, and yet it wasn't—not at all.

"Of course not brown," said Laura in accents of revulsion.

Catherine had thought Matthew's plan ridiculous. And she had told him so. But he had been so taken with the idea of diverting his difficult subordinate from an unsuitable liaison that she had agreed to help.

She had tried to help Laura ten years ago, Catherine thought, when the girl's improvident parents had risked everything for the racing stables that obsessed them, and lost. But Laura had been too proud—or stiff-necked—to accept charity and had gone off to be governess to the Earl of Leith's twin daughters. Catherine had lost touch with her after a year or so— everyone had.

There was no way she could have been prepared for the Laura who received her at Leith House those two weeks past, she told herself. And she had been far from easy in her own mind, of course. She had let Laura's employers assume that she came to offer Laura a new post. The twins had turned seventeen and were to be presented to society, and Laura's job was ended. And when Laura had first entered the parlor, Catherine had been doubly glad for the secrecy, for this was not the Laura Devane she had known.

At eighteen, Laura had been a lively girl with sparkling green eyes and a vivid smile. Though she was always a bit too thin, her raven black hair and milk white skin had given her a certain distinction. Now, after ten years, all of that was gone, Catherine thought. The slender woman who had stood before her in the Leith's back parlor, hands folded, eyes on the floor, hadn't a crumb of vivacity. She was silent, pale, entirely forgettable. Gavin Graham wouldn't waste a glance on her, the general's wife thought, and immediately felt guilty. She would make some excuse for the visit and slip away, she decided.

It was then that she realized she was being observed from behind a fringe of dark lashes, and that the stillness of the figure before her was deceptive. She cleared her throat, aware now of the lengthening silence, and said, "I was acquainted with your mother years ago."

Laura nodded.

There was no sign of nerves, Catherine thought, no fluttering or chattering or anxiety to please such as she had seen in many women in Laura's position. "How are your parents getting on in India?" she added, feeling unaccountably awkward.

"Quite well. My father runs the polo club in Bombay, so he has his horses."

The tone was dry, subtlety ironic. The general's wife was at a loss.

"And he always cared most about his horses," added the younger woman. "You have heard of a post for me?"

The voice was cultivated and musical, but muted, lulling. It was designed to deflect notice, to reveal nothing. Catherine had the sudden notion that she had walked onto a stage and met an actress immersed in her role. She shook her head. She was being fanciful, which wasn't like her at all. Best just to do what she had promised, and go. "A sort of post."

Laura waited.

"Do you remember Gavin Graham?" asked Catherine, plunging in recklessly. She saw, or thought she saw, a flicker of reaction. Then the younger woman was unreadable once more and merely nodded. "Yes. Well, he is assigned to my husband's section at the Congress of Vienna, and there has been some trouble with a Russian spy—a woman. So Matthew thought that you might come to Vienna and divert Mr. Graham's attention from this creature and prevent some sort of…incident."

There, Catherine thought, she had blurted out the whole thing. And it had sounded just as ludicrous as she'd thought it would. Laura would tell her she was mad, and that would be the end of it.

"Incident?" said Laura.

It wasn't the response that Catherine expected. She finally got a glimpse of Laura's eyes. They were still a stunning green, like rose leaves, but far more wary and wise than she remembered. "It's a bit complex," she replied.

"Russia wants Poland," stated Laura. "And England does not wish to give it to her."

Catherine gaped at her.

"I suppose both are trying to win Prussia and Austria to their sides."

The general's wife realized her mouth was hanging open and closed it.

Laura Devane gave her a sidelong glance. "The earl receives all of the newspapers, whether the family is here or in London," she said.

Well, of course he did, thought Catherine, but if Laura read them, she was only one of a tiny minority of women who bothered.

"I do not see what help I could be," Laura added.

Neither did her visitor.

Silence stretched out in the room. The general's wife watched Laura's face. It was obvious that a succession of thoughts was passing through her mind, but Catherine had no idea where they were leading.

"I have no clothes for Vienna," said Laura at last, fingering the pearl gray cambric of her plain gown.

Surprised again, Catherine said, "A wardrobe could be…provided."

This drew the first sign of a smile from this unusual young woman. "Gavin Graham never cared anything for me, you know. He wanted my fortune."

This was almost too much honesty, Catherine thought. One didn't know what to say to this girl.

"However…"

The general's wife waited.

"I should like to go to Vienna."

Suddenly the entire matter appeared to Catherine in a different light. Of course this faded, subdued creature would never interest Gavin Graham; he was rumored to have had scandalous liaisons with an Indian temple dancer, a lady of the king's court in Siam, and who knew how many other ravishing, exotic females. But

Laura might catch the attention of some other eligible gentleman. From what Catherine heard, the congress was turning into a social event such as had rarely been seen before. There would be endless opportunities for Laura to meet potential husbands, and to escape a life that must be indescribably dreary. It was a chance for Catherine to give the help that had been rejected those years ago. "My husband is very eager for you to come," she urged.

"I'm not sure I could really help," began Laura.

"He is only asking that you try."

There was another silence.

"The earl and countess are ready for me to depart," admitted Laura. "They have said I can stay until I find another post, of course, but they are taking the girls to London next week, and I...I am not to go."

"The timing is perfect, then," Catherine suggested.

Laura hesitated. She was looking at the parquet floor as if she could find some answer there.

"I would be happy to help you secure a new post later on," added the general's wife, privately promising herself that it would not be necessary.

Laura was silent a moment longer, then seemed to make up her mind. She nodded.

"Splendid."

Catherine had hurried away then, making all the subsequent arrangements so that Laura could not change her mind. And those arrangements had brought them here, to the shop of one of the leading dressmakers in London, to outfit Laura for her new role.

And to startle her yet again, Catherine thought,

watching Laura run a critical eye over a bolt of material in a luscious rose red. Catherine had expected to be asked for advice, perhaps even to choose the wardrobe that Laura would take to Vienna, but she had been relegated to the background from the first. Laura had very definite ideas on the sort of clothes she wanted, and exquisite taste. It made Catherine wonder why every gown she had seen her wear was drab and forgettable.

"Yes," said Laura to the dressmaker. "I would like that pattern you showed me made up in this fabric. And the other in that green."

"That green" was precisely the color of her eyes, Catherine thought, feeling superfluous. It would bring them out admirably.

They finished at the modiste's late in the afternoon, leaving the dressmaker deeply gratified by the size of their order. As they rode back to their hotel in a hack, Catherine said, "What would you like to do while we are waiting for the gowns to be made up? We might visit some of the sights, perhaps see a play."

"Yes." Laura sounded like someone waking from a sound sleep. "I need to get used to being…out."

The general's wife was touched. Laura appeared to be seeing this opportunity as a second debut, making up for her aborted first one. "We won't be invited to any balls or that sort of thing here in London," she felt obliged to warn her.

Laura turned.

Her whole manner was different now, Catherine thought. She looked at one directly, almost dauntingly. Sometimes, she seemed to see right through one in the most unsettling way.

"Of course not."

They pulled up in front of the small, respectable hotel Catherine had chosen and walked through the reception area and upstairs to their rooms.

"We might make some calls," the general's wife added as they were taking off their wraps. "If you would like to go to…"

"I wouldn't want to encounter the Leiths," Laura interrupted.

No, thought the older woman, much struck. That would be odd. The countess was known to be a flighty, temperamental creature. What would she do if she met her former governess in a drawing room?

"I did not mean that I was expecting invitations," Laura added. "Only…" She paused. "A governess is little more than an upper servant, you know. The post requires a great deal of…circumspection."

Catherine gazed at her.

"I found it was best not to be noticed by anyone except one's charges," she went on. "And perhaps, now and then, by the mistress of the house."

The general's wife frowned in confusion.

"Perhaps you know the Earl of Leith and his set?"

Comprehension dawned. Leith was a womanizer, and not very discreet about it. "He did not…"

"He did not notice me," said Laura. "Nor did his friends. No one noticed me, unless I wished them to, and I almost never did. I was a great success as a governess." She smiled.

Catherine nearly took a step backward in surprise. The vivacity, the charm weren't gone. Apparently, they had simply been in hiding.

"And now I must become accustomed to attracting notice once again," the younger woman finished.

Perhaps Laura Devane would be able to catch Graham's attention after all, Catherine thought. Undoubtedly, she would capture someone's.

# Two

LAURA STOOD IN THE GREAT BALLROOM OF THE HOUSE
that the Danish delegation had hired for the duration
of the Congress of Vienna, her heart racing behind
a calm facade. The roar of a hundred conversations
swirled about her, nearly drowning out the strains of
the musicians playing in the far corner. The huge room
was lavish with white and gold ornament, the tall windows draped in midnight blue velvet. Laura could hear
five languages being spoken just in the area around her.
How fortunate, she thought, that languages had been
one thing the Countess of Leith wished her daughters
to learn. One of the very few things. Teaching them
had kept Laura's skills honed, and even added to them.
She could converse quite easily in French, Italian, and
German. But not Russian, she thought with regret,
listening to two burly men behind her murmur in that
tongue. If she had only known she would be coming
here, she would have learned Russian.

An impish grin lit her features. She automatically
suppressed it, and then shook her head slightly. She
didn't have to do that any longer. For a while—for the

brief period of this unimaginable change in her life, this adventure—she was free. The grin broke loose, making Laura's deep green eyes sparkle.

"Are you all right?" said Catherine, who stood next to her.

Laura nodded.

"They should be along quite soon now."

The sparkle in Laura's eyes deepened. General Pryor was bringing Gavin Graham to this ball—to make sure he showed up for their meeting, Laura imagined. He would hardly be eager. For the hundredth time, she wondered how she would fulfill the task she had accepted. She was determined to do what she could in exchange for this escape—however brief—from the life she had been leading. But how, precisely, did one divert a seasoned man of the world from a lovely foreign spy?

She had absolutely no idea. She was hoping that something would occur to her when she encountered him again. At least she wasn't a naive, ignorant eighteen-year-old any longer, she told herself.

She had to control a spurt of laughter. In the last ten years, she had vastly broadened her horizons by reading almost every book in the Earl of Leith's extensive library. She had learned a great many things that gently reared young women were not supposed to know. She had been startled, shocked, occasionally revolted—and as time went by, more and more intensely curious. This would most likely be her only chance to discover the reality of some of those words on the page. She intended to make the most of it.

"That gown is a most unusual green," said a woman in French behind her.

"Yes," answered her companion in the same language. "Dark, but quite striking."

"A little daring, without going too far. The sleeves are very chic."

Laura glanced at Catherine to see if she was following this critique of Laura's gown, but she showed no sign of understanding.

"She is not French," stated the second observer with certainty.

"No. Yet she has a certain… Spanish, perhaps?"

Laura could almost hear the shrug that followed this guess. She found she was extremely pleased at being difficult to categorize.

"Ah," continued the first French voice. "There is that Englishman, Graham."

At the same moment, Catherine gave a discreet wave at her approaching husband.

"You have heard of him? They say he is a fantastic lover."

"An Englishman!"

"So they say. A veritable poet of the bedchamber."

"Incredible."

Laura had to exert a good deal of control to keep her expression bland. A poet? she thought. What would that mean, exactly? She watched Gavin walk toward them. His hair was still that unusual dark gold, like a sovereign burnished by the years. No doubt his eyes were still a cool gray-blue as well. He still stood half a head taller than most of the others in the room. But otherwise he was quite different from the young man she had known. His figure had filled out—shoulders broadening, chest deepening, arms and legs more heavily muscled. And he moved with an assurance and grace that he had not begun to possess ten years ago. Each move he made seemed slow and deliberate. He drew the eye, Laura thought, seeing people turn and look after him as he passed. He made you wonder, in this city full of Europe's aristocracy, whether he was some great magnate, or even royalty.

"There's Gavin," said the general's wife quite unnecessarily.

Catherine sounded nervous, Laura thought. And perhaps she was just slightly nervous as well. Gavin Graham had no control over her, she reminded herself. No one even expected her to succeed in interesting him. Three days with the Pryors had made that obvious. Catherine had somehow moderated the general's disappointment in his supposed lure, but his hopes had clearly been dashed upon her arrival. The expression on his face when they met had declared the case hopeless. Perhaps, and perhaps not, Laura thought. She prided herself on performing what she promised.

"Very nice," said one of the Frenchwomen behind her. "What a leg he has."

"Umm," agreed her friend. "And what else, I wonder?"

Their laughter chimed out as General Pryor introduced his wife to Gavin Graham. "And you know Miss Devane, of course," he added.

"Of course," murmured Gavin.

Mocking, thought Laura; he had decided to be supercilious and mocking, and he did it very well.

She had a moment's flash of uneasiness, then pushed it aside.

"What do you think of Vienna, Miss Devane?" he asked.

"It seems a pleasant city. And the work going on here is very interesting."

"Work?"

"Of the congress."

Gavin cast a lazy glance around the ballroom, taking in the chattering groups, the faces flushed from too much champagne. "Do you think anyone is working?"

The general cleared his throat. Gavin's hooded gaze came to rest on him as if he were some sort of odd carnival exhibit.

"Splendid music," stated Pryor. "One thing you can say for Vienna—good music."

Gavin continued to gaze at him just too long. Or just long enough, Laura thought. It depended on your point of view. Then he said, "Would you care to dance, Miss Devane?"

It was a waltz. Laura knew this because she had read about the new dance, which was not yet accepted in England. She had heard the steps described, and the scandalous proximity of the partners deplored. She could see that he expected the invitation to unsettle and embarrass her—and to be refused. He would have to do better than this, she thought. "Thank you," she answered, wondering whether she would be able to mimic what she had read without stepping on his highly polished shoes.

"Laura," protested the general's wife, who obviously did not approve of the waltz.

"Good thought," put in the general. With a gesture, he urged them toward the couples dancing at the other end of the room.

"Matthew!" said his wife.

Gavin offered his arm. Laura took it, her head held high.

Laura was surprised at what a pleasure it was to walk with him. Despite his greater height, their strides matched somehow. They seemed to fall into a similar rhythm automatically. It made her feel graceful and powerful and ready for anything. She blinked. Her imagination was running away with her. It had been too long since she'd been out in a crowd, she thought.

At the edge of the circle of dancers, Gavin turned to her, encircling her waist with one arm and taking her right hand in a firm grip. It was very different from a country dance or quadrille, Laura thought. His coat lapel was inches from her face, and warmth was spreading through her back from where his hand rested.

As he guided her onto the floor he said, "Have you ever waltzed before?"

The gloves were coming off, Laura thought. His tone was quite different now that they were alone—cold and uncompromising. She was to be shown what he thought of the general's plots, she realized. "No," she replied.

"Endeavor to follow me, then."

Laura bit back a sharp response. She would show him that she was well able to follow him.

It took a little while. At first, he was almost pushing her in the proper direction and lifting her through the turns. But then Laura caught the cadence and began to really dance. Once again their limbs fell into rhythm with each other, and it felt as if they were floating. She seemed to know instinctively how his body would move, what direction he would choose. It was very odd.

"You learn quickly," commented Gavin, not sounding pleased.

She looked up at him, fully meeting his cool gaze for the first time. She hadn't really known anything about him ten years ago, she thought. Had that intelligence been there then? That wary scrutiny? "Very quickly," she answered.

"And what do you expect to learn in Vienna?" he asked harshly. "Beyond the waltz."

"Something about the world." Laura was shocked at her own honesty. She hadn't even told Catherine that. She had hardly understood it herself until this moment.

"The world?" he repeated sarcastically.

"The larger world, the world where things are decided. History is…" She couldn't finish. It sounded too silly.

"History." It was close to a sneer.

"I wish you would stop repeating what I say."

One of his brows went up slightly.

"It's annoying," Laura added. Immediately, she felt guilty. She had promised to try to fascinate Gavin Graham. Quarreling with him was hardly the way to do so. She remembered the instructions her mother had given her before her first debut. Men liked women who were deferential and admiring, she had said; one should create opportunities for them to show off their superiority. Laura's nose wrinkled at the memory. She hadn't been terrifically good at that even at eighteen. And she had only succeeded as a governess by not speaking at all.

"You look as if you'd encountered a bad smell," said Gavin.

"Oh. Sorry. I was thinking of something else. From years ago."

He gazed down at her as if he was not accustomed to such distraction in his dancing partners.

"You dance very well," said Laura, hoping to salvage the conversation.

He continued to look at her.

"You…you have traveled a great deal, I understand," she added, remembering her mother's admonition that men most enjoyed talking about themselves.

The musicians were making their final flourishes. The dance was about to end. Suddenly, Gavin's arm tightened around her waist. As he turned in the dance, he pulled her close, pressing his body against hers. Her breasts were taut against his chest. The skin at her temple tingled as it brushed his jaw. Vertigo gripped Laura. She was off balance, too startled to react. It was like being suddenly snatched up by storm winds. His arms molded her to his own contours, demanding surrender.

The music stopped. He let her go and stepped away with a mocking little bow, his eyes filled with cool amusement. Around them, other dancers separated and moved away.

Laura felt as if she'd been dipped in fire. Her face

flamed, and so did the rest of her. She was breathless and shaken and utterly humiliated. How many people had seen? How dare he treat her this way? A gentleman would not make such a spectacle of any woman.

Gavin Graham offered his arm. Laura wanted to turn her back and stalk away from him, but that would only attract more attention. She already felt as if hundreds of staring eyes were boring into her. Gathering all her fortitude, standing very straight, she put her fingertips on his forearm and allowed him to escort her back to the Pryors.

∽✥∾

Gavin threw the last of the pasteboard squares back onto the silver tray his man had used to present the mail. Six invitations for next week alone. It was ridiculous, he thought. The congress was turning into a gigantic tea party. The powers had gathered here to settle the fate of Europe in the wake of Napoleon's defeat. Instead they were spending their time dancing and dining and wracking their brains for witty conversation—which damned few of them were capable of.

There was a discreet knock at the door. "Come," said Gavin.

His servant entered, a small wiry man from a country on the other side of the world. He held out another envelope with a look that made Gavin grow alert. "Something interesting?" he asked.

The man made a gesture, half shrug, half dismissal. He was adept at communicating with silence.

Gavin took the envelope. If Hasan thought it

significant, it was. The man had been with him through events that would stagger most of his colleagues, and Hasan had never shown himself less than completely capable and trustworthy.

The envelope was pink and rose-scented, the handwriting full of loops and flourishes. It was a note from Sophie Krelov, expressing her hopes of seeing him that evening. Gavin smiled sardonically. He had promised the general he would not pursue her, and he wouldn't. What Pryor didn't know was that he had never pursued her. On the contrary, almost from the moment he had arrived in Vienna weeks ago, Sophie had been haunting his footsteps, exhibiting her considerable charms, and offering...what?

Gavin fingered the letter. It was odd. Though he didn't underrate his own attractions, Sophie Krelov never wasted herself on simple love affairs. Her favors were exchanged for other kinds of concessions, or for information vital to some country's interests. The name of the country varied with the season and the payment on offer. The question was—what did she want from him?

Gavin was aware that he possessed a great variety of information. He had had postings in many vital parts of the British Empire. He had met powerful people, and he had been involved in a number of delicate and secret negotiations. But which bit of knowledge was attracting Sophie and her employer?

If he could discover the identity of the latter, he might find the answer. Sophie had worked for France. Had Talleyrand engaged her to help him salvage what he could from the wreck of Boney's imperial dreams? Sophie's husband, the deplorable count, was Russian. And the czar was raging around Vienna like a wounded bear, demanding possession of Poland when almost no one wanted to give it to him. Had he engaged Sophie to find something he could use to get it? Or was she working for Austria, or Prussia?

Gavin put down the scented page and contemplated the small city park outside the window of his rented rooms. The winds of early November were whirling the last dead leaves from hidden corners. The day was gray and chill, with a threat of winter. Sophie was only part of the larger question of what he was doing here, he thought. The congress wasn't his sort of posting. It must be clear to everyone in the British diplomatic service by now that he was not suited to these huge gatherings, with their endless posturing and empty chatter. For the last several years, he had received no such assignments. He had been sent to the volatile spots, to small secret meetings convened to further some plot or prevent some explosion. That was what he was good at.

Gavin's jaw hardened. He was no drawing-room diplomat. He worked alone. Trust a colleague with your plans, and they would most likely be spoiled. Trust was always a mistake. He handled matters himself, and presented His Majesty's government with the results when he had them. So what the devil was he doing here, assigned to Matthew Pryor's staff? Gavin frowned. Men like General Pryor were constitutionally incapable of understanding intrigue. They spent their time pushing counters around a map or drafting memoranda. Some damned bureaucrat in London had shoved them together. It was a recipe for disaster.

Thinking of Pryor brought to mind the man's idiotic scheme, and the focus of it—Laura Devane. He had been a bit cavalier with her, Gavin admitted to himself, remembering the outrage on her face after their dance. She wasn't used to that sort of game. It had been rather amusing, though.

Gavin smiled. She'd recovered admirably. He'd been prepared to endure shrieks and accusations, if necessary. But Laura had defied the whole place and walked back to her hosts like a queen. It was almost too bad that he had to get rid of her. But he had no time for squiring an aging virgin around Vienna, however spirited she might be. She must be forced to reject him. Then, Pryor would have to concede—and send her back to England.

It *was* too bad, Gavin thought again. Laura had grown up rather well. The skinniness of youth had turned into a lithe suppleness that had been quite pleasant under his hands during the waltz. She'd become one of those women whose curves are apparent only to the lover, an appealing contrast to those females whose attributes are visible to all. And her pale skin flushed as red as antique roses, he thought. With that raven hair and those eyes… He shrugged. She was striking. But he had more important things to think about.

❧

Laura drummed her fingers on the surface of the writing desk in her room at the general's rented house. They were to go out walking in a few minutes, and there was a chance that she would see Gavin Graham again.

She had come to Vienna on impulse, to help the Pryors and, even more, to have a taste of adventure. She hadn't known what it would be like, whether she had a hope of actually helping. Certainly, she hadn't realized that the effort would involve public humiliation.

She clenched her fists. Gavin obviously intended to thwart the general's plan by intimidating her. Remembering the amusement in his eyes when he let her go after their dance, Laura gritted her teeth. He had already dismissed her as a nonentity, a weakling—in short, a woman who would run from the least hint of opposition or scandal. He had discounted her automatically, just like all the people whose lives she had passed through unnoticed in the last decade.

Laura sat back in her chair and relaxed. He had no idea of the adversity she'd faced, or the skills and fortitude she'd developed. He was acting on false assumptions.

She took a deep breath, feeling her anger fade. He was, in fact, sadly mistaken about her. When she accepted a task, she did it; when she made a promise, she fulfilled it. She didn't abandon obligations simply because they became burdensome. Ten years of being a governess had been rigorous training in that. And now he had made this task more than an obligation. Now it was personal—a contest between them that she had no intention of losing.

Laura's eyes narrowed. The Pryors hadn't seen what Gavin had done at the ball. Too many people stood between them and the dancers. The general had been quite pleased, in fact, believing his plan to be working after all. If they knew, they would call the whole scheme off, she thought. That was exactly what Gavin Graham was counting on. So she would make certain they didn't know. She would formulate her own plans. He wasn't playing fair, neither would she.

The maid knocked and told her the Pryors were ready. Laura rose and took up her gloves. The ideas were already forming. For years she had overcome difficult circumstances by playing a role. She could do so again. These circumstances were very different, of course, and she didn't comprehend them nearly as well. She needed information, background. She would have to ask some careful questions, be unobtrusive. Fortunately, she was an expert at that. Gavin Graham had no idea how expert.

&

They walked toward the center of the city and the Stephansplatz, where the ancient Cathedral of St. Stephan loomed above the pavement. The November air was chilly and kept them moving. But many others had also braved the cold to see and be seen. Laura had never traveled before, except through the pages of a book, and it was thrilling to be in a foreign city and be surrounded by its inhabitants. She also saw a great many conference attendees out strolling. When the general pointed out Prince Klemens von Metternich of Austria, whom she had read about in the newspapers countless times, Laura's satisfaction was complete. "The architect of the balance of power in Europe," she murmured, drawing a startled look from her host.

She was enjoying herself thoroughly when she caught sight of Gavin Graham coming toward them along the promenade. He wore a caped greatcoat and high-crowned beaver hat and carried a curious cane lacquered in black and red. His pace seemed languid, yet he passed walkers who appeared to be moving more swiftly. Occasionally, he acknowledged an acquaintance with a nod. He acted as if he owned the city, Laura thought. And he surveyed the people he met with an absolute lack of feeling, as if they were curiosities that might, perhaps, have some use.

"Graham," said the general when they neared him. "Walk with us."

Impassively, Gavin obeyed this order. It was pleasant, Laura thought, to see him forced to do something he clearly didn't want to do.

"What an unusual cane," the general's wife said. "What is painted on it?"

"A dragon." Gavin held up the object so that they could see the scarlet creature depicted coiling around the cane along its whole length.

"Beautiful. Did you purchase it in the East?"

"It comes out of China," he replied. "I received it in Siam. It was a...gift."

Something about the way he said the word made Mrs. Pryor flush slightly.

"Siam," said Laura. "What is it like there?" She had dreamed of seeing such places, experiencing such different cultures.

"Interesting. The king has more than a hundred wives." Gavin smiled mockingly at her. "Surprisingly, he still finds time for politics and intrigue."

"Mr. Graham," protested Catherine Pryor.

"Ma'am?"

His bland gaze appeared to fluster the older woman. Putting other people off balance seemed to be one of his chief amusements, Laura thought.

They walked in silence for a few minutes. Laura could tell that the general's wife was fuming.

"Oh, there is the baron," said Catherine then, waving to a tall blond gentleman walking toward them.

The man approached and bowed formally. He had the erect bearing of a soldier, though he did not wear a uniform. His pale hair was matched by a small clipped mustache. His eyes were very light blue, and the pale line of a dueling scar marred his left cheek.

"Laura, this is Baron von Sternhagen," said the general's wife. "Baron, a friend of ours from England, Miss Laura Devane."

"Fräulein." The baron bowed again and clicked his heels together.

Laura saw Gavin's eyes flicker with mocking amusement. "It is a pleasure to meet you," she said in German.

"You speak my language?" answered the baron in the same tongue, clearly surprised.

"A little. And not too well, I fear."

"No, no. Your accent is very good," he said, switching back to English. "Where did you learn?"

Laura smiled. "In the schoolroom." Her own and the Earl of Leith's, mainly the latter. Her pupils had not been particularly quick, and she had had to drill them repeatedly.

"Excellent. You have traveled to the German states?"

"Alas, no," answered Laura.

"But you must. So few of your countrymen speak as well as you."

"Perhaps someday." Laura smiled at the baron, pleased with his compliments and rather glad that Gavin Graham was there to hear them.

General Pryor cleared his throat. "Never had much time to learn foreign lingo. Too busy."

"Perhaps I will see you at the ball tomorrow night?" the baron said.

"I don't…"

"At our headquarters?" He cast the general's wife a glance and, when she shrugged, said, "I will make certain that your invitation reaches you. You must save me a dance."

With another bow and a long look at Laura, he moved on.

"So very correct, the Prussians," murmured Gavin.

Laura looked at him. It was interesting, she thought. He and the baron were both blond men, yet so different. The baron had looked bright as a new-minted gold piece; he practically glinted. Gavin, on the other hand, seemed burnished as antique gold, rich with experience and sophistication.

Their eyes met. Laura flushed slightly and turned away. She must give him no opening. He had shown that he would take ruthless advantage of it.

"Wouldn't you say so?" asked Gavin.

"What?"

"That the Prussians are oppressively correct."

"The baron is the only Prussian I have ever met. I thought he was very pleasant."

"Did you?" The tone of the two words implied that she was a fool.

Laura was about to retort when the general said, "There's that dashed painter. Don't look, Catherine. He's trying to catch your eye."

Inevitably, his wife turned. Laura watched a slender man with glossy black hair and brilliant dark eyes smile and hurry toward them. "Madam," he exclaimed, bowing extravagantly over Catherine's hand.

"Signor Oliveri," she responded, taking her hand back.

"Is it not a splendid day? The blue of the sky, the freshness of the air, the movement." He flung out his hands to indicate the people strolling around them.

Catherine seemed to be considering something as she glanced at Laura. Finally, she said, "This is Signor Oliveri. He has come up from Rome to paint the conference. He is working on a great canvas that shows all the important delegates. Our friend, Laura Devane, signor."

"*Bèlla dònna*," he declared, capturing her hand and bowing over it as well.

Laura greeted him in Italian. When she caught the look of surprise on Gavin's face, she felt a spurt of satisfaction.

Oliveri responded with a flood of words and gestures.

"I'm sorry. You'll have to go more slowly," said Laura. "I haven't had much chance to practice my Italian with someone who truly speaks it."

"No, no, you speak like an angel," he answered. "Your voice is music. After the grunts and coughs that pass for speech here!" He threw up his hands. "Danish! May all the saints preserve us. It is as if the farmyard animals began to speak."

Laura had to laugh.

"And I always think the Russians are clearing their throats," he went on, encouraged. "I am only waiting for them to spit."

"Signor," she admonished with another laugh.

"We have to be moving on," said General Pryor, his tone brooking no argument. He was frowning at his wife as if he intended to have a few words with her later.

Turning to look at Catherine, Laura caught Gavin's gaze. Was there actually a hint of laughter in those eyes? She would have wagered, then, that he spoke Italian.

"Yes, we should go," said the general's wife.

Oliveri stepped back, spreading his arms. "I am enchanted to have met you, signorina," he said. "Perhaps you will come and see my work one day."

Catherine took Laura's arm and urged her forward. She was sorry that she had introduced Signor Oliveri, Laura realized. Probably he was not quite socially acceptable.

"No doubt you would find a great deal of pleasure in his 'work,'" murmured Gavin in Italian, close to her ear.

"You think so?"

"No question," he mocked.

"Is he not approved of?" she asked. "How interesting. The last gentleman I conversed with who was not approved of was…you."

He looked distinctly startled.

"My parents thought you utterly unsuitable," she elaborated. "They only allowed you to make an offer for me because of your father's influence."

"Indeed?" he responded. "What a coincidence. My father's influence was the only reason I made it."

Their eyes met. Laura didn't look away. He was sizing her up differently now—still cool, but not nearly so dismissive. She'd given him something to think about, Laura concluded with satisfaction. But it was nothing compared to what she had planned.

❧

The moment that Laura had been waiting for finally came three days later. She had discovered what she needed to know, and the object of her curiosity was moving toward the doorway, obviously getting ready to leave the evening party they had both attended. Laura faded back a step from Catherine's side, and then moved unhurriedly in the same direction.

She found her quarry putting on a long blue cloak in the front hall. When the footman retreated, she stepped forward. "Hello."

The other looked her up and down in frank evaluation.

"You are Countess Krelov?"

The woman nodded, raising her brows slightly.

She was very beautiful, Laura thought. Her hair was red-gold and her clear, deep blue eyes were set at a slight slant in her triangular face. Of medium height, with a voluptuous figure, she also possessed a sharp, intelligent gaze. It was no wonder Gavin was taken with her, Laura thought. "May I talk with you for a moment?" Laura added.

"Who are you?" was the reply. The countess's accent was slight, and unidentifiable.

"My name is Laura Devane. I'm a visitor here from England."

"Married to one of the congress delegates?" A spark of interest entered those blue eyes.

"No. Only observing it."

"What do you want?"

This was the difficult part, Laura thought, feeling a small thrill of excitement. She was stepping out of the careful world of rules and conventions that had governed her whole life so far. She was releasing the safety those things had brought her, along with the boredom and frustration and limits. "I have heard," she began carefully, "that you know a great deal about the people here at the conference."

"You have some information?" was the sharp response.

"No. I should like to learn…that's all."

Countess Krelov blinked in surprise. She looked Laura carefully up and down once again. A smile tugged at her lips, then broke out in a full-throated laugh. "You have heard I am a spy," accused the countess mockingly, "and you have some romantic notion of becoming one yourself. You read too many novels, Miss…Devane."

Laura was already shaking her head. "I don't see anything particularly romantic about it," she replied. "It is a sort of business, isn't it? Anyway, I don't care about that."

"What, then?"

Laura looked around the very public area in which they stood. "Could we meet somewhere else— more privately?"

The countess examined her through narrowed eyes. "Who are you?" she asked again.

"Laura Devane," she repeated. "I was a governess for ten years, before getting the…opportunity to visit Vienna." The idea of returning to a schoolroom and new charges was less and less appealing, Laura thought.

"Opportunity?" repeated the other woman. She was looking at Laura's expensive gown.

"A friend of my mother's invited me here." And that was all she could say, Laura thought. If it wasn't enough, this scheme was doomed.

Countess Krelov looked dubious, but also a bit curious. When voices sounded in the back of the hall, signaling the departure of other guests from the party, she gave a little shrug and dug in her reticule for a card. "Come and see me," she said, handing it to Laura with a mocking little flourish. "Tomorrow… no, the next day, in the afternoon. Three o'clock."

Laura took the card, slipping it quickly into her glove. "Thank you."

The countess made a throwaway gesture and turned to the door. Laura slipped away as a group of people entered calling for their wraps. She was back at Catherine's side before her absence caused any concern.

❧

The Krelovs were lodged in a large house that contained several suites of apartments. When Laura knocked, she was escorted up to the second floor by the landlady, a stoic Austrian who didn't seem to wish to talk even when Laura spoke German. Upstairs, she was admitted by an unusual figure who didn't look at all like a maid. A tall spare woman of fifty or so with gray hair pulled back into a tight bun, she gave Laura several exceedingly sharp glances from under lowered eyelids. She didn't speak, however, as she ushered Laura into the countess's bedchamber. Sophie sat at her dressing table examining her face in the trio of mirrors atop it. "I shall never get old," she declared. She opened a bottle of lotion and began to rub it into her skin. The scent of roses filled the room. "You came," she said to Laura. "I didn't think you would."

"Why?"

She shrugged. "I thought perhaps it was a joke." She examined Laura with acute intelligence. "I have learned never to reject any source of information. But I really do not see what we have to talk about."

"Countess…" began Laura.

"Call me Sophie," said the other, recapping the bottle and putting it back on the dressing table. "And do sit down. It is tiresome looking up at you."

Laura sat in an armchair that flanked a small table by the window.

"In whose house were you a governess?" Sophie asked, surprising Laura with the accuracy of her memory.

"The Earl of Leith."

The other woman frowned, considering. "I have never heard of him. He is here?"

"No. He has nothing to do with politics." Only

gambling, Laura thought, and drinking, and other conventional debaucheries.

"You have some information to sell?"

"No." Laura tried to formulate what she wished to say to this woman. There was a brief silence.

"That color is very flattering to you," Sophie commented, taking in every detail of Laura's deep rose morning dress.

"Thank you."

"I still do not understand what you want."

That wasn't odd, Laura thought. She wasn't sure she understood it herself. She had wanted to meet this woman, the object of Gavin Graham's affections, to see her and learn more about her. This, she thought, would give her clues, ways to win the game between them. This was the kind of woman Gavin admired, she thought, surveying the countess's obvious charms. "My life has become very different, very quickly," she ventured. "I left a nobleman's schoolroom to come here. It has been rather…disorienting."

The countess raised her brows.

"I thought you might have some advice for someone in my…situation." This wasn't terribly convincing, Laura thought, but it was the best she could do.

"Advice?" Sophie looked astonished. "You want my advice?" Her eyes narrowed. "Either you are up to something that I don't understand, or…" She stared. "Or you are a very odd creature," she finished.

"I am rather odd," replied Laura evasively. She hesitated, realizing that she would have to reveal more to get any response from the countess. "I had hopes," she said slowly, "when I was a girl, of seeing things, even doing things that were…significant. Silly hopes. Then the world I had known collapsed." She raised her chin. Sophie Krelov was watching her intently, she saw. "It was just gone. It is a little that way now."

The countess's expression had changed. She looked thoughtful. "What do you expect from me?"

"I…heard of you, and it seemed you had made such different choices. I wanted to see what you were like." Had she imagined that some of the countess's attractions would rub off on her? Laura mocked silently.

"Choices," repeated Sophie. She shook her head. "Do you think women have choices?" Her beautiful lips turned down in a sneer. "I, too, had dreams, once upon a time…" She sniffed. "You have met the count?"

Laura shook her head. She had never even seen him, as far as she knew.

"No. He prefers the society he finds in the gutter. He thought to take me there too. Then he found that my father had taught me to handle a pistol, and my marriage had given me the resolution to use one."

"You shot him?" exclaimed Laura.

Looking haughty, Sophie nodded. "A wound only. But in a spot that…discouraged him from annoying me further." Her grin was feral. "He knew that the next time I would deprive him of parts that he valued greatly."

She should be shocked, Laura thought, but in fact she was fascinated. The story reminded her of things she had read in the earl's library.

"This was in Russia, years ago," added Sophie with a wave of her hand. "Afterward, Ivan would give me no money—not that he had ever been generous. So I was forced to find my own interests." She shrugged again. "I didn't care, as long as he left me alone."

"You couldn't leave him?" asked Laura. She knew this was often difficult, or impossible. A lone woman had few options, as she herself was well aware.

"Once we had reached our agreement, it wasn't necessary," answered Sophie with a thin smile. "And Ivan's work in the foreign service offered opportunities."

"Did you really work for Bonaparte?" Laura blurted out.

Sophie laughed. "Others may say what they will, but I am discreet. I do not wag my tongue about any small…errands I may undertake for friends."

The two women gazed at each other in the ensuing silence. The winter sun was lowering. She had to get back soon, Laura thought, before she was missed.

"So," said the countess.

"How do you fascinate a man?" said Laura.

"Ah, now we come to it. A man."

"An odious man."

"Ah," said the countess in a different tone. "Who? I swear I must know him."

Laura looked away. Gavin Graham was captivated by Sophie. Suddenly it occurred to her that she hadn't considered Sophie's part in this. "Do you… Are you in love with anyone?"

"Love?" Sophie sniffed and tossed her head. "I look on men as the eagle does the mouse." Joking, she moved her fingers like talons. "I don't waste my time with stupidities like love."

Laura sat back in her chair.

"You don't wish to tell me who he is," Sophie concluded. "No, I can see that you don't." She gave Laura a cajoling look. "It would be so much more amusing if I knew."

"I..." Laura searched for an excuse.

"Oh, very well. But I could give you better advice if you told me." Sophie waited a moment to see if this drew an admission, then she shrugged. "How do you fascinate a man?" she mused. She picked up an ebony comb from her dressing table and turned it in her hands. "First, you must take care to look your best, in your own style." She gave Laura a searching glance, nodding as if she approved of her in this regard. "You needn't be beautiful," she added. "I have known some positively ugly women who had scores of admirers. It is much more than looks, you see."

"What more?" asked Laura, truly curious about the knowledge this woman had gained in her unconventional life.

Sophie gave her a sidelong glance. She started to say something, then appeared to change her mind. "It is good to have a bit of mystery about you," she continued. "You should not be someone he can count on—not steady, or reliable, or safe."

Laura wrinkled her nose. "I should be unsteady and unreliable?"

"It should never occur to a man to ask you to dance because he is afraid to ask the one he really wishes to partner," stated Sophie. "He should not think that he will talk with you because you will not unsettle him in any way."

Laura frowned, trying to assimilate this information.

"And then there is…" The countess hesitated, looking at her visitor from under lowered lashes.

"Yes?" prompted Laura.

Sophie made a vague gesture. "Attraction, allure, the…uh…"

"Physical side of things?"

The other woman nodded.

"I have read about such matters," Laura assured her. "I am not some ignorant schoolgirl."

"Read?" answered Sophie, as if the concept surprised and interested her. "What have you read?"

"Books. Portfolios." Laura waved a hand, trying not to look self-conscious. The Earl of Leith's library had included a large collection of works on this subject that he hardly even bothered to hide. The first one she'd opened had shaken her deeply. She had put it away at once. But over the years, she had gone back and examined the materials. What she had learned was astonishing, funny, disgusting, and engrossing by turns.

"Portfolios?" speculated the countess, her eyes gleaming. "What sorts of…?"

"The earl has low tastes," she declared. "So you needn't worry about speaking frankly to me." She sat a bit straighter, trying to look worldly and knowledgeable.

Sophie laughed delightedly. "You are a truly unexpected person. I like you."

She rather liked the countess, Laura thought. "Tell me," she urged, "about allure."

Sophie gazed at her with an indulgent half smile. "Allure," she repeated. "For that, you must discover your own desires. When they are in your eyes, no man can resist."

"My own…?" This was not at all what she had expected to hear.

"If your passions are fired, they illuminate you. They add that final element, that thing the French call *je ne sais quoi*." She turned her hand in the air as if grasping some intangible.

"But I…I don't…" Laura was speechless.

Sophie laughed at her expression. "Did you think I would advise you to wear low-cut gowns and offer kisses in dark corners?" She pushed the idea away with a quick contemptuous gesture. "Men are drawn like moths to the flame of desire. It needn't be *them* that you want. Much better if it isn't. But if you can find the spirit that blazes in you, and set it free, the world will fall at your feet."

Laura stared at her, trying to understand. In all her studies, one topic she had never considered was her own desire.

Sophie took a long breath. "You have turned me into a philosopher!" She laughed.

Where did she look? Laura wondered. She had been in hiding for so long she didn't know where to find herself.

❧

Gavin shifted his position in his chair, crossing one leg over the other and leaning back, trying to ease his frustration and boredom before they exploded into some completely unacceptable behavior. None of the fifteen other men sitting around the table looked as impatient as he was, he thought. A number actually looked interested in the topic of their meeting—drafting a document that set forth guidelines for drafting other documents. How could anyone care about such things? he wondered. And yet a few of his fellows appeared to care quite insanely. One of them was speaking now, droning on and on about forms of address and equivalency of titles from different countries.

General Pryor knew quite well that he hated work like this, Gavin thought. He had assigned him to this committee as a punishment, because Sophie Krelov continued to approach him at balls and evening parties and flirt outrageously. Gavin suppressed a smile. He had known, of course, that holding himself aloof would simply intrigue Sophie all the more. By not pursuing her, he had piqued her interest even further. But the general seemed to expect him to give her the cut direct, or some such foolishness.

The speaker had moved on to the issue of precedence. Gavin gritted his teeth. He imagined the fellow in the hands of Barbary pirates, dacoits from the Indian backcountry, tribes on the steppes of Asia. He had once seen a man sewn into a leather bag and dragged behind the mount of a nomad warrior. That would silence this idiot, he thought.

The speaker droned on. French was supposed to be the universal diplomatic language of the congress, but this man was among the committee members who spoke it execrably. This was a complete waste of time, Gavin thought. He needed to be out in the city talking to people, finding out what was going on. Instead, his life was plagued by irrelevancies like this meeting.

And Laura Devane.

Gavin stopped even pretending to listen and let his thoughts drift to the general's guest. She was more interesting than he had expected, Gavin acknowledged. So far, she seemed impervious to his slights and showed no signs of being driven off. It was annoying. He had never had much difficulty in getting females to do whatever he wished. Admittedly, his wishes usually tended in another direction, but not always. He had discouraged a number of women in his travels. Of course, they had been afflicting him with unwanted attentions, he admitted. Laura wasn't doing that. It was General Pryor who continually nagged him to join some party or outing. Laura scarcely seemed to care.

It was galling, he realized. The woman hampered his freedom. She upset his plans. And yet she remained singularly unaffected by their interactions. The time had come to end this farce. Laura Devane must be made to understand that he danced to no woman's tune and brooked no interference with anything he wished to do.

# Three

"YOU ARE LOOKING VERY LOVELY THIS EVENING," SAID Gavin as he led Laura onto the dance floor at the Austrian embassy ball.

Startled, Laura looked up at him. It was the first compliment he had ever offered her, and she didn't trust it for a moment.

"That gown is unusual. But then, your clothes are all quite elegant."

She gazed down at the folds of her ball gown, fashioned of a silk that shimmered between bronze and deep green, depending on the light. She had been exceedingly pleased with the fabric and design from the moment she saw them. Looking at the gown now, she was filled with suspicion.

Gavin grasped her waist, and they began to dance, falling naturally, once again, into rhythm with each other. It was a waltz. Of course it was a waltz, Laura thought. A country dance or quadrille would offer him less scope to unsettle her.

"You're not usually so silent," commented Gavin, turning her deftly at the end of the room.

The strength of his arm was palpable, and his

hands—on her back and laced with hers—held an unnerving heat. He was a man who demanded notice, Laura thought. You couldn't ignore him, and it would always be a serious mistake to discount him. At the same time, he made it terribly difficult to keep one's wits about one. It was a devastating combination. "Your coat is very well cut," she managed.

His eyes flickered, and one corner of his mouth turned up for a moment. "Thank you."

Evening dress did particularly become him, Laura thought. And he wore it with unmatched ease. She felt a flutter in her midsection, and wondered if her dinner was about to disagree with her.

"Having established that we are both creditably dressed, perhaps we could move on to some other topic," he added.

Always mocking, Laura thought. Did he speak seriously to anyone? To Sophie Krelov, perhaps? "Is Lord Castlereagh here tonight?" she asked him. "I haven't yet seen him."

"I believe so." Gavin turned his head to search for the chief of the English delegation at the congress. "He had planned to be."

"He must be eager not to offend the Austrians." Laura was also scanning the huge room.

"Indeed?"

Laura looked up at his surprised tone.

"And why should he be?" wondered Gavin.

"I assume he wants their support against Russia's demands," she replied.

"Has the general been educating you?" he said, with predictable irony.

"The general shares the common opinion that women understand nothing about politics," she responded tartly. "I believe he would sooner explain such matters to his horse."

"Oh, I think he would speak to the dog first," answered Gavin.

Laura stared up at him, not sure she had heard correctly. A spurt of laughter escaped her.

"Where do you get your information, then?" he added.

"I am quite capable of reading."

"Reading?"

For some reason, the way he said the word made Laura recall the very unpolitical things she had read in the earl's private library. She flushed deep scarlet.

"Newspapers?" continued Gavin, looking fascinated at the reaction his remark had produced.

Unable to speak, she nodded.

"Perhaps not only the English papers? You seem to have a talent for languages."

"I have been reading all the accounts of the congress that I can find," she answered, regaining some measure of composure. "Hard as it may be for you to believe, I am deeply interested in what is going on here."

"It isn't at all hard for me to believe," he replied, in a tone that left Laura wondering whether he meant this as an insult.

"It is oppressively warm in here, isn't it?" he continued. In the next moment, he had whirled her into a tiny alcove and opened one of the French doors. Then they were somehow through it and on a flagstone terrace that flanked the building. A large garden spread into darkness on their left. "There, that's better."

"Mr. Graham!" Laura struggled a little in his grasp. "Excuse me. I wish to go back in." It was quite unsuitable for them to be outside alone.

"But it is such a beautiful night," he argued, his arm adamant around her waist.

"On the contrary, it is quite chilly," she said, trying to step out of it.

He swung her down two shallow steps into the garden. It was all Laura could do to keep her feet. Beyond the squares of light from the ballroom windows, the night was lit by a half-moon, which turned the landscape into a maze of black and silver. Gavin swept her along to a row of shrubbery, inky masses against the stars, which Laura recognized only when their needles brushed her arm.

"Mr. Graham," she protested more loudly, "I ask you, as a gentleman, to—"

"You and the general make the same mistake in thinking I am a gentleman." With a jerk, he pulled her tight against him, his lips capturing hers in a hard, inescapable kiss.

Laura stiffened in surprise and outrage. She pushed against his shoulders—with no effect. She wriggled, and managed only to make herself even more conscious of the contours of his body melded to hers. She had never been in such intimate contact with anyone. One of his hands had slid well below her waist and was pressing her even closer. The muscles of his chest caressed her breasts in the most amazing way. And his lips moved confidently on hers, rousing sensations that she couldn't evade.

It was unthinkable. It was intolerable. It was rather like some of the things she had read, Laura mused dizzily. One couldn't really understand, through mere words, how it felt, how one's whole being could suddenly turn traitor and melt like ice in a conflagration.

In the next instant, she was thrust roughly away and left swaying on her feet at arm's length.

"There," said Gavin unevenly.

Laura could see his face only dimly in the light from the distant windows. She thought for a moment that he looked almost shaken. But in the next, the sneering mockery was back.

"Was that what you wanted?" he said.

"I...?"

"When you allowed me to bring you out here?"

"Allowed?"

"If the general suggested such a ploy, he is even denser than I realized."

"You practically dragged me out of the ballroom," Laura accused.

"Dragged? I think not." He said it in a caressing tone that made Laura's face go hot.

"You...you bastard."

"Tch. Is this language for a lady?"

Sweeping back her skirts, Laura kicked him in the shin with as much force as she could muster. "Be thankful I am a lady," she said over her shoulder as she strode back toward the ball. "If I were not, that might have hurt a good deal more."

His derisive laughter followed her up the steps onto the terrace. Laura turned to glare at him, and he raised one finger in a lazy salute. Her fists clenched, and blood pounded through her temples. If she had had a pistol at that moment, she thought, she would have killed him.

As she turned to go inside, Laura heard Gavin call, "Who's there?" She looked back. Was this another of his vile tricks? she wondered. But he wasn't following her. He was striding purposefully toward the back of the garden.

"Who are you?" he said.

Laura saw a large shadow detach itself from the garden wall and move quickly away.

"Stop!" cried Gavin, starting to run.

The shadow ran as well. But Gavin was obviously catching up to it when the figure stopped and made a rapid movement. With a sharp exclamation, Gavin clutched his shoulder and crumpled to the ground.

The shadow receded. There were scrabbling sounds, and then a thud from beyond the wall.

Laura stepped back toward the doors, which were now closed against the chill of the night. She searched the darkness, but she couldn't see anything. She started to open the door to fetch help.

There was a hoarse groan from the back of the garden.

She turned back and saw Gavin struggling upright.

"Don't call anyone," he said in a stronger voice.

Hesitantly, Laura went down into the garden once more. "Why not? Are you all right?"

"Perfectly."

As he straightened, he stumbled and made an involuntary sound of pain. Laura moved closer. When he swayed on his feet, she risked a few more steps. He was holding his upper arm, just below the shoulder. The hilt of a small knife showed there, and blood welled between his fingers and soaked his sleeve. "My God!"

"It's nothing."

"Nothing? Are you mad? I must get someone."

"No!"

His tone stopped her in midstride. She looked back. "You're wounded. I must—"

"You must mind your own damned business," he interrupted.

"Don't be ridiculous. Wait right there."

But Laura had not even reached the steps again when he grabbed her wrist hard enough to bruise. "You will not tell anyone what occurred here tonight," he said.

Laura jerked away from him, smudges of his blood on her wrist. The blaze of his eyes made her back away.

"It is none of your affair. Forget what you saw."

"But…" At a loss for words, Laura gestured toward the wall where the ominous shadow had disappeared and then at his bleeding arm.

"An interesting development," commented Gavin.

"Interesting?"

He gazed at the wall, then raised his wounded arm experimentally. He winced and muttered a curse. "I won't be climbing tonight," he added. His head moved as if he were examining every inch of the garden, looking for a way out.

"Not unless you wish to bleed to death," said Laura tartly. "What is going on? I don't understand."

"There is no need for you to do so. Go back inside."

He spoke as if she were a highly unsatisfactory servant. Laura put her hands on her hips and glared at him.

"Someone didn't want to be followed," he explained curtly. "Now go…"

"How can you act this way when you have a knife in your arm?"

"It isn't serious."

"Really? You've been attacked so often you can tell without examining the wound?" she asked sarcastically.

"Yes." He turned his back on her, moving slowly to the high brick wall surrounding the garden and beginning to walk along it, checking for a gate hidden in the dimness.

Laura watched him in amazement, trying to comprehend his behavior. He seemed a different man. The mockery was gone; his lazy detachment was revealed as a pose. He was intent and focused—utterly absorbed. It still seemed senseless to her to ignore the aid that waited a few feet away. But he clearly had no intention of communicating with anyone. She couldn't resist moving farther into the dark garden and following his progress around the wall. "Do you think it was a footpad?" she asked after a while.

"Will you go inside!"

"No."

Gavin stopped and looked at her, his face pale in the light from the windows. "Mrs. Pryor will be looking for you," he said.

"Yes, she may even come out here. The general too. They will make a great fuss."

"What is it that you want?" he snapped.

"I want to know what happened."

"Someone threw a knife at me and then escaped over the wall, and if I am to have any hope of discovering…"

"But why do you not summon the authorities? If it was a thief…"

"Thieves do not climb over walls into well-guarded houses when a ball is in progress," he said with exaggerated patience.

"If it was not a thief, then who was it? Who would want to attack you?"

"This is none of your affair."

"An enraged husband?" she asked, remembering the remarks of the Frenchwomen a few days ago.

"What?"

"Or a brother, perhaps?" Laura nodded to herself. "And that is why you don't want anyone to find out—because of the scandal."

Gavin had finished his circuit of the garden wall. Now he came closer. "That's it," he replied. "Crime of passion. Mustn't drag the lady's name in the dirt."

His mocking tone was back, Laura noticed. He was speaking to her as if she were a child. She didn't believe a word of it.

"So you can understand," he added. "This shouldn't be mentioned."

"Your time must be fully occupied," Laura answered dryly. "When you are not dragging me into dark gardens, you are compromising the reputation of some other lady."

"I—"

"And rather clumsily too, if it is so obvious that her

husband must stab you. I suppose that is why you are so often attacked?"

"There is no need for you to be jealous."

"Jealous! You may be sure I do not envy any woman the sort of attentions I have endured from you."

"Splendid! Why, then, don't you go back to the ballroom and let me be?"

"Let you be?" Laura couldn't believe it. "You are the one who forced me to come out—"

"I don't have time for this." He brushed past her and strode onto the terrace.

"Are you going to walk through the ball with blood running down your arm?" wondered Laura, rather wishing to see this.

Gavin stopped with the door handle in his grasp. "Damn." He frowned. "I have to get out of here."

"To find the man who attacked you?"

"It's far too late for that, but there are inquiries…" He bit off the words as if he had not meant to say them and turned to give her a hard stare.

"You need to inquire *which* of the many husbands it might be?" she asked sweetly.

"You are an extremely irritating woman," he replied.

"You are a completely exasperating man," she responded.

They stood looking at each other in the squares of light from the crowded ballroom. Though his gaze was somewhat intimidating, Laura did not allow her eyes to waver. A shiver went through her—not of fear, but of mingled fascination and excitement. This was far more than she had imagined when she took the chance of coming to Vienna.

"Would you get me a cloak?" Gavin said.

"Your cloak?" At once she saw that it was his means of escape. "How will I recognize it?"

"It's black," he answered sardonically.

"But so are a hundred…"

"I don't care whose cloak it is, so long as you bring it at once."

"You want me to steal a cloak?"

He looked at her.

The blood was drying on his sleeve, Laura saw. He looked slightly drawn, and more than slightly annoyed. She had no obligation to help him, she thought. And yet the situation cried out to some instinct in her. "Wait here," she said and slipped into the ballroom.

For a moment, she concealed herself behind the draperies in the recess. No one seemed to be looking at her. Straightening her shoulders and putting a confident expression on her face, she moved out along the wall, heading for the entrance and the rooms where guests' wraps had been left.

She had nearly reached it when Catherine Pryor caught up with her. "Laura! Where have you been?"

Laura forced a calm smile. "I was talking to some people." She gestured. "Over there."

"Where is Mr. Graham? You went off to dance with him half an hour ago."

"We danced," Laura assured her. "And then I met these people, and…"

"What people? Did he leave you alone?"

"No. He…took another partner, and I stayed chatting. I'm sorry if I worried you. I won't do so again."

Catherine eyed her as if she wasn't convinced.

"I am just on my way to…" Laura indicated the direction of the ladies' tiring-rooms.

"Are you all right?"

"Perfectly." Seeing that more reassurance was required, Laura added, "I am having a splendid time. I saw Baron von Sternhagen." It was true, she thought a bit guiltily. She had seen him from across the room earlier.

"Were you talking with him? He's very well thought of. A nice young man."

"Umm," responded Laura. "I'll be right back."

Thankfully, Catherine allowed her to escape. Laura hurried across the entryway to where a troop of footmen watched over the guests' belongings. "Yes, miss?" said one of them, stepping forward.

"Oh. I…" What was she supposed to say? Laura wondered. Ladies didn't fetch gentlemen's cloaks. Providentially, a large group came in behind her, calling for their wraps. "My friends," she muttered, fading back as the footmen came forward to serve them.

Cloaks and hats were fetched. When the servants were occupied draping them over shoulders and waiting for tips, Laura slipped past and grabbed the first dark cloak she saw from the scores awaiting their owners. Moving quickly to the rear of the hall, she was lucky in finding another set of doors that led out onto the terrace. In the next moment, she was through them, her heart beating rapidly, and she hurried along to the spot where she had left Gavin.

He was leaning against the wall, looking rather unwell. "I got it," Laura told him. "Are you all right?"

He nodded and held out his hand for the cloak.

She gave it to him, and he tried awkwardly to swing it over his broad shoulders. "Here," she said, pulling it straight and then stepping back.

"It's short," he commented.

"I beg your pardon. I didn't have time to try it for fit."

"Never mind. It will have to do."

"Really?" said Laura, stung at his lack of gratitude. "You don't want me to go back and find a better one?"

"I doubt you'd be able to."

"You—"

"Go inside. I'll wait a few moments so that no one will connect us."

"That's all?"

"What else would there be?"

"I made some effort to get that for you," Laura pointed out. "Catherine was wondering where I had been, and—"

"Then you'd best return to her at once," he interrupted.

"And I had to sneak around several footmen. It was not precisely comfortable."

"I would have managed it better," he acknowledged, as if she had been confessing some fault.

Laura was speechless. She had not expected effusive thanks, but this was beyond anything.

"Will you go?" he added.

"With pleasure!" she snapped, turning back toward the hall doors and leaving him standing there alone.

# Four

GAVIN SAT IN HIS PARLOR SLOWLY SIPPING FROM A glass of brandy. His arm scarcely hurt now. Hasan, who had skills beyond the imagining of most gentlemen's gentlemen, had bandaged him up, pronouncing the wound minor. They had both seen worse, Gavin mused. Much worse.

For a moment, his mind ranged over some of the perils he and Hasan had endured. Never once had he found occasion to question the man's loyalty, he thought. On the other hand, he had earned that loyalty, Gavin acknowledged. He had included Hasan in his escape from a filthy prison pit straight out of a medieval inquisition.

Gavin's thoughts returned to the present incident. His attacker had certainly been a watcher, not an assassin. He had thrown the knife only to avoid capture and the exposure of whatever plot was brewing.

Gavin moved his shoulder to ease it and turned the brandy glass in his hand. He had sensed he was being watched, but he hadn't known the stakes were this high. He had to find out why he had become a target.

He sipped brandy and found his thoughts drifting again from this vital question to his companion in the night's adventure. Laura Devane's reactions had been surprisingly intelligent, he thought. He hadn't actually expected that she would get him a cloak. It had only been his first scheme. But not only had she agreed, instead of whining or arguing, she had done it. How many gently reared women would, or could, steal a man's cloak from under the noses of a gaggle of footmen?

An unconscious smile tugged at Gavin's lips. He had always judged women at a glance. One look told him whether he was interested, whether he wished to pursue or avoid. But with Laura the process had become more complicated. Her striking appearance might have attracted him. The general's plots repelled him. Her spirit and wit might have beguiled him. Her forced interference in his life annoyed him. He despised manipulation, and though it was Pryor and not Laura who was attempting to manipulate him, the fact remained.

The fact remained that she must be removed from his life, he thought, setting down his empty glass. Indeed, there was even more reason now. He was quite accustomed to danger. She wasn't. And he found he was very reluctant to imagine her in danger.

Who would have thought that kissing her would be so incredibly arousing? Gavin gazed into the darkness beyond the windows. He had done it to frighten her off, of course, to make her reject him once and for all. And she had been outraged—but not predictably so. Laura Devane was never predictable, he thought, the smile appearing once again. He had felt, when he held her, much more than outrage passing through her body. He had felt it in every nerve and muscle. He remembered every nuance of the sensation of holding her in his arms.

What was this? Gavin reached for the brandy decanter. He had kissed many women, enjoyed nights of passion with a number. But with her there was an added dimension. It was as if their bodies sent messages—unseen, unheard, but set in a compelling rhythm that perfectly matched. He had known the contours of her skin, all the depths of her passion. He knew precisely how she could be wakened and roused, and he was absolutely confident that her desires were as fiery as his own. It would be more than pleasure to show her the extent of his knowledge, to take her on a slow exquisite journey, touch by touch, to the blazing end of desire.

Gavin realized that he was gripping the neck of the decanter so hard it threatened to crack. What the devil was the matter with him? he wondered. Had the knifing addled his brains? Only one thing was important just now—finding out why he was the target of such inordinate attention here in Vienna and putting a stop to whatever plot was being hatched.

❧

"This is becoming worse than a London season," grumbled General Pryor as their carriage rattled through the streets of Vienna on the way to yet another evening party. "With the delegations trying to outdo each other in entertainments, we'll never see the end of it. What is it tonight?"

"The Saxons have summoned one of their leading singers to perform for us," answered Catherine in neutral tones.

The general groaned. "A concert!"

"She is said to be—"

"I don't care if she sings like a lark. It'll be dashed uncomfortable chairs and no talking or moving about. And if you do, being hissed at by a pack of foppish 'music lovers.'"

Wisely his companions said nothing. For a while the only sound was of wheels on cobblestones and scraps of German from the street.

"You know," said Laura then, gathering her courage, "if I knew more about Gavin Graham, I might have more success."

"Eh? What more do you need to know?" asked the general. "He's a reckless, insubordinate fellow who won't follow orders. If this was the army, I'd show him a thing or two about command."

"What sort of work does he do?" said Laura.

"Work?" repeated Pryor as if the word was alien.

"I know he is a diplomat…"

The general snorted.

"And he has been sent all over the world. But what does he do?"

"He does as he damn well pleases," was the reply.

"Matthew," his wife chided. The general took this criticism of his language with a grimace.

"It would be easier to talk with him if I had some idea," Laura added. This was quite true, she told herself. It wasn't just curiosity.

Pryor looked grumpy, but he said, "He's sent to talk

with people. The more disreputable, the better. Send a rogue to deal with rogues." He gestured as if making a concession. "Graham will sit on the ground and eat sheep's eyes if that's what it takes to fix an agreement."

"Sheep's eyes!" exclaimed Catherine, revolted.

"Arabs," muttered her husband.

Laura nodded. This made sense. It fitted with everything she had seen of Gavin.

"The fellow's good at it," admitted Pryor grudgingly. "He was with Malcolm in Persia ferreting out Boney's agents during the war. Did some exceptional work. And doesn't he know it!"

"The congress doesn't seem like that sort of assignment," said Laura. "I wonder why he's here."

"As a punishment for my sins!" exploded the general. "Between him and the blasted singers, I may as well cock up my toes at once."

The carriage pulled up in front of a large stone house, and a footman opened the door.

"I'll most likely go early," Pryor warned his wife. "I'll leave you the carriage."

∼

Gavin was involved in some intrigue, Laura thought as they circulated through the rooms. It was all tied together somehow—Sophie, the attack, his presence in Vienna. It was all part of some shadowy transaction, the hidden world that lay beneath the bright veneer of speeches and diplomacy. The thought filled her with excitement and a curiosity more intense than any she had felt before. This was so far removed from the kind of life she had led, and that was what she had been searching for when she took the risk of leaving it.

"Oh dear," said Catherine softly.

Laura turned and then followed her companion's gaze across the room to a sofa against the far wall.

"Matthew will be so angry," the other woman added.

Laura said nothing. Her attention was riveted by the couple sitting on the sofa and apparently oblivious to anything around them.

She had never actually seen Gavin and Sophie together before. Now she watched as they leaned close, Sophie's hair brushing his shoulder, her hand resting on his arm. Gavin was smiling as Sophie gazed flirtatiously up at him. She said something, and he laughed. When he replied, she lowered her lashes and moved sinuously. Laura was almost sure that her breast pressed against him briefly. The look he gave her in response was slow and thorough and appreciative.

It occurred to Laura that Sophie might have lied when she said she was not in love. Gavin, of course, was known to be infatuated. That was why Laura was here, standing in this crowded reception room and feeling an odd constriction in her throat.

Did he kiss Sophie as he had kissed her? she wondered. Immediately, she scoffed at her own naïveté. He didn't drag Sophie into dark gardens and maul her about. That had been mere mockery, an attempt to rout Laura. No doubt he touched Sophie with tenderness. Probably he had some consideration for her... The threat of tears disrupted Laura's thoughts, and she gulped them back, astonished. What was wrong with her? She didn't care a whit about the man or what he might feel.

She was angry, Laura decided. He had treated her outrageously and to see him deferring to another woman brought it all back.

"I'm going to fetch him," declared General Pryor.

Laura blinked. She hadn't heard the general join them, and now she sensed that he and Catherine had had a whole conversation that she missed.

"Should you draw so much attention?" wondered Catherine now.

"Don't care who sees. I've told him not to associate with that woman. He gave me his word!"

Pryor stalked off. Laura watched him approach Gavin and wait while he took his leave of Sophie with pointed politeness. He certainly looked reluctant to abandon the conversation, Laura thought. Sophie looked torn between amusement and annoyance. The general started back across the room with Gavin in tow. Sophie's eyes followed him and then swept over their group. Her gaze paused on Laura and intensified. Knowing herself recognized, Laura had a sudden sharp sense of having made a mistake.

"Ladies." Gavin bowed slightly.

"Where the deuce is this singer?" the general complained, obviously in a foul mood.

There was an awkward silence. Laura saw Gavin move his shoulder as if to ease it, and realized that she was the only person in the room who knew about the wound he had sustained. It was a strange kind of intimacy. She might have said something if not for her consciousness that Sophie was watching their every move.

What would the countess do? Laura wondered. She tried to remember everything she had said to Sophie, since it might now be repeated to Gavin Graham. And would he tell the Pryors about Laura's unconventional visit? Laura felt a profound relief when another gentleman claimed Sophie's attention. She turned back to her own party to find the general scowling, Catherine looking stiff, and Gavin ignoring all of them, half turned away, surveying the crowd with boredom.

"They say Frau von Fursten has a great deal of temperament," ventured Catherine.

For a moment no one replied; then Gavin said, "You think she's throwing some sort of musical fit?"

"Prince Frederick's about to throw something," commented the general with what sounded like great satisfaction. "He's not going to impress anyone with his powers of organization tonight."

"And certainly Prussia will point out how much better they might have managed things," murmured Gavin very quietly. "Just as they would manage Saxony if it's handed over to them."

Pryor gave a snort of laughter. "No doubt."

Laura examined the party with new eyes. Everything that went on here in Vienna had a number of levels, she realized. Each move could be interpreted, by those who knew, as part of a contest of wills, a balancing of powers, a polite struggle that would determine the future of Europe. She looked at Gavin. He seemed to have all this complexity at his fingertips and to be able to navigate it effortlessly. Or, not effortlessly, she amended, remembering the attack. But certainly he was at the center of some critical intrigue.

Catherine Pryor, turning to tell her party that the singer seemed to be taking her place at last, fell silent when she caught sight of Laura's face. Laura was looking at Gavin as if he were the most interesting creature she had ever encountered, as if he possessed secrets she would love to fathom. Suddenly, horrifyingly, it occurred to Catherine that Matthew's idiotic plan might have a disastrous result. If Laura was captivated by Gavin Graham, she would get her heart thoroughly broken. How could she not have thought of this? Catherine wondered. Graham's reputation was all too well known. Some called him irresistible. And Laura had had very little experience with any sort of men. Yet they had brought her here and thrown them together quite heedlessly. This was her fault, Catherine thought. Matthew couldn't be expected to foresee such things, but she should have. The scheme had to be stopped—at once. Laura should not see him again. She should be spending her time with eligible young men who might really be a part of her future.

"Shall we take our seats?" Gavin asked.

Catherine glanced at him, deploring his handsome person and ease of manner. She hurried forward to make sure that she, and not Graham, sat next to Laura for the coming concert.

❧

Laura stood in her room, waiting to leave for a shopping expedition with Catherine. She wore rose cambric, and her hair was dressed in a simple knot, with curls allowed to fall along her temples and jaw, softening her face. She looked lovely but her eyes were unfocused and distant. She was thinking, about history, and risk, and the dark vistas that had opened up with the attack she had witnessed.

Gavin was insufferable, of course. But the life he had led, the secrets he concealed, enthralled her. He had seen and done the sorts of things that she had only been able to read about. He had influenced great events, traveled to countries that were little more than the stuff of fables in London and the English countryside. And now he was in the midst of some such intrigue, and she had accidentally brushed the edge of it. That taste of a larger world had whetted her appetite. She longed to know more, to witness the action firsthand, to discover the taut reality that lay behind the bright veneer of society that was all most women were allowed to see.

Perhaps she could, Laura thought. If she pursued her mission of diverting him—which had not gone well so far, she admitted—she might be pulled in once again. She might see further into that other realm, even make some small contribution.

There was a knock on her bedroom door. "Laura?"

"Yes? Come in."

Catherine Pryor did so. "Are you ready to go? The carriage is waiting."

"Oh. Yes. Yes, I am." Laura looked around for her gloves, feeling as if she had been wakened from a dream.

"Is something wrong?"

"No. I was just thinking." Spotting the gloves, she picked them up and walked with Catherine downstairs.

"It looks cold," she commented, glancing out the window on the landing at the gray November sky.

Catherine merely nodded. They put on warm cloaks in the front hall and went out into a sharp wind to climb into the carriage.

"Do you know anything more about Gavin Graham's history?" Laura asked.

"Why?"

"It is interesting. And I thought it might be helpful—something to talk with him about. He and I have not…" She thought of the way he had treated her, the kiss in the garden, and flushed. "I am not having much success in diverting him. I know that the general…"

"It was a ridiculous plan! I told Matthew that from the beginning."

Laura sat back a bit at the vehemence in her voice.

"We should forget the entire scheme," Catherine added forcefully. "It never had a hope of working."

Stung at this judgment of her powers and slightly hurt, Laura said, "You wish me to go back to England?" Only when she said the words was she fully aware of how little she wanted to return to her previous existence. She imagined looking for another post, visiting the agencies, writing letters. The prospect was unutterably dreary.

"Of course not," replied Catherine.

"But…if you…" Relief and confusion made Laura tongue-tied.

"I am enjoying your companionship far too much," declared Catherine. "You must stay with me until the congress ends."

"The general…"

"I'll manage Matthew," she said with a wave of her hand.

"But I would like to fulfill my part of the bargain," added Laura, conscious of a lingering disappointment.

"Gavin Graham is not a suitable acquaintance for you."

Laura stared at her.

"I should have seen it from the first. I blame myself. I am a fool."

"I don't understand."

"You mustn't associate with him any further. He is far too…dangerous."

Laura thought at once of the stabbing, wondering how Catherine had discovered it.

"He is…not a libertine precisely. But he has a very doubtful reputation." Catherine folded her hands. "You will say I should have thought of this before bringing you here, and I should have. I don't know what possessed me. Matthew was set on his plan, and I…"

Not the stabbing, then, Laura was thinking. "I am aware of his…tendencies," she ventured. "I do not see what they have to do with…"

"If you fall in love with him, it will destroy you," Catherine blurted out.

"Love?" Laura shook her head in astonishment. "What do you mean?"

Catherine gazed directly at her for the first time in this conversation. "He is an extremely attractive man," she said, watching Laura's face. "And he can be very…charming."

"So I have heard," answered Laura a bit dryly. "But you need not fear that I…"

"You know nothing about men like him! You have been living a sheltered existence, hardly seeing anyone. You have no idea of the…the wiles such a man possesses."

Laura started to tell her about the reading she had done in the earl's library, then hesitated. Somehow, she didn't think Catherine would approve. "He is… an interesting character. I find the things that he has done quite fascinating."

Catherine groaned.

"But as for the man," Laura continued, "he is arrogant, rude, and dismissive. I quite dislike him."

The older woman scrutinized her carefully once again.

"And he has shown no signs of trying any wiles on me," she added.

"He is very irritated at Matthew's actions," acknowledged her companion with a sigh.

"I have noticed that," said Laura ironically.

"What a tangle," lamented Catherine.

"Perhaps not."

Catherine looked at her questioningly.

"I will not divert him, er, romantically," she continued. "But he seems very involved in the political matters of the congress. If I can speak to him seriously about those things, I might engage his attention." This was perfect, she thought. It gave her the chance to find out more about the plot she knew he was embroiled in, and freed her from the tedious obligation of flirting.

"I don't know."

"I have no other interest in Gavin Graham," Laura assured her.

"Well…" Catherine appeared to struggle with herself. "I suppose…" She stared into Laura's eyes.

Laura smiled reassuringly at her.

Still looking uncertain, Catherine made a throwaway gesture. "I don't know a great deal about his assignment here. Matthew doesn't speak of such things."

"The general spoke of Persia." The very word had conjured up visions, Laura thought—the shah, the towers of Isfahan.

Catherine shook her head. "I know nothing of that either. Although…"

"What?"

"There is someone who might—an old friend of Matthew's."

"He is here?"

The general's wife nodded. "They asked him to come and observe, offer his advice. He has retired from active service."

"Perfect! You must introduce me."

Catherine looked a little surprised at her eagerness, but she agreed. "And I do have some knowledge of Mr. Graham's family," she added.

"That could be very helpful as well," Laura assured her. She felt as if she were already becoming expert in the art of intrigue.

"You remember his father."

She had met him once or twice years ago, Laura thought. She had a vague recollection of a tall, forbidding man who had looked at her with cold calculation.

"He is dead now, but his chief aim in life was to raise the family's position through his children's marriages. He was terribly proud."

That was one word for it, Laura thought.

"The two daughters made very good matches. They are both older than Gavin by several years. His mother died when he was born, you know."

"I didn't."

"She was older. They had been so eager to have a son, and there were…difficulties."

Laura could imagine them very well, though she knew Catherine would never explain such things to a supposedly ignorant unmarried woman.

"Gavin was a wild young man."

"That, I remember," said Laura.

"He and his father didn't get on. They looked very much alike, however."

No doubt they were alike, Laura decided—proud, ruthless, selfish.

"He more or less forced Gavin into the political service when he wouldn't marry satisfactorily. I've heard he saw it as a kind of exile, a punishment."

"He sounds delightful," replied Laura dryly.

"He was an unpleasant man," Catherine agreed. "Fortunately, Gavin grew to enjoy the work, I believe."

"Where has he traveled, do you know?" Laura thought with envy of the places she had heard mentioned already—Siam, Persia.

The general's wife shook her head. "No. George will."

"George?"

"The man I spoke of—George Tompkins. He can

tell you anything you wish to know—if he will speak to you."

"You think he won't?" asked Laura, disappointed.

Catherine shrugged. "He's...rather eccentric."

"Ah." That didn't daunt her, Laura thought. She was beginning to understand that she was rather eccentric herself.

# Five

GAVIN SURVEYED THE NONDESCRIPT INDIVIDUAL standing before him with an experienced eye. He might have been a minor clerk in a countinghouse or the keeper of a small shop. Nothing betrayed the fact that he was a lurker on the fringes of society, ready to perform a variety of useful tasks for a price. "Good," said Gavin. "No one should pick you out of a crowd. You understand what I wish?"

"You want to know where this countess goes and who she sees," replied his visitor.

Gavin nodded. "I expect a complete record. And I expect secrecy."

"That's what you pay me for."

"It is. And if someone else offers to pay you more…"

The man seemed unintimidated by his threatening stare. "Not how I conduct my business," he said laconically.

Gavin continued to examine him. "So I have been told. If I find I was misinformed, you will not like the consequences."

"That's what I hear."

The fellow was almost eerily emotionless, Gavin thought. He seemed to fade into the wallpaper. No doubt this was helpful in his profession. "Very well," Gavin said, dismissing him with a nod.

When he was gone, Gavin toyed with a quill pen lying on the table in front of him. He had begun to establish contacts in some of the seedier quarters of Vienna, to set up a network that would alert him to any unusual activities. But that sort of thing took time, and with the city full of foreign diplomats and the agents, observers, and hangers-on who trailed after them, it was far more difficult. He didn't have time, he thought. And he didn't have his customary authority and scope. There would be constant interference and a confusing overabundance of information to sift through.

There was only one way to get rapid results, he thought. He had to persuade his adversaries to move. He had to make them uneasy by acting as if he knew their secrets, while putting himself in situations that tempted them to make a misstep. It would be simpler if he knew what they were after, but he had every confidence in his ability to flush them out. They would try something, and he would be ready for them. With a satisfied nod, he rose and went to dress for yet another dinner party.

     ❧

"Friend of the Pryors, are you?" said George Tompkins.

Laura nodded, though they both knew he was simply stating the obvious, since Catherine had brought her here and introduced her.

He took his time looking her over, and she followed his lead, examining her host and his surroundings with lively curiosity.

Mr. Tompkins was a figure from a bygone century. He wore knee breeches and buckled pumps, with a full-skirted coat made of blue satin. His white hair required no powder to give it the look of a previous era. He wore it long and tied back with a narrow blue ribbon. Several rings graced his long white hands, which lay at ease on the arms of a brocade chair.

But it was his face that held the eye, Laura thought. Oval, pale, marked by the signs of age, it had the look of fine sculpture. Those dark eyes seemed to hold the wisdom of centuries, Laura thought. They also seemed to be reserving judgment. It was clear she hadn't been approved just yet.

"You are interested in history," he said, as if it were a mere hypothesis he was testing even though Catherine had told him this.

She was not going to be able to fool him, Laura saw. She had the sudden conviction that no one had deceived this man for a long, long time. "General Pryor invited me to Vienna to divert Gavin Graham. He wanted to keep him away from Countess Krelov."

Tompkins raised his shaggy white brows slightly.

"I thought it was a silly idea myself," she added. "But I couldn't resist the chance to come here and observe the congress, to see the things I had read about really happening. I have always wished…" She faltered a bit under his skeptical gaze.

"I do what I promise," she continued firmly after a

moment. "I cannot match Sophie Krelov on...on her own ground. But I thought if I could talk with Mr. Graham about the political situation, I might...catch his interest."

"You are in love with him?"

"Not in the least! I am only trying to do as the general asked."

Tompkins's brown eyes seemed to bore into her. After a while, he shook his head. "I'm not interested in your romantic intrigues," he said, dismissing her with a gesture.

"This is not—!"

"You haven't told me the whole of it," he interrupted.

Laura hesitated. She hadn't told anyone about the attack in the garden. Gavin had asked her not to—she wrinkled her nose—he had not asked, he had commanded. But she hadn't promised. Perhaps someone in authority should know. She looked at her host. Now that she had met him, she understood Catherine's assurance that George Tompkins had vast, if unofficial, authority. He was not in the government, but he was listened to by everyone who was or would be. Instinctively, she knew that he was the right person to tell. "Something happened," she began, and she gave him the whole story.

There was a long silence when she finished. Tompkins was no longer looking at her. He gazed into the distance with cool calculation. Finally, when Laura was nearly ready to burst, he said, "You imagine yourself as a spy?"

She flushed. "Of course not."

"This…incident. This is why you are here—not to further some plot of Matthew Pryor's."

Her flush deepened. Did this old man read minds? Laura wondered.

For the first time, he smiled at her. It warmed his brown eyes with golden highlights and softened the pale austerity of his features. "If you were a young subaltern, I would send you north of the Hindu Kush to fill in the empty spaces on our maps."

The thrill that went through her at these words matched any champagne she had ever drunk.

Tompkins nodded as if gratified by a successful experiment. Complex ideas seemed to form behind his expression. His smile broadened a little before fading. "I will tell you some things," he said then.

He said nothing, however, until he had called for tea and it had been brought on an odd bronze tray etched with curling designs that made Laura's eyes cross when she tried to follow them. She tried not to be impatient. He was testing her, she thought; he had been since the moment she entered his rooms. She had the feeling that George Tompkins weighed the value of every person he met, and found important uses for some few of them. She found she very much wanted his good opinion.

"Gavin Graham," he said meditatively at last. "I have had my eye on him for years."

Laura sipped her tea, a strange smoky blend, and tried to look only mildly interested.

"He was hopeless at first, of course. So many of them are. Sent out to India to the political service when they only want to stay in London and idle their time away. But then we managed to…catch his interest."

Questions weren't a good idea, Laura thought. She must let him tell the story in his own way.

"Sent him north through the Punjab to meet with a fellow who claimed to have information on Russia's plans for the khan of Khiva. Graham succeeded at the mission, and had a fine time skulking about the frontier as well. Requested another such job at once, I believe. And after a bit, he was given it." Tompkins looked at Laura as if checking to see whether she was following.

"Khiva?" she couldn't help but ask.

The old man put the tips of his fingers together. "A city in central Asia. You have seen Asia on a globe."

"Of course."

He smiled slightly at her offended tone. "Russia has extended her empire across northern Asia, all the way to the Pacific. She controls the great Siberian forests, and so on. Britain is extremely influential in southern Asia—India, Burma, Ceylon. But in between…" He made a gesture.

"The two countries are rivals."

He nodded. "Bonaparte took advantage of that. He offered to join the czar in an invasion of India, you know."

Laura shook her head. She hadn't heard this before.

"They were to march through Persia, another country where we are vying with Russia for an alliance. Graham was one of the chief reasons why the French lost out in Persia. His work there was brilliant."

"What did he do?" Laura still didn't understand the exact nature of this "work" everyone kept mentioning.

"I can't tell you much more about that," was the frustrating reply.

Laura put aside her empty teacup.

"Gavin Graham's talent is his ability to win respect," he went on. "He discovers what the people in a given area admire, and then he does it. If it is horsemanship, he risks his neck on their wildest mounts. If it is skill with weapons, he matches it. If it is intrigue and treachery—well, he's shown a remarkable flair for those for an Englishman. His father's doing, I suppose."

"His father?" echoed Laura, surprised.

"One of the most devious men I've ever encountered."

She digested this.

"This attack on him is interesting," Tompkins added.

"That's what he called it," she replied. "You are both rather cavalier about knife wounds."

The old man smiled. "It is easy for me. These days, I only analyze dangers from comfortable armchairs in well-heated rooms."

"But once you were out in them," guessed Laura.

He met her gaze, amusement lurking in his dark eyes. "Perhaps. That is another story. We are wondering who is showing Graham such marked attentions."

"The Russians?" wondered Laura. "Sophie is Russian. Isn't she?"

"I have heard Hungarian," murmured Tompkins. "I have also heard Swedish and Belgian. She has a new story each time she is asked."

Laura remembered Sophie's advice—to remain a mystery.

"I have never inquired seriously," added Tompkins. He considered this lapse for a moment, then said, "It could be Russia. We are allies now, but it won't last. And Graham has certainly antagonized them. The French hate him, of course. And he *will* offend the Prussians by making jokes at their expense."

"What is he doing here? He doesn't seem at all suited to the congress."

"I may have suggested it," answered Tompkins with studied vagueness.

"You?"

"It is always…useful to add an unexpected element in negotiation. When men are off balance, they trip themselves up." He nodded to himself. "It wasn't a popular request. Of course, a number of his own countrymen dislike him quite intensely."

"You don't think…?"

"I don't have enough facts to form a theory," he responded. "I shall endeavor to gather more."

"I could help," offered Laura, trying to keep the eagerness out of her voice.

His expression said he'd heard it anyway. "Most of my colleagues would politely suggest that you stay in the drawing room and not bother your pretty head about such matters."

"Rubbish!"

He smiled. "Not entirely, I'm afraid. You have no experience, and no organization behind you. This is not a criticism of your intelligence. You are too vulnerable."

"I have looked out for myself for the last ten years!"

He raised his white brows inquiringly.

"I was governess in the house of the Earl of Leith."

"The deplorable Anthony? I am sorry."

"And he never noticed me."

Tompkins looked her over as if he didn't quite believe this assertion.

"No one did."

"It's true I heard nothing about you."

Laura got the impression that he heard about most things that went on in London.

"You never cared to join your parents in Bombay?"

She stared at him in astonishment.

"I don't agree to see people without finding out a bit about them," he told her.

"By the time they were settled there, I had already been employed for two years. And my father was not…optimistic about being able to support me."

"Spends every cent he has on horses," Tompkins commented.

"He always did."

"A convivial man, I understand."

"My father is the best of good fellows unless you have to rely on him for something he finds unpleasant."

"You are on the outs?"

"On the contrary. I exchange regular letters with my parents. We are all quite comfortable with the current arrangement."

"Hah."

Laura didn't know what to make of his tone. Indeed, she didn't understand why he had brought up this subject.

"You may come and see me whenever you like," the old man said, as if he had come to some sort of decision. "I will instruct the servants to admit you."

Because of the way he said it, Laura felt compelled to thank him. It wasn't until she reached home and told Catherine about the conversation that she discovered just how rare a privilege she had been granted.

⚜

Prince Charles-Maurice De Talleyrand had arranged a most unusual entertainment for the members of the Congress of Vienna. He had discovered a huge glasshouse attached to a nearby estate and convinced the owner to let him use it for a night. Lit by a thousand tapers, the orange trees and orchids and other exotic plants made the guests feel they were in a tropical paradise, instead of the chill of Vienna in December.

"Isn't it odd that everyone has come?" wondered Laura as they removed their wraps.

"What do you mean?" said Catherine. "Look at that grapevine. It covers half the wall."

"Well, he is French," continued Laura, "and the head of the French delegation. I'd think people would avoid him, after the war with France and...everything."

"Can't afford to," grumbled the general. "Man's as slippery as a sack of cats. Trying to keep us at each other's throats so we won't have time to give France what it deserves. Shouldn't even have been allowed to come, I say."

"Why was he?"

"Observer." Pryor practically spat the word. "Ingratiated himself with King Louis as soon as he was restored to the French throne. I swear, the Bourbons never had a—"

"Matthew!" admonished Catherine.

"Eh? Oh." He abandoned what he had been about to say. "The champagne should be good, anyway."

"Look at those palms," offered Laura tactfully. "They look just like the pictures I have seen of Egypt."

"I've heard the owner imports plants from all over the world," said Catherine.

"I want to see them all."

The general made a disgusted noise. "I have to find our host. Castlereagh sent me to represent him."

"Won't you come with us?" Catherine asked Laura.

Laura looked imploring. She had discovered that the formal duties of the congress could be quite boring.

"Well...don't wander too far. This place seems to be like a maze."

"I'll take care." Laura hurried off before Catherine could change her mind.

It was like a maze, Laura thought a few minutes later. Although the glasshouse was one giant room, it had been divided into paths and garden nooks by the plantings, some of which looked quite impenetrable. Trees festooned with lianas towered to the ceiling; great bushes loomed, creating corners and arches. At every turn, she found other guests wandering in confusion or delight, and exclamations of amazement floated through the foliage from all sides. Just as she was beginning to wonder how she would ever find the Pryors again, she heard her name spoken. "Have you lost your way?" asked Baron von Sternhagen in German. "You are walking alone?"

Laura smiled up at him ruefully. "I was looking at some purple flowers, and then at a tree with odd green fruits. By the time I took another turn, I found I didn't know where I was. This garden is incredible."

"You should not be walking alone," he answered, as if she hadn't spoken. He offered his arm. "I will escort you."

Suppressing an ironic response, Laura put her hand on his forearm. She was actually a bit relieved to see someone she knew. "Have you mastered the pattern?"

"Of course." He started off briskly.

"Do you know who owns this place?" wondered Laura, walking quickly to keep up. "He must have devoted his whole life to searching for plants."

"A waste of time," replied von Sternhagen, as if he was agreeing with her stated opinion. "A man with a fortune should devote himself to his country's welfare."

"As you have done?"

The baron gave one definite nod.

"You have been a diplomat for a long time?"

"I am a military officer," he answered stiffly. "I am attached to the Prussian delegation here as special duty."

"Ah. It is very interesting, isn't it? There is so much going on under the surface. Each conversation seems to have several meanings."

Von Sternhagen looked at her blankly.

Laura sighed. This conversation wasn't going well, and as far as she could see they were wandering aimlessly among the exotic plants. "You were involved in the war, then?"

This proved a popular topic. The baron proceeded

to tell her every detail of his military career, beginning with his training and first engagement in the field. It could have been exciting, Laura thought, but he had no knack for storytelling. He included far too much, and passed over the thrilling bits with little emotion. He was probably some sort of hero, she concluded, but after ten minutes of his droning she didn't care. She was seriously considering a plunge into the glossy foliage that lined the path when she saw Gavin Graham up ahead. He was talking to a small man half hidden behind a hanging branch. As soon as the latter became aware of them, he stepped back and then was gone. Had he actually done it? Laura wondered. Had he slipped into the plantings as she had been imagining? This question occupied her only briefly, however, banished by her need for escape.

"Mr. Graham," she said. "Are the Pryors looking for me? I would be glad to rejoin them."

Gavin looked at her, then at her companion. Amusement showed in his handsome features.

"Did they send you to find me?" she added, silently commanding him to do as she wished.

He raised one golden brow, taunting her. "Did they?"

"You are to escort me back to them?" she said through gritted teeth.

"I would be most happy—" began the baron.

"Ah, yes, I believe I am," interrupted Gavin. He offered his arm, and Laura took it.

"Thank you for a…a most pleasant conversation, Baron," she said.

Looking offended, von Sternhagen simply bowed his head, clicking his heels smartly together.

"Had enough of the Prussians for this evening?" inquired Gavin as they walked away.

"Shh. He'll hear you."

"I think he has already gotten the message."

"I didn't mean to be rude," protested Laura, "but I couldn't bear…"

"Was it his military exploits, or his theories on education?"

She looked up, surprised.

"I have attended a number of dinner parties with the baron," he explained dryly.

"What he says might be interesting if…"

"If someone else were saying it," he finished.

A guilty laugh escaped her. "Do you know the way out of here?" she said to change the subject.

"The paths are laid out in rough concentric rings. If you keep walking along any one of them, you go in circles."

"How did you discover that?" she asked in surprise.

"I make it my business to learn such things."

"In case of men with knives?" she couldn't resist responding.

"In case of…anything. And I asked you not to speak of that."

"I can't help thinking—"

"You could if you tried harder."

Laura had to pause to get a grip on her temper. Gavin turned onto another path and led her past a fern that was at least ten feet tall.

"Do you think this evening will do Prince Talleyrand any good?" she said then.

He gave her a sidelong glance.

"It is a dilemma, isn't it? People want to punish France for the war, but they have just restored the king there, and I suppose they have to have some consideration for his feelings."

He laughed.

"What?" said Laura, piqued.

"I was trying to imagine the feelings of Louis Bourbon."

"I suppose he is glad to have his throne back."

"Yes, I think it is safe to conclude that."

"You don't like him?"

"From what I have heard, there is little to like. His subjects seem to think so anyway. You are full of questions this evening."

"I am curious. If the French don't like their king, what will—" She was cut off when Gavin suddenly moved, pulling her between two sweeping branches of some sort of evergreen and into his arms.

"Will you give this up?" he demanded, his mouth inches from hers.

"Will you?" she retorted, pulling back against the iron of his embrace.

"I think not." He bent to kiss her, as he had before.

But Laura was prepared this time. She had been expecting him to try something of the sort in these surroundings. She bent and twisted, ducking out of his grasp and stepping quickly back onto the path. "You will have to find some new tactic," she said breathlessly. "That one is shopworn."

He looked angrier than she had expected. So angry, in fact, that when he made a move toward her, Laura fled down the path in the direction they had been going. Very soon, she found herself in a large open space that obviously occupied the center of the building. A number of the guests had congregated there around their host, and she was relieved to see the Pryors among them. "I lost my way," she murmured when she joined them. Catherine looked concerned, but said nothing.

Conversation ebbed and flowed around them. The general was talking to a Frenchman Laura hadn't met. Seeing an empty bench nearby, partly screened by a potted palm, she went to sit down, accepting a glass of wine that a passing servitor offered. Her heart was still beating rather rapidly, and she felt an odd disappointment in the party. She must do better with the information George Tompkins had given her, she thought.

Noticing Sophie Krelov some distance away, Laura ducked farther behind the sheltering palm. Sophie looked gorgeous in cobalt satin; she also looked quite capable of marching over and asking Laura what she was up to. Concealment seemed the better part of valor at the moment.

"Signorina!" said a caressing voice. Oliveri, the artist, sat down beside her. "You are sitting alone? These northerners are idiots."

Catherine wasn't going to like this, Laura thought. Oliveri leaned toward her, his dark eyes intense. "I have been longing to see you again," he added in Italian. "The music of your voice has haunted me."

He was a refreshing change from men who continually ordered one about, she decided. "Have you seen this place before?" she asked, indicating their exotic surroundings with a gesture.

"Never." He pulled the frond of a palm slowly through his fingers. "It is glorious. This man has the imagination of the great god Pan himself."

"Is the owner here? I have not heard anyone mention meeting him."

Oliveri leaned even closer. "I have heard that he is a recluse, and that he is hiding somewhere among the branches, watching us enjoy his creation without speaking to anyone."

Laura looked around. She couldn't decide whether this notion was charming or unsettling.

"I imagine him with wild curling hair and a great bushy beard," continued the Italian, "peering out through the leaves like the ancient statues of Pan and Bacchus in my country."

"You have a vivid imagination, signor," responded Laura, resisting the impulse to look over her shoulder into the foliage.

He laid a hand on his breast and bowed his head a bit, as if accepting an accolade. "I was born to be an artist."

"How is your painting going?"

Oliveri spread his hands. "The background is finished. But it is difficult to persuade the heads of the delegations to come and pose." He smiled wickedly at her, teeth flashing white against his dark skin. "They are too busy posing elsewhere."

She laughed.

"I will probably have to content myself with sketching them at occasions such as this. I always have my drawing materials with me and take every chance to get a likeness."

"That is clever of you."

"Oh, I am terribly clever, signorina." He paused. "Though, not quite clever enough to know how my painting should end up."

"What do you mean?"

"Before I can decide on the final placements, I must know how the congress comes out, eh? Do I place the czar in the center, beaming with triumph? Is Prince Talleyrand in the main composition, or do I put him off to the side, looking disappointed? My painting must tell the observer not only what these people looked like, but also what happened at this momentous meeting. So I wait, and I watch."

Laura nodded.

"But perhaps you have some insight for me, signorina?"

"I?"

"You are surprising, no? You know things one does not expect you to know."

"I don't understand," replied Laura.

His gaze was intense and unavoidable. "Your visit at Mokstrasse. This is quite surprising."

Mokstrasse was George Tompkins's address. How did he know she had been there? wondered Laura, suddenly seeing Oliveri in a new light.

"Very few people go there. And all of them are…powerful."

"I really don't know what you mean."

He leaned uncomfortably close, his shoulder brushing hers. "You can tell me, Signorina Devane. It is only for my art, you see—to make my picture right. I have no other interests."

Everyone at the congress had other interests, she thought. The hard part was sorting them out. Was Oliveri part of the plot she had already brushed up against? she wondered. Or was this some other intrigue entirely? "I don't think I have anything useful to tell you."

"You don't know what I might find useful," he responded quickly, his face too close to hers.

"Signor," she protested.

He pulled back, as if conscious of going too fast. "It is so interesting—all of these leaders gathered here. And I am so anxious to paint it well. This could bring me many other commissions, you see."

That could be all of the truth, Laura thought. And it could be only a small part of it.

"Come to my studio and see my work," he urged, handing her a card. "Then you will understand what I ask."

What meaning lay behind his urgent tone? Laura slipped the card into her glove, putting off deciding.

"Good," he said. "We cannot talk here. It is too public."

As if to confirm this, they were interrupted by a deep voice saying, "Miss Devane?"

Gavin Graham had approached from the side. Laura wondered how much he had heard.

"Mrs. Pryor is looking for you," he added. "She asked me to bring you to her."

Laura stood. "You must excuse me, Signor Oliveri."

"Of course." He had also risen, and now gave her a deep bow. "It was my very great pleasure to speak with you," he said in English.

Gavin pointedly offered his arm. Laura took it, and he swept her off before she could reply. "She really is looking for you this time," he said.

"It was very kind of you to fetch me, then."

He was quite unaccountably angry, Gavin thought. It was all these ridiculous parties—a complete waste of time. "She was shocked that you would stay talking to Oliveri for such a long time. He is not a suitable object for such marked attentions."

"Catherine said that to you?" she answered in an irritatingly innocent tone.

"Anyone would say it."

"We were simply talking, in full view of…"

"Skulking behind a fringe of trees," he corrected.

"Skulking!"

"If you are going to allow yourself to be deceived by the most obvious kind of wastrel—"

"You think he was trying to seduce me?" She looked astonished, as if this hadn't even occurred to her.

She was a very odd combination, Gavin thought, feeling inexplicably lighter. She would speak of things that other women would blush to mention. Yet she seemed to be unaware of the reality of the idea. "It is an obvious conclusion," said Gavin. "He is that sort of man."

"Is he? I suppose that would explain… But then why…?"

He bent his head to catch the murmur, but she said nothing further. "You should be more careful in your associations."

"Indeed?"

She turned her eyes full on him. Gavin experienced a strange shock of recognition.

"I imagine I should avoid men who haul me into dark gardens and assault me, then?"

"I did not assault—"

"You know, Signor Oliveri did not attempt to pull me into the trees and...just what did you have in mind?"

"I was going to kiss you," he said harshly.

"And you dare to warn me about other men?"

"If you would rather kiss Oliveri, be my guest!"

Spotting the Pryors, he pulled her several steps in their direction and then left her to join them on her own. He was furious, he realized, as he strode away. He was as angry as he'd been in ten years of suppressing his hot temper. Laura Devane was impossible, he thought. She was going to get herself into serious trouble, and no doubt General Pryor would blame him for it. Why couldn't she be like other females? he wondered fiercely. Any normal woman would have fled weeping back to England by this time. Instead, she flung his insults back in his face. She pushed him away, and then sat chattering to that popinjay Oliveri for twenty minutes, looking as if she was enjoying herself thoroughly.

He had wanted her to let him be, a small, sane inner voice pointed out. He had wanted her gone. He had set out to frighten her off, not to have her hanging about, flirting with any man who presented himself. She was supposed to be on a boat for Dover by this time. He was supposed to be free, as he was thoroughly used to being.

Gavin pushed aside a hanging branch with unnecessary force. He didn't have time for this. He had far more important things to consider. He had had plans for this gathering, which so far had been thwarted. He slashed at a tendril of grapevine that was curling quite innocently at the edge of the path. He would find Sophie, he determined, and continue to explore her motives in detail. And he would do so in full view of Laura Devane, he concluded with savage satisfaction.

## Six

"ARE YOU SURE THIS IS WHERE YOU MEANT TO GO, miss?" asked the young maid Laura had brought with her on her errand.

It was a larger question than she realized, Laura thought. What did she mean to accomplish by visiting Oliveri? "The map says this is the street," she replied, looking from the city map she had procured to the seedy buildings on either side. A number of them were warehouses, and the pedestrians around them looked as if they spent their days hauling crates and boxes. She was very glad she had brought the maid, Laura thought. She rather wished she had added a couple of footmen. "Here is the number," she added, matching the address on the card Oliveri had given her with that painted on one of the doorways.

The young maid didn't comment, but her expression was eloquent. Laura regretted her fears, but she had required a companion. She wasn't so foolish as to visit Oliveri alone.

But how foolish was she? she wondered as she pushed open the door and stepped into a small entryway. She wasn't very experienced in this sort of game. Yet. But now that she had been pulled into it, she couldn't resist playing a part. She had spent too many years making safe choices, hiding her abilities behind convention. More than likely she would do so again. But not today. She wanted to know how Oliveri had discovered her visit to George Tompkins.

There was no sign of the building's inhabitants, merely a twisting stairway that might once have been grand. Laura consulted the card again. "Third floor," she said and started to climb, the maid trailing reluctantly after her.

The stairway would have benefited from a coat of paint, but it wasn't dirty. Their footsteps echoed. No sounds suggested the presence of tenants behind the closed doors they passed.

"Here," said Laura finally. She noticed with some relief that another copy of the card she held had been tacked to a door on the third-floor landing. She knocked on it.

There was no response.

"Maybe no one's home," said the maid hopefully.

Laura knocked again.

"A moment," called a voice from within.

Footsteps approached the other side of the door. It was flung open. Oliveri looked inquiring, then astonished. "Signorina Devane!"

"Hello," said Laura.

"But...this is wonderful. Come in."

"You invited me to see your work."

"Of course. I am honored."

He ushered them in, and Laura looked around

with a good deal of curiosity. His quarters appeared to be one huge room with lines of windows on two sides. Screens partly hid a bed and washstand in the far corner. To the right was a table and chairs and a small coal stove. But most of the space was taken up by painting equipment and a massive canvas that rested against the left-hand wall. It had to be ten feet long, Laura thought, and half as high. The partially finished painting showed a vaguely classical background, with a great deal of blue sky and some picturesque pillars. In the foreground, human figures were sketched in, but they showed no detail. Signor Oliveri was of the historical school of painting, Laura concluded. She also noticed that the canvas was rather dusty, as if it hadn't been touched in some time.

"You see there is one central figure here," Oliveri pointed out in Italian, bustling to stand in front of the unfinished painting. "He will hold a scroll, representing the treaty." He gave her a brilliant smile. "I am still assuming the congress will produce a treaty, you see. These others will be pointing to it, showing that all are in accord." His smile broadened. "This is the artistic imagination, to bring harmony to chaos."

Laura had to smile. The delegates were certainly exhibiting very little harmony in reality.

"But who is it to be?" Oliveri gestured toward the central figure. "You have a guess, perhaps?"

His gaze was very sharp. Laura shook her head.

"Come, come. You must have some opinion."

"I am simply an interested observer."

"But you have extremely...reliable sources of information."

Laura gazed back at him blandly, as if she didn't know what he meant.

"You hear things, perhaps? You are a sympathetic listener."

"General Pryor never speaks about his work," she replied. "Have you been painting long?" There were no other canvases in the room, she noticed as she looked around. And the tubes of paint scattered over a battered table looked dusty as well.

"Since I was a boy," Oliveri claimed. "But I am rude. You must sit down. A glass of wine?"

"No, thank you. I don't want to keep you from your work."

If he heard the irony in her tone, Oliveri ignored it. "No, no. You must stay a little. You haven't told me how you are enjoying Vienna. You have met many interesting people?" His dark eyes sharpened. "George Tompkins, for example?"

He must be terribly eager to know, Laura thought, to ask so baldly and directly. It must be even more unusual than she'd realized for Mr. Tompkins to receive someone like her. "I don't believe I know that name," she lied.

Oliveri looked frustrated. He frowned in the ensuing silence. "You...you live in London? You have traveled a great deal, perhaps?"

Laura shook her head, rather enjoying this game. "This is my first trip outside England." Let him make what he could of that, she thought.

"Ah. You have family there, I suppose. Perhaps your father, or your brother, is in the government."

"Oh, no. My father cares for nothing but horses."

"Horses."

"And what about you, signor? Your family is in Italy?"

Oliveri spread his hands. "Alas, I have none. I am alone in the world."

"I'm sorry."

"It doesn't matter. Art is my family, and my country. I care for nothing else."

"Naturally. But it is a hard life, is it not? The efforts of an artist are so seldom rewarded as they deserve."

Oliveri's eyes blazed. "Imbeciles! Do they think we can live on air? But a great artist can rot in the gutter for all the world cares."

Here was the crux of the matter, Laura thought. Oliveri was after money. Probably he sold whatever information he could glean to anyone who would buy. He was no more complex than that. "I must go," she said, moving toward the door. The maid, who had understood none of their conversation, followed gratefully.

"But no. You must take a glass of wine, at least. I have not explained to you the allegorical elements of my painting."

"I'm sorry, signor. I have an appointment."

For a moment, it seemed that he would try to make her stay. Then his hands dropped to his sides, and he bowed. "A very great pleasure to see you, signorina. Please come back at any time."

Laura nodded in acknowledgment and slipped through the door. It was rather a relief to descend the stairs and return to the street. Intrigue was quite fatiguing, she thought.

"Do we go home now, miss?" asked the maid.

She was about to say yes when a throaty voice declared, "I don't believe it!" Laura turned and found herself facing Sophie Krelov.

"Michael said you were here, but I did not believe him," Sophie added. She looked splendid, and angry, Laura thought. "Surely you are not one of Oliveri's little tattlers? I thought he could afford only street children."

The maid was gaping at the countess and her magnificent fur-trimmed pelisse. Laura wondered if the guinea she had given her would be enough to quell the temptation to tell such a good story. "Shall we walk?" Laura suggested, hoping to move out of earshot.

"In this part of the city? Don't be ridiculous." With an imperious gesture, Sophie summoned her carriage. When it drew up beside them and a footman hopped down to open the door, she added, "Yuri, go with this young lady and find a hack. You will pay for her to be driven home."

She gave the Pryors' address and sent the maid off with Yuri before Laura could decide whether to protest. She didn't want the maid to hear any more, but neither was she particularly happy about being left alone with Sophie.

The latter practically pushed her into the carriage and then joined her. The vehicle started off as she said, "You deceived me. I don't like being deceived."

"I didn't," objected Laura.

"You told me you were some sort of governess."

"I was…am."

The countess made a derisive sound. "You do not

act like a governess. For that matter, you don't look like one. I was very foolish to believe you."

"I assure you—"

"I don't want assurances. I want the truth. Who do you work for?"

"No one."

"What are your instructions regarding Gavin Graham?"

"I don't—"

"What were you telling that little worm Oliveri?"

"Nothing," said Laura firmly.

"I suppose you will say you went there to look at his painting," Sophie jeered.

"No, I—"

"Indeed, no. No one looks at his painting. It is a transparent sham. What are you doing in Vienna? What is your game?"

Laura didn't know what to say.

"If you think you can beat me, you are an idiot. I will grind you to dust."

"General Pryor invited me here to keep Mr. Graham away from you," Laura blurted out. She didn't know whether this admission was wise, but she was certain that Sophie was a very dangerous enemy.

Sophie stared at her from narrow blue eyes. "Do you think me a fool? No one would do anything so ridiculous. Tell me the truth!"

Wonderful, Laura thought. She had taken the risk for nothing.

"Perhaps you don't realize who you're dealing with," Sophie said softly. "I have friends who can make you speak—make you beg to speak."

She was just trying to frighten her, Laura told herself.

Sophie reached into her reticule and pulled out a tiny pistol. "You doubt me?"

The carriage lurched, even as Laura's heart seemed to lurch into her throat. The vehicle jerked to a halt accompanied by a chorus of shouts outside. Without pausing to think, Laura threw herself against the door and staggered out of the carriage onto the street. She barely noticed a heavy cart blocking the way before turning and running in the opposite direction. People stared at her, but she didn't care. She turned a corner, and then another, and found herself on a busy commercial street. Spotting a drapers shop, she ducked inside and behind bolts of cloth stacked high on a counter. There were several customers, she saw, as well as the shop assistants.

Breathing hard, she pretended interest in a length of worsted and watched the street outside. Barely a minute passed before one of Sophie's burly bodyguards appeared. Sophie herself was right behind him, fiercely scanning the pavement.

Laura stepped farther back. No one could drag her from here without causing a riot, she thought. But it was still a vast relief when Sophie moved out of sight. And it was many more minutes before Laura summoned the courage to leave her impromptu refuge.

❧

Gavin examined the note he had received with a good deal of curiosity. Laura wished to discuss a "matter of some importance," and she asked him to call at the Pryors' residence at two.

What could this be about? he wondered as he read the words again. She had never done such a thing before. Had the general put her up to something?

Somehow, he doubted it. Pryor didn't seem to have any more control over her than...anyone else. He smiled a little at the thought of how that must gall him.

No, Gavin decided, turning the sheet of paper over in his hands, if she said it was important, then it was. Or Laura genuinely thought it was, anyway. Whether he would agree or not would be interesting to find out.

Waiting for Gavin's arrival, Laura couldn't sit still. She was agitated by the experiences of the morning, and even more by what she had decided to do about them. She knew someone had to be told. She couldn't deal with the suspicions she'd inadvertently roused. And she couldn't tell the Pryors. They would be horrified and almost certainly send her straight home.

She had considered calling on George Tompkins and laying her dilemma at his feet. But it didn't seem significant enough somehow. She was rather in awe of him, anyway, and not eager to take advantage of the acquaintance.

No, it had to be Gavin. He was the cause of it, after all. She would never have visited Sophie if it weren't for him. She wouldn't have become involved in the undercurrents of the congress if she hadn't witnessed the attack in the garden. It was practically his fault. And from everything she had heard, it seemed likely that he would know what to do.

She couldn't call on him, of course, after the way he had behaved since her arrival. She would summon him to the Pryors', and she would keep her distance. If he came.

She checked the mantel clock again, then walked over to see if it was ticking. She couldn't believe it was still only five to two.

⌘

Gavin rang the bell and was admitted by a footman. Divested of his hat and coat, he convinced the fellow not to announce him and strolled up the stairs to the drawing room alone. He found Laura pacing back and forth before the fire, looking very impatient.

She also looked quite lovely, he thought, hesitating in the doorway. Emotion tinged her cheeks deep rose and brought a flash to her green eyes. The fire drew reddish highlights from her black hair, and the sleek lines of her gown showed off her slender frame. She fairly crackled with energy, and she moved with a lithe grace that roused an undeniable response in him. Suddenly he cared less about whatever she might have to say and far more about the fact that they were alone together. He shut the door behind him, saying, "Good afternoon."

Laura whirled, her skirts belling out around her. "You're late!"

He raised an eyebrow. It was ten minutes after two, not what any hostess would call late.

"Oh, never mind." She shifted from one foot to the other. "Sit down."

Gavin chose the sofa before the hearth. When Laura took the armchair farthest away from him, he had to smile slightly.

She folded her hands tightly on her lap. "I have to…" She pressed her lips together.

They were delectable lips, Gavin thought, enjoying himself far too much to press her—not thin, but never pouting, a look he despised. And when you kissed them, they…

"Did you know that Signor Oliveri has a network of spies?" blurted Laura.

"What?"

"Apparently, they are street urchins. I suppose no one notices if they are followed by such children. They are everywhere, unfortunately."

"What have you been up to?" demanded Gavin.

"I haven't been 'up to' anything. I was curious about something Signor Oliveri said, so I went to see him, and—"

"You visited Oliveri? Alone?" Remembering the way she had sat beside the man and laughed with him, Gavin's temper flared.

"I took a maid with me," replied Laura haughtily. "But what I am trying to tell you is that he was very inquisitive about—"

"I'll wager he was!"

"Will you stop interrupting me! I am beginning to be very sorry I asked you to call. But there is no one else I can tell."

"Tell what? Did Oliveri insult you?"

"No! He is some sort of spy. He is very insistent about gathering information, and I don't think he has painted in months."

"What do you mean, insistent?"

"What is the matter with you? I thought you would be interested in this."

Gavin struggled to regain control of himself. He didn't know precisely what was the matter.

"Who do you think he could be working for?" Laura asked.

"Oh, you haven't discovered that as well?" he replied, trying to match his customary tone.

"No." She shook her head in disappointment. "But he hasn't much money. If he were connected with someone important, wouldn't he have funds?"

She had a quick mind, Gavin acknowledged. Possibly too quick. "Not necessarily."

"Oh. Well, perhaps if he were watched."

He had a horrifying vision of Laura crouched in a shabby doorway outside Oliveri's apartments cataloging his comings and goings. "You may leave this information in my hands," he said forcefully. "I will see that it is acted upon."

"Oh," said Laura again.

"This is all you wished to tell me?" It wasn't actually so bad, Gavin thought. If he could only discourage her from any further harebrained expeditions, she would be all right.

"Well…"

"There's more?"

She looked extremely reluctant. Gavin found that his fingers were digging into the brocade of the sofa arm.

"This is a bit difficult," Laura allowed.

His imagination ran wild. She had told Oliveri about the attack in the garden. She had approached some other—far more dangerous—personage in Vienna. She had disguised herself as a linkboy and laid dynamite around the Russian embassy.

"The thing is—you must know why General Pryor invited me here."

She threw him a glance, and Gavin nodded sharply.

"Yes. Well. I knew it was a…a silly plan. But I had promised, you see, so I thought I should try my best. I thought if I knew something—"

"What have you done!"

"There is no need to shout at me."

"Isn't there?"

"No! I was only trying to—"

"To what?" cried Gavin.

"To understand the circumstances."

"What circumstances?" he asked through clenched teeth.

"Those the general was…concerned about. So I…" She took a deep breath. "I went to visit Countess Krelov, and I—"

The sound that escaped him was as unfamiliar to Gavin as to Laura. It was somewhere between a gasp and a snarl, a small dispassionate part of his brain observed.

"I thought I would be able to help the general better if I knew what…what interested you," she blurted, her cheeks flooding with crimson.

"Indeed?" He had to regain his composure, Gavin thought, if he was to have any hope of retrieving this situation.

Laura looked at him from under her lashes as if she expected some further comment. "I talked with her," she continued finally. "Actually, we had an enjoyable chat."

Gavin tried to picture it, and was afraid he could.

"But then when she saw me with you and the Pryors, she appeared…agitated."

"You hadn't told her the real reason for your visit," Gavin said neutrally. It wasn't a question.

"No. And when I did, today, she didn't believe me."

"Today?" he echoed. Perhaps he wasn't really having this conversation, he thought. Perhaps he was in the grip of an insane nightmare, and in a little while he would wake up.

"Yes. You see, when she saw me coming out of Oliveri's building—"

Gavin groaned. Leaning on his elbow, he covered his eyes with one hand. If he was going to wake up, he thought, let it be now.

"She's extremely angry with me," concluded Laura. "And I thought I had better tell someone."

Silence fell in the room. "Did it never occur to you that Sophie Krelov is a very dangerous woman?" he asked finally.

"It did today," she admitted. She gave him a searching look again, as if she were trying to figure something out.

"She has friends who…" He didn't even want to think about it.

"I thought you would know what to do."

"I?"

"You have a great deal of experience—"

"I don't have experience in creating incredible muddles," he snapped.

Laura opened her mouth, then shut it. She took in a deep breath, then let it out. She folded her hands in her lap, looked down at them, and took another breath.

"What are you doing?" he couldn't help but ask.

"Controlling my temper," she replied in a tone that suggested she hadn't yet succeeded. "I am very good at it."

So was he, Gavin thought—usually.

"Recriminations aren't helpful," she added, sounding as if she would very much like to make some.

"No," he agreed, fascinated by her behavior.

"If you do not intend to help me…"

"You will do what? Precisely?"

"I will find help elsewhere."

"The Pryors will simply send you home." When she started to reply, he held up a hand. "And much as I might have wished that before, it is not advisable now. You have drawn the attention of some unpleasant people. That attention would follow you back to England." For the first time, she looked a bit frightened. Good, Gavin thought savagely.

"There are others I could ask for help," she said.

"Who?"

Her eyes shifted away from his.

"The judgment you have exhibited so far does not give me much confidence in these 'others.'"

Laura very obviously suppressed a hot response.

This might have been amusing, Gavin thought—trying to break her self-control—if the matter hadn't been so serious. "You must stay out of the way until I discover what's going on. If you don't leave the house—"

"The Pryors will wonder what's wrong," she objected.

"Tell them you're ill. Tell them anything you like. It won't be for long."

"I could help you investigate."

"Out of the question."

"But I have already found out several things." Her expression shifted, as if she was remembering. "There was something else too. Sophie mentioned a name. She said that 'Michael' had told her I was at Oliveri's, but she hadn't believed him."

"Michael?"

Laura nodded.

He pondered this. "Why didn't you tell me at once?"

"You kept arguing."

"I never argue. It is a waste of energy."

"Really? What do you call it then?"

"What?"

"What we are doing right now."

He waved this aside as irrelevant. "Michael," he repeated.

"Do you think Oliveri is part of it?"

Gavin shook his head. "He is insignificant, collecting odd bits of information to sell."

"You knew about him already?" said Laura, sounding very disappointed.

"He is rather obvious."

"Oh." She bit her lip, then brightened. "But the name—Michael—is useful."

"Possibly," he conceded.

"So you see."

"If you come to me for help, you must do as I say," Gavin replied.

"But if I were working *with* you…"

"You are not. And you would be very much in the way. You will confine yourself to the house until I tell you it is safe."

"And if I won't?"

He glared at her.

"You can't tie me up and lock me in a cupboard."

It was an appealing thought, but unfortunately she was right. "Are you attempting to negotiate with me?"

"You are a diplomat," Laura pointed out pertly. "You must be accustomed to compromise."

"You are not a fool," he said confidently. "You won't put yourself in danger merely to annoy me."

This stopped her, but only for a moment. "I can tell the general about the attack on you at the ball," she responded.

"If you like." He tried to sound indifferent.

"I suppose he would look into the matter for you."

He would interfere damnably, Gavin thought.

"I could ask Signor Oliveri…"

He stood up abruptly. Laura jumped to her feet. He took a step toward her. She moved swiftly around a wide table, putting it between them.

"Do you think you can threaten me?" he demanded.

"You cannot tell me what to do," she replied a bit shakily.

"What is it that you want, exactly?"

She met his gaze, her eyes dark with emotion. "To do something important," she said defiantly.

Something about the words, and the passion behind them, arrested his attention. It reminded him of something, though he couldn't recall just what. Where had she come from, this woman who was like no other he had ever met? "What have you been doing for the last ten years?"

Laura stiffened slightly, her hands resting on the tabletop. "What has that to do with anything?"

He simply waited.

"I was a governess," she said, a bit loudly.

He tried to keep the astonishment from his expression, and failed.

"My father wagered everything he had on a young horse from his stables. He was absolutely certain Alliance would win the Derby."

"And he didn't."

"He lost by half a length. I didn't wish to be dependent on anyone, so I took a position as a governess. I was just looking for a new post when Mrs. Pryor came to see me."

"It is hard to picture you in a schoolroom." It was impossible, in fact. This striking creature would have been as out of place as a tiger in Parliament. And she would have drawn the attention of every man in the house. Perhaps she had, he thought. The idea was surprisingly distasteful.

"I looked rather different," she said, as if she knew what he had been thinking.

"Indeed?"

"Not that it is any of your affair."

"Did you enjoy yourself?" Had she been some nobleman's secret mistress? he wondered. Was that the explanation for her unexpected qualities?

Laura gave him a peculiar look. "Must we continue to talk about this?"

Gavin was feeling odd. He wanted to question her closely about her history. He wanted to insist upon the truth. But she was right; it was none of his affair. It had nothing to do with him at all, he thought.

"I will continue to explore matters myself if you do not wish me to help you," Laura added.

He didn't know whether she meant it or was just trying to force him to agree. But he did know that Sophie Krelov's friends didn't take kindly to interference. People who got in Sophie's way tended to regret it, some of them permanently. The thought of Laura wandering into that sort of danger was…unacceptable.

But if he yielded, he would have to be with her whenever she was out. He would have to stay close in order to keep her safe. Gavin surveyed her slender form and lovely face. It would give him some control, he decided. "Very well."

"You agree?"

"If you promise to follow my instructions."

She smiled brilliantly.

Perhaps this wouldn't be so bad, Gavin thought. "Do you promise?"

"Of course."

He felt the beginnings of relief.

"After we have discussed what it is best to do," she added.

"It is not a matter of discussion—"

"And you have explained to me the reasons. We cannot be equal partners unless I know that."

He gritted his teeth.

"I will also be much more helpful if I understand."

"Do you think so?" His voice dripped with skepticism, but she ignored it.

"Oh, and one other thing."

"Only one?" he inquired sarcastically.

Laura frowned at him. "There are to be no more of these…these sudden assaults on me."

"Assaults?" he echoed dangerously.

"Now that we have come to an agreement, you needn't bother with that…sort of thing. You were only trying to frighten me off, after all."

It sounded almost like a question. But Gavin was too irritated to wonder why. "I have never assaulted a woman in my life," he snapped.

"You dragged me into the garden and—"

He moved swiftly around the table. Laura jumped and retreated to the side where he had been standing. They faced each other across the expanse of mahogany.

Gavin struggled valiantly with his temper. How could this one woman make him so angry? "You may be assured I won't touch you again," he said.

She looked strangely unsatisfied by his promise. But she said, "Good. That's settled, then."

"Completely settled."

"It's…it's best to be clear."

"Always."

"I am glad we understand each other."

"Are you?" He would have very much enjoyed smashing something, Gavin thought—which meant he had better get out of here now. Once he was alone, and able to think, he would be himself again. "Good day," he said, turning toward the door.

"Oh. Are you...?"

Before she could say any more, he strode out.

## *Seven*

A DAY PASSED, AND THEN ANOTHER, WITH NO FURTHER word from Gavin. For a wonder, there were no social events arranged by any of the delegations either. When Laura asked General Pryor, he said that the congress had at last begun some real work; at least, the five major powers had. England, Prussia, Austria, Russia, and France had little interest in consulting less influential countries in their deliberations. In fact, by one stratagem or another, they had prevented the entire roster of delegates from ever meeting.

This interesting tidbit merely made Laura restless. She had a sense of things moving, of important developments unfolding outside her knowledge. Had Gavin agreed to her terms simply to put her off? she wondered. Perhaps he had never had any intention of including her in a partnership. Did he imagine that she would sit waiting at home while he…did whatever he was doing?

The idea made her furious, and she decided at once to go out. She would walk, and possibly she would find a hack after a while and drive past Signor Oliveri's apartments, or Sophie's. She would not go in, of course. And she would not let herself be seen. There was nothing particularly difficult or mysterious about gathering information, she thought. Gavin Graham made far too much of it.

Laura did not, however, mention to Catherine that she was going out. Putting on a heavy cloak, she slipped out the front door when the entry hall was empty, pulling the hood up over her head against the cold December air. Outside, she walked briskly for a short distance, to get away from the house, and then slowed and looked in a few shop windows.

Now that she was out, she wasn't sure where to go. The memory of Sophie's anger was vivid. She could well believe that the countess might send someone to threaten her, to find out what she supposedly knew. The street suddenly seemed very cold and deserted.

It was at that moment when Laura realized she was being watched. A slight figure in a long gray coat had been with her since she left the house, and now that she had stopped, he was loitering a bit awkwardly across the way. Laura moved on, turning a corner, and then another. When she waited among the shrubbery of a small square, the figure appeared again, cautiously scanning the area from the street she had taken.

Laura felt a spasm of fear and excitement. This adventure wasn't just in her imagination. Someone had set a watch on her. She had to find out who it was and who had sent him. But first she had to reach safer ground. Walking very rapidly, she started to circle back toward the Pryors' house, choosing the busier avenues, where a few pedestrians braved the cold. Now and then, she risked a glance over her shoulder and always found the gray figure a little distance behind.

As she neared the house, Laura sped up considerably, until she was almost trotting. Rounding the final corner, with the house comfortingly visible ahead, she stopped and waited. Soon, there was the sound of footsteps; then the watcher emerged, hurrying along the same route with his head down.

Laura stepped forward and grasped the figure's sleeve. "Why are you following me?" she demanded.

He gave a kind of squawk and tried to pull away, but she had made sure she had a firm grip on the wool of his coat. His head and face were muffled in a cloth cap and several scarves, so she couldn't see what he looked like, but he was not large and muscular. Indeed, he was smaller than she, Laura realized. Perhaps it was one of Oliveri's urchins.

Emboldened by this thought, Laura reached out and yanked at the scarves wound around the man's face. When she pulled them off, the cap came as well, revealing a cascade of blonde hair and the face of a young girl.

"What are you doing?" exclaimed the girl in German, grabbing for the cap.

Laura stepped back, the scarves dangling from her hand, and stared. This was not at all what she had expected.

"Give them to me," said the girl. This time she managed to jerk the things from Laura's hand. At once she began stuffing her hair back into the cap.

"Who are you?" asked Laura. When the girl simply

hunched a shoulder at her, she repeated the question in German.

"I am a citizen of Vienna," was the reply. "And you accost me in the street."

"You were following me," Laura accused.

"That is ridiculous. I ought to call the watch."

"What a good idea. Let us look for them."

The girl made a move as if to hurry away, but Laura had anticipated it and took a firm hold on her arm, hustling her toward the Pryors' front door.

"I will scream," she threatened.

"That should bring a constable," replied Laura agreeably, without stopping.

There was no scream. They reached the house, and Laura got the door open and pushed her captive through it. Under the astonished gaze of a footman in the hall, Laura thrust her guest into the parlor and closed the door with a click, keeping her back against it. "There," she said, breathing a little hard from the exertion. "Now we can talk."

"You are a madwoman," responded the girl sullenly.

"Possibly. Who are you, and why were you watching me?"

She crossed her arms on her chest and looked stubborn.

"If you do not tell me, I will summon a constable."

"I will tell him that you attacked me for no reason and dragged me in here."

Laura nodded. "And I will tell him that you were following me, and I suspected you meant to steal my purse."

"I'm not a thief!"

"What are you?"

The girl's shoulders slumped. "Papa will kill me," she murmured.

"And who is he?"

She looked frightened for the first time. "You cannot tell Papa what I was doing!"

This didn't seem like the remark of a dangerous criminal, Laura thought. Of course, since she had first unmasked the girl, she had doubted the threat. "I won't tell him, if you explain to me what you were doing."

The girl sighed heavily, looking at the floor. "Heinrick is very ill, you see."

"Heinrick?"

"My older brother."

"Ah?"

"He was supposed to come, but he had a fever and he was coughing so dreadfully. I told him I would watch for him."

"I see. And who asked Heinrick to watch?"

"Papa," answered the girl, as if surprised.

"Your father told Heinrick to follow me. Why?"

"To see where you go and report to the Englishman."

"Englishman?" echoed Laura, surprised in her own turn now.

Under her cloth cap, the girl flushed bright red. "I was not supposed to say that." She put her face in her hands and groaned. "I told Papa I could do this. Now he will say he was right all along, and he will never let me help him."

Laura felt a twinge of sympathy. "Does he say you cannot help because you are a girl?"

Her guest looked up, staring with round blue eyes. "How did you know?"

"It is an opinion I have heard before," she answered dryly.

"You *know* Papa?" She looked stunned and deeply apprehensive.

"People like him," Laura said. "Why don't you sit down?"

"I must go."

"Soon. We will talk first. Would you like a cup of tea? You must have gotten cold, standing outside like that."

The girl looked tempted, then frowned. "You cannot corrupt me. I will tell you nothing."

"Of course not. But what harm could there be in one cup of tea?" Not waiting for an answer, Laura opened the door and asked the footman—who was lingering suspiciously close—for tea. Then she took off her cloak and laid it over an armchair. "I will help you, if you tell me a few things," she offered.

"Help me?" The girl's frown intensified.

"I won't tell anyone that I noticed you, and I'll give you information you can take back to your papa." She watched as the girl puzzled this out.

"What sort of information?"

"Won't you sit down and take off your coat?"

The girl clutched the coat tighter around her, but after a moment she sat on the edge of the sofa.

"What is your name?"

There was a long pause. Laura had decided that she was not going to win her cooperation when the girl finally said, "Annalise."

"Ah. Mine is Laura."

"I know." It was just slightly smug.

"Of course you do." The girl was probably fourteen or fifteen, Laura thought. It was hard to tell in the bulky coat. She wasn't particularly pretty, but she was fresh-faced and very sharp.

The tea arrived. Annalise accepted a cup, along with several of the sweet biscuits on the tray. Laura waited until she had devoured two of them before saying, "Your father watches people?"

Annalise nodded warily.

"And your brother helps him?"

"Sometimes. Heinrick doesn't like it much. He wants to be a shopkeeper." She wrinkled her nose as if she found this ambition utterly incomprehensible.

"Why wasn't your father following me, then?"

"He has more important things to do," replied Annalise, a little contemptuously.

"I see. I am not very important." Laura kept her voice humble.

"No. The Englishman told Papa that you didn't matter, just to make sure you did not get into trouble."

Laura set her jaw. "Herr Graham," she said, her suspicions confirmed.

"Yes, he said that—" Annalise stopped and gasped, aware that she had let another secret slip.

"It's all right," Laura assured her. "We are working together." Or so she had been promised, she thought grimly.

"You are?"

"Yes. Herr Graham is just a little…overprotective."

"Papa is the same." Annalise sighed. "What does he think will happen to me standing about in the street?"

Well, quite a number of things, Laura admitted silently. But some of them might happen to Heinrick as well.

"I am very careful," the girl continued. "I do not speak to anyone, and I stay out of sight. You only caught me because you stood staring at a tray of stale cakes for at least five minutes," Annalise accused. "No one does that!"

"No," agreed Laura absently.

"When those street children came around, I went to the end of the street and waited in a doorway. They didn't see me."

"Street children?"

The girl nodded. "They stayed for an hour or so, then got bored and went away. I would never do that," she added proudly.

Had they come from Oliveri? Laura wondered. "Did you see anyone else?"

Annalise shook her head. "Well, not exactly. Some of your neighbors are very nosy."

"What do you mean?"

"A curtain keeps twitching on the third floor across from here. Some old lady with nothing to do but watch the street, I suppose."

"Can you show me which window?" asked Laura sharply, standing.

Annalise gazed up at her, then frowned again. "Do you think it is…?"

"I would just like to know which."

With each of them on one side of the window, hidden by the draperies, Annalise pointed it out. The lace curtains opposite did not move as Laura looked. It was probably just an inquisitive neighbor, she thought. But with the way things had been going, she wasn't about to count on it.

The mantel clock struck twelve.

"I must go," exclaimed Annalise. "Heinrick is coming to meet me, so I can get back before Papa comes home." She began wrapping the scarves around her face again, looking at Laura to see if she meant to interfere.

Laura merely nodded. She intended to get a good view of Heinrick so that she would know her shadow.

"You won't tell?" added Annalise nervously.

"It will be our secret. Perhaps we could even work together sometime."

The girl hesitated at the door. "What do you mean?"

"I'm not sure. Is there a way I can send word to you?"

Annalise's eyes narrowed as she considered this. Laura thought she was tempted, but still wary. "If you leave a note at Herr Schwimmer's tobacco shop in Friedrichstrasse, I will get it," she said finally. And then she was gone.

Hidden behind the drapes again, Laura watched her leave the house and take up her post down the street. When a tall, thin youth joined and then replaced her, Laura carefully noted his clothes and appearance. So Gavin Graham thought she didn't matter? So he set a watch to keep her out of trouble? He would find that he had seriously miscalculated, Laura vowed—just as soon as she figured out the best way to make it very, very clear.

❧

"It's odd not to be home for Christmas," said Catherine wistfully as they huddled in their cloaks in the carriage, on their way to an evening of carol singing arranged by the congress's Austrian hosts.

"It's ridiculous," responded the general from the opposite seat. "If they don't give up this endless wrangling, we'll be here till summer."

"At least then it would be warm," said his wife as a blast of wind struck the vehicle, making it sway slightly on its springs. "I didn't bring enough winter clothes."

"Send for them," was the unencouraging reply.

Laura gazed out the window at the icy streets. Christmas hadn't been much of a holiday for her in years. When the family gathered at Leith House, the governess wasn't much in demand—except to take the children away when they were overtired or overexcited. Her own family was too far away to visit, so she had spent most Christmases reading in her room and dining alone on the festive dishes sent up to her from the servants' celebration. It hadn't been tragic; often she had enjoyed the respite. But she had lost some of that special attachment to the holidays that Catherine clearly had.

"I've ordered a goose," said Catherine. "We'll have a proper Christmas dinner, at least. And I've asked the Phillipses and the Merritts."

She would be the only person under fifty at the dinner, Laura thought with a tinge of amusement.

"I invited Graham," added the general. After a moment, he became aware that both women were looking at him. "He's here on his own. Besides, gives me a chance to keep tabs on him."

"He has accepted?" replied Catherine.

"Of course. Why wouldn't he?"

"He just doesn't seem…suited for a quiet Christmas dinner."

The general frowned at her.

"I can't picture Mr. Graham being…cozy," explained his wife.

Her husband snorted, whether in derision or agreement Laura couldn't tell.

❧

The palace had been decorated with boughs of evergreen and sprigs of holly. Knots of red ribbon punctuated the green, and there was hot rum punch and a bewildering variety of sweets. Roaring fires lit every hearth, and in a huge reception room a group of singers sang traditional carols in several languages. The warmth and the buzz of conversation were festive. Laura found her spirits rising as she walked through the rooms and greeted some of the people she had met since arriving in Vienna. She accepted a cup of the punch, though it was stronger than anything she usually drank, and sipped it as she enjoyed the ruddy faces and lively laughter of the other guests.

A group of them moved off together, and Laura saw Gavin standing on the other side of the room. His head was bent over a cascade of red-gold curls, and a delicate white hand rested on his sleeve. Sophie Krelov seemed to be telling him something very engrossing, and judging from his smile, very pleasant as well. Laura turned her head, not wanting to be seen staring. But she couldn't stop her gaze from drifting back. They made a lovely pair, she thought; they had a similar elegance. No wonder people looked at them admiringly as they passed.

It bothered Laura that she hadn't been able to discover how Gavin really felt about the glamorous countess. She had been told, of course, that he was infatuated with her. And he did pay her marked attention despite the general's disapproval. But was that because she was part of some intrigue that he was trying to fathom or because he genuinely admired her? Laura had given him a number of opportunities to clarify this question. All he had said was that Sophie was dangerous. Was this a criticism, or a compliment?

Sophie cocked her head and said something. Gavin threw his head back in laughter. Laura experienced a curious pang. Of course he admired her, she thought. What man would not? Sophie was gorgeous and mysterious and sophisticated. And Gavin was notoriously susceptible to exotic females. Laura remembered the phrase that the unknown Frenchwoman had used at her first ball in Vienna—a "poet of the bedchamber." No doubt Sophie knew precisely what that meant, and she was probably well able to reciprocate.

Why was she thinking about this? Laura wondered. It was none of her affair, and it didn't matter to her at all. She turned sharply away, and bumped into Signor Oliveri, who had been coming up behind her.

"Your pardon, signorina," he said, bowing more extravagantly than other men, as usual.

Laura felt her spirits rise. She had been hoping to encounter those involved in the intrigue she was supposed to be helping solve. "Good evening, signor," she replied. "How is your painting progressing?"

He spread his hands. "Alas. Slowly. Until I can discover—"

"Do you know the Countess Krelov?" Laura interrupted.

Oliveri blinked in surprise.

"She's over there," Laura offered helpfully, nodding toward the spot where Gavin and Sophie lingered. The countess was standing on tiptoe now, whispering something in Gavin's ear. Laura's jaw clenched.

"The countess," her companion echoed. "Of course." He tried to look deeply knowledgeable.

"She is very interesting," prompted Laura.

"Indeed?"

"What do you know of her?"

"I?"

"You know so much of what goes on in Vienna, signor."

Oliveri preened a bit at this flattery. "I keep my ears open."

Laura tried not to sound impatient. "So you are acquainted with the countess?"

"Oh, well, as to that…" Reacting to her expression, he added, "They say she was born in Cairo, among the heathen."

"Really?"

"Some say she lived in a pasha's harem as a young girl." He leered.

Laura ignored it. "That seems unlikely," she scoffed.

"She shot two men, escaping," Oliveri countered, his pride piqued. "She fled through the Holy Land, where she met the count."

"Count Krelov was in the Holy Land?"

"Passing through," said Oliveri, smiling. "He is hardly religious."

Laura didn't believe any of this, but she made one more attempt. "What about the countess's friend Michael?" Laura asked boldly.

"Michael?" He raised his dark brows. "Michael what?"

"I don't know."

The artist looked intrigued. "Who is this Michael?"

"I heard someone mention him in a way that made me curious."

"Someone? Who?"

"So you don't know the name?"

His black eyes bored into hers. "It is rather common, signorina. If I knew a little more about—"

"You are always wanting to know more, aren't you, signor?"

"Information is something I trade," he answered, emphasizing the last word. "I cannot afford to give it away."

Laura decided she had gone far enough. She didn't think Oliveri knew much anyway. "What do you mean? I was just asking if you were acquainted with a man named Michael. It was mere conversation."

Oliveri hesitated, as if deciding whether to risk honesty. Finally he bowed a little and replied, "I would never use such a word about a conversation with you, signorina."

"You are too kind," she said, turning to move away.

"Apparently, I am not kind enough," he muttered.

Laura moved through the crowd. Gavin and Sophie were no longer across the room, she noticed. In fact, she didn't see either of them anywhere. Perhaps they had gone off together to a more private place, she thought caustically. Spotting Catherine, she went to join her. Only too late did she see that the older woman was chatting with Baron von Sternhagen.

"Laura. The baron was telling me about Christmas at his home in Prussia. It sounds quite lovely."

"We burn a Yule log that is six feet long," the baron offered. "In the fireplace in our great hall, you can roast an ox."

"Really?" said Laura.

"It was built by Rudolf von Sternhagen, who rode on the Sixth Crusade."

"Wasn't that the one where the Holy Roman Emperor was excommunicated by the pope?"

Her two companions gazed at Laura blankly.

"The pope was angry because the emperor negotiated with the Muslims instead of fighting," she said. When they continued to stare, she added, "I read about it."

"Laura is a great reader," said Catherine, a bit faintly.

"I have little time for such things," responded the baron. "My time is occupied with military duties and my estates."

"Of course." Catherine shot Laura an admonishing glance.

"I am interested in real events, not stories in

books," he stated, as if there could be no other view on the subject.

Laura started to point out that she had been describing real events, then decided it wasn't worth it.

"I understand you are a great breeder of hunting dogs," Catherine said.

"For hunting the boar, yes." There was more enthusiasm in the baron's tone than Laura had ever heard there before. He launched into an animated discussion of the proper characteristics of a hunting pack and the best ways of training young dogs into them. Laura felt her eyes glazing over. She pinned a set smile on her face and settled down to endure.

Watching from the far corner of the large room, Gavin silently wagered with himself that von Sternhagen was prosing on about his dogs. He had that pontificating expression that Gavin had observed—once. He had taken care to avoid it ever since. Everyone had their passions, he thought; some of them were just more interesting than others.

Miss Devane's, for example. Laura was probably quite angry with him. If he approached her, she would no doubt accuse him of abandoning the partnership they had agreed upon in the Pryors' parlor. He *had* been evading it. He kept his promises, but this one was ridiculous, impossible. There was no way she could be involved in the sort of work he did.

Yet she had provided an important piece of information, he acknowledged. The name Michael had suggested a number of possibilities, and he was pursuing them. If only she would be satisfied with that.

Laura gazed around the room, obviously desperate

for rescue from the redoubtable baron. Should he go and save her? Gavin wondered. It was an attractive idea. But before he could move, she had taken matters into her own hands—typically—and excused herself with apologetic gestures. He watched her walk gracefully toward one of the archways draped with pine boughs. She had the air of a sibyl, he thought—composed, intelligent—and she was lovely as a nymph. He continued to follow her appreciatively with his gaze until he realized that she was focused on following something as well. Glancing ahead of her, he almost groaned. Sophie Krelov was making her way around the edge of the room toward the same archway, and she looked as if she was trying to avoid notice. Was Laura actually planning to intercept her? Gavin strode quickly after the two of them.

He reached the archway too late. Sophie had gone through, and Laura had followed after a few moments hesitation. Beyond, Gavin found an empty corridor leading left. He ran along it, and nearly collided with Laura when it turned left again.

"Shhh," she hissed before he could speak.

She was standing beside a curtained recess in the wall, which was a very sensible precaution, Gavin had to admit, and she was bent forward, listening.

"The countess went in there," she whispered softly.

If she thought Sophie Krelov would make some slip in such a public place—he almost laughed. It only showed how little Laura knew of such matters, and how likely she was to get into serious trouble if she didn't stop her interference at once. "I told you to stay away from…"

"Shhh," she said again.

"Are you mad, coming here?" It was Sophie's voice, emanating quite clearly from the room ahead, and speaking fluent French. "I told you I would summon you when I—"

A man's voice interrupted, sharp but unintelligible. Laura threw Gavin a triumphant glance. All very well, he thought sourly; but if she weren't here, he could march right into the room and see whom Sophie was meeting. Now he couldn't, because Laura was certain to go with him.

"I can manage Graham," said Sophie.

Gavin frowned, feeling Laura's eyes on him.

The man made some reply that sounded like an objection. Gavin couldn't resist. He inched forward along the wall, waving Laura back, though he had no confidence that she would obey.

Voices came echoing down the corridor.

"Someone is coming," said Sophie.

There was the sound of footsteps from the room ahead. Gavin stepped back quickly, bumping into Laura, who was, predictably, right behind him. Fortunately, she didn't cry out. He grabbed her arm and pulled her into the curtained niche in the wall.

"Come along this way," urged a voice in French from farther down the hall. "We can be private down here."

The niche was shallow and narrow with a door at the back. This was probably an entrance the servants used, Gavin thought, far too conscious of the fact that Laura was pressed tight against him in the small space. She said nothing, but he could feel the beat of her heart against his own chest. He tried the knob and found it locked.

"This is not a good time," complained another voice.

There were two or three men approaching, Gavin concluded. Applying his eye to the tiny gap in the curtains, he recognized one of them as an Austrian diplomat. He thought one of the others was from Saxony. The third, he did not know.

"The king will never agree," said the Saxon.

"He should have thought of the future before he became one of the little Corsican's allies," replied the Austrian. "He is not in such a good position now."

"Gentlemen," said the third man, whose French was clearly native, "we are trying to come to terms here. Let us not fall into old arguments."

There was no sound from the room where Sophie and her mysterious companion had been talking, Gavin thought. Had they slipped out some other way? Laura moved slightly, and heat flashed along his skin.

"What's the matter with that curtain?" said one of the men.

"What curtain?"

"There, it's got an odd bulge in it."

His shoulders didn't fit into the niche, Gavin realized. They were pushing the cloth outward. If he had been alone, as he always was in his work, none of this would have happened, he thought savagely.

"Is someone there?" Footsteps approached.

Gavin drew Laura into his arms and captured her lips in a passionate kiss.

"I said…" One of the newcomers threw the curtains back.

Gavin pretended to be startled. "What the devil?"

"Ho-ho—a tryst." The Austrian laughed.

Gavin only hoped he wouldn't be recognized. He hid Laura's face from them with his shoulder.

"Can't you find a better place for it than this?" asked one of the others. They were all laughing now.

Gavin yanked the curtain from the man's hand and pulled it closed again. The laughter grew louder.

"Here now, what's this?" one of them said. "Another?"

"I believe I have lost my way, gentlemen," said Sophie's musical voice. "Is the reception down here?"

Gavin held the curtains shut with one hand, his other arm still encircling Laura. If Sophie found them here, the game was up.

But her beauty and manner had diverted the gentlemen. They vied to escort her back to the gathering, and in another moment, their voices were receding down the corridor once more.

"You can let me go now," said Laura quietly.

"Shh," he whispered. "I'm waiting for the man Sophie was talking to."

This silenced her. Gavin waited. But he found he couldn't keep his mind on Sophie's former companion. It kept being distracted by the feel of Laura's lithe body, the intimacy of her breath on his cheek. The sensations gradually took over his faculties until he could think of nothing else. What did she do to him? he wondered. Why did she make him feel as if he hadn't understood passion until now. Unable to resist, he bent to kiss her again.

She was silk and steel, ambrosia, and an attraction more arousing than anything he'd known.

He pressed her back against the side of the niche, intoxicated and a little mad. He knew how to draw an equal response from her. The knowledge was innate, unassailable. Coaxing with his lips, he felt her astonishment, her answering desire, as if they were his own.

Her body softened against him. Her hands slipped from his shoulders and up around his neck. Her lips yielded up everything. Exultantly, Gavin pulled her closer still and deepened the kiss. His hands moved on her back and then up along the subtle curve of her waist to cup her breast. Laura's breath caught, sending a surge of triumph through him. She wanted him; he had made her want him.

He let his lips drift down her neck and left soft kisses above the bodice of her gown, where the skin was even more silken. Then he took her lips again, letting his hands rove, showing her what pleasures they could rouse.

His mind was filled with images of tumbled bed-clothes and flashes of naked skin when a jolt of reality intruded. He had to stop this. How had he let it go so far? With a heroic act of will, he pulled away, jerking the curtains aside and stepping back into the now empty corridor.

Laura remained leaning against the wall as if she needed its support. Her chest rose and fell rapidly, and her eyes were large and dark with emotion.

What the hell had he been thinking of? Gavin wondered. Or, more accurately, why hadn't he been thinking, instead of—whatever he had been doing? What sort of madness had overtaken him? His liaisons with the other sex—pleasurable as they had undoubtedly been—had always aided, not impeded, his work.

Laura was staring at him. He couldn't interpret the look in her eyes. What sorts of damnable complications were in store now?

Her lips parted as if to speak.

They were incredibly alluring lips, Gavin thought. But he had to resist them. And so, of course, he would. He took another step backward.

Laura blinked. She took a deep breath.

Gavin braced himself for a flood of emotion. She would expect vows of devotion, oaths of constancy—possibly even more. He couldn't restrain a slight grimace.

"You promised you wouldn't do that again," said Laura breathlessly.

He gaped at her.

"You said there would be no more assaults—"

"That was not an assault," he interrupted, suddenly furious. "You enjoyed it…"

A bit unsteadily, Laura pushed away from the wall and walked a few steps back toward the reception. "I thought you were a man of your word," she said. "But you have broken it twice now."

"I have done no such thing."

"You said I could be your partner in the investigation only to put me off, didn't you? And now you have…" She gestured, seeming to find no words for what had just occurred between them. "I'm disappointed in you."

"You are…what?" Had he ever been this angry?

Gavin wondered. In a life marked by his struggle with a hot temper, had he ever been this utterly enraged?

"I thought you were a man of honor," she added almost sadly, then turned and walked rapidly away.

Gavin stood where he was, fists clenched, jaw painfully tight, mind in total turmoil.

# Eight

LAURA SAT CURLED IN THE WINDOW SEAT OF HER bedroom, watching the wind blow gusts of snow down the street. The sky was low and gray. Frost rimmed the glass panes in front of her. She shivered, drawing her blanket closer around her shoulders.

If she had found another post, she thought, she would have been in some other bedchamber by now, gazing out at the winter from some nobleman's home, presiding over another schoolroom and set of children. She would know them by this time; she would know their talents and faults and how to manage the combination. The world would be familiar and routine. She would be safely hidden. For the first time, she wondered if she had made a mistake in not going to that unknown house rather than coming to this one.

She rested her head on her knees, hearing the scratching of new snow at the window. Everything was so much more complicated now. She felt so exposed.

Laura turned her head so that her face was muffled by the blanket. Yet again she saw Gavin's face as he stepped back from her in the hallway niche. He had

looked repulsed, apprehensive, and very sorry that
he had kissed her. A few weeks ago, she might have
found that gratifying, Laura thought. She had wanted
to make him apologize. But that seemed like a very
long time ago now.

The trouble was, she had enjoyed the kisses.
Indeed, "enjoyed" was far too mild a word for what
she had felt, Laura thought. She'd discovered whole
new modes of sensation. In a few blazing minutes,
she'd been enlightened about things she'd read, made
sudden sense of what had been only words. It had
been incredible, and thrilling. And then Gavin had
stepped back and looked at her, and she had felt...
sullied, or...that wasn't quite right. But something had
come crashing down when she met his gaze.

She never wanted to see him again, Laura thought.
She pulled the blanket closer and leaned back against
the wall. She had not asked him to kiss her. Indeed,
she had specifically requested that he stop his efforts to
drive her off in this way. Did he think that she would
give up her idea of helping him now? Had that been
the motive for his kisses?

Laura's face grew hot. She could still feel his hands
on her, the contours of his lips, and the way her own
body had responded. Was that the difficulty? Perhaps
he had never expected her to respond. All along, he
had been trying to frighten her, to chase her away. If
he thought his caresses were being welcomed...which
they weren't, Laura thought sharply.

She sat up straighter, feeling inexplicably better.
If he thought that, he would stop. And the matter
would be settled. It was very interesting, of course,

to have experienced some of the intense sensations that she had read existed. But she had no wish for a repetition. Gavin Graham interested her only because of the mystery they were both exploring. If he imagined anything else, he was deluding himself. And if he thought she would retreat now and forget that she had been promised a part in the hunt, he would soon discover his mistake.

Throwing off the blanket, Laura rose and shook out the folds of her gown. How had she allowed herself to fall into such a fit of the dismals? she wondered. It wasn't like her at all. Perhaps it was the weather. She'd never cared much for winter—the cold and the biting damp. And the holidays…well, she was already used to that. But now that she was on guard, it wouldn't happen again. She had far too much good sense and self-control to let it.

❧

A swath of pine graced the mantelpiece, releasing its pungent scent into the room. The fire threw a reflected glow onto the walls, and more pine, tied with red ribbons, hung around the arched doorway. It did look festive, Laura thought, watching the general and his wife talk to the Merritts, the first to arrive for Christmas dinner. Catherine looked happier than she had for several days. Laura was glad she, too, had made some effort, putting on her dark green silk gown and pinning a sprig of holly in her hair.

The Phillipses were announced. They came in glowing from the cold and laughing about something they had seen on the drive over. Only one member of their party was missing now, Laura thought, and she couldn't decide whether she wished to see him or not.

She was no more certain a few minutes later when Gavin walked in. Her heart jumped, but her fists clenched as well. He looked terribly handsome, his dark gold hair set off by a midnight blue coat, his athletic figure moving with such power and grace. He greeted everyone pleasantly and correctly. There wasn't any hint of unease about him, she thought resentfully. And yet the last time they had met... her cheeks flushed at the memory, which *would* keep intruding no matter how often she suppressed it. She placed herself as far from him as possible in the long parlor and joined Catherine and the Merritts in discussing the chances of a blizzard and what effect this might have on the congress's work.

Laura had seen to it that she was not seated beside Gavin at dinner either. Instead she got to observe across the table as he entertained Mrs. Merritt and Mrs. Phillips, apparently with great success. The two women seemed to find him utterly delightful. She spent far too much time watching Gavin being charming from a distance, she thought. And yet he was so irritating at close quarters. Was it some sort of illusion? Did he single her out for insults? Well, of course he did. That was at an end, however, she vowed. She was not going to allow it.

After dinner, the group retreated to the parlor for coffee and further conversation. The guests had brought small gifts for the household, and the Pryors had chosen tokens for them as well. Laura watched Catherine unwrap Gavin's gift—a small Dresden figurine, perfect for his hostess. Naturally.

"I have something for you as well," said a deep voice behind her.

Turning, Laura found that she could avoid Gavin no longer. He was standing right behind her, rather too close.

"Come over here and I will give it to you," he added.

Too surprised to protest, Laura allowed herself to be led a little away from the group around the hearth. Gavin pulled a flat box from his coat pocket and handed it to her. It had no markings or wrappings. Laura gazed up at him in wary amazement. "I thought you would like it," he said.

Her heart was pounding, from what emotion she couldn't say. A bit clumsily she opened the box, and revealed a small, beautifully made pistol resting on cotton wool. Her eyes flew up to his face and then down to the pistol again.

"I suggest you keep your back to the others," Gavin said quietly.

Laura had turned a little. She swung hastily back, hiding the astonishing gift from the rest of the party.

"Have you ever fired a gun?" he asked, as if it were the most commonplace question in the world.

Laura shook her head.

"I will teach you, then."

She met his eyes again. She couldn't fathom the meaning behind them, but she found she couldn't look away either. The sounds of the other conversations seemed to recede. The room seemed close suddenly instead of cozy.

"Since you insist upon taking risks," Gavin explained,

"I think you should know how to protect yourself. We can try it tomorrow."

He deliberately kept her off balance, Laura thought. Just when it seemed that he had broken his promise to let her help, he brought her this. He willfully ignored what had passed between them the last time they met. He pretended that it was not exceedingly odd to present her with a gun.

She lowered her eyes. If that was the game, she could play it—if she wished to. "Thank you," she said. "That would be convenient."

❧

Gavin had become obsessed with Laura's safety. Whenever he thought of her, as he did surprisingly often, his mind veered to the fact that she had gotten involved with dangerous people in a scheme that he himself did not yet understand. She took risks, she roused suspicions—without comprehending what the consequences might be. And she wouldn't listen when he tried to warn her to convince her to stay at home and let him untangle this plot.

That was why he had bought her the gun, and why he was on his way now to fetch her and teach her to shoot it. The pistol was not an ideal solution. But if she insisted on ignoring his orders and striking out on her own… Why couldn't she just listen to him? Of course, it was partly his fault, Gavin acknowledged. His control had faltered in that damned hallway. He shouldn't have given in to… He felt confused emotions rising in his chest, and he suppressed them. The important thing was to keep her safe.

Laura was ready when he arrived. When he found that she had arranged for one of the Pryors' maids to accompany them, Gavin felt a flash of annoyance. "It might be best if the Pryors knew nothing of this expedition," he said in a low voice.

"Gemma is very discreet," Laura replied without looking at him.

He started to protest, then shrugged. He would have no trouble matching this chilling correctness.

The gentlemen of Vienna had a shooting club in which to try out their favorite firearms. It wasn't as comfortable as Manton's, but Gavin had judged it quite adequate when he had made the arrangement for their visit. As he led Laura into the great barnlike room where the targets were set up, he watched her look around with lively curiosity, taking in every detail of the thick wooden walls, the exposed rafters, the stone floor, and layers of hay bales into which one shot.

There was no one else about on this cold December day. They could see their breath in the poorly heated room, and Gavin was happy to see that she had dressed warmly, as he had instructed. As the maid stationed herself near the doorway, Gavin went to one of the tables facing the target range and took a box of ammunition from his pocket. "I will show you how to load the pistol," he said without preamble.

Laura brought it out, and he demonstrated. "You see?"

She nodded.

She had said almost nothing on the drive over, and Gavin found he was sharply disappointed at her silence. He had become so used to her eager questions and objections that he almost missed them. Of course, it was much better to have her listening and following his instructions for once, he told himself. "To aim, you look through here," he said, pointing to the sight on top of the pistol. "The gun may tend to pull to the right or left. You will just have to learn that and make allowances. Are you ready?"

She nodded, not meeting his eyes.

"Very well. Let us try, then." He cocked the pistol before handing it to her. "That target there." He indicated the one directly opposite them on the far wall.

Laura raised the gun and held it out at arm's length, looking as if she wanted to get it as far from her as possible.

"No," said Gavin.

She turned to look at him.

"It will be steadier if you hold it with both hands."

"Isn't this how duelists stand?"

The comment was so like her. He hid a smile that would no doubt make her angry. "So I have heard. But it is not an effective stance for an inexperienced marksman. Your arm will waver."

She brought her other hand up to the pistol.

"Here, like this." He reached to adjust her grip, his arm lying along hers for a moment. He received such a fiery glance in response that he stepped back quickly. "Make sure your feet are securely planted," he went on, as if nothing had occurred. "Concentrate your attention on the target."

Laura drew in a deep breath and let it out. She stared intently at the straw target and then sighted it. Her muscles visibly tightening, she pulled the trigger.

She didn't jump or squeal at the blast, Gavin noted with approval. Indeed, the only perceptible reaction was a flush on her pale cheeks. He walked down the room to check the shot. "You missed the paper target, but you hit the hay bale here." He indicated the spot. "A bit left, you see?"

She nodded.

"We will try again."

They tried innumerable times, until Laura could hit the target two times out of three. She could also load the gun with dexterity and handle it like a familiar object. It was all one could hope for in a first lesson, Gavin thought. "I will show you how to clean it as well. You will not want to give that chore to a member of the household. The general would not approve of your acquiring firearms."

He expected a smile, but got none. She was looking down the room at the targets. "You must be cold. There is a place here where we can get tea."

"If we are finished, I should go."

The flat tone she used, and the way she continued to refuse to look at him, roused something in Gavin. "Nonsense. You must get warm."

"I am perfectly comfortable."

She was practically shivering. "There are matters we must discuss," he said.

"What matters?" Her voice was sharper.

He wanted her to stay. He wanted to make her acknowledge his wishes. So, although he knew it wasn't wise, he replied, "How to discover the identity of Michael, for one."

As he had expected, this caught her interest. She

allowed him to escort her to one of the club rooms and order tea, the maid being similarly provided for at a table a little distance away. "You appear to have a knack for firearms," he said when they were seated. "You picked it up very quickly."

"My pupils always claimed I had a deadly eye," she answered, her gaze roaming the room, surveying its masculine style of decoration.

"How many pupils did you have?"

She turned to look at him then, seeming suspicious of the question. "Two," she said finally. "Twin girls."

"How old were they when you began?"

"You can't possibly care about that."

"I'm quite interested," he insisted. It was only partly a lie. He was interested in fathoming Laura Devane—in order to find ways of protecting her from herself, he thought.

"Seven," she answered curtly.

"And you were, what? Eighteen? That must have been difficult."

"I never had any difficulties with the children," she said.

Implying that she had had other problems. With the gentlemen of the household? Gavin wondered. "I don't believe you said who employed you?"

"The Countess of Leith."

Gavin sat back in his chair as the club servant brought their tea. Though he hadn't been in England much over the last ten years, Gavin had made it his business to know what went on in London, the gossip of the *ton* and the season. He had heard of the Leiths, had mental notes jotted next to their names in his mind, as he had for hundreds of others. The Earl of Leith had never held any interest for him, until now. Looking at Laura across the table—her raven hair and translucent skin, her striking eyes and lovely form—he could not conceive of a way she might have avoided the attentions of a ruthless womanizer like Leith. Ten years in his employ; it had to mean...

Laura raised her head and looked at him. The dark green of her eyes was clear and serious. Her expression was unreadable. "I must get back. Catherine will be wondering where I am."

He couldn't believe it, Gavin thought. But...ten years. Leith would have found it damnably convenient, with her living in his house. And if she had refused him, she would have been dismissed. Such things happened, deplorable as they might be.

"Did you really intend to say anything about Michael?"

"Who?" said Gavin, his mind filled with images that he didn't want to see.

"That's what I thought." Laura rose, picking up her gloves and cloak. "I am grateful for your gift and for the lesson. I suppose I could come here alone if I made special arrangements?"

"Probably, at this season."

She nodded, pulling on her gloves.

Gavin was at a loss for words, a situation with which he had very little experience. Conflicting impulses tore at him. He wanted to know the truth, and he was deeply reluctant to hear it. He believed he knew her character, yet he could see no way she might have evaded Leith. She was far too beautiful and alluring. Hadn't he felt it himself, much more than he wished?

It suddenly occurred to him to wonder whether General Pryor was more cunning than he had realized. Had he brought her here precisely because of her experience? Had everything she had done in the last few weeks been part of some intricate plot to beguile him?

"Shall I summon a hack?" asked Laura from the doorway.

Gavin started, feeling an odd pain flash through him. He stood and threw on his greatcoat. It was impossible, he thought. He trusted his instincts. He would have detected that kind of deceit.

And yet... Walking beside Laura out to the waiting carriage, Gavin was forced to wonder if on this one occasion, his famous instincts had betrayed him.

❧

Laura stood before the mirror in her bedchamber and looked at the past. She wore one of her old gowns, a pearl gray cambric, completely plain. Her hair was bound into a tight knot; her pale complexion was washed out by the color of the dress. But the difference wasn't really the clothing, she thought. It never had been. Making the transformation into the governess—so very long ago it seemed now—had been an inner process. It involved shutting things down, letting vitality drain away. She thought suddenly of what Sophie had said to her about desire. To return to her old self, she had to relinquish desire—to want nothing. And when she did, she would disappear.

Laura stared at the mirror, shaken by this new thought. How had she done this for so long? she wondered. And could she do it again?

Turning away from her image, she picked up the pistol and placed it in a basket she had borrowed from the kitchen, covering it with a cloth. She had practiced with the gun several times now—alone—and it felt familiar. She was glad to have it today, as she prepared to carry out a plan that had come to her one night when she couldn't sleep.

The trouble with the pistol was that it reminded her continually of Gavin. This was all too confusing. She didn't begin to comprehend the man who had kissed her so dazzlingly and then never mentioned it again, who brought her a gun as if it were commonplace, who looked at her with such intensity and apparent doubt. Was it that doubt that had made him break his promise to give her a place in his investigations? But what had caused it? She hadn't been able to think of any explanation.

Laura cut off this line of thought, which was useless anyway and would prevent her from accomplishing her mission. Picking up an old cloak and gloves, and the basket, she slipped out of the room and down the stairs to the front door. It was still very early, and no one was about. She had begged off the round of calls Catherine planned to make today, saying she wanted to spend a quiet day reading. With luck, the household wouldn't notice she was gone.

Putting on her things, she stepped out into the January cold. Fortunately, there was no wind. Laura walked briskly to the corner and waited there until she saw a movement from the opposite side of the street. Annalise, bundled once more into a long gray coat, joined her with a grin.

"Is everything all right?" asked Laura.

"Yes. Heinrick was supposed to watch today, but I made him let me come."

"You're sure he won't tell?"

Annalise's grin widened. "Most sure. I said I would tell Father about his sweetheart and how he plans to marry her and take over her family's shop. He is very frightened of telling him this."

"I see." Laura started walking, and the girl followed her.

"What will we do? Your note only said to come here." Before Laura could answer, Annalise added, "You look different."

"I don't want to be noticed. We are going to follow someone, and then, if you can, you will watch her each day."

Annalise gave a little skip of excitement.

They took a hack, leaving it a distance from their destination. As they approached the house, Laura concentrated on reassuming her old self, that negligible persona who was scarcely worth a glance. It felt like pulling a smothering blanket over her head.

Annalise pulled at her sleeve. "This is the neighborhood where my father is watching," she said, alarmed.

"It is?" Laura hadn't thought of this. "He is observing Countess Krelov?"

"I don't know. But it is a house near here." She looked uneasy.

This was a setback. Laura knew of no one else who could help her carry out her plan.

"You are going to watch the same person?" wondered Annalise.

"Not her. A member of her household."

"My father will see us. He sees everything."

Laura frowned. "The house is in a *cul-de-sac*," she said slowly, remembering it from her visit. "There is only one way out. I can wait at the end, on the busier avenue, and I'm bound to see her. That is better anyway."

"It is easier to watch with more people around," agreed the girl.

"But you must go home. It was stupid of me not to realize…"

"I can stay down the block," Annalise protested. "It will give me time to hide if Father comes."

"I don't want to get you in trouble."

"You won't. He won't see me." The girl seemed to be excited by the challenge now. "Who are we looking for?"

Laura hesitated. She needed help. "You promise to be very careful."

"I am always careful."

She would make sure Annalise stayed well down the block, Laura decided. "It is an older woman. I don't know her name. She is thin with gray hair, and she has a long narrow face with a sharp nose. I believe she is very intelligent, so we must take care."

"She is a servant?"

"She was dressed as one when I saw her." Lately, Laura had begun to wonder about Sophie's unusual maid. She had seemed much more than a servant.

"I will go down there," said Annalise, pointing. "You can pretend to be shopping." She eyed the basket approvingly.

Laura did so, for an endless hour while she grew colder and colder. Tradesmen entered Sophie's street making deliveries, and a carriage clattered by bearing a stately couple. But no one came out.

After another hour, Laura went to speak to Annalise. "I must go. They will miss me if I stay much longer."

"I will watch," replied the girl cheerfully. "I can come every day. Or Heinrick will." She looked regretful. "We must be home before dark, though."

"I think that will do," replied Laura. She hoped so, at least. "Aren't you cold?"

"I have on two dresses, and three pairs of stockings—also the wool underthings my father orders specially."

Laura wasn't entirely reassured. "Will you be all right?"

"Of course." Annalise's grin was enormous.

❧

It was two days before Annalise had anything to report, but when she did Laura was deeply gratified at the result. "She went to a house in Linzstrasse," the girl reported. "The woman there rents rooms. I tried to speak to her, but she was rude." Annalise wrinkled her nose. "She treated me like a child."

"Did you see anyone else?"

"There were some men going up the stairs.

They spoke French. I have studied French," she added proudly.

"You heard them talking?"

Annalise hung her head. "Only a few words."

"You've done wonderfully," Laura assured her, exulting in the fact that she'd been right. The older woman was more than a maid; she was the link between Sophie and her mysterious allies. "You must take me to the house," she told Annalise. "Tomorrow morning, if you can."

"Of course I can," was the prompt reply.

❦

They reached the place by nine, Laura once more dressed as a governess. Once there, she dismissed Annalise with some difficulty and approached the house. The woman who answered her knock was thin and harried. She hardly spared Laura a glance, even when asked about a room. Her eyes kept straying to the back of the building and the work no doubt awaiting her there.

"Upstairs front," she replied, giving the price. "Breakfast and dinner."

"I'll take it," said Laura.

Now she had the landlady's attention. "You are alone?"

"Yes." She was careful to keep her German precise and unaccented. "I am a governess. I go to a post in Salzburg soon."

"You must pay in advance," demanded the woman.

Laura was ready to do so; her stay in Vienna had made few inroads in her savings. But she knew that agreeing would rouse suspicions. "I will pay for one week," she said firmly. "And then we shall see."

The landlady held out her hand. Laura found the requisite coins and gave them to her. "Who else is staying here?" she asked, having purchased the privilege of curiosity.

But the landlady's attention had waned once she had her money. "A German student, a lady from Munich, and some foreigners," she said, waving her hand and starting to retreat down the hall.

"Have they been here long?"

"Wolfgang, yes. The others—a few weeks. Here is a key. The room is at the top of the stairs, straight ahead. Dinner is at five." And with this she hurried away, banging the door at the back of the hall behind her.

Laura fingered the key, listening for sounds in the house. She would have to find an excuse to have dinner here, she thought, and discover whether one of the men was called Michael.

She ought to tell someone about this at once, a voice in her head insisted. She ought, in fact, to tell Gavin Graham. But she didn't know for certain that these were the conspirators, she argued silently. She would wait a little longer, discover more, and then reveal it all at once. The thought of Gavin's astonishment in that moment was very pleasant—too pleasant to relinquish.

Conscious that she was not being entirely wise, Laura walked up the stairs to inspect her new quarters.

# Nine

"BUT WE CANNOT HOLD A CARD PARTY WHEN YOU ARE ill, Matthew," said Catherine at the breakfast table the following day.

"I'm not ill," declared the general, although his hoarse voice and flushed face belied his words.

"You took a chill at the review of the Polish troops," his wife replied. "I knew how it would be, in that wind, but you…"

"Had to be there," he interrupted. "And I didn't take a chill."

Laura drank tea in silence. She wasn't about to get involved in this conversation, though she wouldn't have minded if the card party Catherine had planned was canceled.

"I suppose you were coughing half the night for your own amusement?" said Catherine. "You must get some rest, or—"

"I have no time to rest," snapped the general. "We are finally getting some work done here, after four months of wasting time, and I must be on hand to do my part."

"Surely one of your colleagues could take your place for a few days."

"Who? Ferris? Or Graham? Yes, that would be splendid. Send Graham to my meetings." He turned a bloodshot gaze on Laura. "Damn the man," he muttered.

"Matthew."

"Let me be," he responded, throwing his napkin onto the table and rising. "We will hold the card party, and I will be perfectly all right, and I don't wish to hear any more about it!" He stomped out of the dining room, leaving the door swinging behind him.

"He is irritable because he doesn't feel well," said Catherine apologetically. "He has always hated being ill."

"He likes to be active."

"Yes." Catherine frowned. "Perhaps we can end the evening early, at least. You must help me do so."

Laura, who had been ready to excuse herself from the party early anyway, merely nodded again.

&

By the time the guests had assembled in the Pryors' drawing room, where the card tables were set up, the general was obviously worse, and very obviously in a foul humor because of his illness. His efforts to play the cheerful host tended to turn into barked orders, and his features had settled into an unconscious scowl. Thus, when he directed Laura to partner Gavin at one of the tables, she didn't object. She did, however, resign herself to a long uncomfortable evening. She could easily imagine the kind of partner Gavin would be—impatient, sarcastic, competitive. Her skill at whist was only average; no doubt he would be an expert player, she thought as she sat down. She braced herself for his accusations of incompetence. At least they were paired with the Merritts, an easygoing older couple who shouldn't exacerbate the situation.

"So, Talleyrand has got his wish," said Mr. Merritt as he dealt out the first hand. "He has gotten France admitted to the inner circle of the congress." Picking up his cards, he drew them close to his eyes and peered at them intently.

"I understand the delegates are finally reaching some agreements," replied Laura, much more interested in this than in cards.

Mr. Merritt laughed shortly. "The five great powers are making agreements. No one else is getting to put their oar in." He laid down a card.

Gavin, on his left, considered a moment, then added a card of his own.

"And Poland will go to Russia?" said Laura.

"Most of it."

Mrs. Merritt put down a card.

"You are not going to play that!" exclaimed her husband.

His wife started like a rabbit hearing hounds, and Merritt made a sound like "Pah!" with his breath.

All of them looked at the three cards lying in the center of the card table. Laura couldn't see anything particularly culpable in any of the choices.

"Well, are you going to play?" Merritt asked her.

Her heart sinking, she did so—and waited for Gavin to add his objections to what was clearly going to be a very unpleasant game.

He said nothing.

Mr. Merritt gathered up the trick, which he had won, and laid down another card. When his wife played the next time, his cheeks began to take on a purplish hue as he cried, "No, no, no. You must save your clubs for later. You can be sure they will be doing so. Do you wish to make it easy for them?"

Mrs. Merritt's shoulders began to slump, and she clutched her cards as if she had fallen into a familiar desperation. Laura glanced at Mr. Merritt with some astonishment. He looked so gentle, so unassuming. As she turned back to her own hand, her gaze encountered Gavin's and caught a distinct glint in his eyes. He raised his brows slightly, sharing her surprise. The next time he played, he said, "I often think cards bring out people's true character."

Laura watched Mrs. Merritt push a card onto the table as if she hoped no one would notice it. "Do you?" Laura added her card, winning the trick.

Mr. Merritt growled softly.

"Yes," said Gavin, a laugh in his voice.

He was relaxed in his chair, and he held his cards with elegant negligence. His plays were quick and clever, yet he didn't seem terribly attached to their outcome. Was this his true character? Laura wondered. It was not what she had expected from the game.

"We are pitted against one another in a series of small contests that end in winning or losing," he added. "It tends to bring out all one's instincts and training. Of course, if there are wagers involved, it becomes even more obvious."

"I never gamble," said Mr. Merritt sanctimoniously. He snapped down a card with a triumphant look, then gathered up the trick.

"You enjoy cards, though," commented Laura.

"A friendly game," he agreed. "Lydia, how can you put down a queen at a time like this? You should have played it on Miss Devane's knave."

"She went after me," ventured his wife.

"What? Nonsense."

No, it was perfectly true, Laura thought.

"You should have known she would play it," Mr. Merritt added. "Why do you never learn to keep track of the cards and anticipate?"

"How could she know what was in my hand?" Laura couldn't help asking.

"It is a process of elimination," was the pompous reply.

"But you might have had the knave, or Mr. Graham."

Mr. Merritt's lips turned down. "Can we play? I abhor talk across a card table."

Laura stared at him, wondering what he called his criticisms of his wife.

"Very diverting," said Gavin.

Laura met his eyes again and saw ironic amusement and an amazing depth of understanding. His expression also held a warmth that was very unsettling. Completely distracted, she made a stupid play. Mr. Merritt couldn't contain his delight; he practically bounced in his chair.

One corner of Gavin's mouth jerked in response, and then he smiled at her.

He was so very handsome, Laura thought. His features and coloring and bearing all conspired to attract the eye. But until now, she hadn't realized how much these outward attributes were enhanced by intelligence and wit and a curious compassion she hadn't recognized before. The combination raised her pulse and made it a bit difficult to breathe.

"I believe we take the game," said Mr. Merritt, laying down his last two cards to show this.

"Congratulations," said Gavin.

Laura noticed the way the skin crinkled at the corners of his eyes when he was amused but not smiling. She watched his strong hands as he prepared to deal. Did he really not care about winning? she wondered. But even as she asked, she knew the answer. He cared very much indeed. He simply had the discrimination to choose his game so that winning really meant something.

Gavin looked up and Laura flushed. A sense of danger overtook her that had nothing to do with the game, or even with the larger events in her life outside it. She was skirting the edge of some abyss, she thought. And if she fell, she would never find her way out of it again.

❧

Walking back to his lodgings later that night, Gavin thought how odd it was that he had enjoyed the card party. He wasn't fond of cards, or of any of the games that people substituted for real risk in their lives. He had plenty of actual jeopardy to occupy him. But tonight, something had been different. The play had had a charm he'd never experienced before, and he had been genuinely sorry when General Pryor's worsening illness had broken things up early.

Despite the deplorable Merritt and his timorous wife, Gavin had had a fine evening. There was, of course, only one explanation for it. Laura.

A gust of wind whipped his cloak and threatened to capture his hat. Gavin settled them more securely and walked faster.

He didn't understand the wordless communication that occurred with Laura at times. They would somehow fall into the same rhythm, look up at the same moment with similar expressions or gesture in tandem. Yet they certainly didn't agree on everything. Gavin smiled wryly. They seldom agreed on anything, in fact. It wasn't a matter of thought, he decided. It was something else. Temperament? Spirit? He didn't know. But it added piquancy to every meeting. And when he held her...

Gavin turned a corner, nearly home. He had to resolve the plot that Laura had stumbled into, he thought. Once that was done, he would be able to think clearly. Order would return to his life. Very likely this odd feeling of...connection would dissipate.

He gave a satisfied nod. That was it. Her inconvenient involvement in his real life—his hidden life—must be the cause. Remove that, and she would become like any other woman he'd known. He would regain his perspective, his ability to choose the relationship he wanted.

Gavin took a deep breath, feeling as if a weight had been lifted. This was clear. This was logical. All he had to do was find the elusive Michael and discover Sophie Krelov's purpose, and all would be well. He breathed again. Any time now, he would find him. He had a number of hirelings combing Vienna. They had unearthed three Michaels of no consequence. But soon, they would find the one he wanted, and he would act. An anticipatory glint lit Gavin's eyes. That was the moment when he felt most alive—when he had the facts in hand and made his move to use them. Everything else became irrelevant then, and so would Laura Devane.

❧

Two days later, Laura made ready to go downstairs for dinner with her fellow residents of the house on Linzstrasse. She had escaped the Pryors because of the general's rapidly worsening illness. All Catherine really wanted to do was sit with her husband. Laura felt a bit guilty about abandoning her hostess, but she told herself Catherine was relieved, really, not to have a guest hovering.

Laura shook out her plain gray gown. Once again she was wholly the governess, a shadowy figure who faded into the background. She had given the landlady a German name and spoken only German to her, deciding it was better to give no hint of her true nationality. She had also come by the house as often as she could to allay suspicion. But in fact, the landlady seemed to have no interest in the habits of her boarders except when they might save her a few marks on the cost of food. Laura's excuses about spending time with the family she was leaving had been accepted without comment.

Laura took a breath. When she let it out, she tried to let her present life go with it and to become what she had been at the Leiths'. It was much harder now, when she had an important purpose behind her actions. But she knew that her appearance was reassuringly drab. It was like a reflex, she thought. She had learned it so well that the persona slipped on like a familiar old gown.

Walking downstairs, she could hear male voices from the dining parlor. Moving slowly down the hall, she tried to sort them out. They were speaking French, which was both encouraging and daunting. She could hear no other languages. And she thought she discerned at least three different speakers. With one more deep breath, she entered the room.

Sitting around a long table were five men and one woman. In the pause that greeted her arrival, Laura quickly slipped into a chair next to the latter, keeping her head down and her eyelids lowered. She murmured, "Good evening," in German almost too low to hear.

The landlady pushed through the rear door carrying a large, steaming platter, which she plunked down in the middle of the table. A servant followed with another, then returned to the kitchen for pitchers of ale.

"Fräulein Schmidt is a governess," said the landlady, giving the name Laura had used. With nods she indicated the others, "Frau Bach, Herr Dupres,

Herr Lebrun, Herr Genet, Herr Chenveau, and Herr Klemper."

The last was the German student, Laura concluded. He seemed interested only in his dinner. The rest were hard-looking men past their first youth. They gave her searching looks, but seemed to find nothing noteworthy. With murmurs of "Fraulein," they turned back to the food and immediately began abusing it roundly in French.

It appeared that no one else in the household spoke French, Laura thought, keeping her face carefully blank. Or the group didn't care, if they did. The men made insulting remarks about the landlady, the city, and about pudding-faced Austrian women, which Laura took as a comment on her own appearance. They all seemed to be in foul moods and ate as if it were a penance.

It was true that the meal relied rather heavily on dumplings, she thought. And the half of one that she managed to consume sat in her stomach like a stone. But they could hardly expect roast beef for the rent the landlady was charging.

Just then, one of the men called Herr Lebrun "Michael." Only her years of practice kept Laura from reacting. From beneath lowered lashes, she examined the man, and soon noticed that the others deferred to him as if he were their leader. He was dark and compact and exuded a rough impatience that made her very glad he had no idea who she was.

Michael was not a French name, she thought. And the man had distinctly said, Michael, not Michel. Listening more closely, she decided that these men were not Frenchmen. Though their French was very good, an occasional hint of an accent slipped through. They were using the language as a further disguise, she concluded, feeling quite pleased with her deductions.

"Someone is asking in the city for a man named Michael," said one of the others. "Duclos says so. He doesn't know how long it has been going on. They are very discreet."

Michael's scowl was ominous. "Damn him."

"You think it is—?"

Michael cut him off with a savage gesture. "Of course."

"We could—"

"Say no more about this." Michael threw a threatening glance around the table, and Laura concentrated on her plate. "We will talk later."

The table was mostly silent after that. Frau Bach, a plump, nervous woman, ventured a remark to Laura, to which she replied in a barely audible murmur, but the men were silent. The student shoveled in all the food he could get and then excused himself. The other men were not far behind. Laura gave them a few minutes, then returned to her room and sat on the rickety bed.

There seemed nothing else she could do. It would be very unwise to draw the attention of Michael and his friends; she had no doubt about that. She also felt certain that this *was* the Michael that Sophie had mentioned. She even thought his voice was the one they had heard from the palace corridor, though she couldn't be sure of this. She should go home now, Laura thought, and tomorrow report what she had found to Gavin.

And have the whole matter taken out of her hands as if she hadn't tracked Michael down when no one else could find him, she added silently. And be ignored still further.

Resentfully, she rose and paced the bare floor. Boards creaked as she stepped on them. From downstairs she heard the landlady berating the maid for dropping a plate. The walls were cheap and thin, she thought. The noise must be unpleasant for those who actually lived here. She heard the maid begin to cry and was suddenly struck by an idea.

Laura moved to the door and opened it. There was no one in the upstairs hall. The voices of the landlady and her unlucky servant had receded toward the kitchen. Warily, Laura stepped out and closed her door. Then she began walking slowly down the hall, straining her ears for any sound.

At the first closed door, there was nothing. The second was the same. But when she approached the third room from her own, she heard voices. Checking behind her and seeing no one, she moved on until she was directly in front of the worn panels.

"We must stop him," said a man inside.

"If only Jack had killed him with that knife," said another.

"We cannot afford to kill him," said a harsh, commanding voice. Laura thought it was Michael.

"That servant of his has been searching the backstreets like a wolf," said another of the men. "He is uncanny. His eyes make you shiver."

"Kill them both," suggested another of them.

"The British would turn Vienna upside down to

find the killer," Michael answered. "We cannot have that sort of disturbance. Matters are too delicate. It is only a few weeks until the escape."

A pause followed this warning.

"He should not be here!" Michael burst out then. "It makes no sense!"

No one replied to this. The floor creaked, and Laura tensed, ready to run back to her own room.

"I must speak to Sophie," said Michael's voice, much closer now. "Come."

The floorboards creaked again, and Laura fled, racing down the hall to her own room and throwing herself inside. She heard a door open and footsteps. Breathing hard, she waited. They passed by without pausing.

Weak with relief, she dropped on the bed again and waited for her heartbeat to return to normal. These men were deadly serious, she thought. She had to tell someone what she'd heard, and soon, before it was too late.

⤫

Laura hurried through the cold dark streets, muffled in her cloak. They were nearly empty on this winter night, and any passersby had no attention to spare for others. They were concentrated on reaching their destinations and getting out of the icy wind.

She didn't blame them. As the wind tore at her cloak and whined about her ears, Laura searched in vain for a hack to save her the walk. She, too, wanted to go home. But she had to find Gavin first.

She knew his lodgings. Catherine had pointed them

out once when they were driving through the city. And all thoughts of the impropriety of visiting him had gone with the urgency of her errand. Something dreadful was being planned. He would know what to do.

Her hands were almost frozen when she at last came to the street. She ran the last few yards and slipped inside the outer doorway with intense relief. There was no sign of a concierge or attendant. She hurried up the stairs, checking all the doorways for cards announcing their inhabitants. She found Gavin's on the second floor and knocked at once.

There was a long pause. She knocked again. This time, the door opened. Behind it stood a small, dark wiry man whose English clothes could not disguise his more exotic origins.

"I must see Mr. Graham," said Laura.

The man examined her—not critically, but carefully, like someone cataloging the features of a potentially dangerous animal. Remembering that she still wore her drab governess garments, she wished for her finest silk dress. "It's very important," she added.

His dark eyes were preternaturally shrewd. It would be extremely foolish to try to push past him, Laura decided. He might be small, but he gave the strong impression of physical power.

Finally, he spoke. "Not here."

Laura's spirits plummeted. For some reason, she had not expected this. "Mr. Graham has gone out?"

The man nodded. He made no move to invite Laura inside, but neither did he seem to urge her away.

"Do you expect him back soon?" she asked.

He made a noncommittal gesture, as if he wasn't about to give out such information to a stray woman on the doorstep.

"I must speak to him," repeated Laura. "I have very important information."

The man's dark gaze ranged over her face. After a moment, he stepped back and indicated that she should enter. Laura felt as if she had passed some rigorous test and been admitted to a select company. This man was much more than a servant, she thought. The sharp awareness in his expression made it clear he was privy to Gavin's secrets. She felt a pang of envy.

"You can write," he said.

For an instant, she thought he was asking her if she had the ability; then she understood. "I can write him a note."

He gestured. "Paper, pen."

She went to the desk and sat down, pulling off her gloves. When she had opened the inkwell and dipped the pen into it, she found her mind blank of words. How could she possibly explain everything that had happened in a note? She would be writing here for an hour. And perhaps Gavin would return in that time, responded a hopeful inner voice. But her thoughts refused to be marshaled into a coherent narrative. She fumbled and frowned, and in the end she wrote simply, "Please come at once. It is vital that I speak to you."

She folded and sealed the message, then laid it on the desk. "He must have this as soon as he returns. I will be waiting."

The man nodded, and Laura handed him the note with a curious relief. She felt she had put her request in the best of hands.

With that thought came a great weariness. Pulling on her gloves again, she braced herself for the long walk home. She stood, pulling her cloak more tightly around her.

"I will get a hack," said her companion.

"There are none to be had, I'm afraid," answered Laura. "I looked everywhere."

"I will get," he responded, without a shred of doubt in his voice.

She was torn between the hope that he could and reluctance to send him out into this cold night for nothing. "I can…"

But he was already putting on his cloak and opening the door. She allowed him to usher her out and down the stairs.

"Wait," he said at the bottom.

She stopped. He disappeared into the darkness outside. Laura scarcely had time to worry about him before he was back with a hack, its shivering driver so wrapped up that only his eyes were visible.

Astonished and grateful, Laura stepped out into the wind. "Thank you. How in the world did you…?"

He interrupted with a gesture that seemed to say that it was his job to perform small miracles. He smiled suddenly, briefly, and indicated the open carriage door.

Laura stepped into it. "What is your name?" she asked, feeling an odd connection with him even though they had hardly met.

He hesitated, watching her.

The driver complained in German about the delay. Laura got into the carriage, but she leaned out the window as it started off.

"Hasan," he said at the last possible moment and raised a hand in farewell.

With the feeling that she had passed another test, Laura relaxed against the worn cushions of the seat.

⁓

Riding home, Laura felt as if a great responsibility had been lifted from her shoulders. Gavin would know just what to do. He had dealt with men like Michael before. He would make sure nothing dreadful happened.

It was very pleasant to have someone you could truly rely on, she thought as fatigue descended more heavily over her. She hadn't known such a person in a long time. Perhaps, suggested a small voice in her head, she had never known such a person. Her parents had certainly not been reliable. And her employers had not imagined that they owed her anything beyond her meager salary.

Huddling in her cloak, Laura rejected the notion. There had been people she could count on, she insisted silently. But when she considered the question further, she couldn't think of anyone but Gavin.

Why did she believe in him so completely? He had treated her quite shabbily in a variety of ways. But here Laura felt a calm certainty. In this matter, at least, Gavin was beyond question. He would not fail her.

⁓

But he did. Though she waited deep into the night, there was no response from him. The morning passed with no reply to her note. Could Hasan have failed to pass along the message? She didn't believe that.

At midmorning, Catherine came into the drawing room, looking tense and anxious.

"How is the general?" asked Laura.

The older woman shook her head. "I've summoned the doctor. I don't think we can wait until his regular visit tomorrow."

"The powders aren't helping?"

"No." The single word was bleak.

"I'm so sorry." Laura went over and led her to a chair. "Can't I help? I would be happy to share your nursing."

"I have to be there with him," Catherine said forlornly. She looked around the room as if she didn't recognize it. "If only we were home."

Laura nodded. The general had been pronounced too ill to travel, even if he had been free of duties.

"This must be dull for you," Catherine added. "Perhaps the Merritts would escort you to—"

"Don't be silly," interrupted Laura. "I don't want to go out. I want to be here, helping you." Catherine gave her a smile that made Laura feel guilty at how little she had actually been able to help and how she had appreciated her freedom from engagements. "Please don't worry about me."

"You are a sweet child," said Catherine, increasing Laura's guilt tenfold.

There were sounds of an arrival in the hall below. Automatically, both of them rose.

"The doctor," said Catherine, hurrying out of the room. Laura followed, hoping it was the doctor *and* Gavin Graham. But when she looked down over the stair railing, she saw only the old Viennese physician who had recently become a mainstay of the household.

❧

Laura's patience came to an end in the early afternoon. Leaving Catherine still occupied in the sickroom, she set off for Gavin's. It was still cold, but the wind had died, so the walk wasn't unpleasant. This time, she found the front hall occupied by a very large Austrian lady. Laura asked for Gavin in German without embarrassment. "His colleague General Pryor is very ill," she added, as if this were the reason for her unescorted visit.

The woman frowned, her broad face creasing into a hundred wrinkles. "Herr Graham is gone," she said.

"Gone?"

"He didn't even give me notice. Just packed up and left in the middle of the night. I went this morning to see if he wanted tea, and *pfft!*" She made an eloquent gesture. "Nothing."

Laura was having trouble taking this in.

"The rooms were paid until the end of the month, so he did not cheat me. But it is rude, is it not? If he had told me he was going…" She gestured again, not seeming to have an ending for this sentence.

"He didn't leave a note, or…?"

"Nothing. No address to send on his mail, no word of thanks. It is not what I expect from my gentlemen."

"Could…could I see the rooms?" She wouldn't be able to believe it until she did, Laura thought.

The landlady eyed her suspiciously.

"I don't think the general knew he was going either. He may ask me."

Evocation of the military title seemed to impress her. "You may look if you like," she said, opening the door wider. "But there is nothing there."

And there wasn't—only the disorder of a hurried packing. Laura examined a few scraps of paper on the floor, but they were of no consequence. "You're certain he didn't leave word for the general?" she asked.

"No note, nothing for the maid, not so much as a word of thanks or farewell."

Laura looked around the hastily vacated room. This wasn't like Gavin, she thought, and then wondered. Did she really know what he was like? The general was always complaining about his flouting of authority and disregard for proper procedures. Perhaps this was exactly what he would do. But where had he gone?

Walking back downstairs and into the cold street, Laura tried to imagine. If he had discovered something about Michael, he might have gone off in pursuit. But would he have packed up all his things and taken them along? It didn't seem logical. And no matter what the general said of him, Laura didn't believe he would go without informing his superior.

Perhaps he had, she thought suddenly. The Pryors weren't paying much heed to letters just now. Perhaps Catherine had simply forgotten to mention it. Driven by this possibility, Laura walked swiftly toward home. She was halfway back when a street sign caused her steps to slow as a new idea emerged.

She stopped and looked up at the sign. She bit her

lip. This was foolish. But she couldn't help herself. She turned down the street and made her way to a residence she had visited once before. "Is the Countess Krelov in?" she asked when the door was opened to her.

"Gone out of town," was the laconic reply.

"Oh." Laura's heart sank. "Do you know when she will be back?"

The woman shook her head.

"I don't suppose you know where she has gone?"

The response was the same.

Laura started to turn away. The door was shutting when she thought of something more and said, "Is the count here?"

The landlady's mouth turned down in a disapproving grimace. "He's here—when he bothers to come home, that is. I don't know whether he's in just now."

"Thank you."

Laura resumed her walk toward the Pryors' more slowly than before. Had Gavin gone off with Sophie? If not, it was quite a coincidence that they should both leave town at just the same time.

Laura suddenly remembered the evening of carol singing and the way Gavin had stood with Sophie, his head bent close to hers, his smile warm and encouraging. She remembered Sophie's hand coming to rest so naturally on his arm. The whole reason for Laura's presence here was the general's concern about Gavin's infatuation. Undoubtedly Gavin had gone off with Sophie. He was no better than her old employer, the Earl of Leith.

To her horror, Laura found there were tears in her

eyes. She bent her head and walked faster, avoiding the gaze of passersby as she struggled for control. She had been living in a silly fantasy world, she thought. She had imagined that Gavin saw her differently, that they were partners in solving the mystery of the attack on him. But what grounds had she ever had for such ideas? He had not included her. He had never told her anything unless forced to do so. And on top of that, he had taken inexcusable liberties with her person.

Laura flushed and had to fight harder against the threatening tears. The last time he had held her, she had enjoyed it! After all her years of resistance, she had been captivated by a heartless libertine. She had fallen in love with a rake.

Gasping at the shock of the realization, Laura almost ran the rest of the way to the house. Once there, she went immediately to her room and stood in the middle of the carpet with burning eyes and clenched fists. It wasn't love, she insisted silently. She was in the grip of mere infatuation, and she could conquer it—particularly now that Gavin was gone and she was unlikely ever to see him again.

The word seemed to echo in her ears—ever. She had had this one chance at a more expansive life, and she had wasted it on a man who cared for nothing but himself and his own pleasures. How could she have been such a fool?

Laura unfastened her cloak and threw it over the chair. She went to the mirror and smoothed her hair, noting dispassionately that her eyes were still over-bright. It didn't matter, she thought. She would have all the time she needed to recover; she would have all of the rest of her life.

Someone tapped on the door. "Laura?"

"Come in."

Catherine entered, looking more cheerful than she had in days. "Laura, Matthew is feeling a little better, and I have gotten permission to take him home!"

"Oh, good," she replied, trying to sound natural.

"We are leaving as soon as we can get packed up."

"All right."

Catherine looked suddenly concerned. "This will cut your visit short, and you have not...that is, perhaps I could arrange for you to stay with..."

"No." It all seemed futile, Laura thought. It was over. "I am ready to go home."

The other woman looked distressed. "Are you sure? But you haven't... I thought you would meet someone here in Vienna—a suitable husband."

If she had not been so unsettled, Laura would have laughed. "I don't think I'm destined for a suitable husband," she replied a bit hollowly.

"The Merritts would very likely be glad to..."

"Of course I will go home with you."

Catherine's expression did not lighten.

"The visit has been much longer than I expected already," Laura added. "You and the general have been very generous."

Catherine seemed torn between trying to arrange something for her and wanting to prepare for the journey. "You will stay with us in London for as long as you like. There is no need, you know, for you to look for a post. We would be more than happy to—"

"Let us not think of that just now," interrupted Laura. Indeed, she never wanted to think about it. "We need to get the general home."

"Yes." Catherine wrung her hands. "I will feel so much better when we are in our own house."

"Of course you will. I will supervise the packing, so that you are free to sit with him."

"Would you?" She looked immensely relieved. "You must come and ask me if there is any question."

"I will."

"The trunks are in the cellar."

Laura nodded.

"And, let me see, don't forget the teakettle. I brought ours from home, because I didn't know, you see…"

"I remember," said Laura gently.

Catherine laughed. "I am so distracted."

"Don't worry. I will take great care."

"This is so kind of you, Laura."

It wasn't really, she thought. A task was exactly what she needed to occupy her mind, and keep her thoughts from straying—as they continually did—to Gavin Graham.

# Ten

THEY ARRIVED IN VENICE IN AN EARLY FEBRUARY DUSK
that threw purple shadows on the glorious old buildings and made the water glow in rippling stripes of
gold. Catherine had decided to return to England by
ship rather than the more taxing land route. Privately,
Laura wondered whether it was really because she
didn't want to spend the long journey shut in a carriage with an extremely irascible patient. Illness had
made the general short-tempered and morose.

Laura herself was not in the best of tempers. Her
great adventure had ended badly, and she had nothing
to return to but a life that had begun to seem pointless.
She tried to keep from brooding over her situation by
staying busy, volunteering to do Catherine's errands
and manage the details of their travel. It didn't help.
She was perfectly able to think as she visited shipping
offices and dealt with innkeepers. It was ironic, she
thought as she crossed one of Venice's beautifully
arched bridges, her mind had always been her refuge.
Now she longed to escape from it. She paused at the
top of the bridge and gazed down the canal. It was

busy with gondolas carrying people and goods. She watched a load of cabbages pass beneath the bridge, then turned an idle gaze to the next boat. Its contents made her stiffen.

In front of the gondolier sat Sophie Krelov, her red-gold hair gleaming in the sunlight. And close beside her, their shoulders touching, was Gavin Graham. Laura stood frozen as the boat approached a landing. Gavin stepped to shore and then turned to offer Sophie his hand as she followed. Laura hadn't really believed their departures were connected. She had expected some other explanation to surface. She would hear later, she had imagined, that Gavin had been sent on some critical mission or been called halfway across the world by some exotic crisis.

She watched the countess take Gavin's arm with a proprietary air. His head bent to catch something she said, and Laura could see his elegant profile quite clearly. He looked unruffled, and perilously handsome. Laura's hand went out and gripped the balustrade of the bridge. She had to close her eyes to weather a wave of pain that made her sway on her feet. She couldn't believe how much the sight hurt her.

Her distress was so obvious that a woman walking across the bridge stopped and asked if she needed help. Laura swallowed, straightened, and assured her that she did not. The exchange caused a few heads to turn, Sophie Krelov's among them. But Laura was too occupied to see the countess's quick frown and angry glance from her to Gavin. When Laura was able to look again, the pair had started off along the canal, arm in arm, strolling as if they hadn't a care in the world.

Laura told herself that it was none of her affair. The matter was now closed, and she should get about her legitimate errands. But somehow her feet took her in the same direction. It was simple to follow them. Gavin towered above the other pedestrians, and his golden hair was like an irresistible beacon luring her on.

They walked to a large inn near the waterfront. In its courtyard, Sophie stopped and leaned against Gavin seductively. Her arm went around his waist. She raised her head and kissed him, slowly and passionately, prolonging the embrace despite the ribald comments from loungers around them.

Laura couldn't bear any more. She turned away and started to walk blindly over the uneven cobblestones. She didn't see Sophie signal to a man lurking in the inn yard or notice when he fell in behind her. It was all she could do to find her way back to the Pryors' lodgings and into her own small room. There, at last, she could let herself cry.

✎

It was fortunate for her that the general was so ill, Laura thought the next morning as she set out to do some shopping for Catherine. If he had not been occupying her mind, Mrs. Pryor would surely have noticed Laura's dejection and tried to discover the reason for it. She would never tell her, or anyone, Laura vowed silently. She had been a fool but no one need know about it.

She rounded a corner and crossed a narrow bridge over one of the smaller canals. At least she had seen

Venice, she thought. She took a deep breath and
gazed at the beautiful stone buildings on the other
side of the canal. She was imagining how she might
have enjoyed the place under other circumstances
when a hand closed around her upper arm and
jerked her into a dim passageway. Laura opened her
mouth to scream. A rag saturated with chloroform
was immediately thrust into it. She struggled and felt
more than one assailant pinion her limbs. As she lost
consciousness, she felt herself smothered in heavy
cloth and lifted off the ground. After that, everything
was black.

Laura woke in dimness. She was curled into a ball
on some hard surface that seemed to sway beneath her,
making her queasy. Her head hurt, and there was a vile
taste in her mouth.

She had been attacked, she remembered, sitting up
quickly, and then regretting it as dizziness made her
clutch the wall.

It was an odd wall, she was able to notice after a
while. It was made of horizontal planks, and it wasn't
straight but curved. Was it her vision? Laura shook
her head and blinked, but the wall remained bent. She
raised her eyes further and found that the room was
illuminated by a small round window faced in metal.
A ship, she realized, slightly relieved. And so this shelf
behind her head was probably a bunk. She hoisted
herself off the floor, hoping for no more than a soft
place to lie down.

On the bunk built into the wall lay Gavin Graham,
lashed in and unconscious.

Laura fell back to her knees. "Mr. Graham?"

There was no reaction.

"Gavin?"

He was very pale and absolutely still. Suddenly frightened, Laura put out a hand and touched his face. It was clammy. She felt for a pulse and was profoundly relieved to find one. "Gavin?" she said again. She shook his shoulder.

He gave no sign of awareness. She checked for wounds. There didn't appear to be any blood on his clothes. His hair was tangled though, and she soon found a lump on the side of his head. But that didn't explain his current state. He must be drugged, she concluded.

Laura looked around the cabin. Where was Sophie? she wondered irrationally. She tried the metal latch on the door—locked. There were cupboards in one wall, but when she opened them, she found only a tin cup, a tinderbox, and two squat candles.

The ship rolled. Probably they were casting off. It rolled again, and she put out a hand to steady herself. There was nowhere to sit but the bunk. Gently pushing Gavin's feet aside, she settled beside them.

Voices from beyond the door made her muscles clench.

"I don't see why the damned prisoners had to be put in *my* cabin," complained a man in French. "Why should *I* be the one cramped in a hammock all the way to Marseilles?"

"I don't think they'll be with us for the whole voyage," answered a deeper voice. "I heard the lady tell our passengers to get rid of them as soon as they could."

"The devil you say? She gives the orders, you think?"

"So it seems."

"I would not be commanded by a woman."

The other sailor laughed. "A woman like that? With hair red as sunset and a body from my dreams? I would be happy to fulfill all her demands."

"Or she mine," responded his companion. "On her knees, eh? We could put those lips to good use."

"I would rather be between *her* knees."

"Too bad she didn't sail with us."

The other agreed with a grunt. "This Michael of hers is a hard man. He and the captain have secrets."

"What kind of secrets?"

"My friend, I think it is better we do not ask."

The two men's footsteps faded down the corridor. Laura relaxed, thinking over what she had heard. It seemed the countess had had them imprisoned here and that Michael was on the ship. It sounded as if they were to be killed, she thought with a chill. What were they going to do?

Gavin would know. She watched his still, white face, wondering if he realized that Sophie had betrayed him.

&

Laura started awake to a stream of curses. It was pitch black, and the room was heaving around her as if in some sort of earthquake. Her first thought was—"The children!" Then she remembered she was in Vienna. Had some catastrophe struck the city?

The curses continued—vividly.

Laura moved and found she was curled in a confined space next to someone's legs. Startled, she sat up.

"Who's there?" demanded the deep male voice that had been swearing so colorfully.

The ship, thought Laura. Venice. It all came rushing back. Gavin was at last conscious.

"Sophie?" he said.

Laura froze. Was he accustomed to waking in the dark to find Sophie Krelov beside him? Groping in the dark, she opened a cupboard, found the tinderbox and candles, and clumsily lit one. She looked for a candlestick, but there was none.

Turning, she found Gavin staring at her. "What the devil?" he said.

"Are you all right? How do you feel?"

"Vile." The ship heeled over and it felt as if it was skidding down the trough of a wave. "Are we at sea?"

Laura nodded.

"What the bloody hell are we doing there?"

"I believe Michael abducted you."

"Michael?"

"I've forgotten his last name," said Laura.

Gavin moved his hand and found that his arms were bound to his side. He cursed again.

"Here, I will untie you. I was afraid you would fall before." Laura leaned over and found herself hampered by the lit candle. She looked around for a place to set it down. Finally, she saw wax drippings in one spot on the exposed timbers of the cabin. Adding to them from her own candle, she started to affix it in order to get both hands free.

"What are you doing?" demanded Gavin.

"Making a place for the candle."

"Do it later," he ordered.

"I can't untie you with one hand," she pointed out.

He cursed again.

Finished, she turned to the rope. It appeared that one long piece had been wound round and round the bunk, which was separated from the wall by a narrow gap. There was only one knot, at the back.

Laura reached for it. The placement was awkward; standing by the bunk, she could just touch the knot, but she couldn't work with it. She leaned forward, and the deck lurched, throwing her onto Gavin's lower regions. "I beg your pardon," she said, regaining her balance with a stumble.

"Will you just untie me?"

"I am trying to do so!" Laura looked at the knot. She put a knee on the edge of the bunk, but that position was quite precarious. She knelt there, and her skirts hampered her every movement. Finally, she hiked them up and pushed them out of the way, then bent over Gavin and grasped the knot.

It was complicated and tied very tight. She tugged at the coils with no effect. The ship heeled, and Laura fell onto Gavin's hips and legs again, her bare knee braced against his thigh. He made a sound. "I'm sorry," said Laura. "The boat keeps—"

"Just get the ropes off," he snapped. He sounded as if he might be choking.

Laura braced herself more securely and went to work again. The movement of the ship kept interfering, and she couldn't keep her breasts and torso from brushing Gavin at intervals. The cabin began to seem very warm. Laura was flushed and flustered. "It is a very difficult knot," she said, to excuse her slowness and to break the silence, which was beginning to feel uncomfortable.

"Undoubtedly," answered Gavin, his voice thick.

"I don't think it was tied by a sailor," she added to keep the conversation going. She didn't add that she was finding it almost impossible to concentrate on the rope in such close proximity to him. "I have read that sailors chiefly use—"

The ship gave a particularly violent lurch. Laura grabbed the ropes to keep from falling off the bunk. Momentum pressed her hard against Gavin, the fine wool of his coat rasping her cheek, the contours of his body impressed upon hers. The scent of him evoked the memory of his arms around her and his lips on hers. Her flush deepened painfully as she scrambled up. She felt dizzy, and her mouth was dry. She told herself it was the motion of the waves.

Gathering her scattered wits, Laura attacked the knot. At last, she worked one finger under the widest loop. Feeling it give a little, she yanked and managed to get another of her fingers into the gap. When she pulled again, there was a definite movement. "I think I'm getting it," she said. She shifted position to gain more leverage; her elbow brushed Gavin in an extremely awkward place, and he let out an almost inaudible groan. "Sorry," stammered Laura.

The cabin had become unbearably hot, she thought, focusing her scattered attention on the coils of rope. It was hard to breathe. She tugged at the knot again. "It is definitely coming loose," she told Gavin.

"Splendid," he said, sounding as if his teeth were clenched.

Laura worked at the knot. The ship continued to toss and force their bodies together and apart in an irresistible dance that made her fingers fumble and her cheeks burn. At last, when she was about to give up in frustration and embarrassment, the coils gave and fell away. "There!" she cried and sprang up out of her awkward position.

Gavin pushed against the rope. It didn't give. "Are you sure?" he said.

"It is untied."

He flexed his shoulders. "It doesn't move. There are too many windings. You will have to pull it off."

Laura swallowed, wishing her pulse would slow down. She bent over him once again to pick up the end of the rope, and then she began to unwind it, pulling it across his body and through the narrow gap behind the bunk over and over again.

It seemed to take forever. Gavin was holding himself rigid as the coils slid over him. His face looked like stone in the flickering candlelight. Laura tried to hurry, but that only tangled the rope and forced her to lean across him to free it. His breath touched her cheek and seemed almost to burn it.

At last, with only a few coils left, Gavin burst up out of them. He pushed the rope off himself and onto the floor, then sat up against the wall. He was breathing as if he had stayed under water too long, and his eyes seemed hot. "Damnation," he said.

Laura hung on to an exposed timber as the ship lurched yet again.

"I suppose we are locked in?" said Gavin.

She nodded.

"How the devil did you get here?"

The deck heeled in the other direction. Laura swayed with the movement.

Gavin drew his feet closer to him. "Sit," he commanded.

Gingerly, she settled on the opposite end of the narrow bunk. They faced each other warily in the dim light.

"What are you doing here?" he repeated.

"I was abducted as well."

"From Vienna?" he asked incredulously.

"No." Laura tried to order her scattered thoughts. The past half hour had wreaked havoc on her logical faculties. "I came to Venice with the Pryors," she began. "They are going home because of the general's illness. I was out walking, and I saw you and…" She trailed off, uncertain whether she wanted to mention the countess just now.

"And someone saw you."

"I suppose so." Was he going to mention Sophie? she wondered.

Gavin groaned. "Of all the ill luck."

"What?"

"Of course they decided we were involved in some sort of conspiracy," he told her. "And they decided to eliminate both of us. You've ruined everything."

"I?"

"If you had not interfered, I would have gotten the information I need by now."

"Interfered? I did no such thing!" Laura paused,

remembering that she had followed him through the streets of Venice.

"And now I am burdened with your presence—"

"Burdened! If it were not for me, you would still be tied up and—"

"I would not be here at all."

"You would be at the inn with Sophie Krelov!" Laura accused.

"Precisely."

This left Laura speechless for a moment. He said it without any discernible emotion. Did he mean he longed to be with Sophie? Or only that he wanted to get information from her? "Sophie ordered the kidnapping," she said. "I heard some sailors talking."

"Once you were seen," he responded. He put a hand to his head as if it hurt. "And now I must look after you. I am perfectly capable of looking after myself, but I do not—"

"Oh, perfectly capable," she interrupted. "That is why you were drugged and shanghaied onto a ship for Marseilles."

"We are headed for Marseilles?" he interjected.

She nodded.

"Marseilles," he repeated, diverted from their dispute. "Why Marseilles?"

Laura bit her lower lip to keep from shrieking. He was so completely exasperating.

Gavin took a deep breath and rubbed his face with his hands. "Have their drugs completely addled my wits?" he asked himself. Raising his head, he added, "Did you hear anything else?"

She shook her head.

He sighed. "With you here to hamper my movements, I cannot—"

"Hamper? I untied you!"

Gavin met her eyes. After a long moment, they both looked away.

"I have been in worse situations," he said. "And gotten out of them. But then I was alone. I work alone. The necessity of protecting you will—"

"I can look out for myself!"

"You got yourself imprisoned on this ship," he pointed out.

"So did you!"

"Because you spoiled my plan," he countered. Something seemed to occur to him. "You didn't see another captive?"

Surprised, Laura shook her head.

"Hasan got away then. Good."

"He looked as if he could get out of anything. Did he give you my note?"

He frowned at her. "I had no time for social calls."

"Social?" She glared at him, outraged. "I went to your lodgings after I heard Michael and the others plotting. To tell you."

"Plotting," he repeated, as if unfamiliar with the word. "What the devil are you talking about?"

"I found Michael. If you had just waited until I…"

Gavin put two hands to his head and pressed his fingers into his temples. "Stop, or I will go stark mad."

Laura bit her tongue to keep from protesting. She hoped he had a horrible headache.

"Tell me the whole tale, from the beginning," he commanded.

"Well, I am not sure what *is* the beginning…"

He made a sound that caused her to rush on.

"I had an idea about Sophie's maid."

Even in the dimness, she could see his surprised expression.

"I saw her when I visited, and she didn't seem at all like a maid, you see."

"No," he answered. "I don't."

Laura took a breath. It was hard to reason clearly when he was staring at her. "I thought she might be more than a maid, perhaps involved in Sophie's spying."

"Ah."

"So I spoke to the girl who was watching me—"

"What girl?"

"Oh." She had almost betrayed Annalise. "Never mind that."

"On the contrary—"

"We kept watch on the maid and eventually followed her to a house where Michael and his friends were staying."

"A fact you neglected to tell me," he said in a dangerous voice.

"I wasn't sure at first. And then when I was, you were gone. If you had honored our agreement to be equal partners, you would have—"

Gavin's teeth ground together. "What else?"

"I took a room at that house, to find out more, and one night at dinner…"

She stopped as Gavin let his head fall onto his hands.

"Are you all right?"

"I thought you said that you had eaten dinner with Michael and his gang."

"Yes. Well, I didn't know whether he was Michael until then. It seemed the only way to find out."

"Aside from telling *me* of his existence," he snapped.

"Well, I would have if you had not—"

"Have you no conception of the danger—?"

"Of course I did. But I have spent years avoiding notice, and I thought I could do so again. I suppose spies are different," she added.

"Years… What are you talking about?"

"It doesn't matter."

"This is not some parlor game we are playing at." Gavin leaned his head against the ship's timbers. "I have to think," he muttered. "Please be quiet."

Part of Laura wanted to object. But the grim set of his mouth made her decide to save her complaints for later.

❧

"She must be given a cabin of her own," Gavin told the crewman who had escorted him to the sanitary facilities. "Tell the captain I said—"

"Ain't none," was the reply. "She can come along to the fo'castle," he added with a gap-toothed grin. "We'll give her a warm welcome, we will."

This silenced Gavin as he realized that if Laura was taken from the cabin they now shared, he wouldn't know what was happening to her and would have no way to guarantee her safety. He cursed under his breath.

"What's yer beef?" asked the crewman. "Ya got a female in your cabin. Ya don't have to do no work, and they're feedin' ya anyhow. Ye're on a pleasure cruise, mate."

More like a penance, Gavin thought. It was driving him mad being so close to Laura. He was very much afraid his control would break down before he got them out of this.

They reached the cabin, guarded by another sailor of daunting proportions. The crewman opened the door and pushed Gavin inside. The lock clicked behind him.

Laura was sitting on the end of the bunk looking alert and inquiring—not at all as if she had spent a day cramped in a small space aboard ship. Tendrils of dark hair curled at her temples and along her cheeks. Her legs were tucked under the froth of her skirts. She was the loveliest thing he had ever seen, Gavin thought. He edged over to the other end of the bunk and sat. He had to avoid touching her, he thought. It set him afire. But the motion of the ship continually threw them together. Simply trying to move in the cabin was likely to cause a collision. And then he would find himself holding her, and every part of him would be united in one desire, and it took all of his considerable will to step back politely and deny the need that drove him. This was intolerable, he thought for the hundredth time. He couldn't bear it.

"Did you see him?" asked Laura.

His thoughts were scattered to the winds. "Who?"

"Michael."

"Oh. No. But from your description I am sure it is the same man I knew in Persia. He was one of Boney's best agents."

"He is not French," Laura declared.

Gavin looked curious. "How do you know that?"

"The way he speaks. He is very good, but there is still a small accent."

"I had noticed that…"

"But you are astonished I did. Why can you not admit that I possess a fair degree of intelligence?"

"Experience is needed here, not simply intelligence."

She glared at him.

She would addle the brains of a saint, Gavin thought. He had to concentrate on the task at hand—defeat the plot they had disturbed. This was his work and he took great pride in his abilities. He was not subject to distractions, even those held out by beautiful women. Yes, Gavin thought. Sophie Krelov was clear evidence of that. Most men would have judged her far more alluring than Laura Devane, and yet all he wanted from the devious countess was answers. He had not lost his edge—or his mind.

"What do you think they're up to?" Laura asked, having apparently conquered her temper.

"Bonaparte is exiled on a small island off the west coast of Italy," Gavin said. "We are sailing down the coast of Italy—the east coast, I admit. But if we are headed toward Marseilles…"

"We will go up the west coast," Laura finished. "You think we might be going to Napoleon?"

"I believe there is a strong chance."

"But why?"

Gavin shook his head, remembering the long years of war with Napoleon's armies, the huge costs in money and lives. "Escape? They should have sent him farther from Europe. Many of the French still support him, you know."

Laura rose. "But this is terrible. We must get word to someone. We must stop him."

"I shall endeavor to do so."

Laura turned and fumbled in the pocket of her gown. "I brought my pistol," she said, holding it out to him.

Gavin took it, feeling suddenly much better with the smooth grip in his hand. "They didn't find it?"

"They didn't think to look."

Gavin hefted the gun. He could use it to overcome the guard the next time he brought them food. But then what? There was nowhere for them to go and a ship full of opponents. "Keep it for now," he told Laura, reluctantly returning it. "We will hold it in reserve for the right opportunity."

She put the gun away again. As she straightened, the ship heeled over, and Laura staggered, putting out a hand to restore her balance. It landed on Gavin's thigh, sending a jolt of desire through him that drove all other thoughts from his mind.

"Sorry," she said, snatching her hand back and flushing that luscious rose red.

He very nearly reached for her. He wanted her more, in that moment, than he had ever wanted anything. But even if she felt the same, he thought, even if she fell gratefully into his arms, what could they do with a guard outside and the chance that their captors might open the door at any time? How was he going to endure this voyage? he wondered. It was going to be the most difficult mission he had ever undertaken.

❧

The cabin door was opened without warning later that day, revealing a group of armed crewmen. They bound Gavin's hands tightly behind him and then took both of them along a narrow gangway to the captain's more spacious quarters. It was not the captain who awaited them there, however, but Michael and his companions.

The former smiled when his two captives were pushed into the room. He was seated at a round table bolted to the deck in the center, while the others lounged about the edges of the chamber, which occupied the bow of the ship.

"Graham," said Michael silkily. "Come in."

The crewmen pushed them until they stood before him.

"A little different from the last time we met, eh?" he continued in French. "I told you then that I would make you pay for cheating me."

"You were the one cheating the hill tribes," Gavin answered. "How did you convince them not to kill you?"

He spoke as if he were inquiring about some commonplace, Laura thought. His manner appeared completely unconcerned. She tried to emulate it.

Michael's face reddened alarmingly. "Bastard!" he spat. "You left me there to be spitted like a roast pig."

"As you had attempted to do to me," Gavin responded.

Michael started to speak, then stopped himself. Laura watched him struggle for control. "That doesn't matter now," he said finally. "I have you, and you will not escape me. Nor will your little friend." He eyed Laura.

"She has nothing to do with this."

"No? You sent her to spy on us in Vienna. Something new for you, eh, Graham? You always boasted of working alone."

"I didn't send her. You have made a mistake."

"I don't think so." He looked Laura up and down again. "She is rather good at disguise. I might not have recognized her if it weren't for those green eyes. Like a cat, eh? Does she show you her claws in the bedroom?"

"Perhaps we should see," suggested one of the other men.

Michael waved him aside with disdain. "We are on an imperial mission."

"Imperial?" said Gavin. "Those days are over. There is a Bourbon king in France again."

"Pah." He made a rude gesture. "King Louis the coward. He is nothing."

"Who would you put in his place?" asked Gavin softly.

"He who belongs there—the emperor!"

The other men murmured their approval.

"Bonaparte abdicated."

"Words on a piece of paper, forced on him by a pack of rabble. It means nothing."

"So you intend to restore him?"

"I do," was the reply. "And then…many things will be possible."

"When does he land?" inquired Gavin in a deceptively even tone.

Michael gave him a crafty glance. "That is not for you to know. You are out of this game, Graham. Checkmated very neatly by our little Sophie."

Laura risked a glance, but Gavin's face showed nothing.

"And now, we must part company. We have many things to do, and your presence is…awkward."

"Let Miss Devane go," said Gavin.

"Go and report to your friends? I fear not. We are going to have to dispose of both of you."

"What do you mean to do?"

Gavin didn't ask as if it were a real question, Laura thought. It was more of a challenge.

Michael grinned at him maliciously. "I believe we will let that be a surprise. Yes, I think so. Do you like surprises, Graham?"

Laura saw a vein standing out in his neck, but he said only, "As much as you do."

Michael threw back his head and laughed. "You won't be surprising me this time. You are helpless. How do you like the feeling?"

The two men stared as if they could annihilate each other with a glance.

"About as much as I do, eh?" added Michael finally. "It is a pleasure beyond measuring to turn the tables on you, Graham."

"We shall see," he answered.

"I fear all has been seen, and foreseen." Michael waved his hand. "Take them back."

They were returned to their cabin by the group of crewmen. "You think he means to kill us?" asked Laura as she untied Gavin's hands. She tried to match his air of unconcern.

He shrugged as if he didn't want to answer.

"You don't think Napoleon can win?"

His hands free once more, Gavin turned to face her. "He is a master strategist. If he has the advantage of surprise…" He let the sentence trail off.

"We must see that he doesn't."

The look Gavin gave her was unreadable. He had been full of inscrutable looks throughout this voyage, Laura thought. He had made it very plain, however, that he didn't want her here. He was incapable of admitting that anyone could help him, she thought. He believed he was the only person who could accomplish anything useful. It was incredibly annoying.

Being shut in a small room with Gavin Graham was like being caged with a tiger, she thought. He filled the cabin with an aura of menace. And though she knew it wasn't directed at her, that didn't make it any less difficult. He jumped whenever she touched him, she thought. She tried her best not to touch him. But the ship would unbalance her; the space was tiny.

Tucking herself into the corner of the bunk, Laura felt a qualm of guilt. She wasn't being entirely honest, she admitted. She didn't always avoid touching him as assiduously as she might have. Sometimes the excitement of it tempted her, and she let the motion of the deck sway her, let the cramped quarters seem an excuse. The jolt that went through her when their hands brushed or their bodies pressed together was so thrilling. It had become a pleasure she couldn't resist.

Had Sophie grown to feel the same way? she wondered. What was really between them? The countess was so beautiful. She was mysterious, exotic, dangerous—just the sort of woman Gavin was rumored to prefer. It was inconceivable that he would ever choose Laura over Sophie. Wasn't it?

Laura felt a tremor of fear. This was far more dangerous than any tiger, she thought. What had become of her celebrated detachment? And what was going to become of her, bewitched by a man like Gavin Graham?

# Eleven

THE FOLLOWING AFTERNOON GAVIN HEARD THE sound of the anchor chain rasping across the deck above them. After a while, the movement of the ship lessened. Straining his ears, he listened for the bustle of an Italian port town. But he could hear nothing except the familiar sounds of the creaking timbers and the exchanges of the French crew. Still, if they were anchored, there might be some chance for escape. Though he knew it was futile, he went over and tried the cabin door. The lock held as well as ever.

Footsteps approached. The key grated and the door was pulled open to reveal Michael and a party of armed crew members. "Come," he said. "You are getting off here."

As Laura scrambled up, Gavin said, "Where is 'here'?"

"You will see soon enough. Come along."

"If you had given me some warning, I would be ready to come," responded Laura.

Gavin smiled slightly. Nothing seemed to quench

her spirit, he thought. She really was one of the most amazing females he had ever encountered.

They were herded along the gangway and up a ladder to the deck. The simple touch of fresh air heartened Gavin. He had never endured imprisonment well, though he had probably suffered more of it than most honest men in England, he thought wryly. He remembered a time in Persia when he had nearly gone mad before escaping. He stretched his arms, and one of the sailors trained a musket on him.

"Come," repeated Michael, urging them toward the ship's rail. Gavin looked over it to see a small island a hundred yards away. This, then, was their anchorage. On the waves below was one of the ship's longboats, with several crewmen already aboard. "Into the boat," said Michael.

Gavin hesitated. But he could see no alternative. He turned and offered Laura a hand, helping her over the rail and onto the rope ladder that hung over the side. As she descended precariously, he threw a leg over the rail and prepared to follow. The muzzles of a number of guns moved with him and remained trained on him when they reached the smaller vessel. Michael and two of the other crew members joined them, and the crewmen rowed them toward shore.

The sea was calm, and they soon reached a tiny, ramshackle dock. Urged out by gun barrels, Gavin stepped onto it, giving Laura a hand as she joined him. Michael also came ashore. The sailors began unloading some boxes.

"There is a house of sorts at the top of that path," said Michael. "We are giving you provisions."

"You are leaving us here?" said Laura.

"I am giving Graham the same chance he gave me," sneered the other.

Laura looked around at the rocks and sand that made up the visible landscape. "What is this place?"

"A forgotten little island that one of the crew knows. His uncle lived here until he died recently." Michael glanced at Gavin. "Don't think you will escape it, my friend. No ships come here, and old Tomaso used to shoot at any local men who ventured to land, so now they don't."

The sailors returned from wherever they had carried the boxes.

"All stowed?" said Michael.

One of them nodded.

"Good. Let's be on our way, then."

The others climbed back into the boat and took up oars. Michael moved to join them, keeping his pistol carefully trained on Gavin.

He might be able to overpower him, Gavin thought. He gauged his chances of taking the boat if he held Michael hostage. They weren't good. And the longboat was a poor vessel for travel to the mainland. Laura would very likely be hurt in the ensuing melee. He stepped back.

"Very wise," said Michael, getting into the boat. He grinned. "Enjoy yourselves."

The sailors were already rowing. The boat pulled away from the dock and out into the deeper water. Gavin watched his only link with the outer world draw slowly away and wondered if there was anything else he could have done. Should he have tried to commandeer the ship? Impossible against so many.

"I never properly appreciated *Robinson Crusoe* until now," said Laura.

He gave a curt laugh. "We had best explore our new prison."

The small stone house at the top of the path looked as if it had been there for generations. The slant of the roof did not inspire confidence, but when they peered inside, it seemed weathertight. One large room, with a wide fireplace at the back, held a battered table and chair, a sagging bed, and a tall cupboard. The windows of oiled paper let in little light. The boxes from the ship were piled in the middle of the floor. "It smells of mice," said Laura.

"No doubt." He surveyed the place again, seeing no likely dangers. "Wait here. I'm going to look around the island."

"I don't want to wait here." She came back through the door with him. "At least it is not too cold. There's firewood."

He followed her gaze to a stack of twisted branches and logs beside the house. Nodding, he strode up the hill into which the building was nestled, looking for a broader view of their situation.

He soon found it. The crest wasn't far, and from there he could see all of the island, a dot of perhaps ten acres in a circle of blue water. The only signs of life were the departing French ship and a scattering of seabirds apparently nesting in the cliffs opposite. There were some twisted trees bent from the wind and some grass. Gavin heard a distant bell and spotted a little herd of goats grazing near the far shore.

"There must be water," said Laura.

"I imagine we will find a spring near the house." Gavin tried to keep his voice level, but a tinge of frustration crept into it. Unless another ship materialized, he was trapped here while great events were going forward outside. There was nothing he could do, no effect he could have. His knowledge of the threat to British interests was useless. It was a damnable situation. "Why don't you go and see," he suggested to Laura. He very much wanted to be alone until he could get this raging impatience under control.

But, as usual, she couldn't accede to a simple request. "There are goats down there. Perhaps we can get milk."

Gavin felt as if he might explode. "We did not come here to settle into domesticity," he snapped. "We are prisoners. While you chase after goats, Europe may go up in flames!"

"I was only—"

"Interfering, as you never seem able to resist doing."

"You are the most infuriating man I ever—"

"Do be quiet."

Her green eyes blazed at him. Even in his agitation, Gavin noticed how lovely they looked.

"My 'interference' might have been of real help if you had only been able to acknowledge that—"

"Will you go away!"

She looked as if he had slapped her. Standing straighter and raising her chin defiantly, she turned and walked down the path away from him.

At last, Gavin thought, and took a deep breath of the salt-laden air. Now he would be able to think. But for some reason, all he could think of was Laura's face and the look she had given him as she went—compounded of outrage and surprise and hurt.

She didn't understand, he thought, a bit defensively. He couldn't bear to be relegated to the sidelines when he had been right in the thick of it—this was abominable, insupportable. All his experience and work of the last ten years suited him for action. His fists clenched. Laura could have no conception of this. She couldn't possibly know this need to affect events, to be one of those who steered the outcome.

A gust of wind swooped over the hilltop. Clouds were massing in the northwest, promising a squall. Gavin sighed and forced his muscles to relax. He had been in worse spots, he told himself. He might yet find a way out. The important thing was to maintain control, be watchful, take advantage of whatever presented itself.

He took a long breath. Laura's presence was disruptive, he decided. He had not reacted so violently on past missions. She disturbed his concentration, distracted him from vital concerns. What was it about her that was so unsettling? She was beautiful, but he had known scores of beautiful women. She was intelligent and quick-witted, but again, such females were not wholly outside his experience. She had courage—too much perhaps. She was tenacious and spirited and damnably alluring. She matched him, somehow; she moved to the same rhythms and resonated to the same signals.

What the devil did that mean?

Gavin frowned, oblivious to the seabirds wheeling before the approaching clouds or the goats clattering over the rocks in search of shelter from the coming storm. He must take more care. Laura Devane was intruding far too much into his consciousness. He couldn't afford that sort of preoccupation. It was perilous for someone like him. Resolving to put a stop to it this moment, Gavin turned and started back down the path.

∾

The rain began in early evening, a cold soaking rain that enveloped the house. Laura had swept the floor earlier and asked Gavin to make a fire, so the scene might have been cozy. It wasn't, however, Laura thought. Gavin sat brooding in the chair, staring at the flames as if they were ranks of enemies. It was like waiting for a storm to break, she thought, or for the arrival of news that was bound to be bad. The force of his personality made the very air seem charged. She felt that any word she spoke would spark an explosion.

She wasn't frightened. But she didn't relish the idea of a confrontation. He had already been quite rude enough. Eventually she would have to do something. They couldn't spend much time here in this kind of atmosphere. For now, however, she went quietly about the business of toasting some of the cheese their captors had left them and combining it with ship's biscuit into a kind of dinner. She didn't know whether to be glad or sorry that they would be drinking only springwater until they left this island.

The cupboard had revealed a few tin plates and cups and minimal cutlery. She filled two of the plates and set them on the table. Gavin continued to glare at the fire from the only chair in the house. After a moment, Laura took her dinner over to the bed and sat on the edge of it to eat.

"I feel as if I am back in the schoolroom," she said tartly. "Are you going to go on sulking for a long time?"

Gavin grunted.

"You're very welcome. I was happy to go through the stores and prepare your dinner. I try to be of service where I can."

He made no further sign. His back remained to her.

"We may very well be able to escape," she ventured. "Michael might have been lying about ships coming here."

He made a dismissive gesture.

"And what about the person who lived here? He must have had a boat of some kind."

"Michael is no fool," Gavin growled. "He will have seen to that."

"Perhaps. We should search to be sure."

"I will search. I have nothing else to do."

Laura ate another few bites. "Perhaps we could build something?" she said then. "A raft, or a—"

"There is not enough wood on this island to build an ale cask," he snapped. "You saw the trees; they are dwarfed and twisted by the wind. Rest assured that I have thought of all these things, and rejected them, already."

"I *beg* your pardon." Laura finished her meal in

fuming silence. Then she took her plate to the table and set it beside his untouched one. "Do you intend to eat anything?"

"No."

"Perhaps I'll just throw your dinner out for the goats, then."

"You may send it to perdition for all of me."

Laura clicked the tin plate down on the tabletop. "When I was a governess, if one of my charges behaved as you are, I would have—"

"Governess!" he jeered.

She stiffened. "There is nothing wrong with being a governess."

"Indeed not. If that is what you really were."

"What do you mean by that? I was a—"

"No woman who looks like you could have been a *governess* in the household of the Earl of Leith." He finally turned around. His expression was as supercilious and sneering as it had been when they first met months ago. "*Governess*," he repeated as if it were an obscenity. "What did the earl have you governing?"

"How dare you!"

Gavin surged out of the chair and took hold of her upper arms in a harsh grip. "Ten years, you said? You stayed with him for ten years? Why did he throw you out?"

Laura was so angry that a haze of red seemed to tinge her vision. "Leith never touched me," she hissed.

"Really? He altered the habits of a lifetime for you? Of all the women who came under his power, he spared *you* his attentions? Why? Out of chivalry? Gentlemanly restraint?"

She twisted away from him. "He doesn't know the meaning of those words."

"So I have heard."

"As had I, before I took the position in his house."

"And yet you didn't hesitate," he sneered. "I suppose it was a kind of opportunity."

"How dare you speak to me this way? What I have done or not done is none of your affair."

Gavin stood quite still. His hands, which had been clenched, opened. His frown smoothed out, leaving behind something that almost looked like sadness. The fire in his eyes receded. He bowed his head then, conceding her point. "None of my affair at all," he said.

"I took the position because it was the only one offered me at the time," she added in clipped tones. "I had no money, just a few gowns suitable for *ton* parties. My father asked me for my pearls—to sell—and I gave them to him."

"I beg your—"

"Pity is as insulting as your accusations," she interrupted. "I haven't the least interest in it."

He was silent.

Satisfied with this, she went on. "I was warned about Leith, of course. And I considered what I should do. I was young, but not stupid."

"Never that," he said in a different tone.

"I decided to make certain he never noticed me, and thus avoid having to fend off his…advances."

Gavin raised a skeptical eyebrow, but he didn't speak.

"You don't understand. I didn't really understand myself until recently. You see, I became one of the invisible women."

"The…?"

"You have no idea what I mean, because you have never noticed them yourself—all the governesses and maiden aunts and poor relations with their drab clothes and downcast eyes. They are expected to want nothing for themselves, to care for the children and run the errands and listen if there is no one more interesting to talk with."

"I have encountered a number of such women who were hardly invisible," Gavin objected.

"The discontented ones," she agreed. "There are many of them, of course. But this is what I have learned recently. If you can manage to really want nothing, you vanish." Somewhat to her surprise, Laura had to gulp back a sob.

"Do you want nothing?" asked Gavin in an odd voice.

"I did. To live in that household, I learned to want nothing. And I disappeared."

Silence fell over the room. The rhythm of the rain embraced them.

"And now?" His voice held a peculiar intensity.

Laura looked up at him. She couldn't tell him that everything was different now, and that it was his fault. She couldn't say that his presence in her life had shattered forever her ability to fade into the background. He had brought the excitement of great events, the satisfaction of being useful, and most of all—himself. Her old life was mere memory, Laura thought. She could never go back to not wanting. "I've forgotten how," she murmured and felt a tear slide down her cheek.

"Laura." He stepped forward and enfolded her in his arms.

She rested her head on his shoulder, listening to his heartbeat. She felt as if she belonged in this place, as if all her worries could be set aside for the moment. Her breath sighed out, and the anger that had been sustaining her ebbed with it.

"Laura," he said again.

This wasn't wise, a part of her warned. She shouldn't have spoken to him so freely. She shouldn't be at ease in his embrace. He hadn't revealed anything of himself. She had proffered her confidences and asked for none in exchange.

She raised her head. His gaze was warm, questioning. His body spoke to hers in a myriad of silent, fiery tremors. Not wise, the inner voice repeated, promising regrets. What was wise? she responded. The years she had spent becoming nothing—was that wisdom? Reading about desire and having none? Was she never to have anything she wanted? Was she to return to invisibility and die there?

His hand moved slightly on her back, leaving a trail of heat.

"I want you," Laura whispered.

He bent his head a little. "What?"

Could she not, for once, take what she wanted as others seemed to do? Trembling with excitement and her own daring, she brushed her parted lips across his.

Gavin looked startled. His eyes darkened and his arms around her tightened. "What are you…?"

Throwing wisdom to the winds, Laura kissed him again.

The result was breathtaking. He took her unpracticed kiss like a gift and deepened it until she was dizzy. She clung to his shoulders as her knees went weak, then let her arms slip around his neck and draw him even closer. He pulled her against him, his arms wrapped around her as if he never intended to let go. His lips drew out her desire, coaxing it as a man does tinder to the flame. Every inch of Laura's skin prickled with the need to be touched by his hands. As if he knew, his fingers grazed her side and came up to caress her breast. She caught her breath.

His other hand found the buttons at the back of her gown and unfastened a few. Pushing one sleeve off her shoulder, he dropped kisses down her neck. When he teased her with his tongue, Laura was astonished by the sensations that jolted to her very core. "Oh," she breathed. "I didn't know it would be like this."

"Did you not?" he murmured, pushing down her other sleeve and letting his mouth roam.

When he captured her lips again, his hand stayed busy with the buttons. With an amazing lack of concern, Laura felt her dress peel away. It was as if some annoying impediment had been swept aside. But when Gavin drew back and gazed at her, standing before him in a shift that was already half off, she pulled one of the straps back up. "What about you?" she said.

"Me?" His eyes devoured her.

"You haven't undressed."

He glanced down at his clothes and then up again. "I haven't, have I?" He grinned, almost feral. "Would you care to help?"

Feeling at once shy and excited, Laura moved

closer. Taking the lapels of his coat, she eased it back over his broad shoulders. He moved them, and the garment slipped off. She began to undo the buttons of his waistcoat. He ran his hands up her sides, over her breasts, and down again. Laura's breath quickened as she tried to concentrate on her task.

The waistcoat went the way of the coat to lie at his feet. Laura started on his shirt. With each button, her fingers brushed his bare skin, while his brushed hers in an extremely intimate way.

The shirt slipped away. Laura ran her palms over his chest, marveling at the sculpted muscles and the curling golden hair.

"Enough," Gavin said thickly. In one swift movement, he picked her up and carried her to the bed in the corner. When he had settled her there, he sat on the edge and pulled off his boots in two quick motions. Then he was beside her, kissing her more intensely than ever.

Laura had never imagined such a flood of sensation. All of his body seemed to speak to hers, communicating secret desires and wishes long hidden. When his hand slid up her thigh, pulling her shift along with it, she wriggled out of the thin garment gladly. His next touch was so intimate, and so arousing, that she gasped aloud.

He murmured her name, but Laura was overwhelmed by a need that was building beyond all reason. When he pulled away from her, she reached for him like a drowning woman.

"A moment only," he said, stripping off his breeches with one rapid gesture. Then he was with her again, his lips and hands driving her nearly mad.

Just when she felt that she could take no more without dissolving, Gavin shifted, and she felt him inside her. There might have been a flash of pain. She wasn't sure, because it was immediately followed by an explosion of pleasure that reverberated through her as Gavin moved. Waves of delight crashed from her core through all her limbs. Her breath came out in a soft cry. In that moment, she felt utterly physical, as complete as a wild creature in the forest depths. She wanted to laugh and cry at once at the sheer unassailable beauty of it.

Gavin groaned and held her in a viselike grip for an instant. Then he came to rest above her, his heart pounding, his breath coming hard. Laura held him. It seemed to her that all the difficulties and tensions of the last few days had been whirled away, leaving the two of them alone together.

❧

The fire had fallen into ash. Faint dawn light filtered through the windows, muted by the rain that drummed on the roof as if it meant to continue for some time. Tendrils of cool, damp air edged around the door and into the room, bringing the scent of wet grass and stone.

Propped on one elbow, Gavin looked down at Laura, sleeping beside him. Her hair spilled out like a cloud of ink. Her skin was milk white in the dimness, and the delicate outline of her face, with its thick fringe of black lashes, was blurred. A twenty-nine-year-old virgin, he thought, recalling a phrase he had used months ago when he had first heard her name again. She really had been.

He still found it incredible. Not that he'd thought she was lying when she told her story of living in the Leith household; he simply didn't understand half the things she'd said. Invisible women and disappearing—it sounded like a fairy story. And yet, she had, in fact, escaped the villain. He shook his head. It was just one more thing that made her such an extraordinary creature.

The wind blew a spattering of rain against the oiled paper of the east window. It was chilly in the house. He should make up the fire, bring in more wood from outdoors. Later, he would see about the drafts around the door. Perhaps something could be done.

As he looked back down at Laura breathing softly, an inner voice asked what the devil he was thinking. He wasn't some settled householder to worry over winter drafts. Comfort hadn't been his prime consideration for years and years. He had discovered vital information; it had to be conveyed to his government. His only concern was getting off this island and fulfilling that mission. There was no space in his life for…entanglements.

What was she going to expect when she woke? he wondered. Some sort of declaration? What had become of his careful policy of taking his pleasure only with women who understood the game, who knew quite well what he was offering?

The anger at being trapped, which had affected him so deeply the previous day, returned to Gavin with even greater intensity. He hated having the power to act wrenched from him. If Laura was disappointed, it was her own fault, he thought. She hadn't played the innocent last night. She hadn't held back.

The memory of what she had done coursed through him, and he felt himself becoming aroused. He wanted her. Of course he wanted her. He wasn't made of stone. And their bodies spoke to each other in a simple, utterly compelling language that asked nothing of the future. But the result wasn't simple. It was so complicated that he had begun to dread the moment when she opened her eyes. If there had been anywhere to go, in this moment he would have chosen escape.

Moving very gently, Gavin eased himself off the bed and pulled on his shirt and breeches. The floor was cold; he added his boots before going to stir the coals and put wood on the fire.

He was ravenous. Seeing the plate Laura had left for him last night still on the table, he went and began to eat the cold biscuit and cheese. His mind started reviewing all possible ways off the island, with as little success as yesterday. There had to be some means at his disposal. He had never been outwitted before.

Gradually, the sensation grew on Gavin that he was being watched. He looked up, and found Laura's eyes focused on him, her expression unreadable. "Good morning," she said.

"Good morning."

"You've dressed already."

Did she sound disappointed? The idea startled Gavin. "Yes."

"I wanted to see if you were like the drawings."

"What?" He would have sworn she *was* disappointed.

She flushed. "Nothing. I don't think I'm quite awake."

"What drawings?"

"Never mind." Laura looked around as if not sure what to do. She saw her shift and reached for it, pulling it over her head and wriggling as she pulled it down.

Gavin experienced a twinge of desire and regret. "What drawings?" he repeated, curiosity overcoming his earlier concerns.

She shrugged. "The earl had a number of portfolios in his library," she said, speaking rather quickly. "With drawings."

"Portfolios often contain drawings. What was their subject?"

Laura raised her head and looked at him again. "You are teasing me," she commented. "They were drawings of men and women in…in various intimate positions."

"The earl left these where anyone could examine them?"

"*He* didn't care. And he was often away, of course."

"And you took the opportunity to, er, familiarize yourself…"

"I was curious."

"Indeed?"

Surprisingly, she laughed. "I was shocked at first. But then I began to find them rather…interesting."

Gavin was silenced.

"And the…experience of last night was so much more overwhelming than what I had read about it that I wanted to see if…"

"If I differed in any particulars from the drawings?" he finished, his voice unsteady.

She nodded, rather more flushed.

"I take it the earl had books as well as pictures."

"Yes."

"And you availed yourself of these also?"

"You needn't sound so superior. You would have looked at them if you had been there."

"Undoubtedly." Gavin didn't know whether to laugh or be scandalized. The implications of her knowledge were fascinating. Her naïveté about it was touching.

"There is no need for you to stare in that way. I read a great many other things as well."

"I'm sure you did."

Laura looked at her dress, which was lying in a heap on the floor some distance from the bed. She hesitated, then rose and went to pick it up, and slid it over her head. She began, a little awkwardly, to do up the buttons in the back.

Her hair was tumbled about her shoulders. Her bare feet showed below the hem. Gavin couldn't resist. "Can I help you with those?" he asked, rising and placing his hands over hers.

Laura looked over her shoulder at him. Her eyes were shifting pools of dark and light. "Thank you," she murmured.

He did up the buttons slowly, letting his fingers linger along her back. Laura's breathing quickened.

"I don't know…" she began. "How does one behave after…? Is there some sort of…?"

"Etiquette?" The scent of her perfume and the feel of her under his hands was erasing all other thoughts from his mind.

"I suppose you could call it that."

"I can think of only one." Tempted beyond bearing, he bent and placed his lips on the soft skin of her neck. His arms slid around her and pulled her against him.

She leaned there. He let his mouth and hands rove, exulting when he made her breath catch and her body tremble.

After a while, just as he was wishing her to, she turned into his embrace and laced her arms around his neck. Their kiss was like oil on flames. He held her hard against him and felt her yield in every limb to his demand. He ached with wanting her.

"Are you undoing my gown again?" she said dreamily.

"I am."

"Oh, good."

It fell from her shoulders. Laura looked at him with wide passion-blurred eyes, and then pulled her shift up and off, standing naked in front of the fire. Her slender curves showed all the allure that was usually hidden. Her gaze seemed to dare him. Responding, he shed his own clothes and faced her, feeling at once taunting and tender.

She blinked and breathed, "Oh."

"Do I match your studies?" he asked hoarsely.

"You are all golden."

"Some parts are hard as metal," he acknowledged and stepped forward to sweep her up and into bed.

Once again he coaxed from her the passion he had recognized in the beginning. Once again, their bodies fell into an inevitable rhythm with each other, and desire rose unspoken. There was no place for thought or reason, no chance of hesitation. She touched him and he almost cried out.

"Not cold as metal though," she whispered.

He couldn't speak. He couldn't wait. He had to have her now. It was all he could do to hold back until she moaned in release. And then he let go and allowed the sensations to crash through him like a storm battering jagged cliffs. The pleasure was so intense it made him shudder. It rebounded from every part of him and left him utterly spent. He was so shaken he was afraid to collapse on her, afraid he would crush her with his weight. With his last strength, he turned, holding her close and pulling her onto his chest. He came to rest on his back, pulse hammering, breath ragged, and waited for the world to return from the whirlwind.

Minutes passed unheeded. Slowly, his heart resumed its normal beat. His muscles regained some resilience. He was aware of his surroundings again. The rain was heavier; droplets strayed down the chimney to hiss in the fire.

Laura's head rested in the vicinity of his collarbone. Her legs straddled him. One of her hands cupped his shoulder. Gavin's earlier qualms came rushing back. He hadn't meant to do this. Uneasy, he cleared his throat.

Laura pushed up on her hands and looked down at him, her black hair falling around them. "You're very good at this, aren't you?" she said.

He blinked.

"I heard some Frenchwomen talking about you once. They said you were 'a poet of the bedchamber.'"

"I beg your pardon?" Gavin hastily searched his memory for Frenchwomen and came up with none. "I assure you that I have not..."

"And now I know what they mean." She smiled down at him.

She sounded like a scholar pleased at some new bit of learning, he thought. And she looked rather like the cat who had managed to unlatch the canary's cage. She was an incomprehensible woman.

"I wish we could stay here forever," she said, looking around the shabby house with far more fondness than the furnishings deserved.

This was more what he had expected. Gavin cleared his throat again. "Ah. I realize that my behavior has gone beyond the bounds of propriety."

Laura turned to look down at him again. She appeared astonished.

"The situation was irregular," he continued. "Though I do not mean that it excuses—"

"You didn't seduce me," interrupted Laura bluntly. She straightened, pushing her raven hair back behind her pale shoulders. "Please don't begin talking of proprieties and convention and reputations. As far as I am concerned, they have nothing to do with me."

Gavin found himself speechless.

She moved to kneel beside him on the bed. "I will be going back to England to find a new post when we escape, as I had always planned to do." She got up and went to put on her shift. "There is nothing else to discuss," she finished. "Are you hungry? If only we had some tea."

She continued to dress as Gavin stared at her. After a while, his only option seemed to be to follow suit.

"Bacon," she said, looking through their stores. "Just the thing."

# Twelve

GAVIN SPENT THE AFTERNOON WALKING THE BOUNDS of the island, climbing over stone and sand, searching the seas for a sail. The rain had stopped at last, and the clouds were beginning to break up. He could see for miles across the water, all of them empty. Accompanied by seabirds and, for a while, goats, he walked.

As he moved, he tried to formulate plans for escape. But he had difficulty concentrating. He was suffering the restlessness of a man who has gotten what he wanted.

He put it down to frustration. He had to get to the mainland, and he couldn't. But what he kept thinking was: Laura wanted no declarations, no promises. She expected nothing from him. She was going back to England and taking up her life as if they'd never met.

He would be able to go his way, free of entanglements, just as he had wished, just as he had always done. She would become just another of the pleasant interludes in the long series of them that punctuated his career. He would leave her behind and go on with his work, venturing into new places, facing new dangers. All was well.

Why, then, did he feel unsatisfied with this resolution?

Her behavior made no sense, he told himself resentfully. She wasn't like the other women he'd known. She'd apparently been as isolated as a nun for years. She had no experience in dalliance. She should not be acting as she was.

Gavin kicked a stone out of his path. She ought to be railing about her shattered honor, insisting that he offer marriage, weeping at the cruel advantage he had taken of her innocence.

His lip curled in distaste at the picture. If she had been... But that wasn't the point. It was the way she *ought* to be reacting. He had been braced to deal with that. He had been readying responses. Damn it, he had wanted to comfort her, to show his nobility. Indeed, it almost seemed to Gavin now—when the question was moot—that he had *meant* to propose to her. It would have been damned inconvenient, of course, really an imposition. He had no interest in marriage, no place for it in his life. But he had been ready to make the sacrifice. He had known his duty. He had some respect for the conventions that supported society—unlike the maddening, incomprehensible woman who waited back at their prison.

Rounding a point of land, he pushed a straggling shrub savagely out of his way. She had dismissed the civilized proprieties with a snap of her fingers, he thought. It was...unnatural. All that reading she'd spoken of must have turned her brain.

The thought of her reading roused a memory of the morning. Gavin smiled reminiscently and felt his body respond to the images thus evoked. He imagined her in an empty library turning the pages of some scandalous portfolio and absorbing the images with wide-eyed curiosity. He almost laughed aloud. Surely there was no other woman like her in the world, he thought.

An odd regret came with the idea. Back in England, she would vanish into the mass of people there, and he would hear no more of her. He would miss those moments of amazement at her remarks and reactions. And, of course, he would never touch her again.

Gavin stopped, feeling momentarily breathless. The terrain was rougher than he'd realized, he thought. He'd been climbing too fast. He put a foot up on a rock ledge and leaned an elbow on his knee.

Separation was inevitable, he reminded himself. He worked alone. And the places he went were wild and brutal. After being exiled, practically disowned by his family, he'd learned to be independent—and he'd learned to love it. He loved the freedom, the risk, and the sense of achievement when he triumphed over great odds. He wasn't giving up any of that.

Gavin started walking again. Of course he wasn't. There was no question about it. What was he thinking? Laura's attitude was a profound relief. He was grateful for the lack of complication. He was extremely fortunate, in fact, considering that he had violated his own code by becoming involved with her. Everything was going very well.

Except for their imprisonment on this lump of rock, he added silently. Rounding the last bend and seeing the sagging dock ahead, Gavin turned all his considerable intellect to the question of escape.

~~~

"I have an idea," said Laura when he returned to the house.

"Do you?" Gavin's own lack of viable ideas for escape had put him in a foul mood that had lasted now for hours.

"Yes. The native tribes of North America sent signals with smoke. They can be seen from a great distance, I understand."

Once again, he was taken aback by the sheer unpredictability of her thought processes.

She gazed back at him, waiting.

"Is this something you found in a book?" he asked.

"Yes. They use green wood, I believe, and—"

"How in God's name did you come to read such a thing?"

"You can become very, very bored in ten years. You would be surprised at the volumes I waded through."

"I already have been," he murmured.

She flushed a little, but showed no other awareness of his insinuation. "The smoke might be visible from the mainland. And someone would come to investigate, don't you think?"

"Why should they? A column of smoke—"

"Not a column. The tribes make it into a code. They cover the fire with blankets and then remove them to make a pattern of...clouds."

Gavin frowned. "We don't know the code, nor does anyone hereabouts."

"Of course not. But such an unusual phenomenon would cause curiosity. They would come to see the source."

"Possibly." He looked for flaws in the idea.

"I would think certainly. Besides, what other way do we have to send a signal?"

Gavin had an overwhelming desire to present a stunning counterplan. Unfortunately, he had not thought of one. "Perhaps we could try it," he conceded.

"You gather some green branches. I'll get the blanket."

"We have only one blanket," he objected. "And it will end up covered with soot."

"True," she said, pulling the gray wool from the bed and bundling it in her arms.

Her calm competence was beginning to annoy him. "I suppose we will find other ways to keep warm," he taunted, and he was obscurely gratified to see her flush a deeper red.

She didn't look at him, however. She had been avoiding his eyes since he returned to the house. Gavin needed her to look at him. "You are very eager to flee," he said.

This brought the desired result. Wide green eyes focused on him. "It is vital that we communicate with the authorities."

He searched her face for more than this. It was unreadable.

"Just yesterday, you were railing about the need to escape," she pointed out.

Her logic infuriated him. "Let us go and ruin our only blanket," he said, striding out into the cool air.

After a moment, he heard her footsteps on the path behind him.

"It's no good trying this now," Gavin said when they stood on one of the headlands beside a pile of logs and branches. "There are too many clouds."

Laura nodded. "The smoke wouldn't be noticed among them."

"We will have to wait for a clear day," he said, scanning the sky and for some reason feeling gratified.

Picking up the blanket, she turned and started back down the path toward the house. Gavin remained behind, looking out over the empty sea. It was rather a good idea, he acknowledged to himself. An obvious pattern of smoke might well attract a passing ship or a local fisherman. It would be far more noticeable than a beacon fire, which he had already determined to light. They might have a real chance to escape.

Wondering why he didn't feel more elated by this development, he followed Laura down the hill. The winter day was waning, and the wind was chill. He started walking faster.

Laura had done what no other woman in the world could do, an insistent inner voice argued. She had discovered Michael, courageously endured an abduction, and now she had formulated a possible escape plan. And through all this, she had not let…personal concerns interfere. He could not have asked more of Hasan or any colleague, the voice pointed out.

It was all luck, he retorted silently. She didn't really know what she was doing. But his own inner honesty forced him to concede that many times, she certainly seemed as if she did.

❧

Laura placed another log on the hearth and straightened. She listened for Gavin's footsteps outside, but heard nothing. Perhaps he was still on the headland, wishing for a ship. Part of her longed for his return, while another part hoped he would stay away a while and leave her some tranquillity.

Too much had happened in too short a time, she thought. It was difficult to adjust. But that wasn't really the problem, and she knew it. The thing that was making her hands tremble and her heart ache was the memory of Gavin's expression when she'd awakened this morning. Still fogged with sleep, she had seen him sitting in the chair, and when he met her eyes he looked as if she were a burden that had been forced upon him, which he was trying to find a way to shed. He couldn't hide it from her. It had been clear in the lines of his body, which spoke to her more eloquently than words. He was regretting the night that had seemed magical to her. He was wishing for escape from more than this small island. Was he also wishing for Sophie Krelov?

Even when he touched her, making her forget everything in the world but him, that knowledge lingered in the background, waiting. It made her heartsick. It made her furious. Lying in his embrace later, she had remembered a conversation she once overheard at Leith House. A friend of the countess's was rejoicing in her daughter's luck. The young woman had been forced by circumstances into a compromising situation with one of the greatest catches of the season. The young man had done the honorable thing—even though nothing had really occurred—and offered marriage. They had accepted, and the mother was exulting over the brilliance of the match. Despicable, thought Laura. And Gavin had expected something similar from her.

Yanking the wooden bucket from the floor, she went out to the spring to fill it. How could he think that of her? Had he seen so little in the time they had been together? Couldn't he feel when they touched...? She stumbled, and water splashed out of the bucket onto her skirts. She hauled it inside and set it down by the fire. At least she had shown him his mistake, she thought with grim satisfaction. He would have nothing to reproach her with. She had behaved like a creature that no one believed existed—a woman of honor.

Holding her wet skirts out to the flames to dry, Laura swallowed tears. She hoped pride in that accomplishment would sustain her when she was once again in a dreary schoolroom.

The door opened, and Gavin walked in. At once, every fiber of her body was aware of him.

"The smoke really was a good idea," he said carefully. "I think it may well work." He nodded in acknowledgment.

Something twisted in Laura's chest. She loved him. More than she had ever loved anyone—or ever would again, she realized. The enormity of the knowledge made her sway on her feet.

"Are you all right?" He took a step toward her.

"Of course." She turned her attention back to her wet skirts, afraid to meet his eyes. "I am afraid there's only cheese, bacon, and ship's biscuit for dinner. That is all they left us."

He didn't answer.

Daring a glance, Laura found him watching her as if he sensed her turmoil. He was so handsome, she thought—antique gold and bronze and formed like an ancient Greek statue. But even more, he was so intelligently aware, so compelling, and aligned with her in some subterranean way that she didn't understand. It beat in her as steadily as her heart.

She couldn't have helped falling in love with him, she realized, any more than she could help breathing. She might know it was a mistake. She might despair of the result. But she couldn't have stopped it. From the moment they met and danced together so naturally, the outcome had been inevitable. She had met her match, Laura thought a bit wryly. In more ways than one.

"Did you fall?" he asked, as if still trying to interpret her expression.

"No, the bucket spilled." She gave her skirts a final shake and prepared to turn and face him.

"You should have waited. I would have gotten water."

"I'm perfectly able to do so. I was clumsy, that's all." She turned, and found him watching her. He was everything she wanted, Laura thought. But he didn't wish to be burdened by love. They had these days together, and then it was finished. She would take full advantage of the time, she decided. She would have at least that memory for the rest of her life.

"Sit down," he commanded. "I can cut cheese."

She took the chair and let him examine their stores of food. "Have you really eaten sheep's eyes?"

"What?"

"The general said you had."

"Pryor? Why would he say such a thing?" He unwrapped the block of cheese and began slicing off pieces.

"Actually, I believe he said you were the sort of person who *would* eat sheep's eyes, if it was necessary to make an alliance."

"Fortunately, the matter has never come up." He laid the slices out on a tin plate.

"Too bad. I wondered how they tasted."

He raised an eyebrow. "I suppose I could catch a goat for you. They are quite similar to sheep."

"No, thank you," she responded hastily.

He looked at her as if still sensing something unusual. "Why this sudden curiosity?"

Laura wondered if he could feel a change in her now that she had realized the truth. Did it show in the way she sat, the angle of her head? "I am always curious. I've always wanted to travel and see how other peoples live."

He gestured with the knife, which he was preparing to use on the ship's biscuit. "Well, you are traveling now. What do you think?"

She was surprised into a laugh. "This isn't precisely what I had in mind."

"A great deal of my work is like this, or worse. It isn't all exotic scenery and sheep's eyes."

"You sound as if you don't really like it."

"I would be a strange creature indeed if I liked being soaked to the skin and hungry, while being hunted through impassable mountains by hostile tribesmen."

"Then why do you do it?"

He smiled. "Perhaps I am somewhat strange."

She laughed again. "I wouldn't mind hardships on such journeys. It would be worth it to do something important."

"A woman could never venture into those regions." He sounded shocked.

"Why?"

"For a thousand reasons. It's unthinkable." He filled two cups from the bucket of water. "Dinner, my lady," he added.

Laura took the plate he handed her without meeting his eyes. It could hardly be clearer, she thought. There was no place for her in his life. He couldn't even imagine such a thing. She ate a bite of cheese and found she wasn't at all hungry.

Awkwardness descended with full night. Gavin seemed restless, abrupt. He moved around the room without lighting anywhere. Laura longed to feel his arms around her, but she was reluctant to make any demands. From the way he paced and the curtness of his remarks, it seemed that he wished to be far away from this ramshackle house, and her.

Finally, they fell into strained silence. The fire sputtered and crackled. The wind rushed over the cliffs outside. The sea murmured below. Laura sat in the chair, her hands folded tight.

She grew positively afraid to speak, afraid that if she

did, she would blurt out all her feelings, the depths of her love, and then have to face the rejection in his eyes.

When she could stand it no longer, she rose, pretending normalcy. "I'm tired. I believe I'll go to bed."

Gavin turned as if she'd thrown something. "I'm going to check outside," he answered.

Check what? she wondered. The goats? She waited a few minutes, but he didn't return. Laura undressed and got under their blanket. It was a long time before she heard the door creak open. Gavin didn't join her.

❧

The day dawned bright and clear. Gavin wasn't in the house when Laura woke, but he came in a bit later, flushed by the wind and looking very handsome. Had he slept? she wondered. Where?

"I've taken more wood up to the headland," he said. "The sky is clear, ready for our experiment."

So they were concentrating on the signal project, Laura thought. Not on anything so trivial as what had gone on between them. Gavin wanted to get off this island and run.

They lit their fire at midmorning, building a good blaze and then piling on green branches to maximize the smoke. When a broad column was rising above the headland, Gavin cast the blanket over it, then removed it again. Waiting for a brief interval, he repeated his actions, producing an obvious, satisfying interruption in the flow. He did it again.

"Someone must notice that," said Laura, gazing up at the intermittent pattern of smoke rising into the sky.

Gavin merely kept at his task. After an hour, there was a trail of smoke shapes fading off to the horizon—some very short, others quite long. Gavin was sleek with sweat from the heat of the flames, the bare column of his throat gleaming. He had rolled his shirtsleeves to the elbow, and his forearms had streaks of soot. He looked rather magnificent, Laura thought, his hair glinting in the sun.

"That should do it," he said, throwing down the blanket. "If anyone is going to notice, they will notice that." He wiped his forehead with one hand.

Laura nodded. She thought some ship would come to investigate the signal, but she found the prospect didn't fill her with unalloyed happiness.

"You can go back to the house if you like," Gavin said. "I'll watch up here."

Without answering, she went. This was what everyone expected her to do, she thought as she negotiated the twisting trail down the cliff—wait in the house while great deeds were done elsewhere. Efface herself, attract no attention. She had come out of the shadows, and now she would go back in, one brief emergence in what might seem a very long life. She suddenly remembered something she had read in the earl's library. A poem spoke of a bird that flew from the night sky into a brightly lit banqueting hall, where torches burned and people celebrated, and then out again; an ephemeral flight from darkness to darkness. She felt a sharp kinship with that bird.

Reaching the house, Laura went in and sat in the chair before the fire. Low spirits threatened to overwhelm her. She had battled such feelings many times during her years at Leith House, but they seemed even worse now. Back then, she had had so little to lose.

Impatient with herself, she rose and began to pace the uneven wooden floor. Was she just going to give up? Was she going to trot meekly back to a life she didn't want and wasn't sure she could bear any longer? Was she going to accept others' definitions of what she could, or could not, do?

She wanted to say no. But she knew it wasn't so simple. She had made it clear to Gavin that she wasn't a whimpering miss ruled by convention. When they returned to civilized land, however, she would be bound by certain constraints. If she wasn't to earn her living as a governess, what would she be? There were few other choices, and none of them appealed.

She paced some more. If Gavin loved her, she thought; then stopped herself. He didn't. On the contrary, he saw her as a potential entanglement and a threat to his happiness. She mustn't include him in her calculations. He wished only to leave her.

Catching her breath on a twinge of pain, Laura turned and paced in the opposite direction. She was facing reality here, she insisted to that part of herself that wanted to weep. There was no time for mourning. And regrets were useless. There must be something she could do.

An idea struck her. She stopped in the middle of the floor and contemplated it. Arguments emerged before her mind's eye in orderly rows. Points of persuasion presented themselves. It seemed to her a compelling case. Would it to others?

She started to pace again, taking the idea apart and putting it together piece by piece, testing for weaknesses. Her energy returned as she found very few. It might very well work, she thought, and the future opened out in a whole new way.

❧

It was hours before a sail appeared. But when it did, it was obvious that the vessel was heading for the island. They tossed more branches on the fire and began to send their signals once again. With excruciating slowness, the ship drew nearer. It seemed eons before they could make out figures on the deck. "It looks like a local fisherman," said Gavin. "The boat is small, and there's no flag."

"Will they take us to shore, do you think?"

"For a price."

She nodded. "Do you have any money? I have a little."

"Enough. It's fortunate Michael thought himself above thievery."

She nodded again.

Gavin gave her a sidelong glance. There was something different about her, had been ever since she came back to the headland. Her step was lighter, her gaze more sprightly. It was puzzling. She had changed before there was any sign of rescue, and he hadn't been able to elicit any reason for it. "It's better, actually, that we didn't attract a merchantman or a navy ship. They would be much less likely to alter their course, and any navy commander would have a great many questions."

"Unless it was a British ship," she replied.

Even her voice was different—more carefree. Gavin felt inordinately irritated by the mystery of it. "They might have more questions than anyone else. We can't waste time on explanations. We need to move fast."

She raised her eyebrows, looking quizzically amused. And what, Gavin wondered, had he said that was amusing? This new, enigmatic Laura was beginning to be annoying. "I'm going down to the dock," he said. "You stay here and wave them in that direction, so they can find the landing."

"All right."

He started toward the path, then was struck by a thought. "I'll tell them our boat was wrecked. And… it will be easier if I say you are my wife."

"Whatever you think," she answered airily, keeping her eyes on the now rapidly approaching fishing boat.

Gavin frowned at her back briefly, then dismissed his questions from his mind. The critical thing now was to convince the sailors to take them off the island. Deciphering Laura's odd behavior would have to wait.

❧

Laura stayed on the headland until the fishing boat hove out of sight around the cliffs below. Then she returned to the house, where she soon heard voices approaching. They were lively and punctuated by laughter. As they came closer, she took in that they were speaking Italian.

Gavin entered first. "Laura, Luigi and his crew have agreed to take us to the mainland."

He was followed by three dark-haired men in
rough work clothes—one barely more than a boy. All
of them eyed her with great appreciation.

Since Gavin had addressed her in Italian, she
expressed her gratification in the same language.

"This is Luigi, his son Roberto, and Gianni."

She acknowledged the introductions. Roberto
made as if to kiss her hand, but his father pulled
him back.

Gavin indicated the boxes of food stores, and the
men went to pick them up. "I told them they could
have this, since we won't be needing it any longer."

"Of course." Did that mean that he hadn't had to
pay them? Laura wondered.

"Are you ready?"

She nodded. Gavin came and took her arm, which
surprised Laura until she noticed the approving looks
of the Italian men. She remembered what George
Tompkins had said about Gavin—that he fitted himself
to any group he encountered. Listening to him banter
with their rescuers on the way down to the dock, she
understood what he had meant. Gavin seemed almost
one of them. He made them laugh, but he also spoke to
them as if they had all known each other a long time.
And his manner was different—more animated and
open. It didn't seem like an act, she thought; it seemed
as if he had absorbed their ways just by being near them.

The fishing boat was tied up at the old dock. Laura
was surprised to see a large dog standing alertly on the
deck, watching the path with close attention.

"Alto," called Luigi. "It is all right. We are back."

The dog gave one sharp bark and leaped onto

the dock, jumping amazingly high. He ran to the little cavalcade and capered excitedly around them, especially Roberto, who was carrying the box with the bacon.

"We call him Alto because he jumps so high," the young man told Laura. "He guards the boat when we are on shore."

The dog, whose short brown coat and pointed ears belonged to no particular breed, looked up at Laura as if he knew he was being described. His tongue lolled out in a kind of grin. "Hello, Alto," she said.

His ears swiveled, but he didn't approach her.

Luigi put his box down on the dock and turned. "Alto," he said. The dog trotted over to him immediately. "This is Signor and Signora Graham," he told the dog. Looking up at them, he added, "Would you give him your hands?"

First Gavin, then Laura extended a hand to be sniffed.

"They are friends," Luigi said. "They are coming with us."

As if he understood, Alto now came over to Laura and offered his head to be patted.

Gavin helped Laura step over the rail and onto the small boat's deck. She didn't really require help, but she knew her part now and played it. A blanket was thrown over a large coil of rope, and she was seated as if she were breakable. Only then were the lines untied and the boat cast off from the dock. The fishermen turned the hull with poles and then raised the sail to catch the wind. The boat drew away, picking up speed when it left the lee of the tall headland.

Laura watched the landing, and then the island,

recede across the water. She would never forget this place, she thought. It held far more memories than seemed possible for the short time they had spent. But the memories were such an intense mixture of good and bad that she wasn't sure how she felt leaving it behind.

The day was clear and cool and the waves calm. They encountered no difficulties, and as sunset approached, they sighted the long line of the Italian mainland ahead. Laura was aware of Gavin's voice, discussing with the fishermen where they would be set ashore, but it receded into the background of her thoughts. The sky was washed with crimson in the west. Lights glimmered here and there on the coast. The wind, picking up a bit, brought scents of salt and pine. It felt as if they were moving from one world into another, she thought. Soon, they would be back to the one where she was a governess in need of a post, and Gavin wished only to be free of her. Laura's sigh joined the currents of the wind floating out over the sea.

Darkness fell, and they had only the stars to guide them. This didn't seem to cause any concern, however, and after a while Laura found she was getting drowsy. Her head was nodding when Gavin came over and knelt next to her. "They have agreed to take us back to Venice," he said. "Once there, I can find out where Sophie went and follow her."

This was an unexpected blow, and it was a moment before Laura could answer. "You wish to follow Sophie." She was wide awake now and a little breathless.

"I thought of going to Marseilles," he replied, as

if she were arguing with him. "But we can't be sure when the ship will arrive, or even if they will really land there. No, Sophie is the key."

But to what? wondered Laura. However, she said only, "We can tell the English authorities in Venice what we have learned about Bonaparte."

"Umm," was his noncommittal response. "I wouldn't mention that name again until we are safely ashore. Loyalties are complicated in this part of the world."

Stung, she didn't answer. Let him go chasing after Sophie, she thought. Let him do whatever he pleased!

Soon after this, Laura was shown to a tiny cramped cabin below deck that contained two bunks and a minuscule cupboard. Roberto indicated these amenities with a flashing smile and then vanished. A few moments later, Gavin joined her. "The others will sleep on deck," he said, sitting on the bunk opposite.

Laura watched his expression gradually shift from concentrated animation to fatigue. This fitting himself to circumstance must be difficult, she thought. It must require every faculty and unwavering attention.

Without looking at her, he lay down with his back to her and pulled up a blanket. She did the same, though it was a long time before she actually slept.

❧

They docked in Venice late the following day. Gavin made their farewells, which entailed a great deal of gesturing and compliments, and then led her along walkways beside narrow canals to an inn. After a moment, Laura realized it was the same one where she had seen Gavin and Sophie together.

There was only one room available, and he took it with a sidelong glance at her. Laura was too delighted at the prospect of a real bath to think of anything else. And when she had bathed, she found that she was so tired she nearly fell into bed. Her last coherent thought was that it had been eons since she had been this comfortable.

She woke sometime later with the sense that there was someone in the room with her. Blinking, she saw that Gavin stood beside the bed, illuminated by a single shaded candle. His back was to her. He was taking off his shirt.

Laura watched the light flicker across his shoulders and the muscles of his arms. It gleamed in his hair like ancient gilding. He bent to pull off his boots and then set them outside the door to be shined, quietly slipping the bolt as he shut it again. When he turned, Laura shut her eyes and pretended to be asleep. She didn't know what to say.

There was a silence, and she *felt* that he was gazing at her. Her body recognized his presence and his attention. Time seemed to stretch into some other dimension. The air seemed to thicken, and Laura's skin tingled with the memory of his touch.

Then he moved. She heard the floorboards creak and a rustle of cloth—and then nothing.

A few muted sounds drifted up from the taproom below. Outside the window the jingle of harness passed. Cloth rustled again. Laura risked a look through her lashes.

Gavin was wrapped in a blanket and sitting in the

armchair that was the only other piece of furniture in the room. His head was resting on its back at an uncomfortable angle. He looked tired and resigned.

"What are you doing?" said Laura.

He started and sat up straight. "I didn't mean to wake you," he said.

"You don't intend to sleep there?"

"Yes."

"You have as much right to the bed as I do."

"It is not a question of rights."

"Well, there is no reason I should have the bed, and you that chair."

"There is every reason."

"Nonsense. Just get in the bed."

An odd expression crossed his face. Not quite a smile, and not quite a grimace. "Now that we are back in civilization—" he began.

"You already told them I am your wife."

"I was obliged to do so," he agreed. "But I don't intend to take advantage—"

"We can both use the bed without…anything more."

"Can we?"

The change in his tone reached deep inside Laura and set something trembling.

"*I* can't," he added.

She sat up and looked at him, one strap of her shift falling off her shoulder.

"Go back to sleep, Laura," he said almost harshly.

She kept looking, wondering if he felt her gaze as she did his. The memory of his touch was so vivid that she shivered a little.

"You're cold. Lie down." It seemed as if tenderness had brushed his voice.

"Gavin." His name slipped out, and her longing and uncertainty vibrated in the word without her conscious volition.

The sound drew him out of the chair. As the blanket slid out of his hands, he was revealed wearing only his breeches, golden hair glinting on his chest. He looked magnificent. "You try me beyond bearing," he said.

Laura couldn't seem to recall any words. Her hand came to her throat and rested there. She could feel her pulse beating under her fingers.

"How am I to resist when you sit there looking…?" His chest rose and fell. His eyes burned as she would not have thought possible with their cool color.

He wanted her, Laura thought. That, at least, was undeniable. His desire was proclaimed by every line of his body. The knowledge excited and gratified her. And every part of her responded to the message he sent. Her hand dropped to the coverlet. "Must you resist?"

And then she was in his arms.

❧

Gavin sat in the inn's front parlor, a tankard on the table before him. Through the small window at his side, he could see that the sky was overcast on this mid-February day, threatening rain. He toyed with the bread and cheese that were the innkeeper's idea of breakfast. At least the man had given him no trouble. For a few coins he had happily revealed that the "delectable redhead," as he called Sophie, had hired a coach and set out for Vienna. Why she had done so was another question, one that would have to wait until Gavin saw her again.

The countess was a damned nuisance, he thought. He was tired of pretending that he found her irresistible. And she had obviously ceased to believe it in any case. The thought of her reaction when they showed up in Vienna once again made him smile slightly.

It faded when he realized that he pictured Laura with him. She had no reason to undertake a wet and chilly journey to Vienna. Perhaps she would refuse to come. The idea made his jaw clench.

He couldn't leave her alone in a strange town far from home, he told himself. He was responsible for her safety. And what more? he wondered, taking a deep draught of ale. After what had passed between them, shouldn't he be responsible for far more? Yet she didn't want that from him. She intended to go back to England and be a governess. Gavin turned the tankard between his hands, bewildered by this unprecedented situation. Women always wanted a man to stay, he thought, feeling resentful at Laura's perversity in this matter. She never acted predictably.

Something made him look up. Laura was standing in the doorway, dressed in her green gown once again, its wrinkles and stains removed by an inn servant. She looked beautiful—her ivory skin and raven hair enlivened by a dark green gaze full of emotion and intelligence. A tremor went through Gavin. The tankard wobbled slightly under his hand, and he closed his fist on the handle.

"Good morning," she said, coming into the room

and taking the chair opposite him. "I don't suppose they have any tea?"

"No." His voice sounded odd in his ears.

"Coffee?"

He nodded, wondering if he was coming down with a chill.

"Good." She hesitated, as if about to say something else, then picked up a piece of the brown bread and broke it into fragments.

Gavin tore his attention from her slender white fingers, which had reduced the bread to crumbs. "Sophie went back to Vienna," he told her.

Laura went still. Gavin couldn't interpret her expression. "Did she?"

"I've hired a chaise to return there as well."

"Ah."

He could tell nothing from her face or her tone about what she meant to do.

"Should we not find a British consul, or some sort of official and tell them what we have discovered?"

"He would delay us sending messages to get instructions and permissions and exceptions. By the time he was satisfied, Michael would have accomplished whatever he is plotting."

Laura raised her eyebrows. "I take it you do not consult the local officials when you are on one of your missions?"

"I work alone," he replied forcefully. It was a salutary reminder.

Laura drew back a little from the table. She had destroyed another slice of bread, he saw. So did she apparently; she put her hands in her lap.

In the clear light of morning, last night seemed like a dream, Gavin thought, or something that had happened long ago. "I will notify the appropriate people in Vienna," he said.

Something about this statement made her brighten, though he couldn't imagine what it was.

"I...I have some acquaintances in Vienna," she replied. "I should...I should like to go back there before I return to England."

The news that she would not be leaving him was so welcome that Gavin didn't even think to question this rather odd itinerary.

◆

They set off just before noon in the hired chaise. The rain held off, though the cold, heavy dampness of the air promised that this couldn't last. They went quickly; with little talk, and perhaps too much time to think, Laura decided. She would catch herself watching Gavin, remembering the feel of his lips and hands, the words he murmured when he held her. She found herself memorizing his features as if this were the last time she would ever see them.

And perhaps it was, she thought. Wouldn't he abandon her in Vienna and go about his work? He would take her at her word and have her sent home, going off gladly on his pursuit of Napoleon's agents.

Not "abandon," Laura scolded herself, and she would not be "sent" anywhere. She had her own plans. She simply had to see that she was able to carry them out.

The rain started around four, darkening the

February day nearly to twilight. By the time they stopped for the night at a farmstead, Laura was almost too exhausted to eat the bowl of stew she was offered. She fell into the bed and knew nothing until Gavin woke her early to set out again.

Three more days passed in this way. The rain disappeared on the second, making things easier, and on the fourth Laura found that she was actually becoming inured to travel. She was less fatigued by the end of a day and able to converse a little in the evening with the families who sheltered them. She had some attention to spare for the future.

"When we reach Vienna," she said to Gavin one afternoon.

He turned to look at her.

"I believe...I think it would be best if we took our news to George Tompkins."

He blinked in surprise. "Where did you hear that name?"

"I am a little acquainted with Mr. Tompkins, and he seems the best—"

"How?"

Laura shrugged. "He will know just what to—"

"Very few people even know that he exists," he interrupted.

"Well, I am one of those few," she responded tartly. "And I think that he will know precisely what to do about our news." There was no need to mention that she very much wanted to speak to him about other matters as well, Laura thought.

"No doubt," was the curt reply.

Laura rather enjoyed the irritated look on his face.

He really hated relying on others in his work, she thought. He wanted to do everything himself. "And just who should take care of the matter," she ventured.

"You have to exercise some caution in these things," he snapped, "not simply push blindly in."

"I'm sure—"

"You have to have some subtlety, to allow things to come to just the proper point, and then to move."

"I imagine Mr. Tompkins is well aware of that."

This silenced him.

"So we are agreed that we will go to him as soon as we reach Vienna?" Laura pressed.

He growled.

"Unless you would rather go to the embassy or the congress delegation?"

As she had expected, these alternatives pleased him even less, and he eventually gave in. Really, he wasn't all that hard to manage, Laura thought, as they entered the final leg of their journey. One didn't even have to be that subtle.

When they drove up to George Tompkins's house in Vienna the following day, there were no protests about an unexpected visit. They were ushered inside at once and directed up the stairs to the drawing room.

"I will make the report," said Gavin as he climbed.

Laura looked up to answer him and saw another figure at the top of the steps.

"There you are," said George Tompkins cordially. "I have been expecting you for three days now."

# *Thirteen*

MR. TOMPKINS, LOOKING LIKE SOME IMMACULATE phantom from another age, came slowly down the stairs. His full-skirted coat was purple satin. Silver buckles gleamed on his shoes, matching the silver of his hair. He made Laura feel like a half-dead bird the cat had dragged in.

"I have a report to make," said Gavin.

The old man nodded, not seeming at all surprised. "I am eager to hear it. Are you both well? Not hurt?"

"We're all right," said Laura.

"Good." He looked at her kindly.

"Aren't you going to ask why we have come to you, where we have been?" demanded Gavin, sounding goaded.

Tompkins smiled. "I thought you were going to tell me."

"You," confirmed Gavin. "And not the embassy or the delegation."

His suspicions seemed to amuse their host. "My dear Graham, I know you better than to suggest you go to either of those places." Seeing Gavin about to speak, he held up a hand. "And no, I do not claim to be *utterly* omniscient." His eyes twinkled. "I did have some warning from a friend of yours."

"Hasan," said Gavin at once.

"He is here. As is your luggage, and Miss Devane's."

Gavin gaped at him. "Miss Devane's? Hasan retrieved her things as well?"

Tompkins nodded. Gavin looked positively stunned. It was rather surprising that Hasan would bother with her belongings, Laura thought.

"I must say I was very impressed with Hasan's actions during the, er, uproar that followed Miss Devane's disappearance," Tompkins added.

"The Pryors?" cried Laura. She had not even thought of them and what they must have endured, she realized guiltily.

"They were extremely worried. After Hasan contacted me, I did my best to reassure them."

"They went on home then?"

He nodded.

Laura relaxed a little.

"Does anyone care to hear my report?" wondered Gavin sarcastically.

"Yes indeed. If both of you will come along..."

"I can tell you everything," he interrupted. "Miss Devane is tired."

George Tompkins looked from one of them to the other. One of his eyebrows twitched. "Is she?" he said. "Well, we will try not to keep her too long."

Laura felt her spirits lift as she followed the old man up the stairs. He wasn't going to shunt her aside as if she had had nothing to do with the adventure, as Gavin apparently intended. Perhaps there was some hope.

When they had told Tompkins all they had learned, he sat frowning for only a moment before summoning messengers and sending them out on a variety of errands. Very soon thereafter, officials began to arrive, and the house began to hum like an overturned beehive.

Laura was taken to an opulent chamber on the third floor. There she found her trunk already unpacked and a bath ordered. The maid assigned to her took her wrinkled gown away to be laundered. Laura enjoyed the luxury, but she began to feel oppressed by the silence and space of her rooms. It was as if she had been walled off from the flow of events, wrapped in a cocoon of cotton wool and placed on a shelf for safekeeping.

When she had dressed in one of her Vienna gowns, she went out into the corridor and along it to the stairs. In the front hall, messengers were still coming and going, and a dignitary speaking German was admitted and hustled away.

"Do you know where I can find Mr. Tompkins?" she asked a passing servant.

"I believe he is with the ambassador."

"Oh. And Mr. Graham?"

"I don't know, miss."

"Oh. Thank you."

She wandered a little while longer, then returned to her room. She felt cut off and forgotten. Crossing her arms over her chest, she fervently hoped this wasn't an omen of the future.

Sometime later, the maid came to summon her to dinner. There were a number of guests, though no one bothered with introductions. The talk was all of Bonaparte and what could be done to stop him. It would be days before the couriers could reach his place of exile and the garrison there.

After a welcoming smile from Mr. Tompkins, Laura was ignored. She might have been a governess again, summoned to fill an empty chair at her employer's table. The conventions of society had fallen back into place around her, she thought, like a net over an unwary bird. She understood the system quite well; she had used it as a place of concealment for years. But she didn't wish to any longer.

She would never look for a new post in a schoolroom, Laura realized. She wouldn't be able to tolerate that sort of cage again.

They were rising from the table when the clatter of hooves sounded outside. A lone messenger was brought in, swaying on his feet. "Bonaparte has landed in France," he announced. "He is rallying the country behind him and moving toward Paris." The messenger staggered with fatigue.

The room erupted in exclamations and fevered conversation.

"Quiet," shouted Gavin. "What else, man?"

"He took the brig *Inconstant* and sailed on February 26th," the messenger added. "He landed near Cannes two days ago."

"The country rallies behind him?" asked Gavin sharply.

"So they say, sir."

"We must leave at once," said a young military man near Laura. "It will be war. We have to rejoin the regiment before Wellington beats him."

His companion agreed. "Will they give us permission, do you think?"

"They'll need every fighting man they can find." The young man's grin was fierce. "I'm going to pack my gear right now."

The two hurried out.

Laura made her way over to where Gavin was standing. "I suppose it will be war," she said.

Gavin turned and looked down at her. "Undoubtedly."

"I wonder if Michael is with him."

His mouth hardened. "I'll find out if he is."

"You?"

"They'll be wanting good intelligence. I'll go north tonight."

Laura waited, feeling as if they were isolated together, cut off from the shouting, gesturing men in the room. But he said nothing further. Nothing about what had passed between them, or what he might feel at this final parting. Laura couldn't believe it. Now that the moment had really come, she knew that she had hoped for more. Despite her brave words, she had thought he might discover love for her. She couldn't speak. Her throat was full of tears, and they threatened to spill into her eyes. She bit her lip. She would not humiliate herself by weeping over him in public. Turning on her heel, she left the noisy room, unaware that Gavin watched her with regret in his gaze.

Laura didn't go far. In the entryway outside, she struggled to master her feelings, keeping her back to the people rushing back and forth. Finally, when she judged that almost everyone must have left the room, she ventured in. As she had hoped, George Tompkins was alone, sitting in an armchair in the corner.

He looked up when she joined him. "I am too old for another war," he said. "I thought we had settled this one."

&#8766;

Gavin returned to his bedchamber to order Hasan to pack. He needed to leave first thing in the morning, he thought, which no doubt he would be commanded to do. This was what he had been waiting for. He would be on his own, traveling into enemy territory. His life had returned to the perilous adventure that he saw as normal.

Laura might have at least said good-bye, he thought. When he had told her he was going, she'd turned away as if it were a matter of little interest to her. Not that he wanted a hysterical scene, of course. Far from it. It was much better this way.

Gavin went to the window to look out over the street below. She might have shown some sort of sentiment, he thought. They had shared more than a casual acquaintance.

Desire for her burned through his veins. She felt it, too; he knew she did. The certainty had been in every touch of her hand, in the arch of her body and the rhythm of her breath.

Yet she couldn't even say good-bye.

Gavin realized his jaw was clenched and he was breathing rapidly. How did she do this to him? She was maddening, incomprehensible.

This made him remember another mystery, and he turned away from the window. "Hasan?"

The small, silent man looked up from his packing and faced him.

"Why did you fetch Miss Devane's luggage from Venice?" Hasan had never done such a thing before. He had shown no consideration for any of the people Gavin encountered—female or male, friend or enemy.

Hasan gave a one-shouldered shrug. "She is *tandek*," he said and returned to his work.

Gavin gazed at him in astonishment. This word from Hasan's native language had a complex meaning. It referred to a person who was trustworthy and important to the tribe. It also implied unusual ability or skills of some kind. It conferred respect.

Noting that his mouth was open, Gavin closed it. Somehow or other, Laura had impressed Hasan more than any other European he had met in the course of their association. And Gavin had reason to trust Hasan's judgment of character. It had saved his skin more than once.

What was it about her? What sort of creature was Laura? Intelligent, obviously. More devious than seemed possible. She had apparently spent years evading the attentions of the English aristocracy. Involuntarily, he grimaced. She had come to him untouched, and wholeheartedly. Now she seemed to be treating the experience as something to be passed off and forgotten. It made no sense.

Movement outside his window caught Gavin's eye. Another messenger was arriving, mud-spattered, on an exhausted mount. There would be further news. He took a deep breath. He had been longing for this—the old excitement, the urgency of great affairs. He had what he wanted. But as he left the room, he found himself wondering why so much of the savor seemed to have gone out of it.

❧

Silence had fallen in the front parlor. George Tompkins's voice had held such weariness and regret that Laura had been reluctant to intrude. Yet this might be her only chance to speak to him. She had to take advantage of it.

"I don't suppose Mr. Graham told you," she blurted out, "but it was my idea that allowed us to escape from the island."

The old man looked up. "Actually, he did."

Astonishment silenced her for a moment. "Oh. He did?" She was so touched by this that it took her a bit longer to recover her momentum. "Well. You see, then, that I have certain abilities."

"It was a very clever scheme," he acknowledged.

"I am quite knowledgeable about history and politics as well. I have always done a great deal of reading."

Tompkins waited.

"And I...I am in need of employment." Laura let out her breath in a rush. She wasn't sure whether what she felt was relief at having said what she had planned to say, or mere nerves.

"Employment?" repeated Tompkins.

"I am fluent in several languages," she said. "And I'm sure I could learn others. I have always had a facility for—"

"My dear young woman," he began.

"No, wait."

Her tone stopped him. He looked at her with interest and reservation.

"I have thought a good deal about this," Laura went on, marshaling her reasons carefully. "You gather information. That is the true center of all your work, isn't it?"

Tompkins nodded.

"I know you have many sources, but I believe there may be some you are neglecting."

"Indeed?"

Laura couldn't tell if she had really caught his interest, or if he was merely humoring her. "There are women who see and hear a great many things because people forget they are present. Companions, governesses, poor relations. No one bothers to hide things from them, any more than they would from a piece of furniture. They are not thought to have any interests or opinions, you see."

Tompkins was examining her with care.

"Such women would never talk to…Mr. Graham, for example, or an embassy aide, or…anyone like that. But they would talk to me."

"To you?"

"Yes! I could discover all sorts of things. Who is caring for Bonaparte's young son? Perhaps they would like him to learn languages."

Tompkins appeared to be thinking this through. "You would take a post in the household and observe what goes on there?" said Tompkins slowly.

Laura nodded. "And I would make friends with other women in similar positions. It would be a kind of…network."

He looked thoughtful.

Laura held her breath as he considered.

"I could not place you in the Princess Marie's entourage," he said regretfully.

She leaned forward. "But somewhere else?"

"Perhaps. I will need to think about this. We have informants who are servants of course." He held up a hand as she started to protest. "But this would be of a different order altogether."

"I would understand things that a servant would not," she said a bit stiffly.

"Naturally. But whether I could expose you to such danger…"

"I am not afraid of danger."

"So you have shown." He held her gaze. "You don't want to go home?"

"I would only have to find a post there."

"I received the impression that you could stay with the Pryors for as long as you like."

"As a sort of poor relation," she agreed. "Though we are not actually related."

"Catherine Pryor—"

"She would be very kind to me and never make me feel my position," Laura interrupted. "But nevertheless, I would."

"You might marry," he pointed out. "Living in the

Pryor household, you would have the opportunity to meet eligible young men."

"I shall never marry."

Something in her tone appeared to startle Tompkins. He frowned slightly. His eyes bored into hers again, until Laura had to look away.

Silence fell over the room. Footsteps could be heard passing in the entryway outside. A voice was raised. Another responded. Laura wanted to speak, to ask for his decision, but she was afraid to hear it.

The door opened and one of the ambassador's aides looked in. "There you are, sir," he said. "Another messenger has arrived. The ambassador requests your presence."

"I'll be there momentarily," Tompkins replied.

The aide nodded and, with one curious glance at Laura, shut the door again.

"I will think about your suggestion," he added, rising from the armchair.

"How long?" she couldn't help asking. She stood to face him.

He smiled. "Not long."

She had no choice but to agree. "I…I have always wanted to do something important," she told him.

"I know."

"I *can*, if given the opportunity."

"You must have patience, child."

"There has been too much patience in my life," she blurted out.

"In my business, there is no such thing as 'too much patience.'" And with a gentle smile, he left her standing there.

Laura clasped her hands tightly together, then turned and walked over to the window. The courtyard was bustling with stablemen bringing horses and cloaked and spurred travelers catching the reins and setting off. Laura looked for Gavin, afraid to find him. But he wasn't among those leaving just now. Maybe he was already gone, she thought. A cold numbness spread through her at the idea that she might have seen him for the last time.

∾

A little later, Gavin Graham was summoned to the study. Expecting to receive orders to depart, he went at once, and found the room empty except for George Tompkins sitting serenely behind the large desk. "Come in," said the old man when he hesitated in the doorway.

Gavin did so and took the chair he indicated with a gesture.

"I wanted to consult you about a matter that has come up."

"Of course," replied Gavin, feeling flattered. Tompkins was a legendary figure in diplomatic circles. The idea that such a man wanted his advice was very gratifying.

"It is about Laura Devane."

Gavin's body went still, while his pulse accelerated. Had the old man's uncanny powers of discernment picked up something about their sojourn together? Gavin decided he would blatantly lie, even to Tompkins, to preserve Laura's reputation.

"You have had ample opportunity to observe her," the old man continued.

Gavin simply stared at him, not sure what this was supposed to mean.

"I am interested in your judgment of her abilities."

"What do you mean?" He sounded hostile, Gavin realized. He must get control of his voice.

"She has suggested a somewhat unusual arrangement. She wants to work for me."

This was so unexpected that Gavin had no immediate answer.

"Her idea is to take a post in a…sensitive household and keep her ears open, gathering information. She seems to think that people talk very freely in front of governesses and such."

Gavin remembered all her talk of invisible women. Did she truly imagine that she could go unnoticed into danger? He was overtaken by a surge of rage. "That is ridiculous."

Tompkins raised one white brow.

"Out of the question. You cannot be seriously considering it."

"The plan has a certain appeal. That is why I wondered if you—"

"It's madness. Putting herself in the power of our enemies? Becoming a dependent who is prying into the private affairs of such men? I forbid it!"

There was a silence.

Gavin realized that he had said far too much. Not that he hadn't meant every word, but clearly George Tompkins was wondering at his vehemence. What was it about Laura that continually destroyed his finely trained powers of control? He cleared his throat. "Miss Devane and I, er, became friends

during our...ordeal. I would not like to see her put
in jeopardy again."

"She seems to have handled it rather well." The old
man's tone was very dry.

Gavin realized he had truly aroused his suspicions.
He had to allay them before he could squelch this
ridiculous plan. "She was quite amazing," he said
and immediately wished he had put it another
way. "She, er, showed no sign of hysterics or other
female weaknesses."

"And she seems to have exhibited a good deal of
initiative."

"Yes. She...she is full of ideas." Far too many ideas,
he thought bitterly, and none more outrageous than
this one.

"A young woman who can think on her feet,
respond to circumstances."

"I was with her," replied Gavin stiffly. "I recom-
mend that you refuse her request. It is a very bad idea."

Another silence ensued.

Tompkins was looking at him as if he were a
fascinating puzzle, Gavin saw. He felt the intelligence
of his scrutiny very keenly, with the clear sense that
he had revealed things he was unaware of and told far
more than he knew.

"You care very much about Miss Devane's safety,"
Tompkins said.

Determined to expose no more, Gavin said, "As I
would about any woman's."

"Ah."

Did he think to trick him into some admission by
saying, "ah," as if he had already made a slip?

"Commendable. Yet she seems rather above the common run of women."

He remained stubbornly silent.

"Would it not be a waste to send her back to England to preside over a schoolroom? She appears capable of much more."

Gavin was not to be caught out again. He had clamped down every ounce of his formidable self-control on his emotions. "Women do not belong in such positions."

"It is unusual."

"It is impossible. She would make a mistake and…" He couldn't think about the consequences.

"But if no one associated her with us… And why should they? As you say, women do not hold such positions. Then her mistake might appear unimportant. It is an interesting proposition."

"You asked for my opinion. It is negative."

The old man nodded.

"Is there anything else?"

"No. That was all."

"Very well." Gavin rose. "It is an extremely bad idea," he repeated.

Tompkins nodded again. Gavin did not see his lips curve in an ironic smile as he strode out of the room.

~✦~

The outrage that Gavin had been suppressing came roaring back to life as soon as he was alone. He couldn't believe she had suggested such a thing. Fuming, he went in search of Laura.

She wasn't in any of the common rooms. She

wasn't in the library. He headed up the stairs. He knew which was her bedchamber. He had made it his business to know.

She opened the door to his knock, and looked surprised to find him there. "What in God's name were you thinking of?" he asked.

She blinked at him.

"Do you know what some of these people are like? They're ruthless. They live to scheme and manipulate. They don't hesitate to kill. And you would put yourself in their hands?"

"What are you talking about?"

Gavin pushed past her and strode into her room. "I've forbidden it. Do you understand me?"

"Forbidden what?"

"Your idiotic idea of going into the houses of conspirators and gathering information." He made a chopping gesture. "Do you know what they would do to you?"

"Mr. Tompkins told you?"

"He asked my opinion," Gavin replied with savage enjoyment. "I told him it was out of the question."

Laura looked at him as if betrayed. "He is letting you decide?"

He didn't like her expression. And despite his anger, he couldn't lie to her. He didn't know what Tompkins was going to do. "You told me you were going back to England," he accused instead.

"I thought I was. It seemed the only option. Then, after all that happened, I formed this plan."

"Ridiculous," he snapped.

"I don't see why. No one would suspect me of anything. I would simply be the—"

"Don't start that nonsense about 'invisible women' again."

Laura flinched as if he had slapped her.

"You are not invisible, and you would get into serious trouble if you attempted to…to infiltrate a dangerous household."

She looked away from him.

Gavin took a step closer. Other emotions were tangled up with his rage, and the result was an incendiary mixture that made it difficult to think. "You told me you were going back to England to find a new post," he said again.

She continued to gaze at the carpet. Gavin had to fight the impulse to seize her and force her to meet his eyes. "Well?" he added.

"I didn't see what else I could do," she said, so quietly he had to bend closer to hear.

"You mean you didn't want to go?"

Finally, she raised her eyes. But she looked at him as if he were an idiot, as if there was something very simple that he should be understanding.

"I told you something about the life I led."

Gavin tried to recall all the things she had said. There had been the speech about invisible women, and something about hiding, and other things he couldn't bring to mind just now. They hadn't made a great deal of sense at the time, and they hadn't stuck in his memory.

"You couldn't have imagined I wished to return to it," she said coldly.

"You said you did!"

"I said that I was returning—not that I wished to."

He felt a strong desire to throttle something.

"I saw no other choice. Under the circumstances."

"You could marry me!" he exploded.

Laura stared at him. Gavin didn't blame her. He'd had no idea he was going to utter those words. But the way she said "circumstances" had shaken him. His mind had filled with images of her in his arms, gallantly facing their captors on the ship. Something irresistible had spoken for him.

Her lips soundlessly formed the question "Marry?"

In the ensuing silence, Gavin became aware of the fact that they were alone in her bedroom, standing only a few feet apart. Her hair curled beside her ears. The amber satin of her gown clung to the lines of her body. Words deserted him completely.

Laura moved slightly. The satin of her dress whispered. Desire gripped Gavin like a river at full flood.

She was looking at him. She was waiting for him to say something.

"That would be the…the normal course of action," he managed.

"Normal?"

"Under the…circumstances." That was a nice touch, he thought—throwing her word back at her.

"Because we…?"

"Precisely." This was better, he thought. He was getting the upper hand again. And he was right, of course. This was the way things ought to have happened. He didn't wish to be married, of course. It was a damned inconvenient complication. But Laura was definitely alluring. Perhaps something…

"And what do you mean by 'marry'?"

Gavin heard a noise—like "*Ehh?*"—and realized he had made it.

"What do you mean?" she insisted.

"What anyone means."

"And what is that?"

He fumbled slightly. "Standing up in church?" He wondered how he had lost the initiative so quickly. "Taking vows? Friends and relatives? Music, flowers?"

"And then?"

"Er…" Extremely vivid pictures of the wedding night rose before him. But surely that wasn't what she meant?

"What about your work? Do you mean to abandon it?"

"Abandon?"

"Or would you be leaving for some distant country right after the wedding?"

"Not right after," he protested.

"So I would sit in England while you traveled the world?"

She looked belligerent. And completely unreasonable, Gavin thought. "Many wives do so," he pointed out. "There is the navy, the East India—"

"And quietly keep house until you chose to return?" she interrupted, ignoring him. "How often? Once a year?"

"More than that."

"Indeed? How generous."

Only Laura could make an offer of marriage into an insult, he thought.

"And while I sit alone, waiting…"

"You needn't be alone." He began to improvise.

"My sisters are in London for the season each year. I'm sure they would be happy to introduce you to their friends." He didn't know whether they would or not, he thought. Actually, he didn't know them very well. But it didn't matter. He had ways of ensuring their cooperation.

"Your sisters?"

"Baroness Monfort and Lady Sloane."

Laura gave him an odd look. "Baron Monfort is a constant companion of the earl's."

"What earl?"

"Leith."

"Oh." Gavin had known that he didn't like his eldest sister's husband. Until now, he hadn't known why. "Well, I don't see that that would—"

"No doubt, your sisters would be delighted to take the Leiths' former governess into society. So amusing."

"They will do as I say."

Laura grimaced. "Wonderful."

"As my wife, you will be accorded—"

"How would you know what I am accorded? You would be a thousand miles away."

He had no answer for this. Indeed, he had more than a suspicion that his sisters would do just as they pleased.

"I suppose I could make my own friends," she went on. "I would be very lonely."

Gavin suddenly saw the matter in a new light—a woman as lovely as Laura left alone amidst the sharks of the *haut ton*, with no outlet for her considerable passions and time on her hands. Her character would not permit her to stray, of course, but...

"I would have money for clothes, and that sort of thing?" she asked.

"I have a moderate income," he answered stiffly.

"Oh, good. And you won't be needing much of it, wandering about with hill bandits and so forth. I might set myself up very comfortably in London. I understand it is quite fashionable to have a whole string of admirers. What do they call them? It's an Italian word."

"If you think that I would tolerate—"

"*Cicisbeo*, I think it was."

"I know that you would not stoop to—"

"Many women would find such a prospect quite appealing."

Gavin found it appalling. It was all too easy to imagine Laura surrounded by ranks of lascivious opportunists, falling prey to the wiles of society rakes. He had known marriage was not for him, Gavin thought. He had simply not foreseen all the reasons why.

"Unfortunately, I have no interest in society," she said. "I want to accomplish something with my life. I prefer my own plan."

"You are refusing me?" Instead of feeling relief, Gavin was surprised by a flash of pain.

She looked at him. Her gaze was steady.

He tried to read it. Was there yearning in those depths? Regret? Desire? He couldn't tell.

"Yes," she said crisply.

"Tompkins won't go along. I'll see to it."

"You will keep me from having what you have?" she exclaimed. "Out of spite?"

"What I have?" She always managed to disorient him, Gavin thought. She would have made a wretched wife.

"Important work to do. Respect. Adventure."

"You are not—"

"I am not to have those things because you are worried about my safety. You would prefer to store me in England like unused furniture, taking off the dustcovers a few times a year when you deign to visit. How would *you* like such a life?"

"Surely it's better than being a governess?" he snapped.

Laura blinked. She shook her head a little as if to clear it. The anger that had flashed in her eyes seemed to fade. "I suppose the pay is better," she murmured sadly.

He felt as if she had escaped him somehow. His sense of grievance increased. "There is something wrong with you."

She cocked her head at him.

"This is not the way most women would respond to an offer of marriage."

"No flutters of gratitude? No shy maidenly glances? No little sighs of relief at a spinster's dream come true?"

He tried to relieve his feelings with a gesture.

"I am quite perverse," she responded sympathetically. "I trace it back to the time I was five and finally realized that my parents would always prefer a promising young colt to their only daughter."

She was laughing at him! Gavin closed the distance between them in one stride. He swept her up and held her hard against him. His kiss was a demand and a challenge. He would *make* her be serious.

He succeeded. When he let her go, Laura was wide-eyed and trembling. He could have her here and now, he thought. He could show her what she was throwing away.

"It isn't enough," she whispered.

He frowned at her.

"I'd rather have nothing."

She would rather have nothing than have him? The rejection crashed through him. This was the second time she had refused his offer of marriage, he remembered suddenly. The first, ten years ago, hadn't mattered; in fact, he'd been profoundly relieved. This time…this time felt as bitter as a failed mission, the worst disappointment he could imagine in his life.

Laura moved away, putting an armchair between them.

She would rather have nothing, he thought. Let her, then. Without another word, he turned and went out, resisting the impulse to slam the door.

The click of his boots on the parquet floor receded. Laura burst into tears.

## *Fourteen*

"THANK YOU FOR COMING SO PROMPTLY," SAID George Tompkins from behind his wide desk. Laura and Gavin faced him in straight chairs placed several feet apart. "Events are moving rather swiftly, as you know. Bonaparte is gathering an army as he travels north."

"I should be..." began Gavin.

The old man held up a hand for silence. "His return has had one good effect. It appears to have sharpened the minds of the allied leaders marvelously. The Congress of Vienna is going through the items on its agenda with commendable speed and amity."

Laura wondered why he had summoned them, and together. She had not seen Gavin since the previous evening when he had come to her room, and sitting near him now, she felt an uncomfortable mixture of uneasiness and longing.

"And of course the plots and counterplots are multiplying like rabbits," Tompkins continued.

She had had to refuse him, Laura thought, wondering if she was trying to convince herself.

"Indeed, it is hard to judge loyalties from moment to moment."

But if she hadn't, she would at least have seen him for some few months a year, a part of her argued. She would have been acknowledged as his wife.

"What is decided in Vienna may determine the course of the war," Tompkins went on.

But she didn't want to spend her life waiting, Laura concluded. She didn't want to be always hoping things would change. She was sick to death of the sidelines.

"There are a number of matters we need to explore," said Tompkins.

"We?" replied Gavin.

It took Laura a moment to absorb the implications of the word.

"I don't belong in Vienna," declared Gavin. "I must go into France, seek out people I know there, discover Bonaparte's plans."

"His plans appear straightforward. He is raising an army to fight for his throne."

"But when and where he will—"

"These things will be easily discoverable. It won't require a man of your...talents."

Laura stole a glance at Gavin. He looked thunderous.

"This is ridiculous," he said. "I shall protest."

"If you like." Tompkins didn't seem at all concerned at the idea. He put the tips of his fingers together and gazed at them from under lowered lids. "Now, the question of Sophie Krelov."

He had gained Laura's full attention. Noticing, he smiled at her benignly. "She is still very active, you know. She has been talking to an interesting collection of men…"

"Sophie is always talking to men," growled Gavin. Laura threw him a look, but could see nothing but anger and frustration in his face.

"Indeed. And about what, I wonder? I believe there is something more to her plotting, something we have not yet uncovered. And you have the advantage of having observed her closely for some time."

He had observed her all right, Laura thought.

Gavin started to speak, then clenched his jaw.

Tompkins smiled almost imperceptibly, like someone used to winning and too generous to gloat about it. "Our work will also give me an opportunity to test Miss Devane's abilities."

"What?" said Gavin and Laura simultaneously.

"Perhaps we will even find her a new post. Vienna is still full of people with valuable information." His smile broadened slightly.

"You can't be serious," said Gavin.

Laura wasn't able to speak. She had gotten her wish. She was to be given a chance.

Gavin stood. He looked furious. "And if I refuse?" he demanded. "I can ride north without anyone's damned permission!"

The old man acknowledged it with a calm gesture, as if it were a matter of indifference to him. "Do you think you could learn Russian in a few weeks, my dear?" he said to Laura.

"Russian?" Gavin looked as if he were about to explode.

"I have a talent for languages," she replied a little unevenly.

"I'm sure a tutor could be arranged."

"This is insanity," muttered Gavin.

They turned to look at him.

"Has the whole world lost its mind?"

Tompkins raised one elegant white brow. Laura clasped her hands together.

"Isn't Boney enough to deal with?" Gavin accused.

They gazed at him.

"Well, isn't he?"

He was shouting. Laura noticed that Mr. Tompkins seemed to almost approve of this vehemence.

"Deuce take it!" With a scorching glare, Gavin stamped out of the room. He didn't bother to close the door behind him.

"An amusing young man," commented Tompkins.

"Would you call him that?" Her voice was distinctly unsteady now, Laura realized. Gavin affected her whether she willed it or not.

The look Mr. Tompkins gave her carried an obvious twinkle. "Ah, well, as one gets older, things look a bit different."

"Do they?" she said, rising unsteadily. "That is comforting."

Tompkins remained at the desk when she had gone, his smile now broad and satisfied. From a very young age, he had been addicted to intrigue, but up to now he had confined his interests to politics. Was this new effort a sign of senility? he wondered. They were so amusing, though—both of them.

People seemed to grow more and more transparent

with each year that was added to his age. He had gained
a reputation for omniscience simply by observing their
antics and applying lessons from many others he had
known. These two were rather special, however.
They reminded him of himself long ago. Both of them
did. That was something he had never seen before,
and the implications were positively fascinating.

It had been a long time since he was last fascinated,
the old man thought, rising and making his way to
his chamber. It was a sign he had learned to heed. It
meant that something important was in the making.
Was this, at last, the legacy that he had hoped to leave?

He walked along the corridor ruminating on the
possibility. After a while, he began to chuckle. He was
still chuckling when he entered his room, but his valet
paid no attention. He was used to it.

❧

Gavin held out his hand to help Laura down from the
carriage in front of the headquarters of the Austrian
delegation. Gathering her skirts, Laura took it and
stepped lightly to the pavement. She took his arm, and
they started together up the steps. Something about
the gesture—the whole evening ahead—felt very
right, Laura thought. They were moving together,
in matched rhythms, against an adversary. They had
made a plan, and now they would execute it.

But that was not how Gavin felt, she reminded
herself. He had not wanted her to come at all. He had
wanted to confront Sophie Krelov alone. Was that
because he actually yearned to see her again? Laura
wondered as they made their way up the main stair to

the noisy reception rooms ahead. Or was he really so fearful for her safety?

They neared the archway, and Laura's muscles tightened. Mr. Tompkins was certain that he had kept their return to Vienna secret. And what the old man stated, Laura believed. They would surprise Sophie by their sudden reappearance and, it was hoped, shake loose some information.

Laura had her doubts about this, but she kept them to herself. She wasn't going to do anything that threatened her chance to prove herself to Mr. Tompkins. And to Gavin? inquired an insinuating inner voice. She gave it a defiant yes. What if she could prove her worth to him? Might that not change things between them?

She stole a glance at his handsome profile. He was totally focused on the crowded room they faced. As she should be, Laura thought. But for just one more wistful moment she contemplated the change in their situation. The closeness of the island seemed gone forever, dissipated like the smoke they had used to call for rescue. It was as if it couldn't survive in the actual world, as if it were a dream she had once had and now could only remember.

Standing straighter, she turned to the mass of people in front of them, pushing aside regrets. She *would* show them. She had already contacted Annalise and set her on the trail of Sophie's supposed maid once again. Something important would come of that, she told herself. But now, there was Sophie herself to be faced.

"I don't suppose you would leave this to me?" said Gavin.

"What would you like me to do? Go and sit in a corner with my hands folded?"

"If you had done as *I* liked…" he muttered but didn't bother to finish the sentence.

"There is Sophie," replied Laura calmly. "We should go and speak to her before she sees us." She glanced at him. His expression was focused, impassive. She could find no emotion there.

They moved forward together, maneuvering around other guests, and approached the other woman from the back. She was talking to a young man Laura didn't recognize. Gavin caught his gaze over Sophie's shoulder and gave him a look that made him step back a pace, then excuse himself and move away.

Sophie turned. When she saw them, she went completely still.

"Countess," said Gavin.

Laura merely nodded a greeting.

"You cannot be here!" she hissed.

"Do you think us phantoms?" asked Gavin. He reached out and grasped her wrist. The skin whitened under the pressure of his fingers. Had he wanted to touch her? Laura wondered.

Sophie jerked her arm free. "What have you done to Michael?"

"Your plans are spoiled," he responded, not answering her question. "You will never succeed."

She started to reply, then caught herself. In silence, she looked them over, seeming to see a great deal, Laura thought uncomfortably. After a while, she began to smile. "I?" she said. "What sort of plans could I have? I am just a woman, nothing more than a…messenger."

"Bonaparte will be defeated," Gavin told her. "The cause is hopeless."

Her smile widened. "Hopeless causes. Unattainable dreams." She fixed her gaze on Laura, taunting.

Her stare was unsettling, Laura acknowledged. She looked as if she knew all one's inmost secrets and was mocking them. It was a pose, Laura told herself. Their task was to shake her out of it, out of all her many poses, and find the truth that lay beneath. From some unknown part of herself came a question. "Where was it that your father taught you to shoot?" she asked.

Gavin looked startled, but Sophie's reaction was much more marked. She stepped back. Her eyes widened, then narrowed dangerously. Her lips thinned. "You have never been what you seemed, have you?" she said to Laura. "You deceived me once. Believe that you will not do so again."

With a rustle of silk, she turned and left them.

"What the deuce was that about her father?" said Gavin.

"Something she told me once. Something real, I think."

"Real?"

"No one seems to know where Sophie comes from. She tells everyone a different story. If we knew her origins…"

Gavin waited.

"We might know her loyalties better."

"If she has any," he murmured, but his expression was interested.

"I think she does," Laura responded, though she knew he hadn't meant it as a question.

"Why?" His gaze on her remained keen.

She shook her head, having no good reasons for this intuition.

"Instincts are all very well," said Gavin after a moment. "But they are no substitute for information. We should speak to some of my acquaintances. Form a picture of what has been going on in Vienna while we were…away."

"I can talk to people I have met."

"You are to stay with me!"

For an instant, Laura couldn't speak. She wanted nothing more than to stay with him, she thought. But he hadn't meant it that way. "We can reach more people if we separate. And some might talk more readily if—"

"You are not to go off on your own."

She would never prove her abilities unless she did, Laura thought. "Nonsense. I will be in plain sight." And she walked away before he could object again.

∾

Gavin watched her move away from him, her head high, her slender figure rigid. She was angry again. She was always angry lately. She didn't wish to marry him; she didn't wish to hear his advice, or even to admit that ten years of practice in these delicate matters might make his opinion valuable. She only wished to drive him mad worrying over her safety and wanting a woman who had definitively rejected him.

She was going to talk to von Sternhagen, he saw. At least that was relatively safe. The worst the estimable baron would do was bore her to death. And he would take a very long time to do it.

Watching Laura march up to the man and engage him in conversation, Gavin felt once more that odd sense of recognition that she occasionally elicited. She reminded him of something—someone. She stirred memories of the past in a way that unsettled him even more than thwarted desire. What was it? But the more he groped for an answer, the further it receded. At last, he had to shrug off the feeling and dismiss it. It was so very difficult to get anything done with Laura nearby, he thought.

With a sigh, Gavin went in search of his own sources of information. He spoke to Austrians and Frenchmen and Poles; a Russian attaché and a Saxon nobleman. He talked with the wife of an Italian delegate who had an obvious *tendre* for him. He chatted with a Dutchman who had vast shipping interests. But all he could discover was that Sophie had continued to enjoy the society of Vienna while they were imprisoned, attending nearly every event with apparent enjoyment.

Through it all, he remained constantly conscious of Laura, moving about the huge reception room on her own rounds. He found he could sense her location without looking, feel her presence, like a light that catches in the corner of the eye or a sound that rings at the edge of hearing. When she was nearby, he relaxed; when she strayed to the far end of the chamber, he was uneasy. Finally, on one of the latter occasions, he abandoned his questioning and turned to find her among the press of guests.

Once he did, he couldn't turn his gaze away from the grace of her form, the vivacity of her expression. Some primal part of him insisted that she was *his*, that she should be at his side, smiling up at him. Yet there she was, as far out of reach as the moon. She seemed to be enjoying herself too. With a spurt of rage, he realized that she was talking with that idiot Oliveri. Unconscious of the stares he provoked, Gavin strode through the crowd to her side.

"What do you think Bonaparte will do?" the Italian was saying.

"He'll raise the largest army he can and try for one of his great victories," interrupted Gavin curtly. "He'll hope for one decisive battle. The French are as tired of war as the allies."

Oliveri nodded in agreement. "And the other side will hope for the same."

He didn't say "our side," Gavin noticed.

"I can't believe the French countrymen are joining him," said an Englishwoman Gavin hadn't even noticed, who was standing next to Laura. "How can they?"

"Bonaparte made them great," responded Laura. "The old aristocracy had nothing but contempt for the people. But Bonaparte is like them, and yet he was emperor as well."

Gavin felt a flash of pride. She really understood the intricacies of the situation, he thought. She took the time to learn, and she had the intelligence to interpret the things she read.

"Very true," said Oliveri unctuously. Seeing the look he gave Laura, Gavin had to suppress a strong desire to throttle him.

"He's nothing but a jumped-up commoner," said the woman. "His mother wanted to keep pigs at Versailles, and he has the manners of a costermonger."

"Have you met him?" asked Laura.

"What? Er, no, I... It's well known."

Laura had deflated the woman's pretensions rather neatly, Gavin thought. And though her expression had been innocent, he could have sworn that she'd done it deliberately.

"From what I have heard, Bonaparte's manners are liable to vary with the situation," said Oliveri.

"Will he summon his wife to Paris, do you think?" said the woman.

"I have no doubt he will."

"Will she go?" asked Laura.

Gavin nodded in approval. That was the crux of the matter.

Oliveri gave an eloquent shrug. "Like many others, she will wait to see what happens, I suppose."

"So that is the danger?" Laura's inquiring glance brushed his, and Gavin couldn't suppress a smile. "That his old allies will rejoin him?"

"Precisely," Gavin said. She went right to the heart of things. "We have some unpredictable period of time to defeat him. Weeks or months. After that, he can only gain power."

Laura looked thoughtful.

"We will finally see some action from the congress," jibed Oliveri.

Gavin's lip curled. The fellow wouldn't have recognized real action if it marched up and planted him a facer. Shaking his head, he caught Laura's eye. She was obviously thinking the same thing. Their gaze held for a long moment. When she looked away, Gavin felt somehow abandoned.

"Wellington will defeat him," said the woman, sounding as if she wanted to convince herself.

"Wellington has never faced Bonaparte in battle," commented Oliveri.

"Nor has Bonaparte faced Wellington," replied Laura. Her gaze met Gavin's once again, and she smiled.

Gavin had the sudden sense that he had made a mistake. Had he forgotten something? he wondered. Had his report been incomplete? He shook his head. It wasn't that. No detail of his work had been neglected. Yet he continued to have that sinking feeling that had surfaced on the few occasions when he had jeopardized a mission and was in danger of losing everything at one throw.

"Are you all right?"

He looked up to find Laura close beside him. The others were a little distance away.

"You looked so odd. I was afraid you were ill."

Had he become so transparent? Gavin wondered. He was known for his skill in masking his feelings. He looked around, but no one else was paying any attention. His gaze shifted back to Laura, and held.

"I...beg your pardon," she said. "I didn't mean to pry."

She stepped back, but he held her with his eyes, refusing to let her go. She *was* his, reiterated that powerful inner voice. He ought to be free to take her home and demonstrate that fact to her so thoroughly that she could never forget it again. His lips and fingertips knew every contour of her body. His desire moved to the same rhythm as hers. This was undeniable, whatever she might say.

Laura flushed, and he knew she read this message in his face. The same memories that were rousing him drifted like shadows in her eyes.

Gavin stepped closer, towering over her. He was unaware of anyone else in the room. He was going to take her out of here, he decided. He didn't give a damn about the consequences. He didn't give a damn about anything, actually, except hearing her breath catch and feeling her respond to his touch as she always did. His hand reached out to grasp her.

"Mr. Graham?" asked a deep, gruff voice.

Gavin and Laura both started, pulled back from some private world by this inquiry.

"Yes?" Turning, Gavin confronted a stranger—a burly, middle-aged man whose face showed signs of hard living. He wanted to tell the fellow to go to the devil.

"May I speak to you? I have some information you might find useful."

Gavin examined him. Such an offer couldn't be refused, no matter how much he might wish to. Years of control snapped into place, and he was impassive once more. What he'd wanted was impossible in any case, he acknowledged. He had no right to Laura. She had told him so. The driving inner conviction that he did was wrong, and if he couldn't eradicate it, he would have to resist it.

"If we might speak more privately?" The man gestured toward a partly curtained alcove, out of earshot of the crowd.

With an impatient nod, Gavin headed for it. "I'll be back in a moment," he told Laura.

The stranger followed him to the recess, standing so as to block Gavin's view of the room. He had better have something extremely useful to impart, Gavin thought. And if he didn't begin to do so immediately, he was going to shove past the fellow and sweep Laura out of here.

∞

Left alone, Laura watched the people—their animated faces and gestures, the kaleidoscope of colors shifting around her. It looked different to her now. When she had first arrived in Vienna the crowds at parties and the din of conversation had been almost overwhelming. At the same time, it had seemed distant, like a play she was attending rather than an event in her own life. Now the chatter and busyness was revealed as simply a shell beneath which all manner of fascinating things went on. Laura felt as if she could discern some of them and would soon recognize others. She belonged here, she thought—not in the way Catherine Pryor hoped she would, but in quite another, more complicated way.

Sophie Krelov was approaching her. She was coming from the side and a little behind, hoping to catch her unawares, Laura saw. And in that moment she realized that the unknown man had removed Gavin just so this might happen. Curious, and a little apprehensive, she turned and waited for the countess to reach her.

When she did, she wasn't smiling. "Have you told me anything that was true?" she asked.

"Everything I told you was true," answered Laura.

Sophie brushed this aside contemptuously. "I won't be beaten. You may have slipped through Michael's fingers, but you will not stop me." She moved in closer, as if trying to force Laura to take a step back.

"It isn't Bonaparte, is it?" she responded, not moving. She was remembering the way Sophie had spoken when they first talked.

The countess's blue eyes narrowed, and she leaned even closer. "Have you fascinated him? Do you imagine that you have?"

Laura couldn't help but pull back a little.

"You are a fool if you think so," the other woman went on. She peered into Laura's eyes. "You are, aren't you? And even more than a fool. You hope for something beyond fascination. Love, perhaps?" Her soft laugh was deeply derisive. "Oh, this is better than any threat I could make. You have destroyed yourself!"

Laura concentrated all her faculties on showing no reaction.

"Gavin Graham has no heart. He has hands, and lips, and…other pleasurable parts, and he is very good at using them." Sophie smiled gloatingly. "Very, very good. Isn't he?"

The last two words were like the sudden strike of a cobra. Laura couldn't suppress a start.

"Yes. We both know that. We both know how he—"

"No," interrupted Laura, conscious only of wanting to stop her.

Sophie smiled, looking very pleased with this reaction. "Gavin only uses women. Everyone knows that's how he gets his information, manages his spectacular 'successes.' And afterward, he throws them away. I could tell you stories that—"

"Is that what he did to you?"

Sophie's smile broadened. "Oh, with us it was quite the other way around. I set out to use him. He found that very…exciting, I think."

"You failed."

The countess gave a lovely shrug. "Perhaps. But it was a most *enjoyable* failure." She leaned closer again. "Tell me, did he ever come up to you in the midst of a crowd and slip his hand beneath your…"

Laura turned and walked away. Sophie's bell-like laughter followed her across the room. Her hands were shaking, and she felt cold despite the stuffiness of the room. All this time she had been worrying about whether Gavin truly cared for Sophie, she thought. And the truth was he cared for no one.

Fingers closed on her arm and pulled her around. "What was she saying to you?" Gavin demanded.

It was all Laura could do to stay on her feet. She gulped a deep breath.

"Did she threaten you?" he asked. "I promise you I will—"

"No." Once again, Laura didn't know if she was answering or simply protesting the last few minutes.

"What then?" He was frowning at her. He looked half angry, half concerned.

"Nothing," stammered Laura. "She said nothing important."

"Then why are you so upset?"

"I'm not."

"Don't be ridiculous. I can see that you are—"

"I'm not being ridiculous!" She spoke so loudly that several heads turned nearby.

"Laura, what is the matter?"

He had never used her first name in such a public place before. Laura felt the danger of tears very close. And if she cried…

"I'm tired," she said. "I need to go home." The word seemed to echo slightly in her mind. Where was home?

Gavin appeared to become conscious of the inquisitive people surrounding them. Looking dissatisfied, he offered his arm in silence.

# Fifteen

LAURA MADE IT BACK TO HER ROOM AHEAD OF THE
tears. Oddly enough, once she was there, she found
she no longer had any desire to weep. On the contrary, she threw her cloak into the window seat and
sent her gloves flying after it. Still unsatisfied, she
kicked off her evening slippers in high arcs that ended
with gratifying thumps in the corner.

"I am sick to death of being treated like an idiot,"
she said aloud.

The words surprised her considerably. She blinked,
then sank down at the desk to try to figure out what
in the world she meant by them.

"No one believes that I know what I'm doing."

Laura nodded in response to her own statement.

"No one understands what my life was like for the
last ten years."

This was not only true, it was somehow calming.
Laura's finely honed intelligence went to work and
began to offer her hypotheses. First, Sophie had obviously arranged their talk together. Her maneuvers
hadn't been particularly subtle. She had certainly

also planned what she was going to say. Every word she'd uttered had had a purpose. Was this simply to hurt Laura?

She shook her head at the empty room.

Sophie's motives always went beyond the purely personal. Even her tantrums furthered some scheme. She used emotions for her own ends.

Laura frowned. Sophie had very much wanted Gavin out of the way, and once she had associated Laura with him, she had wanted to be rid of her as well. No doubt she still wanted this. She'd been furious when they confronted her this evening.

She would do anything to get what she wanted. She would tell lies, Laura thought.

Perhaps everything she'd said was untrue.

Laura felt her spirits lift. She wanted to believe this. She wanted to dismiss the whole conversation, erase the picture of Gavin with Sophie and the assurances that he cared for no one. She wanted to deny the character Sophie had given him, to obliterate the man she had described and replace him with...the man she loved.

But he had never said he cared for her, an inexorable inner voice declared—not in their time together on the island, not when he proposed marriage, not at all. Everything she knew of him suggested that Sophie was right.

At this, tears threatened again. But Laura did not allow them to fall. She rose and began to prepare for bed. She was on her own, she thought. She knew that, had known it for years and years. If she was to have a future, she must make it herself. She must prove beyond a doubt to Mr. Tompkins that she was a valuable addition to his organization and create a place for herself within it. Once she did, it wouldn't matter what Gavin Graham thought of her.

But though she repeated this silently more than once, Sophie Krelov's words echoed through Laura's dreams, making them painful and the night very long.

⟡

Right after breakfast the next morning, Laura sought out Mr. Tompkins. "You said Countess Krelov had been seen talking to an unusual variety of men," she said. "Do you have a list of them?"

He eyed her. "One could be prepared."

"I could speak with them as well, and see if they have some interests in common or if Sophie revealed anything to them." She didn't tell him the rest of her plan just yet. There would be time enough for that if it worked.

Tompkins frowned. "Perhaps some. These are not all men of good character."

"All," replied Laura firmly. "I should only approach them in public places, of course."

"I'm not sure even that would be wise."

Laura put her hands on her hips. "Mr. Tompkins, do you have any intention of letting me work for you—really?"

He raised one brow at her vehemence.

"Because if you do not, it would be a kindness to—"

"I have a great many intentions," he interrupted. "Some of them quite clear; others not yet fully formed.

But all of them must be thoroughly thought out and correlated. I do not accept an idea the moment it is brought to me."

Chastened, Laura looked down.

"Not until I am certain it is a good idea," he finished.

"What is a good idea?" inquired Gavin, coming into the room behind Laura.

Tompkins looked at him with an amused calculation that Laura did not understand, and then explained her suggestion. Laura braced herself.

"Absolutely out of the question!" Gavin exploded. "An idiotic scheme. I forbid it."

"Why?" asked Laura, keeping a tight rein on her feelings.

He glared at her. "Why? Because it is dangerous, and useless, and completely unnecessary. I will find out everything we need to know in a very short time."

He was extremely agitated, Laura thought—more so than she would have ever imagined he could be when she had first met the cold, supercilious Gavin Graham. He cared about *something*. But what, precisely? "I don't see why I can't help," she ventured.

"I don't need any help! I work alone."

Instead of anger, Laura felt a curious shivery sensation, as if shutters were folding back to reveal unexpected vistas. "Has anyone ever helped you with anything?" she asked.

Gavin looked distinctly startled. "What?"

"Has no one ever done anything for you?"

He frowned, at a loss. "I have always had servants. I don't know what you—"

"Not servants. When you were small, did no one—"

"What sort of nonsense is this?" he interrupted. "If you are trying to divert me from the subject, it won't work."

Laura noticed that Mr. Tompkins was watching her with what seemed like approval, as if he had set some sort of test and she was performing well. If only he would be so good as to explain it to her, she thought wryly, rather than leaving her to flounder.

"You have no business speaking to that sort of man," Gavin added.

Did she hear a hint of jealousy? Laura wondered. She didn't dare believe it.

"It's rather the same idea you had with the countess, I believe," commented Mr. Tompkins.

Gavin stared at him as if he had said something incomprehensible.

No one had ever helped him, Laura thought. She remembered what she had learned about his family. His father had treated him as a pawn, and when Gavin had failed to perform as his father wished, he had been banished from everything he knew. Gavin had had to prove his worth to his superiors, she thought, recalling things Mr. Tompkins had said. And he had had to do it alone. His friends... Did he have friends? She couldn't remember hearing of any.

"This is outrageous," he declared.

Laura felt a deep tremor. She wanted to help him. Along with all the other things she wanted, she wanted this very much. But to say so would be foolish.

Gavin had turned to Mr. Tompkins. "How can

you even consider sending a young woman with no experience to mingle with the likes of Girard or Slanski?"

"The only way to acquire experience is to…" began Tompkins mildly.

Gavin cut him off with a slashing gesture. "I won't allow it." He turned to Laura. "I shall be with you every moment you are out," he told her. "You will have no opportunity to do anything foolish."

"So we will work together," she dared. "As partners."

Something flared in Gavin's eyes. Probably rage, Laura thought. He made a sound like an animal goaded past endurance.

"Splendid idea," said Mr. Tompkins.

With a searing look at both of them, Gavin turned and left the room.

Silence fell in his wake. Laura was trying to sort out a welter of feelings and to decide what Gavin had really meant by some of the things he had said—or hadn't said.

"That went rather well," commented her companion.

She looked at him. "Do you think so?"

"Oh, yes."

He looked quite self-satisfied, she thought, rather like a gardener surveying a successful planting. "Why?" she asked.

He gave her one of his charming smiles, but no answer.

She very much wanted to press him, to ask him about Gavin and whether he had seen some of the emotions she imagined in him. But she didn't quite dare.

❧

The next few days were among the most maddening of Gavin's life. He had never allowed any other
woman to lead him such a dance, he thought, as he
watched Laura making her way around the room at
the Saxon delegation's ball.

She accepted his escort without protest, but at
each of the events they attended, she waited until he
was engaged in conversation with an acquaintance
and then slipped off to accost some blackguard who
knew Sophie. She seemed to have no difficulty
interesting such men. And why should she? Gavin
thought sourly. They all of them had an eye—and
more than an eye—for an attractive woman. He
got her away from them as quickly as he could, but
not always as quickly as he would have liked. And
he was developing a reputation for rudeness as he
dashed about trying to keep her safe. Not to mention
the whispers that were rising over his obvious interest in the lovely Miss Devane, he thought bitterly.
Traveling faster than a diplomatic courier, the gossip
had even reached as far as London. He had received
an irritating note from his eldest sister asking just what
he thought he was doing.

He *thought* he was keeping Laura from getting into
serious trouble. Gavin gritted his teeth as she paused
on the other side of the ballroom to reply to a sally
from a disreputable Polish nobleman. She was going to
dance with the fellow, he saw with outrage.

"She's doing rather well, isn't she?" said George
Tompkins at his side.

Where had he come from? Gavin wondered. He
hadn't seen him approach, and indeed had thought

that the old man meant to spend this rare excursion from his home in the cardroom.

"I believe she has a knack for this sort of thing."

Gavin grunted, too irritated to speak.

"Just needs a bit more experience," Tompkins added.

"What sort of experience do you expect her to get from a rakehell like that?" growled Gavin, watching Laura turn in the fellow's arms.

"She is learning to take care of herself."

Anger washed over Gavin like a pail of scalding water thrown in his face. A red haze pulsed across his eyes. If that blackguard made the slightest move toward Laura, he thought, he would find an excuse to call him out and put a bullet in him.

The Pole bent to say something to Laura. She laughed in response.

It came home to Gavin suddenly that he could really lose her. Not to this jumped-up idiot, but there were other men in the world. And if not a man, then time and distance would separate them—or something worse. Gavin's pulse pounded. He had to convince Tompkins not to send her off into danger.

But when he turned, the old man was gone.

The music was ending. But Laura's partner was not letting her go, he saw. He was making some jest, but there was no doubt about his motives. Gavin strode over to them just as Laura slipped free of the idiot's arm. "Miss Devane," he said in a tone designed to convey all his objections, "may I have the honor of the next set?"

Ignoring his furious look, she nodded a serene

farewell to her previous partner and walked with Gavin onto the floor.

"I will not always be here to rescue you," he said.

"You didn't rescue me. I was perfectly all right."

"Indeed? Do you have any idea what that halfpenny 'count' had in mind?"

"Of course. But since he had no chance of getting it, I…"

The musicians struck up and Gavin pulled her into his arms with a bit more force than necessary. The relief of having her close, of feeling her safe, was extraordinary. With her scent drifting around him and her body moving in perfect rhythm with his, he almost forgot his complaints. The world seemed right in that moment. She was in her proper place, in his arms.

"How can Tompkins allow you to do this?" Gavin exploded.

There was a short silence. An echo of his irate tone seemed to vibrate between them.

"I suppose he trusts me," said Laura quietly then. "As you apparently do not."

"Trust has nothing to do with it!"

They turned in the dance, their bodies exquisitely synchronized. To Gavin, their rhythm was almost painful. "You could be deceived, or attacked. You don't belong in this situation."

She looked at him, her eyes wide, her skin pale as cream. The candles drew a highlight from her black hair. "Where do I belong?" she murmured, so softly he wasn't certain he'd heard it.

Gavin felt something twist inside him. He was

being pushed too far, he thought, and then wondered what the deuce that meant.

Laura drew in a breath as the dance made them sway together. "I can do this. It is perfectly reasonable that I should."

Reasonable, thought Gavin. He clung to the word as a shipwrecked man might a floating spar. "Reason," he echoed, "would suggest that things be left to me."

"You got no information from Sophie," she answered. "Whatever else you may have gotten."

"I beg your pardon?"

Laura looked away from him. Her profile was lovely against the moving frieze of dancers. "It must have been a very...enjoyable assignment."

"What are you talking about?"

"Sophie," she said baldly.

"She was hardly an assignment."

"Ah."

He didn't like her tone. He didn't much care for her expression, either. "Pryor did everything he could to keep me away from her."

"Yes, he did, didn't he?"

Gavin had forgotten the reason for Laura's presence in Vienna. The general's scheme seemed like something that had happened years ago.

"Rather like you are doing now, with me," continued Laura.

The comparison was odious. "Nonsense! This is completely different."

"Why?"

"Because I knew what I was doing!"

He saw by the flash of her gaze that he was getting

nowhere. The music was ending. She would slip away from him again. "Laura," he began.

He could see in her face that she meant to do exactly as she pleased, no matter what he might say, what arguments he might bring to bear. She thought she knew better. The recurring feeling of familiarity was there again, Gavin noticed. She reminded him of something—or rather, someone. What was it about her?

Laura's gaze shifted to the crowd, she was clearly planning her next step.

And then, in one astonishing moment of clarity, he had it. She reminded him of himself, a decade ago, when he had embarked on his first real mission and discovered his true calling in the diplomatic service. He could see the same eagerness and focus vibrating through her. He knew that look of confident disdain and the qualms of doubt it hid so effectively.

Realizations cascaded like a row of falling dominoes, one after the other. Things she had said to him suddenly made sense. Invisible women, he thought. A decade ago he had felt, not invisible, but insignificant. Living under his father's thumb, he had looked forward to a meaningless life, ruled by oppressive conventions and other people's desires. And then he had been sent into exile, but instead of punishment he had discovered freedom—a way to use all his faculties and abilities, to have some role in the shaping of events.

He and Laura were kindred spirits. She had emerged from her own exile into the kind of liberty he had felt those years ago, with the same certainty that she was meant for this sort of adventure.

"Mr. Graham." Something tugged at his sleeve. "Gavin!"

"What?" It was Laura.

"The music has stopped." She was pulling out of his embrace, glancing here and there at the amused people around them.

Jerked back to reality, he let her go.

"I know what I'm doing," she said. "Why can't you give me credit for that?"

Hadn't he spoken those exact words years ago to a panicked subaltern? Gavin wondered. He thought he had.

"I am not reckless," Laura insisted.

Gavin nodded. That, too, he had said.

"I have thought this out very carefully."

Nothing would stand in the way of what she was feeling, he thought, the excitement of those first days vivid in his memory. But she was a woman, he protested silently. And she was *his*.

"Can't you acknowledge that?"

Not his, another voice reminded him. She had refused him. She would not listen, and she would not be stopped. He had never been so frightened in his life, Gavin thought.

❧

"These are the ones the countess's maid goes to see?" Laura asked Annalise.

The girl nodded. "And sometimes they give her parcels to carry back."

"Large parcels?"

"No." She made gestures in the air, indicating

the size. "Like a cake, or a box of cigars from Herr Schwimmer's."

Laura studied the list Annalise had compiled. All of the men on it were also on the one Mr. Tompkins had provided, but Annalise's was much shorter. "I would very much like to know what is in those parcels," she murmured.

"Shall I steal one?"

"No!" She didn't want to get Annalise in trouble. So far nothing she had done was illegal, and Laura wanted to keep it that way. She studied the list again, thinking about each of the men on it and what she had been able to glean about their characters from short conversations. It didn't take long to make a decision. "This one," she said, pointing to a name. "The next time the countess's maid visits him, come and fetch me."

Annalise nodded.

"You have done a very good job," Laura added. As the girl beamed at her, she promised herself that she would do something for her when this was over. Perhaps Mr. Tompkins could find some work for her. "How is your brother?" she was moved to ask.

Annalise grinned. "Papa found out about his engagement and his plan to run a shop. He was *so* angry. But Heinrick stood up to him! He never did before. I think Papa liked that, actually. And now Papa pretends he has resigned himself." She shrugged as if to say that she didn't believe it.

"But he still does not let you help him?"

The girl looked shocked. "I have not asked him, when he is in such a bad mood. Later, when Heinrick is really gone, we shall see."

"You are a most intelligent young woman," answered Laura.

Annalise grinned at her again. "I must get home."

Laura walked with her out into the front hall. "Thank you, Annalise."

"It is I who thank you," was the reply. With a final grin and a wave, the girl departed.

Turning, Laura discovered Mr. Tompkins standing on the staircase watching her. She had to suppress a start. He was always turning up in unexpected places. And one never noticed his approach, only his sudden, penetrating presence.

There was a short, charged silence.

"Good afternoon," Laura said finally, wanting to escape scrutiny. "I was just on my way to…"

"Are you confident you know what you're doing?"

Laura flashed him a startled glance.

"I would be deeply distressed if you were harmed in any way," he added.

She blinked. He spoke as if he knew every nuance of her plans.

"And yet I hate to discourage…initiative."

She wouldn't have imagined that anyone could appear kindly and implacable at the same time, Laura thought. She was strongly reminded of the tests of mental agility her teachers had subjected her to at school.

"So?" he said.

Laura swallowed. She took a breath. She was going to pass this test. "I am confident," she answered, as steadily as she could. She made the mistake of meeting his gaze. It felt as if he looked right through her. When he finally nodded, she nearly sagged in relief.

He watched her a moment longer, then smiled.

She waited for him to say something else. But he didn't. He let the silence stretch until she couldn't stand it. "I'm a little tired," she said. "I think I'll go up to my room."

Mr. Tompkins merely bowed. Laura took this for permission and fled past him.

He watched her climb the stairs, his smile lingering. Things were progressing very nicely, he thought.

# Sixteen

GAVIN LEANED AGAINST THE WALL IN THE LONG SALON where the English delegation to the Congress of Vienna was holding its final reception. Glass doors were open to the soft spring air. People were exchanging farewells; many of them were already packed and ready to leave the city, to return to their own capitals or to ride for the battlefield in the north. Decisions had at last been made, documents signed. All that remained was to defeat the military genius who had held Europe in thrall for years and caused this momentous meeting in the first place.

Gavin smiled briefly. Everyone spoke as if this defeat were simply a matter of time, but most would be barring their doors and waiting to offer their allegiance to whoever was the victor.

Part of him chafed at his distance from the coming confrontation and longed to be in France, gathering intelligence. But another, less familiar part, was fascinated by what was going on right here, in this room.

He watched Laura move through the crowd, speaking to some people, smiling at others, invisibly calculating friend and foe, useful and negligible conversations. He understood exactly what she was feeling and the thoughts that were running through her mind. He had been just the same in the early years, at once excited and careful, daring and circumspect. It was like spreading wings too long confined in a tiny cage, he remembered. The exhilaration was unmatched. Or, almost unmatched, he amended. He had since found something that was even more heady.

She was making her way back to him now, with some bit of information to share. She looked pleased and intent and ardent in her new role. It excited him to watch her, Gavin thought, although it terrified him, too. It was a shame that some of his former superiors would never know of this moment, he thought wryly. They would enjoy it so much.

Watching her, he remembered that feeling of having accomplished a mission—found the thing he was sent for, made the connection with a vital source. His pulse sped up as he knew Laura's had.

This was bizarre, Gavin thought. He had trained himself to read the expressions and gestures of others. But he had never found himself feeling *with* anyone he observed. The link with Laura moved him in tandem with her.

For some reason, this brought to mind the questions she had asked him recently. Of course, many people had helped him over the years, Gavin thought. What had she meant? When he was small there had been nurses, tutors. His father had… For a moment, Gavin tried to tell himself that his father's incessant criticisms had been an effort to help. But he didn't believe it. The old man had wanted a way to a fortune, not a son. When he'd failed to marry an heiress, Gavin had become an outcast, banished from everything—and everyone—he'd ever known. And when he'd appealed to his sisters for aid, they had simply reproached him for incurring their father's wrath.

An old pain stirred, but Gavin had long ago come to terms with it, and it was easily suppressed. What lingered—inexplicably—was the image of Laura's face when she had asked the question. Something about it made him very uneasy. *He* was helping *her*, Gavin told himself. He didn't need help—he'd found his proper—solitary—place in the world.

"Are you feeling all right?" asked Laura, joining him just then. "You look a bit bilious."

She was always asking him how he was, Gavin thought. Untying him, advising him, whether he wanted advice or not. He felt an odd uncertainty, as if he had left some critical detail out of his calculations.

She took his arm and unobtrusively guided him across the room and out onto the flagstone terrace. "A Frenchman pulled Sophie this way," she told him quietly. "He seemed quite agitated."

Gavin's attention focused immediately. "Who?"

Laura shook her head. "I didn't know him." As they walked a bit faster, she assumed a virtuous expression. "But you see I came to tell you at once instead of following them on my own."

"Commendable." He knew quite well that this was a mere sop to his strictures and that she would do precisely as she pleased another time.

The sprinkling of new leaves offered little concealment, but there was evergreen shrubbery ahead, and
they slipped quickly into it. Sophie had apparently
had the same thought, for they soon heard her
voice ahead.

"We cannot speak of this here," she hissed in
French.

"The moment is come," replied a man's voice.
"We cannot wait longer."

"In one week," said Sophie. "Everything is set. It
will happen then."

"You must be certain—"

"I am certain! And *you* must not speak to me again.
There are watchers all around us."

Gavin pulled Laura into the outer branches of the
shrubbery.

"If I find anyone watching, I will kill them,"
boasted the Frenchman.

"Put that away!" exclaimed Sophie. Her voice had
risen, and it was more controlled when she added,
"You cannot wave a pistol in such a place."

"It is war now," declared the man loudly. "I can do
as I please. Bonaparte will crush these *canaille* and…"

His arm around Laura's waist, Gavin pulled them
still farther into the shelter of the evergreens. A twig
snapped beneath their feet.

"What was that?" exclaimed the Frenchman.

Footsteps rushed toward them. In one smooth
motion, Gavin crouched and folded Laura and himself
into the heart of the shrubs that lined the path. Small
sharp branches poked him from all sides.

"Who is there?" called the man. The shrubbery

swayed as he beat it, and Gavin could see his feet quite clearly under the sweep of needles.

"Stop it!" hissed Sophie's voice, far too close for comfort. "Do you want to attract every person here? You will ruin everything."

There was a soft thud, and the Frenchman's feet stumbled. Gavin drew Laura closer, and waited.

Another thud; Sophie was hitting her reckless ally, Gavin thought, trying to drive him along. There was a flurry of French curses, and then the feet retreated. He listened as the footfalls grew fainter, straining to determine whether it was one set or two.

A bird began to sing in the trees above them. The clink of glasses and the buzz of conversation floated on the soft breeze from the reception. Relaxing slightly, Gavin realized that Laura was trembling against him. In the same instant, his blood flamed with the feel of her, tucked into the curve of his body, pressed along every inch of him. His arms were laced across her chest, his cheek was pressed into her hair. And he didn't want to let go. "It's all right," he murmured into her ear, which was only inches from his lips. "They've gone. There's no need to be afraid."

"I'm not"—her breath caught in a tiny gasp— "afraid."

She shifted against him. Desire blurred his vision and tightened his muscles.

"We…we have to get out of here," breathed Laura. She moved again.

Every fiber of Gavin shouted, "No!" But his throat was too thick with longing to speak. He let her struggle out of his embrace and push her way through the branches, and followed after a brief, titanic effort at control.

"Oh, God," said Laura when he emerged beside her.

For a moment, he thought she would say that she wanted him as fiercely and inevitably as he wanted her. She would admit it, he imagined, and fling herself back into his arms.

"Do I look as dreadful as you do?" she said then.

Gavin blinked and forced his mind back from the far reaches of longing.

Twigs were stuck in Laura's hair, which was falling out of its pins, and in the lace of her sleeves. Bits of dead leaves clung to her skirts, which also showed green stains from the moss they had crouched in. He put a hand to his own hair, brushing out bits of twig and needles.

"We can't go back inside," protested Laura. "People will think we have been…" She flushed and bent to shake out her skirts.

If only they had, Gavin thought, another jolt of desire rocking him. If he had done as he wanted and let his hands rove, felt the silk of her skin once again, would she have responded as she had on the island? She wasn't looking at him. He couldn't keep his eyes off her. Slowly, Gavin reached out and pulled a twig from her hair.

She stood still. Her hands shook in the folds of her gown. He let his fingers brush her cheek, which blushed under his touch. "Laura."

She looked at him then, her eyes clouded.

He must say something, he thought—the right thing, the thing that would dissolve the barriers separating them and open out the future. But he couldn't think, much less speak. He was submerged in her beauty, the feel of her, the echo of words they had said, and not said, over the last few weeks. She took a step away from him.

"There's a back gate," she said unsteadily. "If we go out that way, perhaps no one will notice." She began brushing at her dress again.

If they were blind, they might not notice, Gavin thought. How could any observer miss the rhythm that pulsed between them? But then, most people were blind to the important things. It was rare to discover another human being who could see.

∽

Late the following afternoon, a servant knocked on Laura's door with the information that she had a visitor. Downstairs, she found Annalise moving from foot to foot in one of the parlors. "The countess's maid has just gone to his house," she said as soon as Laura entered. "I ran to tell you."

Laura's pulse speeded up. This was the moment she had been waiting for, when her plan would show its merits and she would prove herself once and for all. She had chosen her target carefully. She had thought it through. She was ready. Giving Annalise an approving nod, she said, "Splendid."

"Do we go there now?" replied the girl, obviously excited.

"Yes." Laura hesitated. She could not go without telling someone, but anyone she told would ruin everything by trying to stop her. Biting her lower lip, she stepped into the front hall. "Is Mr. Graham here?" she asked the footman.

"He is out riding, miss."

"Ah. Is Mr. Tompkins in his study?"

The servant shook his head. "He was called to the ambassador's."

This solved one problem, Laura thought as she returned to the parlor. But it raised another. She needed just enough time for her errand. Rescue that came too early or too late would be fatal. And she needed to leave now. Frowning, she cobbled together a plan.

"I will go to the house alone," she said to Annalise. "You must search for Herr Graham, who is riding. You remember what he looks like?" She had made certain to point him out to the girl.

Annalise nodded.

"Send him after me. He will know what to do. As soon as you have done that, return here and ask for Mr. Tompkins. I will give you a note for him. Bring him to the house as well."

"I will."

Laura experienced a sudden qualm. "If you cannot find Mr. Graham…"

"I can find him," promised the girl.

She had to, Laura thought, as she sat down to write the note for Tompkins. This had to work perfectly, or she would end up proving Gavin right rather than demonstrating her abilities. And that would be intolerable.

"You understand what you are to do?" she asked Annalise when she gave her the folded paper.

The girl simply nodded and slipped out the door.

❧

Laura ran to her room and gathered the items that she had prepared for this moment. A few minutes later, she was in the street. She walked at a measured pace, hoping to show no sign of anxiety, though she felt a good deal.

All her preparations were in place, she thought. She had been over them a hundred times, and they were good. Mr. Tompkins would be impressed. Gavin—she stumbled over an uneven cobblestone—she couldn't think of Gavin right now. She couldn't be distracted by her feelings.

She walked along a row of shops and around a corner. The house was just ahead. Squaring her shoulders, Laura marched up to the front door and knocked.

There was no problem getting in, not even much surprise at the appearance of a solitary female. Which wasn't a good sign, Laura thought, as she was ushered upstairs into a large reception room. This was going to require all her fortitude and skill. She fingered the object in her pocket for reassurance.

"My dear Miss Devane," exclaimed Count Slanski when he came into the room. He was rubbing his chubby hands together and looking extraordinarily pleased with himself. "What a charming surprise. You have refused my invitations so often I had given up hope of your calling on me."

Laura tossed her head and did her best to pout. "I have come only to tell you that I have discovered your false heart, Count."

"False?" He put a hand to his breast as he circled closer.

It was too bad they had to converse in French, Laura thought, moving a little farther around a table in the center of the room. Things sounded more intimate in that language. But she had no Polish and the count no English. She blinked at him reproachfully. "All the time you were claiming to adore me, you really preferred someone else," she accused.

"Who has told you so?" Slanski came closer. He moved very quickly for such a pudgy man, and he stayed between her and the door.

"It is well known that you constantly send gifts to Sophie Krelov. You have never given anything to *me*!"

"Sophie...?" The count looked startled.

"How could you be so fickle and cruel?" Laura added. She wanted to keep him from thinking too much, and she was counting on his stupidity. Slanski was by far the stupidest of the men Sophie had been cultivating, and thus the most likely to let information slip.

"What makes you think...?" he sputtered.

"Her servant comes here to fetch your presents," Laura accused. "You are faithless!"

"No, no, not that at all. No such thing. Sophie and I are—"

"You admit it," cried Laura. She clasped her hands and turned half away, gazing back at his round face from under her lashes.

"Sophie's just politics. There's nothing else..."

"Politics!" Laura gave him a searing look. "Do not try to confuse me. What politics could you and the countess—?"

"She has a scheme in mind," Slanski interrupted, eager to redeem himself. "And it has possible... advantages for my country. So I have provided funds to support it."

"Money?" It was a great effort to maintain her tone of reproach. She was about to find out the truth, and her heart was pounding.

"Others have done the same," Slanski assured her. "It's nothing personal. There is no one but you..."

"But what is it for?" Laura hoped she sounded bewildered and half persuaded.

"She is organizing an uprising—"

To Laura's deep chagrin, his revelation was interrupted by a sound at the door. They turned to find Sophie Krelov's maid standing there with fire in her eyes.

"*D'anam don diabhal!*" she cried.

They both stared at her. Slanski took a step backward.

"What is she doing here?" the older woman added in English. Seeing that the count didn't understand her, she switched to French, "She is an English spy!"

Count Slanski gaped.

"You are a fool!" pronounced the maid. She turned to Laura like an avenging fury.

But Laura had taken this opportunity to remove something from her pocket. She leveled her pistol at them both.

Slanski looked astonished. "You have a gun," he said, as if to verify the evidence of his own eyes.

"And I have spent a great deal of time learning to shoot it, so you needn't think I won't."

"A gun," he repeated incredulously.

She gestured with it. "Stand side by side."

His dark gaze shifted to her face. He looked as if she had betrayed him. "You are a woman."

And you are a half-wit, Laura replied silently. She gestured with the pistol again. She needed to work her way around them and reach the door. She had all the information she needed.

Slanski moved. But he kept turning his head to gaze at the gun as if he couldn't maintain belief in its reality. Sophie's maid, on the other hand, simply watched her. The ferocity of her gaze made Laura a bit nervous. She was thus only partly prepared when the older woman leaped at her and fastened both her hands around the gun.

They struggled violently for possession of it.

"Help me, you fool," screamed the maid to Slanski. Jumping like a startled hare, he did so, and the two of them wrestled the pistol from Laura's grasp.

The woman took charge of it, holding it aimed at Laura's heart. She drew back the hammer and started to squeeze the trigger.

"What are you doing?" cried Slanski.

"She must be killed," was the laconic reply.

"Are you mad?"

"She will betray us." Her finger tightened.

"You cannot kill her here, now, in my house. Gunfire will bring every servant running."

"Aren't your servants trustworthy?" she asked contemptuously.

"Most of them came with the place!" Slanski replied frantically. "Put down the gun."

She didn't lower the pistol, but she eased the

hammer back, frowning. "Send someone for Sophie," she ordered.

As Slanski ran out to do so, Laura had the satisfaction of knowing that she had been right about this woman. She was no maid. The way she referred to the countess by name was evidence enough of that.

The count returned, panting, a sheen of sweat on his forehead. "The footman's gone for her."

Laura ignored them. She was listening for sounds below. Surely Annalise had found Gavin by now, she thought.

❦

"How could she have left without anyone knowing?" raged Gavin.

The two footmen standing before him visibly quailed.

"What's your name?" he demanded.

"John, sir," said one of the servants.

"Well, John, why did you let her go out alone?"

"But, sir, I…I only accompany Miss Devane when I'm summoned. I'm not aware of what she—"

"Your job is to keep her safe!" Gavin snapped. "And you've botched it."

"She must have slipped out the side door," put in the other footman, who had been stationed in the front hall. "Begging your pardon, sir, but the staff can't be responsible if—"

"Who is responsible, then?" Gavin would have enjoyed finding someone he could blame. It would have been some relief to his feelings.

"Good afternoon," said a calm voice from the doorway. Gavin turned to George Tompkins, who looked maddeningly unconcerned. "You know that Lau... Miss Devane is gone?"

"It appears she left the house about three."

Gavin swore. "I told her she was not to go out without me!"

Tompkins looked at the two footmen. "You may go," he said.

They hurried out.

"She had some plan in mind, I believe," he added.

Gavin couldn't seem to think as quickly as usual.

"And she is a very clever young woman," Tompkins added.

"She has not dealt with real villains," he replied.

"We don't know that she is attempting to deal with them," the old man pointed out.

"Do we not?"

Tompkins looked concerned.

"She is alone," railed Gavin. The word was like a knell.

"I believe I will send out some men to look for her."

"I'm going," Gavin assured him.

"It might be best if you stayed here. Others will search more efficiently."

Gavin felt as if the blood might burst from his veins. "Do you doubt my abilities?" he snapped.

The look Tompkins gave him was kind. "I doubt your sensibilities. It is difficult to keep a clear head when one is deeply worried."

"I'm not worried. I'm furious."

"Even more so, then."

"Do you intend to have me bound? Nothing else will keep me here."

"It could be arranged." Tompkins showed no reaction to the savage look that had made more than one bandit chieftain cower.

"Excuse me, sir." The footman came only halfway into the parlor where Gavin and Tompkins were arguing. He looked as if he hadn't wanted to come at all.

"What?" snapped Gavin, who wasn't feeling very charitable toward footmen just now.

"There is a young person at the door. She insists upon speaking to you. She won't see anyone else, and she won't go away."

Gavin was pushing past him before he finished speaking. He ran down the hall to the front door and confronted the girl waiting there. His hopes faltered when he took in her youthfulness and fresh open face, but he demanded, "Who are you? What have you to tell me?"

The girl looked uncomprehending, and his heart sank.

"You are Herr Graham?" the girl asked in German.

"Yes!"

"My name is Annalise. Fräulein Devane sent me to find you."

"Where is she?"

She recited an address some distance away.

His horse might still be saddled, Gavin thought. He started to run for the stables. "Tell him," he called over his shoulder to Annalise, gesturing at Tompkins, who had materialized in the hall.

It was one of the longest journeys Gavin had ever taken, despite his thousands of miles of travel. Try as he might, he kept thinking of Laura lying wounded, her life bleeding away. Every word she had spoken to him, every caress they had exchanged haunted him as he raced through the streets of Vienna.

~

"I cannot be involved with this any longer," Slanski was stammering. "I did not bargain for anything like this. I cannot afford to—"

"Do be quiet," said Laura and the other woman at the same moment. They exchanged a quick startled glance.

There it was, Laura thought, a stealthy sound downstairs. "What exactly is it that Sophie is planning?" she asked. She hoped to divert their attention and also to convince them that she did not know their secret.

The supposed maid gave her a contemptuous look.

"If you are going to kill me, there's no harm in my knowing. And it would be rather satisfying."

Slanski nodded as if agreeing with this argument and opened his mouth.

"Keep quiet, you imbecile," said the other woman.

His mouth snapped shut.

Laura moved, drawing their attention to herself. In the next instant, Gavin erupted into the room, struck the gun from the maid's hand, and trained his own weapon on the two of them. "Get the pistol," he commanded.

Laura had already lunged for it. She felt much better when she held it trained on Sophie's confederate once again. "You were rather slow in getting here," she said to Gavin.

"Your young friend was slow in finding me."

"I'm sure she—"

"Could we discuss this at a later time?" he replied through clenched teeth. "We should be going."

"Oh…yes. Sophie is on her way."

"Indeed?" Gavin was backing toward her, keeping his gun steady on their adversaries. "Will you move?"

Together, they made for the door. When they reached the corridor, Gavin turned and took her arm. "Run!" he said.

They raced down the stairs and into the entryway. When Laura would have gone to the front door, he urged her in the opposite direction, heading for the back. But this did them no good. Even as they burst into the open air, they were caught and held by four very large men wearing Sophie's livery.

The woman herself appeared behind them. "If you have hurt Bridget, I'll kill you," she hissed. She ran into the house.

"She's going to kill us anyway," said Laura. Gavin gave her an odd look.

Sophie returned with the older woman, but there was no sign of Slanski. "Tie them," she said to her men, and Laura and Gavin were bound and gagged before being hustled into a carriage and forced down onto the floor for a very uncomfortable ride.

"We cannot take them to your house," said Bridget. "They will be searched for."

"I know exactly where I am taking them," declared Sophie.

# *Seventeen*

THEY CLATTERED THROUGH THE STREETS FOR NEARLY twenty minutes. Gavin fought to keep his sense of direction and feel in the sway of his body the turns they made. But being unable to see anything except the carriage floor and several sets of feet, he soon lost track. He could tell only that they were traveling into a poorer quarter of the city. The sounds and smells were clear evidence of that.

When the vehicle finally stopped, scarves were tied around their eyes before they were half carried, half pushed into a building and up several flights of stairs. The slam of the door and the sound of a key turning told him that they had been imprisoned. Immediately, he used his bound hands to tear the scarf away.

Laura was there, standing very still and seeming to listen intently.

His chief fear relieved, Gavin worked at the knot of his gag and soon had it off. The ropes on his wrists would take longer, but he was confident he could get them off as well. He had used his teeth for such a task before. Seeing that Laura was already at work on her own bonds, he began to examine their prison.

It was a small attic room with a slanting ceiling. The furnishings consisted of one dilapidated straight chair and a sagging wooden bedstead with a straw pallet flung on top. There were two dormer windows. He strode to one of them and looked out. They were four stories above one of Vienna's less savory neighborhoods. He didn't recognize the nearby streets, but the towers of St. Stephan's could be seen in the distance. He could easily find his way back.

"Where are we?" asked Laura.

The emotion Gavin had been holding in check burst out in sheer rage. "We are locked in a small room in a back slum, where we would *not* be if you were not an utter fool."

She drew in a breath.

Gavin didn't give her time to speak. "How could you go off alone to that scoundrel's house? Telling no one what you meant to do, putting yourself helplessly into the hands of—"

"I sent Annalise for you!"

"Having no idea where I was or when she might find me." She deserved the wounding sarcasm in his voice, Gavin thought. No woman—no one—had ever frightened him as she had today.

"You came alone," she accused.

She was impossible, he thought savagely. "I have the experience to deal with such people!"

Laura looked around the room and then back at him as if to point out that they were both captives.

Gavin clenched his fists, which reminded him of the ropes that still confined him. He started to pull at one of the knots with his teeth.

"I could untie that for you," said Laura.

"I can do it!"

"I'm sure you can, but why gnaw at it when I could do it more easily?"

If she were anyone else, he'd throttle her, Gavin decided.

"Here," said Laura.

She was at his side in an instant, and when her fingers touched his wrists, Gavin felt as if the breath had been knocked out of him. The delicate brushes of her fingertips as she struggled with the bonds were as arousing as intimate caresses. "You seem fated to untie me," he said a bit unevenly.

This reminder of their imprisonment on the ship brought a tinge of rose to her complexion. She kept her eyes on her task.

Gavin's gaze followed the curve of her eyelids, with their fringe of dark lashes, and dropped to her cheek and then to her lips—slightly pursed in concentration. He couldn't look away. He couldn't break away. Something irresistible pulled his head down closer; he was determined to take those lips for his own.

"There."

In the same instant, the ropes fell away from his wrists and Laura looked up. He had come so close that her lips softly brushed his, a brief galvanizing touch, like a butterfly's wing dipped in fire. Her startled gaze met his; her lips were still tantalizingly parted.

Gavin could feel her breath on his lips. His pulse

pounded in his temples. He had never wanted anything as much as he wanted her, he thought.

She took a step back, retreating from whatever she saw in his gaze.

He grasped her hands to keep her near. "I must free you," he murmured, sliding his fingertips over hers and up to her wrists.

The quickened rise and fall of her chest gratified him amazingly. He began to work at the ropes, taking his time, letting his fingers stray over her forearms, the smooth skin of her hands. When at last the bonds fell away, he caressed the scrapes they left behind, lacing his fingers around her wrist. "Are you all right?" he whispered.

The expression she gave him was so filled with longing that he could wait no longer. He stepped close, to take what was his.

Outside the locked door, there was a hoarse, deep cough.

The sound struck Gavin like a whiplash. Of course they had left a guard, he thought. What was wrong with him? He had never, in all the years he had worked for the British government and with all the pleasant dalliances he had fitted into those years, so forgotten himself in the midst of a mission.

He stepped back, still damnably aroused but now outraged as well. Any slip would put Laura in danger, too. It wasn't only himself he risked. Had he gone mad, to be thinking of…?

Gavin moved farther away from her. His eyes fell on the chair. Picking it up, he jammed the back under the doorknob, bracing it firmly. When he turned back, Laura was watching him. "I don't like people entering my room uninvited," he said. It sounded curt, Gavin thought, but he couldn't help it.

"There is a guard."

It wasn't a question. He simply nodded, then went to check the windows again. It was a long fall to the street.

"How shall we escape?" Laura asked.

She had come up behind him to look over his shoulder. Gavin moved away. "I'll think of something."

"I must get back to Mr. Tompkins. I have figured out what—"

"You might have thought of that before you went wandering off on your own," he cut in. She seemed to have no understanding of how hard it was to be near her.

Laura's eyes flared. She shut her mouth firmly and went to sit on the bed.

"That is probably full of fleas," Gavin informed her and watched her jump up again with savage satisfaction. So she wanted an adventure, did she? How would she like crawling on her belly through freezing mud, infested with a small army of such vermin, as he had done in Persia?

But the image offered him no gratification. He wanted her safe, he thought. He wanted her far away from blackguards like Slanski and vixens like Sophie Krelov. He wanted her...

Gavin turned to the door and examined it more closely. It was suspiciously sturdy for such a building. No doubt it was new. He would not be able to kick it in and overpower the man who waited outside.

"Perhaps they don't mean to kill us after all," said Laura. "If they keep us locked up until—"

"I wouldn't count on that."

"Sophie will be reluctant to kill *you*, at least."

Gavin continued his survey of the walls. "Why should she be?"

"Well…when one has been…that is…when there have been such intimacies…" she stammered to a stop.

Gavin frowned at her. "What the deuce are you muttering about?"

Laura stood straighter. "Sophie mentioned…that is, she told me that you had…she was…"

"What?"

"That you were lovers!" she blurted out. "She may wish to kill *me*, but surely she will not—"

"Sophie cares no more for her lovers than a black widow spider."

The look he got in response startled him. It seemed positively despairing.

"And in any case, we were never lovers. I managed to evade that particular sacrifice for my country—barely."

"You didn't…?"

Something in her face dissipated all Gavin's remaining anger. "No," he said very clearly.

"But she told me things. She said you…" Breaking off, Laura looked at the floor.

Was it relief he saw in her expression? Sophie was a bitch, Gavin thought. But for some reason, he felt almost grateful to her in that moment. "The countess has a variety of…experience. I'm sure she was able to make up something convincing."

"She wanted to divide us," murmured Laura.

Gavin had to strain to hear it. She spoke as if it was a thought she had had before, but hadn't dared believe. His pulse was speeding up again, he realized. He couldn't afford that. "I'm certain they are only waiting for a convenient time to dispose of us. We mustn't allow them the opportunity."

As soon as he said it, he regretted his bluntness, but Laura simply nodded. "What shall we do? We could rip up the pallet cover and make a rope."

"It wouldn't be long enough."

"Oh. No." She looked around the room.

"It wouldn't reach the ground," he added meditatively.

She turned to him again.

"But it might—"

"To a lower floor!"

Her mind was remarkably quick, he thought. She was already reaching for the cloth that covered the straw of the pallet, ready to dare the fleas. Then she drew it back. "Will they hear it ripping?" she whispered.

Amazingly quick, he thought. "Can you manage it? I will distract them."

"Certainly. I don't suppose you have a penknife?"

"They took everything from my pockets."

Laura nodded, and without further conversation, she lifted the dusty fabric and tore a beginning rent with her teeth.

Surprise and admiration held Gavin immobile for a moment. But when she threw him a questioning look, he went at once to the door and began to pound on it and shout, effectively covering the sound of cloth tearing. There was no other woman like her in the world, he thought.

Some minutes later, Gavin felt a tap on his shoulder. Looking back, he saw that the pallet had been reduced to a pile of dusty straw and a number of long strips of cloth. Adding a curse and a sharp kick on the door for good measure, he abandoned his distraction and went to kneel beside these materials. "We will have to wind two strips together or it won't hold," he murmured, beginning to do so.

Laura followed suit. "A bowline?" she asked when they were ready to be tied together.

When he gazed at her, she flushed.

"I once looked through a treatise on knots," she said.

He couldn't suppress a smile.

"The ones on the ship were *not* tied by a sailor," she declared, her flush deepening. "They were a tangled mare's nest."

"A bowline would be quite suitable," replied Gavin, a warmth that was only partly laughter swelling in his chest.

They worked quickly together, and the makeshift rope was soon finished. "Does it look long enough? I could rip up my petticoat…"

"It will do. Help me carry the bedstead over to the window. Quietly."

He chose the side window, thinking them less likely to be spotted from the alleyway than from the street in front. Tying the rope securely to a bedpost, he pulled the bed up against the wall under the window. "I will climb down and break into the lower floor. Wait here until I come back for you."

"But…"

"Here," he commanded.

"What if you—?"

"You will obey me in this!"

She subsided—into obedience, Gavin hoped. He wanted to say something else, something less preemptory, but he couldn't find the words. Instead, he put one leg over the windowsill and ducked under the open sash. He yanked on the rope to test its strength, then looked at her a final time. "I'll be back for you," he said and swung out over the long drop.

∼≈∽

With a mixture of hope and foreboding, Laura watched him descend. One of her chief fears was that the rope wouldn't hold. The cloth had been ancient and nearly rotten.

The bedstead banged against the window, then creaked with the strain of supporting Gavin's weight. Laura braced herself against it, glancing worriedly at the door. Had their guard heard the sound?

Peering out once more, she saw that Gavin had reached the window they had spotted on the lower floor. He was working with one hand to open it—without success. After a moment, he pushed against the house with his legs, swinging out and then back, his feet smashing the panes. As he disappeared inside, Laura clenched her fists. Everyone would have heard that.

She waited, every muscle tense. There were shouts

below, then a thump and a crash. What if Gavin was in trouble? she thought. What if he was overpowered? They might kill him in the fight.

The doorknob of her prison rattled. The key turned in the lock, and the door moved slightly before jamming against the chair Gavin had placed there. If it was Gavin, he would call to her, she thought. An expletive in Russian confirmed her fear. The guard was trying to get in.

There were more shouts from below. Pounding began on the door panels. Taking a deep breath, Laura pulled up her skirts and climbed over the windowsill. The drop was daunting. The thought of trusting herself to the flimsy rope made her feel ill.

She grasped the rope with both hands and eased out of the window. Swinging sickeningly over empty air, she strove to brace her feet on the rope as she had seen Gavin do; then she began the descent.

It wasn't that far, but the climb down was frightening. The rough cloth chafed at her hands; her feet slipped. She was trembling all over by the time she came even with the lower window and was able to rest on the sill. A series of shouts and a crash drove her on immediately.

The opening was full of broken glass and the jagged remnants of the frame. Laura kicked at them before carefully lowering herself through. One of the remaining spears grazed her shoulder and left a line of blood behind.

Twisting, she landed on the floor of an empty room. With another deep breath, she straightened and went to the door. The sounds were coming from the stairs. She looked around for a weapon, but found none.

Trying to hurry and be cautious at the same time, she made her way along a hall. Gavin was there, grappling with one of Sophie's guardsmen on the steps. As they teetered back and forth, Laura spotted a cudgel on the floor. She picked it up and approached the pair, looking for an opportunity. When Gavin saw her, he bared his teeth in a grimace that might have been encouragement or anger. But he jerked away from his opponent for a moment, and Laura brought the cudgel down sharply on the man's head.

He went down with a crash that seemed to make the whole house shake. "I was coming for you," panted Gavin.

Laura decided that a nod was the best response. She still couldn't tell what emotion was animating his features. And there were sounds from above and from below. She handed him the cudgel. Gavin snatched it and started down the stairs, motioning for her to stay behind him.

The volume of sound increased as they went down. It was clear that some sort of struggle was in process on the ground floor. Gavin went more slowly. At the foot of the steps, he said, "Wait here," and moved toward the source of the noises.

Laura followed. The scene they discovered in the front room was as unexpected as it was welcome. One giant Russian lay crumpled in the corner. Another was being held at bay by Hasan, who held a wicked-looking knife.

Gavin didn't hesitate. He strode forward and struck the man smartly with the cudgel. "There's another upstairs," he said.

Indeed, Laura could hear feet pounding on the staircase.

"This way," said Hasan, gesturing.

"I have to get…" Gavin half turned, saw Laura right behind him, and grimaced. He grabbed her arm, but Laura didn't need any urging. All three of them ran.

Hasan led them out a rear door and then through a twisting maze of streets and alleys where poorly dressed people scattered before them. When they finally paused, Laura was breathing hard. But there was no sound of pursuit. "How did you find us?" she asked Hasan.

"I followed you," was his reply. He looked up at his employer. He hooked a thumb in Laura's direction. "*Tandek*," he said and grinned.

Gavin looked disgruntled. Laura glanced from one to the other, trying to puzzle out what this might mean.

"*Tandek*," Hasan repeated with more emphasis.

"Yes, all right," replied Gavin. "Are we going to stand about here for the rest of the day?"

His grin widening, Hasan turned to lead them onward.

# Eighteen

HALF AN HOUR LATER THEY REACHED MR. TOMPKINS'S house. Before they could ring the bell, a figure emerged from a nearby doorway and ran toward them. Gavin and Hasan turned defensively at once, but Laura called out, "Stop. It's Annalise."

The girl joined them. "You are all right," she said. She patted Laura's arm as if to make sure. "I could not go home until I knew."

"We escaped. You did very well, Annalise."

She glowed. "You will tell my father what I have done for you?"

"I'll do even better. Come." Laura marched up the steps and rang the bell. "I'll ask Mr. Tompkins if he has work for you."

Gavin watched her smile at the girl, wondering that she could think of this now, when she had just endured experiences that would have reduced most women to hysterics. There had never been any question of that, he thought with a smile. Hysterics were not part of Miss Laura Devane's repertoire.

He would have hated it if they were, he

acknowledged. But her courage and composure were sometimes disconcerting. They severely limited a man's opportunities to come gallantly to her rescue.

Mr. Tompkins was waiting for them in the study. Before anyone else could speak, Laura recommended Annalise to the old man as someone who might be very useful to him in Vienna.

Tompkins seemed a bit disconcerted too, Gavin saw with distinct pleasure. He was happy not to be alone in this. And the old man's unshakable equanimity could be maddening.

"I will give the matter serious consideration," Mr. Tompkins responded. "She certainly did well today."

Annalise departed happily, and Gavin gave a quick report of what had happened. "If Miss Devane had condescended to inform me of her plans, she would not have been put in such jeopardy." Surely Tompkins would see, now, that Laura could not be sent out alone, he thought.

Tompkins raised one brow. "Does Miss Devane have anything to add?"

He spoke as if he knew she did, Gavin thought.

Laura, who had been staring at the floor, raised her head. "Sophie Krelov is plotting an uprising in Ireland. She has been gathering the money for it here in Vienna, from those who oppose England's interests. It is to begin in six days."

Gavin gaped at her. He had to run the words through his mind a second time to make sure he had heard correctly. "What sort of a fantasy have you—?"

"Count Slanski told me some of it," Laura continued. "He has given her money. Other parts I overheard at a reception. But the most important piece came from Sophie's maid."

"Maid?" exclaimed Gavin.

Laura nodded as if he had pointed out something important. "As I suspected, she is not really a maid. She has been with Sophie from the very beginning, more as a friend, I suppose. It was from her I learned that Sophie must be Irish."

"She *told* you that?" Gavin was beyond astonishment.

"No." Laura smiled slightly. "But she slipped and swore at me in Gaelic."

"Gaelic." He repeated the word because his mind was refusing to keep up with the speed of events.

"It is a language spoken in Ireland and—"

"I know what it is!"

Laura looked away from him. "The woman's name—Bridget—was another clue. And Sophie's red hair."

"You are familiar with Gaelic?" asked Mr. Tompkins. Gavin was savagely pleased to see that he looked a bit stunned as well.

Laura shrugged. "My father was acquainted with a number of Irish horse breeders. I occasionally heard them speaking Gaelic among themselves." She smiled slightly. "And they were prone to cursing. One of them taught me several phrases that got my mouth washed out with soap."

Tompkins had recovered his composure by this time. He reached for pen and paper and wrote quickly. When he had sealed the note, he went to the door and gave it to a footman, who set off at a run at his muttered instructions. When he returned to his desk, he was smiling. He folded his hands on top of a pile of papers and regarded them both. "Well," he said finally, "I think we must say that Miss Devane has done a very fine job indeed. Wouldn't you agree, Graham?"

Gavin felt Laura's gaze on him, an almost tangible pressure. He knew what she was feeling. He had been in the same position himself, waiting for a bit of praise, a validation from his superiors. She wanted him to admit her abilities, to acknowledge her. Did it perhaps matter even more because they had been lovers? he wondered. But he had to put that question aside. It complicated things far too much.

She deserved the acknowledgment. He couldn't deny that. Indeed, he was still astonished at what she had done. She had gathered the pieces and put them together brilliantly. But if he spoke the words, Tompkins would no doubt take them for approval of his mad scheme to employ Laura.

Gavin wanted to protest that he had been with her, that he had helped and protected her. But he couldn't take the credit for what she had done.

He glanced up. Tompkins was looking at him, one corner of his mouth quirked up as if he was fully aware of, and enjoying, Gavin's quandary. Laura gazed at him with a face full of hope and apprehension. Gavin felt a tearing sensation in his chest. He wasn't capable of ignoring that gaze. He wanted to be. But he wasn't. "She did an extraordinary job. I know of few men—and no women—who could have done it."

The joy that filled Laura's face then was his reward and his punishment. She would get what she wanted,

Gavin thought, and he would spend the rest of his, no doubt truncated, life in torment, worrying about her.

"A splendid job," reiterated Tompkins, beaming.

Gavin couldn't bear any more. Muttering something about cleaning up, he fled from their smiles and from whatever mad plan Laura intended to propose next.

Laura was too full of emotion to try to stop him. Tears of triumph and love overwhelmed her voice. He had spoken for her, she thought. He had publicly recognized her skills, given her the thing she had so longed for.

"You really are an extraordinary creature," commented Tompkins.

Laura swallowed. "Then you will have a place for me?"

"Very likely. We shall see."

"See? But I—"

"I am expecting some developments that will allow me to make that decision."

"Developments? In France?"

He smiled. "A bit closer than that."

She tried to imagine what he could be referring to. Perhaps there was some important figure in Vienna who would be needing a governess? But Gavin filled her thoughts, pushing everything else aside. He had acknowledged her. Couldn't they be partners now that she had proved herself?

"Come and see me in the morning," Mr. Tompkins added. "I may have a task for you."

"What sort of task?"

He waved a hand. "It isn't yet clear. Come at ten, and we shall see."

It was a dismissal. Laura climbed the stairs to her room. She tidied her hair. Where was Gavin?

She went to the door and opened it. The quiet of late evening lay over the building. No one was about. She walked down the corridor to Gavin's door and knocked. There was no answer. Indeed, there was no sound except the ticking of a clock on a side table.

A wave of loneliness washed over her. She had felt very close to Gavin over the last few hours. They had worked well together, she told herself. Surely he had noticed that? Where had he gone? She wanted to know how he felt. She wanted to know what her future held. But there was no one to ask.

❧

Gavin walked quietly along the hall that stretched the length of the house. Passing the door of Laura's bedchamber, he paused unconsciously and listened. But no sound penetrated the solid oak. She slept just a few feet behind its panels, her black hair tumbled about her shoulders, her face smooth and a little child-like. Gavin stood alone in the middle of the corridor remembering other nights. The memories had a fire, and a sweetness, that went through him like a stiletto.

That was over, Gavin thought, making himself move. It had happened in some other realm of existence—outside reality. He had to stop thinking of her in that way. But in the depths of the night, the feel and the scent of her kept returning to his thoughts, and a part of him remained convinced that she was his forever.

He walked past the closed doors of the other

residents, taking care to make as little noise as possible. Reaching his own room, he eased the door open and slipped through. He tossed his cloak on a chair and set the candlestick beside the bed. Shedding his coat, he stretched, easing tense muscles and the fatigue. Walking hadn't helped. He wondered how he would sleep.

Gavin was pulling off his shirt when he heard a sound behind him in the far corner of the room. After an instant's stillness, he gave no sign of having noticed. He merely continued removing his shirt, then bent to place it on top of his discarded coat, deftly retrieving his pistol from its pocket as he did so. When he had the gun in his hand, he straightened and turned, pointing it at the dimness in the corner.

"It's me," said a familiar voice.

The pistol barrel wavered. Was he having some sort of hallucination? Gavin wondered. Or had he finally lost his senses completely?

Laura rose into the candlelight. She had been sitting in an armchair that was half turned away from the door, he saw. Slowly, he lowered the gun, still not believing this was real.

"I'm sorry I startled you," she said. "I was waiting and I fell asleep." She smiled sheepishly. "I suppose I'm rather tired."

She couldn't be in his room, Gavin thought. He must be dreaming. And yet she looked quite solid and heartbreakingly lovely.

"But I needed to speak to you," Laura said. "To thank you."

He was seeing her on the island, with the strap of

her shift falling away and her lips parted in surprised pleasure. He was losing his grip.

She walked toward him, the skirts of her silk gown rustling in the silence.

"I couldn't wait until tomorrow."

She was so beautiful, Gavin thought. She had become so intertwined with his thoughts and emotions. He was suddenly conscious of the pistol dangling from his hand, of his bare chest, and of the unmistakable signals his body was sending him. "You shouldn't be here," he said hoarsely.

"I know. But when you told Mr. Tompkins..."

She moved a step closer. Was she trembling? Gavin wondered.

"We have...I mean, it's not as if we never..."

Gavin forced himself to look away from her. He put the gun down and picked up his shirt. "I simply spoke the truth," he managed.

"Even though you didn't want to."

How did she know that? When he met her eyes, his heart seemed to turn over in his chest. If he didn't look at her, perhaps he could regain his senses, Gavin decided. Perhaps he could think clearly, even convince her that she had to go before he did something irredeemable.

Laura came closer.

"It meant a great deal to me," she said.

Her perfume intoxicated him. His shirt slipped from his fingers and whispered to the floor.

"I don't think you can imagine how much," she added.

He had to look at her. She drew his gaze, tugged at

all his senses. "Yes, I can. Exactly as much as when I returned from my first real mission and..."

She gazed at him, recognition and understanding of their kinship blooming in her deep green eyes. It was as if he looked into some enchanted mirror, Gavin thought. He didn't see his own physical image, but a reflection of his spirit stood before him.

She murmured his name.

Gavin had never experienced such a state of tension. Desire possessed him, goaded him to crush her body to his. She was here in his bedchamber, it shouted. What else could she expect? She must want it. But other feelings held him rigidly motionless. They reminded him of her gallantry, her wise innocence. He wanted more than her body, he realized. "You have to get out of here." The pounding of his pulse was making him dizzy.

"I had to tell you..."

He shook his head to clear it and took a step away from her. Somehow, his feet tangled in his discarded shirt, and he stumbled. He had gone mad, he thought. He never did such things.

"Are you all right?" She put a hand on his arm. The touch seared him; it was more than he could bear.

"Do you think I can stand this?" he said through clenched teeth.

Her eyes were huge and green as the depths of a forest. Her hand, feather light, moved up his bicep to his bare shoulder. Gavin broke. He pulled her against him and kissed her. All the longing he had been suppressing burst out and mastered him. He couldn't have let her go to save his life.

"Gavin."

He didn't know whether it was a protest or a welcome. He didn't have the faculties to judge. He could only kiss her more deeply and woo her to come to him.

He felt her arms around his neck, her fingers in his hair. Her body yielded to his embrace with a familiar pliancy that excited him even further. He let his hands explore the curve of her hip, the lithe suppleness of her waist—as he had wanted to do every hour since they had been separated. Pushing her gown off her shoulders, he set his lips to her pale throat, the rosy tips of her breasts. When she moaned his name, he pulled at the fastenings of her dress, not even hearing something tear as it fell away.

He was wild to touch her everywhere, all at once. With one swift motion, he stripped off her shift, then let his fingers travel from her knees to her collarbone. Laura's head fell back, eyes closed. He scattered the pins from her hair and let it cascade down over her shoulders.

She swayed a little. He picked her up and put her on the bed, stripping off his boots and breeches almost before he let her go. When he joined her, she reached for him and raised her mouth to his kiss, her lips parting under his and demanding more even as they yielded.

She was rose and ivory in the candlelight. Her hair gleamed blue-black. Her hand drifted down the muscles of his stomach and then caressed him in a way that made him gasp. "Don't," he murmured, afraid he would lose control.

"No?" she breathed, touching him again so that he cried out.

He groaned. "If you don't stop…"

"What will you do to me?" Her smile was teasing and something more—something mysterious that made his desire for her intensify in a way that was new to him.

In answer, he pulled her on top of him, settling her knees at his sides and letting his hands slide up her inner thighs. "Drive you mad as you do me," he murmured and touched her.

"Oh." Laura arched her back, stretching her arms out behind her. Her eyes were closed, her lips parted.

He knew every rhythm of her, Gavin thought. Heartbeat, breath, the pulse of desire. Their bodies matched each other. He let one hand move up to cup her lovely breast as the other still caressed her.

"Oh," she said again. "Gavin, please."

Feeling triumphant, he shifted slightly so that he could enter her. When he moved, she moved with him, perfectly in tune. The sensations were exquisitely wrenching, a tidal wave overwhelming reason.

Her legs tightened on his ribs. She bent to kiss him as they rode the crescendo together. Every muscle in Gavin's body pulled taut as the feeling rose and rose until it burst through him like living flame. He was in a thousand pieces and yet complete, utterly spent and yet filled.

He felt her collapse against him, equally satiated. Her hair fell over his shoulders. Her cheek rested on his chest. Watching her head rise and fall with his breathing, Gavin felt a sudden sting of tears, and blinked them away, astonished.

His throat was tight, his chest constricted. "This is impossible," he muttered.

"What?" said Laura languidly.

"I'll go mad wondering what you're up to and what danger you are in."

She pushed up to look down at him, her hair falling like veils of ink around her exquisite face.

"You must promise me that you will never take such a risk again." He grasped her upper arms. "To be alone in some aristocratic ruffian's house…" The memory of it, and the desperation he had felt, made him feel ill. "To work there, at his mercy. You can't do it, Laura!"

She slipped away from him, moving to sit cross-legged at his side on the bed. Gavin didn't know whether to laugh or groan. She looked so serious and intent, yet she was gloriously naked before him.

"I have done it before," she said.

"What do you mean?"

"I worked at the Leiths for—"

"You were not trying to ferret out information! And besides Leith is—"

"A fool," she finished, nodding.

"And the men you propose to dupe would be far from fools. They would find you out and…" He ground his teeth in frustration. "If I had not been there, you would have been killed," he pointed out. "And I will not be there if you do such a thing again!" Simply stating this fact drove him to distraction.

"You won't…"

It sounded almost like a question. But of course she knew he wouldn't. "If you would go back to England—"

"Would you have done so, after that first mission you spoke of?"

This silenced him. She wouldn't marry him, Gavin

thought, and she wouldn't retire to safety. She was the most obstinate female on the face of the earth.

"Gavin."

Her hand on his chest was a torment and a goad.

"Is there no other possibility?"

He frowned, trying to fathom her tone.

"We said once that we would be partners." Her voice was trembling. "We worked well together, didn't we—?"

"I won't be there! Don't you understand? That's the whole point. I'll be a thousand miles away. I won't be able to do anything but lose my mind worrying over you."

"Because you work alone."

He couldn't comprehend why she was repeating phrases that they had spoken eons ago. Phrases that made no sense and offered him no reassurance for the future. She wasn't going to listen to him, he saw. She never had listened to him, not once in their entire infuriating, delicious history. There was only one thing to do that would guarantee her attention and wholehearted cooperation.

Gavin pulled Laura into his arms so fiercely that she gasped. Silencing her mouth with his own, he made love to her as he never had to any other woman in his life.

❦

Laura watched the candle guttering in its holder and listened to Gavin's slow, even breathing beside her. It was time to go. She didn't want to. She wanted to give herself up to sleep, to nestle close to him, to wake here in the morning by his side. But even if that had been possible, even if they weren't in a house full of strangers who would ruin her, she would have had to go.

There was no tomorrow for them. There were stolen moments—on the island, tonight—when they flamed together like two souls meant for each other. But when the smoke of passion cleared and they returned to reality, the way was blocked. She wouldn't be a sometime wife, waiting alone in England for his visits—even if he still wanted her to be. He wouldn't have her with him on his missions. She had hoped that he would, Laura admitted silently as she began to dress. She had proved herself, she thought a bit defiantly. She had shown him that she wasn't afraid, that she could stand at his side. But it hadn't been enough. He could see her skills and her determination, but he couldn't see her as his partner.

If Mr. Tompkins gave her work, Laura thought, she and Gavin might meet like this from time to time. They might steal moments like tonight, radiant with tenderness and glory. But that was not nearly enough either, she acknowledged. She wanted everything. She wanted his love.

Her dress was torn and wouldn't fasten all the way. She did it up as best she could and then stood in the middle of the room and looked down at Gavin's sleeping face.

He looked like a knight carved of marble and gold, or a fairy-tale prince under an enchantment. Some of the hardness left his face during sleep, and he looked younger too. She couldn't think of anything but how splendid he was and how desperately she loved him.

# *Nineteen*

GAVIN WOKE TO SUN STREAMING THROUGH THE WIN-
dows of his room. For a moment, all he knew
was that he felt extraordinarily good. He stretched,
enjoying the pull of his muscles and the feeling of satisfaction that coursed through him. Then
he remembered. Laura was still with him in the
body's memory.

He looked around. From the slant of the light, it
was late. He stood and went to the window. It was
a brilliant spring day. He stretched again, relishing
his own strength. Ringing for Hasan, he ordered
a bath.

Gavin went down to breakfast expecting to find
Laura there. He didn't know precisely what he would
say to her, but he was eager to see her. She would
flush at the caress in his gaze. It would be amusing to
tease her just a little. And with any luck, they might
find themselves alone.

But when he entered the breakfast room, he found
only Mr. Tompkins, resplendent in ivory satin, sipping
a cup of coffee. Gavin suppressed an astonishingly

sharp stab of disappointment and filled a plate from the silver chafing dishes on the sideboard.

"I hope you slept well after your little adventure?" the old man said.

Gavin eyed him as he nodded. Tompkins was so canny that one might think he was omniscient. But there was no way he could know how Gavin had spent the night.

"Splendid." He sipped from his cup. "It appears that Miss Devane got it right. There have been a number of packets sent to Ireland from Vienna. And sent to some very suspicious addresses. I've forwarded messages to Whitehall. We should be just in time to stop whatever they plan."

Gavin grunted.

"The countess was clever, taking advantage of Bonaparte's planned escape. She thought to win by splitting the English forces."

Gavin nodded, wondering why he found this so uninteresting.

"Sophie herself slipped through our fingers, however," Tompkins went on. "She and her husband took refuge with the czar's delegation."

"That sounds like Sophie," he muttered.

"Yes." Tompkins raised his cup again, watching Gavin over the rim. "So you think Miss Devane is fit for our sort of work after all?"

Gavin went still.

"At one time, you were of a different opinion."

"I said she did well yesterday," Gavin answered carefully. "At least, once she had gotten herself into trouble, she was able to—"

"Of course, if she hadn't gotten into trouble, we would not have uncovered some vital information," the old man interrupted.

"*I* would have—"

"You have fallen into worse scrapes, I believe, during some of your missions."

"I am not a woman, alone, and vulnerable to…" He couldn't even say it. "If I had not been there, the outcome would have been…different." Disastrous, he thought.

"Indeed." Tompkins looked meditative. "So you think Miss Devane should work with someone, perhaps?"

"She should be safe at home!" Gavin replied, too agitated to contemplate the suggestion.

"Ah, well, perhaps we should all be safe at home."

Gavin rejected this with a savage gesture. "Some of us are suited to risk. We enjoy being alone in strange places, discovering an enemy's plans. But that does not mean—"

"And Miss Devane is *not* that sort?"

"She…" Frustration and fury held Gavin rigid. He wanted to lie, to say she wasn't. But he knew that would be an unforgivable betrayal, the sort he had vowed never to commit.

He had fought his own father's manipulation. He had spent his career watching men moved like chess pieces across the globe. He had seen scores of young men out to prove themselves trample on anything that got in the way. He had seen his sisters ruthlessly cut down whoever interfered with their families' advancement. He had promised himself he would never behave in such a way, no matter how important it was, no matter what he wanted.

Gavin was shaken by a spasm of pain such as he had never experienced in ten years of perilous missions. Where was it coming from? What was happening to him?

He called on the resources that had sustained him through danger and physical hardship, through deprivation and anguish. He summoned every ounce of fortitude and control. The sensation was like windows shutting, one after another, all along the wings of a great house. The openings closed, and the pain lessened. The light dimmed, and the loneliness increased. But he was used to that, he thought.

❧

"I beg your pardon for keeping you waiting," said Mr. Tompkins to Laura a few minutes later. He had kept her safely out of the way in the study while he interviewed Gavin, and now his final decision was made. "I am in need of a confidential messenger. Someone who will not be noticed and will not be connected with my…usual practices."

Though obviously disappointed by the smallness of the task, Laura assured him she could do it.

"There should not be any danger involved," he added.

She looked as if she wished there were. Indeed, she looked as if she would like to throw herself in front of a runaway coach-and-four. Tompkins allowed himself a small smile. Very intelligent people could be amazingly obtuse, he thought.

"I will give you a letter, and you will carry it to a certain location and deliver it to the person you meet there."

"That's all?" She sounded almost insulted.

Mr. Tompkins's smile widened. "There may be some…negotiation to be done. Indeed, I'm sure there will."

"About what?" she asked, looking a little cheered. "What am I to say?"

"I will leave that to your own good judgment."

"But what is the issue, what is in the letter? I cannot…"

He shouldn't enjoy her consternation, Tompkins admonished himself. "It will all be clear when you are there. You have my permission to use your initiative and make whatever agreement seems right to you."

She frowned at him.

"Is this another test?" Laura asked.

"You might look at it that way."

"Haven't I already shown that I—"

"Or you could consider it a favor for an old man."

Her lip curled, as he had expected it would when he played that particular card. It was such a pleasure to work with people who couldn't be gulled, Tompkins thought.

"Is there even a real messenger?" Laura asked.

"Oh, very real," he assured her. "And I consider the transaction extremely important. Vital, in fact. I will be dreadfully cast down if it doesn't go well." It was easy to sound sincere when you were telling the truth, he thought with amusement. And how often did one get the chance?

"Oh."

"Go and get your things. I will have the letter for you when you come back."

Laura nodded and started to rise.

"Oh, and Miss Devane?"

She turned.

"You mustn't speak of this to anyone."

She looked deeply offended, as he had known she would. But it would keep her from stopping to chat with…anyone on her way to her room, Tompkins thought complacently.

❧

When Laura returned to the study, Mr. Tompkins handed her a heavy sealed envelope. "You must take this to number sixteen Mariastrasse. Do not ring. Go inside, to the second floor, the room at the back. The messenger will meet you there."

Despite herself, Laura felt a thrill of excitement. This *was* far better than life as a governess. "I am to wait while he reads the letter?"

He made an affirmative gesture.

"So it will be a man?"

Tompkins smiled at her small trick, but he didn't admit anything.

"And then…deal with him?" She still hoped for a bit more guidance.

He only nodded.

There had to be more to it, Laura thought. There was something she wasn't grasping. As she left the room, she vowed that whatever it was, she would show him that she could handle it.

Spring was well along in Vienna now, and despite the armies massing to the north, people were delight-ing in the warmth and the buds beginning to swell on the trees. The streets were full of smiling strollers, and children romped and laughed in the sun.

She found the address without difficulty. It wasn't far. Approaching number sixteen, she looked for signs of anything unusual. There were none. With a sudden qualm she imagined walking into the house of some Viennese burgher and trying to explain why she hadn't bothered to ring or knock.

But she trusted Mr. Tompkins more than that. His plans would be impeccable, she thought. Marching up the two steps to the front door, she tried the handle. Unlocked. She opened it cautiously and stepped inside. A mundane entryway. Shutting the door, she listened and heard only silence. The place might have been empty.

Laura walked up the stairs to the second floor, and then along the central hallway to the room at the back. Its door was ajar. Taking a deep breath, she went through it, and came face to face with an impatient-looking Gavin Graham. "What are you doing here?" he said.

"I…Mr. Tompkins sent me."

"Why?"

Not entirely recovered from her surprise, Laura looked around the very ordinary room. "He said there would be a messenger to meet me."

"He sent me here to retrieve a letter from a messenger," declared Gavin.

Confused, she held out the letter.

After a moment's hesitation, he tore open the seal and pulled out the folded sheets inside. They were blank. "What sort of game…?" He frowned at her.

Laura shook her head. Had Mr. Tompkins meant her to negotiate with Gavin? she wondered a bit wildly. About what?

"This is ridiculous," he said. Striding to the door, he grasped the knob to open it. It didn't turn. "What the deuce?" He rattled the panels violently. The door didn't budge. "It's locked."

"It can't be."

"Well, it is."

They gazed at each other. Laura was putting together certain twinkling looks Mr. Tompkins had given her and remarks he had made, with today's mission and the locked door. It was an odd sensation, becoming a piece in one of the old man's plots. What was he hoping for?

Gavin rattled the door again. It remained solid. "Someone followed you here," he accused.

"No." She was sure of this.

"You didn't see them. You haven't the experience to—"

"I saw the watchers *you* set on me right away. Indeed, I convinced one of them to work for me instead."

He had no answer for this. He kicked the door. "If you are so clever, you must know who has locked us in."

Laura thought she did, but she wasn't going to say so.

Gavin went to examine the room's single window. It was heavily barred. "We are trapped here."

She was supposed to negotiate with Gavin, Laura thought. But she had already tried to talk to him, and gotten nowhere. Mr. Tompkins didn't know that. What did he expect from her? She hid a smile. Perhaps he had concluded that if she could negotiate with Gavin Graham, she could face any challenge the world might throw at her.

Gavin took a penknife from his pocket and inserted it in the keyhole of the door, probing the mechanism.

A mixture of excitement, nervousness, and elation rose in Laura. She was to risk everything on this one encounter, she thought. Mr. Tompkins must think there was some chance of success. She had to use every faculty she possessed to fight for what she wanted. "If we think it through together, I am sure we can get out," she said.

"I will get us out. Don't worry."

"I'm not worried."

Gavin threw her a look. "Whoever locked us in here is probably waiting for reinforcements," he pointed out.

"That is why we should join forces. How can one person alone think of everything?"

He turned and really looked at her for the first time since he had opened the letter.

Laura felt as if the air had rushed out of the room, making it very difficult to breathe. "We worked very well together the last time."

"After you had gotten us both into serious trouble."

"I'm sure I could do better, with a good teacher."

Letting go of the doorknob, Gavin took a few steps back and drew a ragged breath. He felt as if he were in the last safe place on earth, beleaguered, surrounded by threats on every side. And with him was the one person in the world he most wished to protect. He could feel all those inner windows that he had slammed shut opening. "Don't you understand?" he asked her. "Sophie Krelov may have sent men after us, or perhaps it is someone else…" There were so very many people it could be, he thought with despair.

"We'll find a way out!" declared Laura.

He knew the spark in her eyes. He had seen it there before, and he had seen it in his own. It held an ardent desire for life and hope for approval, a determination to act, a delight in walking the edge.

Gavin stood rigid, trying to contain emotions that held him like iron shackles. He swallowed, the muscles of his neck and shoulders bands of iron. He couldn't live without her, he realized. The talk of her leaving or taking some dangerous post—it had been all talk. She had been there, in the same house. He had seen her every day, spoken to her. It had been simple to put off consideration of how he really felt. But now he couldn't deny it any longer. He loved her as he had never loved another living being. He would sacrifice whatever was necessary to keep her by his side, he understood with a terrible mixture of despair and exultation.

He needed to say something.

"Uh." Gavin looked at the wall behind her head, searching for salvation.

She gazed at him as if she knew something unusual was happening.

He took a jerky step toward her. "It's no good," he said. "You must marry me."

Laura blinked. "But—"

"I'll find some post at home," he added passionately. "There must be something I can do in London."

"But your work?"

In two strides he was beside her. He caught her upper arms and pulled her close. "Don't you understand? I can't leave you." He shook her a little. He was furious and yet vastly relieved to have said it.

"Can't?" she whispered.

"I won't be able to work without you. I'll be continually diverted. I'm a ruined man." Pulling her hard against him, he kissed her. "I love you," he finished, and it felt like an ending indeed—and a beginning. She was his, she would always be his. Wouldn't that make up for anything?

He pressed her closer. His lips demanded all her attention. He felt a wild reckless joy when Laura gave herself up to his embrace. Nothing else in his life had ever made him feel this way.

Somewhat later, when both of them were breathing rapidly, Gavin raised his head. "That's settled, then. We will find someone to marry us here in Vienna."

"Gavin—"

"I won't wait until we're back in England," he interrupted, his hands proprietary on her. "Don't even suggest it."

"No, but…" Laura shook her head. "Your work, your travels, you can't give them up."

"There's no more to be said on that score."

She pushed a little away from him, eyes soft from his kisses. "You'll miss it. You'll be unhappy." She tried to move farther back, but he wouldn't let her.

He didn't answer her objections, however. "It won't work," she protested, her voice full of heartbreak.

"If you think you are going to refuse me again…"

"How can I not?" Laura grasped his lapels as if she could shake him as he had her. "You'll hate being back in England," she declared, her eyes filling with tears. "You can't say you won't."

He couldn't.

Laura struggled, but he wouldn't let her go. "I won't be the cause of your unhappiness. I love you too much."

Gavin felt a sudden lightness at her admission. He tightened his arms around her.

"We would destroy each other in England," said Laura.

"We will find some way to—"

"You said I could be your partner," she added breathlessly. "Well, I will be."

"My wife," he agreed.

"And your partner," she repeated. "You have seen that I am not afraid. I will join you in your work."

"Laura. That isn't possible."

"What about the ship? Do you think I cannot endure hardship?"

"You cannot imagine the kind of—"

"Don't you trust me?" she accused. "Even now?"

Gavin looked down at her, and some final barrier gave way. "I would trust you with my life and everything I have. But I do not trust myself to function if you are in danger. I couldn't let you go off and…"

"Then I would simply sneak away without your knowledge," replied Laura, attempting to tease him.

His laugh was half a groan. "You would drive me mad in a month, worrying over what you would do."

"No, I wouldn't. Because I would tell you, as a true partner does."

Their eyes met again, and held. His arms tightened around her. Each could feel the other's heartbeat.

"Could we really…?" Gavin desperately wanted to believe.

"Ahem."

Laura and Gavin turned at the sound and discovered George Tompkins standing inside the open doorway. Neither of them had heard the key turn or his entrance, or had any idea how long he had been there.

"Perhaps I can suggest a solution."

Laura stared at him, not daring to hope.

"It is true it would involve some compromise," Tompkins continued.

Gavin watched him like a predator.

"You would have to give up certain habits, like galloping off to join the hill tribes in Afghanistan, Graham."

Laura started to protest.

"And you, Miss Devane, would have to admit the value of experience in the field, and occasionally even defer to it."

"I have never denied…" she began.

"Tell us," commanded Gavin at the same moment.

Mr. Tompkins allowed himself a moment to look at the two of them. He had rarely seen such a handsome couple, he thought. But more than that, he didn't believe he had ever encountered such a canny pair. They were going to cut a swath through the foreign service, he concluded with immense satisfaction. "I am very much in need of a source of information in Cairo," he told them. "And I cannot afford the least suspicion to arise about that source."

Gavin's hand slid down and enfolded Laura's. They both watched him like cats at a mouse hole.

Tompkins smiled. "A honeymoon couple visiting the ancient sites of Egypt would hardly be suspected. They could poke about the bazaars and contact certain people in whom I…have an interest."

He enjoyed the dazzling sparkle that lit Laura's eyes and the way Gavin immediately concentrated, obviously forming plans already. The grip of their hands tightened visibly.

"Of course, it would be a rather odd sort of honeymoon," he finished, wondering if any moment of his long career had offered greater gratification.

"It is *exactly* the sort I want," replied Laura.

Gavin looked down at her, then threw back his head and laughed. "I give up," he said. "I will take you with me to the ends of the earth if nothing else will satisfy you." He pulled her tight against him once more.

"Nothing else but you," she murmured.

"Splendid," said Mr. Tompkins. "Shall we consider it agreed, then? You will be partners."

He waited a moment for an answer. Then he realized that no one else had been listening. With a complacent smile at his success, he slipped out of the room.

JOHN BEXLEY STRODE DOWN THE GANGPLANK ONTO the Southampton dock and paused to look over the busy port town. For the first time since he'd left English shores in February 1816, everything felt familiar—the shape of the buildings, the faces and dress of the people, the sounds and scents and voices. And yet, they also felt strangely changed. His twenty-month journey to the other side of the world had reduced England to just one corner of a vast globe. A noble corner, without doubt, a corner with a proud history and admirable ideals, but still just a smallish island among continents. And so his home looked not only natural and welcoming but also a bit…constricted.

Speaking of constricted, John wiggled his shoulders, trying to get more comfortable in a coat that no longer fit. He'd gained more muscle than his clothes could accommodate. The binding cloth contributed to the mixed emotions of this moment. He'd outgrown his raiment. What about his old routines, or the wife he'd left behind?

John looked at the English faces on the docks around him, pale even under the August sun. For almost two years, he and Mary had led separate lives—his active and public, hers domestic and small. So many things had happened to him that she would never comprehend. And a thousand domestic details that newly married persons usually shared had gone by on opposite sides of the world.

Worse, John wondered now whether he'd done the right thing, giving in to his family's plan for him. The young man he'd been before this voyage had let his family urge him into a lifetime bond without really thinking. If the foreign secretary's letter about the China mission had come a few weeks sooner, would he have offered for Mary? The answer was too uncomfortable to contemplate.

John looked out over the town. His world of two years ago seemed like a dream to him now, pale and insubstantial, the people distant shadows. Swept away on a grand journey, he'd found inner continents as surprising as the discoveries of ancient explorers. The impulses that had risen in him and answered the challenge of storm-wracked seas still burned—more vibrant perceptions, fiercer ambition, a determination to make his mark.

But a suitable wife—one with important connections and social skills—was practically required for advancing through the ranks of the Foreign Office.

A bale of silks rose from the ship's hold, pulley creaking as the navvies hauled on the rope. The heavy cargo swung out over the dock and plunged down just as a street urchin emerged from between two stacks of crates. John took three steps, snatched the boy from its path, and pulled him well out of the way. "Careful there," he said.

Pale and wide-eyed, the grimy child nodded his thanks and scampered away.

The planks of the dock vibrated as the bale thumped to the boards. A brawny dockworker rounded the corner of a warehouse and hefted it—no easy task, John knew. He should head into town, find transport, and begin the last sixty miles of his journey. To Mary. But his tumbled thoughts kept him standing near the ship.

He remembered his first sight of her at the Bath assembly. Neither of them came from the sort of grand families who went to London for the Season; Bath was the center of their social world. She'd stood with her mother by the wall—a small, delicate girl with chestnut brown hair and huge dark eyes; a full lower lip that seemed made for kissing; pretty little hands. She'd looked as sweet and timid as a sparrow. In that moment—which now seemed long ages ago—his family's mandate that she was the wife for him had seemed no burden at all. He'd walked over, been presented. Mary had smiled at him…

After that, events were a bit of a blur. They'd danced, walked the streets of Bath together, taken teas and dinners at their families' tables. He had offered for her; that moment had been between the two of them. At the time, it hadn't seemed as if he had a choice. But once the words were spoken and she had accepted, their mothers had swooped in and taken over. He didn't remember being consulted about a single item after that.

He was simply told things. Mary's father had lectured him about how the combination of their two inherited incomes would allow them to live very comfortably, as if John couldn't work that out for himself. His brothers had teased him relentlessly, as usual. He'd overheard his parents agreeing that this was a good enough match— for him, for Mary—and for some reason, incomprehensible to him now, he'd made no remark.

There'd been a whirl of a wedding and a seaside week in Weston-super-Mare, with dolorous rain and intimacies that had been clumsier than he'd have liked. Then the Foreign Office summons had arrived to take over his thoughts and change his life.

John sighed. His life, not Mary's. What would a little sparrow like Mary think of the intricacies of Foreign Office etiquette? What would she think of him, now that he'd…come alive? He took a deep breath of the seaside air. That's how it felt—as if he'd been half-asleep for years and finally woken. Now, he intended to plunge into the drive for advantage and jostling rivalries he'd generally ignored in his three years on the job. Work was going to occupy much of his time. Where did Mary fit in all this?

John loosened his shoulders, chafing at the tightness of his coat once again. Done was done. Mary was his wife. She would have to fit. She was young, unformed, eager to please. Though she didn't have the family connections that were so useful in government work, she was a taking little thing. She'd welcome his guidance. Indeed, she would probably be awed by his new sophistication. There was a curiously attractive notion.

❧

Sitting at her easel in the back parlor of her great-aunt's house, Mary was swept by a wave of loneliness so strong it made the brush tremble in her hand. In this household, she had no one to talk to or laugh with. No one within a decade of her age. Instead of a house of her own with a husband and perhaps by now a tiny addition to their family, she had a group of elderly... charges. There was no other way to look at it.

A shriek rent the air. Mary's brush twitched. A streak of yellow flicked across the painted face, muddling one eye, slashing across a cheek like war paint.

Mary lowered her brush, sat back, and sighed. Apparently, she would never become inured to these disturbances. Who could? Yes, she no longer leaped to her feet and ran, heart pounding, to discover the emergency. But she couldn't help reacting when Alice the housemaid screamed. It could only be Alice; past forty, and she still delighted in shrieking at the least excuse. Setting her brush in a glass of water, Mary rose and went to see what it was this time.

She found her Great-Aunt Lavinia, Alice the housemaid, and Voss the aged butler in the morning room, looking down at a shattered vase, a scatter of pink roses, and a puddle of water. The once formidable Lavinia Fleming was wringing her hands and trembling. Humid August air wafted through the open French doors.

"Drat that boy!" said Voss.

Mary didn't question his attribution because...well, there simply was no question about the origin of the disturbance.

"Something must be done," Voss added, clearly addressing Mary.

Mary looked back at him with wry resignation. When she'd first arrived, into this household that had lost its rudder and fallen into chaos, she'd hung back, of course. She was a guest, and anyway she hadn't known what to do. But then it had risen in her, like a great wave looming from the sea, an irresistible need to set things right. Perhaps it was an inheritance from her mother—not an entirely comfortable thought. But she found she could no more resist than she could alter the deep brown color of her eyes. The household had been like a workbasket jammed with snarled thread. She'd been forced, really, to discover her own way of untangling it. She'd been surprised at her daring and then amazed at how eagerly her intervention was welcomed.

"Ma'am?" said Voss, waiting for her to solve the household's most recent problem.

"I'll go and speak to him," Mary said, and she walked into the hall toward the front door of the manor.

Outside, she scanned the parkland for her quarry. There was no sign of him on the lawn or in the front garden. Mary turned toward the stables, rounded a corner, and there he was.

Ten-year-old Arthur Windly squatted at the edge of the stable yard, searching for more round pebbles. Here was the one remaining source of mayhem in her great-aunt's household.

She walked over to Arthur, who pretended to ignore her. The son of Great-Aunt Lavinia's supremely competent estate manager, Arthur was a constant conundrum. Mr. Windly was vital to the workings of the manor and must not be offended. He was also a prickly, distant man, especially, Mary had been told, since his wife's death three years ago. Her attempts to speak with him about Arthur had confirmed this characterization. He'd treated her like a nuisance and a busybody, and she was certain he hadn't listened to a word she said. Using her own newly discovered skills, Mary came to understand that Arthur was desperate for his father's attention and that the boy would take a whipping if that was all the notice he could contrive.

Trailing from Arthur's pocket was a length of brown cord with a woven pouch in the center, the source of many recent disasters. The local vicar had taken it into his head to show his young parishioners the instrument that had vanquished Goliath. She held out her hand. "You'll have to give me the sling, Arthur."

The boy sprang to his feet and glared at her. "No, I don't."

"That was our agreement—the last time."

"I never agreed!" Arthur's lower lip jutted out; his hazel eyes narrowed. Rebellion showed in every line of his skinny little body.

Suppressing a sigh, Mary stood and thought. She could threaten to go to his father, and Arthur would dare her to do it, and they would repeat a cycle of punishment that accomplished nothing. Arthur wasn't a bad child. Still, he couldn't be allowed to break vases, or knock ripening apples from the trees, or crack glass windows on the upper stories. Providentially, a scrap of overheard conversation came back to her. "I understand the hayricks in the north field are infested with rats."

"What?" Arthur frowned at the non sequitur.

"Still, I don't suppose you could kill a rat with that sling."

Arthur stiffened in outrage. "'Course I could."

"Really?" Mary strove to look merely interested. "Your father is desperate to be rid of them. Indeed, the idea of a whole colony of rats…" Her shudder did not require much acting. "But it must be much more difficult to hit a moving target than, oh, a vase or a window."

"I could, though." Speculation and hope passed visibly over the boy's triangular face. "I could do it!"

"I'm sure *everyone* would be very grateful," Mary replied.

Without another word, Arthur rushed from the stable yard. Mary walked back to the house with some bounce in her step and cautious optimism in her heart.

Inside, all was quiet once more. Great-Aunt Lavinia dozed on a sofa, the strings of her lace cap fluttering with her breath. Mary returned to her painting to see what could be salvaged but found herself picking up her sketchbook instead. She wanted to capture the image of Arthur sifting through stones in the stable yard, with his intent expression and irrepressible cowlick.

She opened the drawing pad and came upon a portrait of John, done during their brief honeymoon journey to the shore. For a disorienting moment, memory wavered in Mary's mind. But that was ridiculous. Of course she remembered her own husband. Here he was. Medium height, wiry, with reddish brown hair, a broad brow, straight nose, and crystalline blue eyes. The direct gaze of those eyes had been one of the first things she noticed about him.

She stared at his image. He'd been away longer than

all the time she'd known him. And with the great distances involved, they'd had only occasional dispatches to let them know he was alive and well. What would it be like when she saw him again? Mary's heart beat faster at the question. With anticipation, or worry? She felt nothing like the heedless girl who had married him. She didn't know what she felt like as she gazed at the man she was expected to live with for the rest of her life. The rest…that might be forty years, fifty, all resting on one unconsidered choice.

Pushing such unsettling thoughts aside, she turned to a blank page. At once, her fingers itched to draw. Under the golden afternoon light slanting through the open casement, her soft pencil moved over the paper as it so often did, as if it had a mind of its own.

She didn't know why she'd loved to draw since a teacher first put a pencil in her hand and explained some of the principles of art. She didn't know why she had a talent for capturing human figures, particularly faces. Her landscapes were wooden and characterless, her still lifes stiff and uninteresting, while people sprang to life on her pages. The process held a kind of magic that she was reluctant to probe.

Using her pencil and the tip of one finger, Mary shaded and sharpened, added detail, and clarified line. A sharp, foxy little boy emerged on the page, scrabbling for stones to fill his pouch, ready for any sort of mayhem. He looked as if he would leap up in the next moment and set off on yet another escapade.

When she felt finished, she surveyed the result. Arthur's likeness was accurate, the expression true to life. It was good.

Sadness jumped from the page. Although she'd been thinking of the Arthur who continually disrupted the smooth workings of the household, her pencil had found more in the angles and lines of him. The poignancy of the boy's life tightened her throat and stung her eyes. A kindred loneliness plucked at her. It was time—past time—for her real life to begin. But had she chosen the right life? Looking back at the… girl she'd been, she didn't feel as if she'd chosen at all.

Mary set the drawing of Arthur aside, along with the self-pity. Done was done. She'd made her vows. And right now there was plenty of work awaiting her, chiefly readying quarters for the housekeeper/companion she'd hired for her great-aunt. The woman was due to move in next week, and Mary wanted everything perfect for her arrival. Mrs. Finch had seemed the perfect solution to the problem of Great-Aunt Lavinia and all her household. She wanted her to feel warmly welcomed and pleased with her situation.

Alice came in with a letter, brought by courier, she said. Mary opened it quickly, fearing bad news, then caught her breath. "John's ship has landed at Spithead. He's home."

# About the Author

Jane Ashford discovered Georgette Heyer in junior high school and was captivated by the glittering world and witty language of Regency England. That delight was part of what led her to study English literature and travel widely in Britain and Europe. She has written historical and contemporary romances, and her books have been published in Sweden, Italy, England, Denmark, France, Russia, Latvia, the Czech Republic, and Spain, as well as the U.S. Jane has been nominated for a Career Achievement Award by *RT Book Reviews*. She lives in Los Angeles, California.